SHIFTING TIDES OF CHAOS

THE GATEWAY SAGA #2

ERIN THORNTON

No one was harmed in the making of this story. Although, my boobs were sacrificed for the greater good. Now I feel like we should have a moment of silence in memory of my girls…Ok now get on with the story!

CHAPTER ONE

$\mathcal{D}$ropping yet another dusty, browned photo back into the stack, Aggie wished her mother were there to help her through all of this. There was so much going on that she didn't know how to handle it all. The Fae powers were one thing, as she used her power over the earth to dust off the next box and lifted the lid. Now she had Mathius' powers as well, not that she knew what that meant completely. The training to learn the gamut of unknown that comprised his powers was exhausting. It seemed the power over matter was relative and endless. Now, sifting did make her life that much easier, as she no longer had to walk from point A to point B if she chose not to or was in a hurry. Though she almost forgot the rules one day when she wanted a snack and the house was empty of what she wanted. Thankfully it was dark that night in the grocery parking lot.

Aggie's mind drifted to the night she had gained her powers. *Mathius was frantically trying to find her, and about ripped the door of the hinges. Had she not been so scared about having just vanished only to reappear, thankfully clothed, in the hallway where anyone could have seen her, she might have been turned on again by his display. Instead, when he found her, she was shaking a bit and laughing hysterically. "What is wrong?"*

Mathius placed his hands on her shoulders that were still bouncing from her insanity.

"Nothing—I guess you're officially my new mate," she said through bouts of giggles. Aggie didn't really know why she was laughing, only that she was a bit lost after trying to figure out what that meant. Moments later, the doors in the hallway started flying open. The rest of the guys had been awoken by the chaos happening in the hall.

"What's going on?" Eldon's soft, sweet voice wafted over her and relaxed her instantly. She loved that he had that power over her and wondered if she would love it as much when she wanted to be mad at him.

"It seems we have ourselves a part demon gatekeeper now," Mathius supplied for them, not bothering to hide the pride in his voice. He was now her second mate and not concerned in the least with toning down his boastful lilt. Now there was no way they were hiding it, not that Aggie had intended to, but this was all new to her.

The memory faded and Aggie continued her mission to clear out the attic while looking for memories to claim. Her Gran never let her come up here as a child and never mentioned the wonder it would contain for Aggie. She had found so many pictures and relics from her mother's childhood, and even a few of Gran with her late husband whom Aggie never had the pleasure of meeting. He passed years before she was born. The light from the sun, while faded at the late hour, was still catching the floating dust particles and lighting them up like glitter in the air. Aggie found herself lost in thought as she contemplated each picture.

"Mom, why did you have to go so soon?" Aggie spoke out loud without fear of anyone hearing her. It was never an issue before and the guys were off doing their duties, leaving her to pursue her thoughts and learn her duties as well. "This is all so much to take in. I'd rather do it with you, or even Gran. I feel lost." Her voice dropped as the words spilled from her mouth, ending on barely a whisper.

"Did you say something, love?" The hypnotic tone that was Kyrel's voice rang through the attic. He had been helping her sort through things today, as he didn't have anything else to do. Thankfully his hormonal imbalance had dissipated, and staying in the same room alone with him was easier. Lost in her thoughts, she forgot he was there.

She was pouring her heart out to the pictures; it wasn't because she thought her mom could hear her, but she just needed to say them out loud. Everyone had fears and things that held them back, but this was more than a roadblock and more of a blackout. She didn't know what her role really was as Gatekeeper and Ninth Guardian. While she helped the guys, or so she thought, get through the demon kidnapping, there was always a better chance they would have done it themselves just as well. Not to mention, there was no one around to help her figure out what this gatekeeper job entailed. Surely, she had more than this as a role. It felt like she spent her days walking around her house, waiting for something to happen.

"No, I was just thinking out loud. I seem to do that more and more these days. I sort of forgot you were here. I've gotten used to you guys being off doing things these past few weeks. I just tend to talk to the empty rooms more often than not." Aggie barely glanced in his direction and continued going through her box.

Occasionally, when she was alone, she would walk into the gateway and walk around the room. Not knowing what to do, she ran her hands along the walls and would feel the energy beneath them. "Is that the doors, or the energy from the wall itself and its connection to the earth?" Questions went unanswered because she was alone. She knew the guys had their responsibilities to their people, but without any family left for her Aggie was feeling the effects of the quiet. Not that the guys were much help in sorting out the gateway. None of them had spent much time lingering in it or studying it. They used it as a means of travel. No different than the average Joe not knowing how an airplane functioned, only that it did what was necessary for their needs.

In that time, Aggie learned a lot about the doorknobs. She was brave enough at times to touch them, and realized they did give off the slightest energy. She wondered if that was because of the Fae powers and Demon powers, or her gatekeeper role finding a connection. Those were questions that would be left for another day and time, unanswered as well. The ones that resembled the lava handle that led them to Ahael were warm, but not melting hot like she originally wondered. That had taken weeks to gain the courage to figure out. Though she touched one that looked like icy tundra before she gained the nerve. While the individual doorknobs had different elements and features, she hadn't tested them all. Though she did consider licking a couple that wouldn't harm her. She feared her tongue sticking to a frozen one and opted out.

The lush green that looked more like grassy plains or full bushes were the first she touched. She could almost feel the leaves scratching her hands and cool grass slipping between her fingers as she embraced the metal. She wondered if metal was the right word, because many of them didn't feel or even look like metal, but there was a firmness to them that wasn't foliage or lava or even water. After examining the knobs with a keen eye, she had a better understanding of where they might lead. Not that she had been brave enough to actual venture into any of their hidden depths. She feared not knowing where she was and becoming lost, or even captured by the inhabitants for being an intruder. There were so many fears, rational or not, that it kept her from opening any doors. Instead, she chose examining the space and the room was enough to satisfy her current level of curiosity.

Those days were perfect to take a break of the clutter of boxes that littered the attic. It felt like she would never reach the end of the memories stored in its depths. Box after box memories were uncovered, and with most Aggie had no idea how they mattered. Having Kyrel there was a nice break from the emptiness she normally felt from being alone.

Then she came across a simple picture of a couple. A man, unknown to her, and a woman, clearly her mother, caught in a moment of joy. Her mother laughed at something this mystery man had said and someone had captured them. Forever caught in happiness. Frozen in time forever. Aggie wondered what they had been talking about and remembered her mother's laugh. Because she was very young when her mother died it wasn't so much a precise memory, but something that came to her once in a while as though brought on the tail of a strong wind, never letting her forget the beauty of it.

Staring at the image in her hand, she studied the man. He was tall and had a chiseled jaw. With dark wavy hair that looked a bit unruly. His smile was captivating and his eyes splintered in wrinkles as they lifted. He, too, was enjoying the sound of her mother, Adalade Wasley's, laugh. She had a way of captivating everyone around her with a simple laugh or a smile, or even just a glance. She was beautiful and knew what she wanted out of life. At least that was one of the few things Gran had mentioned once when Aggie was growing up. Aggie figured she had caught her on a day of reminiscing, and therefore wasn't told to stop dwelling in the past.

Looking between her mother and the man, Aggie wondered if by some strange instance this man might be her father. She shook her head at the idea. If her father and mother had been this in love, why would he have left them? Then she looked closer. Perhaps it was her mind playing tricks on her, but it seemed that the two of them, the man and Aggie, had some similarities. Like the texture of their hair. Aggie reached up and felt her own curls pulled back away from her face, allowing her fingers to get caught in the tangles that were inevitable. She also saw something in his eyes that was familiar. Unable to put her finger on it, she let it go for now. Instead, she placed the picture in her pile that she planned to take downstairs. She was planning to frame some and just keep others close. The memory of her mother wasn't going to be hidden any longer.

*A*fter a long afternoon of cleaning and clearing, Aggie and Kyrel had made a significant dent and could now walk through the attic without fear of tripping and falling. Gathering her small box of things to go downstairs, she said, "I'm going to take this downstairs and I'll get us something to eat."

"I think you need a bigger distraction than lunch. You have been working so hard trying to get your life back on track and organize a little here and there now that you are the keeper of this manor. Why don't you let me take a little of that stress away from you?" Kyrel's intentions were clear and Aggie's arousal was instant, but she decided to play coy.

"Oh really, and what did you have in mind? I'd love a back rub or a foot rub right about now." She purposefully bat her eyelashes at her incubus lover.

"I could do both of those things but I have another sure-fire method to ease the tension that I can see radiating through your entire body." Without waiting for permission, Ky walked right up to her and captured her lips with his. His hand clasped her neck and pulled her snug against his front. She could feel the evidence of his very large erection. Aggie remembered the feel of it against her lips and shivered at the memory.

Ky's hand traveled down her back and to her ass. His hand kneaded the flesh; she didn't realize how tight her muscles had gotten and a moan slipped out.

"You are so tense, my love. Let me take care of you." Given the amount of traffic in and out of the attic, the floor was practically clear of dust. Ky lifted her without relocating his hands and expertly navigated her to the floor. "I've been looking forward to this moment." He nudged his nose into her fully-clothed apex still and playfully sank his teeth into her. Even though it wasn't hard, the action made her gasp.

He made quick work of her pants and underwear. Then he settled himself between her thighs. A nibble to her right calf and she was distracted enough to once again be startled when his fingers brushed her nub, which was throbbing for more attention.

She didn't have to wait long. Kyrel's tongue ran the length of her slit with just the right amount of pressure. "Oh, that feels amazing." He had rendered her to shortened phrases.

"You are as perfect as I imagined. I could do this all day long and never tire." He slowly tasted her and paid close attention to all of her sensitive places, a few she hadn't realized were quite so much. His fingers splayed out on her stomach just beneath the fabric there. They moved so slowly it was almost painful.

Ky didn't rush. He was enjoying her in his own time. Working her up so tight that she wanted to scream, but she was afraid he would stop. Pressing her hips up and tighter against his mouth, she tried to encourage him without words. A laugh rumbled out of him and it buzzed along her clit, causing delicious friction she desperately wanted.

"Ky, stop tormenting me. I'm so close." She begged shamelessly for climax that stayed just out of reach.

"You think this is torment? I could never torture you, my love. All I wanted was to please you." His tongue plunged inside her, pumping in and out as though it were the tip of something else. His right hand that was still free pressed two fingers to her clit and pinched it lightly, causing her to break her silent enjoyment. Her climax built again quickly and his left hand pressed her shirt up higher and under her bra like a sneaky snake. It latched onto the closest nipple and pinched hard. Her climax broke through her like a roaring wave. Her body arched off the floor but Ky didn't slow his actions. All three continued. His mouth pierced her, and fingers flicked and pinched throughout her orgasm, pulling every last drop out of her.

She dropped as abruptly as she had arched. The room grew quiet save for her heavy breathing as she tried to catch her breath. "That was perfect and just what I needed." She struggled to lift her sated body from its place on the floor. Propped up on her elbows, she lifted her foot to his swollen crotch. "I'll gladly return the favor, seeing as you've worked yourself into an unfit state." Rubbing with her foot, she was still trying to push energy into her limbs to do exactly what she said.

Ky gently moved her foot from him and leaned forward to place a gentle kiss to her lips. "This was all for you, my love. I want nothing in return but to see you relaxed and happy." He helped her back into her panties and pants so she looked like nothing had happened. A guy had never done that for her before. It was always a give and take or, in some cases, just a take on their part. Her previous lovers hadn't always been so considerate.

Ky helped her to her feet and she let out a groan of displeasure to be upright again. "I'll stay here and stack the rest of these boxes you haven't finished with and get them out of the way." Aggie blew him a kiss. Kyrel caught it in a cheesy way, sticking it into his pocket, causing her to laugh. She rolled her eyes at his antics. Turning away, she made her way out of the attic. Aggie took her time so she wouldn't fall with her newfound treasures.

Suddenly, the stairs began to tremble. Not enough to call an earthquake but significant enough that she froze and braced herself on the wall. Then it was as though the walls of the house were vibrating and not the ground actually shaking. After a moment, her body regained its balance and she was able to walk with the tremors. It felt like the current was drawing her in a single direction.

"Is there a giant troll walking through my house? Did he just fall down or just sit to take a rest?" Aggie made her way through the halls, part of her truly wondering if she was going to bump into some dangerous being that could or might at least consider eating her on sight. Absently, she thought Kyrel would be there to assist if need be. Though the fact that he didn't run after her when the house began to quiver was strange to say the least. As she turned the last corner, she was a bit surprised to find the house calm as she stood directly in front of the mysterious door that, up until a few weeks ago, had remained sealed her entire life. The Gateway practically hummed its approval that she had made her way to answer its call.

"Did that just happen?" Aggie didn't know what to do but she placed her hand on the door cautiously, still unsure of what all was happening. It was as though the entire house came to life around her and brought her to this room. Not the first time she was drawn to this room, but definitely the first time to this extent and with so much force.

Slowly she pushed open the door, and to her surprise a man stood in the center with his back to the door. Hands crossed behind his back, he surveyed the space. His dark hair was cropped neatly above his ears. Aggie's hand flew to her mouth to contain a gasp as she tried to remain quiet, taking him in. The slight wave to his hair had a familiar feel and he was rather tall, and she knew if she stood next to him her head would be straining in order to see him clearly. He was wearing what she would consider business attire. A pair of dark colored slacks that fit him as though a tailor had made adjustments just for his shape, and standard white buttoned shirt under a sport coat, the color of which Aggie couldn't make out in the low lighting of the Gateway. With a tie wrapped around his neck, he looked as though he wore these clothes everyday out of habit and not for stylistic choice.

As she stepped further in past the door, the room suddenly felt as though a great wind passed around and the door she was just standing in sealed completely. Aggie gasped at the sudden change and spun to see that the wall looked no different than any other wall in the room. Doorknobs covered every inch, but there was not a single doorway. Panicking slightly, she tried to calm down and not think about being trapped in the Gateway for the unforeseen future.

The commotion didn't go unnoticed by the stranger, as he

turned quickly to face her but never altered his stance. Arms still clasped behind him, he had a serene look to his face. It was like he knew it would happen or was used to the strange happenings going on in this space that once seemed smaller to her but now, with her only escape closed, seemed vast and endless. She glanced around the room and looked for any possible way out or protection from this stranger if things should turn bad. Then she remembered she was part Fae and part Demon. Should things go bad, she could whip up some sort of whammy to defend herself.

"Who are you and what do you want?" she practically shouted, as she was nervous and still trying to sound brave and in control of the situation.

The man slowly turned around, and she was struck with recognition. His face was the same as the one she tucked away from the attic, just a bit older now. The man standing with her mother all those years ago. "Agatha? Is it really you?" His voice was deep and tainted with disbelief. She took an involuntary step back in shock.

"How do you know who I am?" While she had her suspicions as to who the man in the worn picture was, it wasn't seated in any level of fact.

"You probably don't remember me, as I only saw you a couple times when you were younger and mostly from a distance." Aggie was a bit freaked out; his words made him sound like a pedophile or even worse. "My name is Eckard Gnash, and the Gateway brought me here." His words didn't make complete sense and the room shuddered in response. She didn't know what to make of that. Was it a reaction to his words?

"The Gateway? It brought you here?" Aggie didn't understand what he was saying and wasn't sure what was going on. Was that tremor in the house the Gateway calling her? That was a pretty convenient security system if that was the case. Aggie glanced behind herself quickly, not wanting to give this stranger any upper hand. The door was still missing and she was a bit concerned for her safety, but in the same token relieved that he wouldn't be able to invade her personal space. She could at least use her magic in here to protect herself, as this was a magically safe space. The room seemed to purr at her thought, giving Aggie the suspicion that it was connected to her on a deeper level. Was the room reading her thoughts or just her feelings? Knowing the room had never hurt her before, somehow she knew that when it was completely safe again the room would show her the way home.

"Yes, it brought me here. I felt a pull and knew I was needed somewhere. When I arrived here, I realized you must need my help. Seeing as I'm likely the only one alive who could give you any insight as to what you're supposed to be doing here. As in how to control the Gateway." The room flared a bit at his choice of words, giving Aggie a bit of caution. "Forgive me," Eckard said to the room more than to her directly. "I merely meant that you needed to better understand your roll as the Gatekeeper." The room of knobs calmed a bit and Aggie felt it was still on guard, but sensed it lessen slightly.

"So let me repeat myself, because your previous answer wasn't exactly clear. Who are you, and how do you know who I am?" Aggie's hands migrated to her hips in a defiant pose. She was tired of vague answers and wanted more information before her level head was gone, to be replaced by her trigger-happy demon side. Since training with Mathius she was more of a mind to shoot first ask questions later because it was easier. The Fae in her worked more with her instincts, and for that she was grateful, as they balanced each other.

When Mathius began training her, they spent hours talking through the possibilities. While his demon powers were isolated around the ability to control matter, no one knew where Aggie's skills would lie. Even though Mathius was very knowledgeable, his words sounded to Aggie as though he were speaking a different language.

"*If you share my powers of manipulation, I can train you in a direct path. Though, if your powers differ in any way it could result in life-altering consequences.*" Confusion filled Aggie's face, but that didn't stop Mathius from breaking everything down to the tiniest detail.

"*If you use too much force, the matter will become misshapen and won't return to its original state. But if you use too little it won't even get off the ground. I made that mistake once in my youth and almost obliterated my family home by impaling an object deeply into the foundation.*"

"*Stop, stop, STOP!*" Aggie had to do anything possible to shut him up before her head spun off her shoulders. "*There has to be a different way to figure out what my demonic powers are.*"

"*What if we tried the meditation method that she did with her Fae powers?*" Eldon chimed in after noticing Aggie was becoming more frustrated than gaining any actual training or skill.

Mathius considered that option. "*I guess I hadn't thought of that. I got so excited that she had a power I could help her with, I didn't consider the best way to train her.*" The three of them proceeded to sit down in a makeshift circle to prepare to find her headspace again.

"*I'm not sure this will work. I haven't had a conversation with my inner self since my Fae powers manifested. I even didn't seem to get to my completely relaxed state until the twins helped me.*" Aggie was so nervous and anxious about succeeding, she had begun rambling and was unable to stay focused.

"*You seem to have forgotten that they just redirected your focus; you fell into your state of mediation on your own. There is no need to be concerned this go-around.*" Eldon's sweet voice danced over her skin and eased her frazzled nerves. Releasing the breath that she hadn't realized she was holding, Aggie attempted to allow her body to release so she could find her inner demon, or whoever she was going in after. All she knew was that she was going to find her Fae self again using this method.

Closing her eyes, Aggie took deep breaths to clear out any clogs that might inhibit her transition. Not wanting to think about anything distracting, she tried to wipe her brain of any lingering thoughts. Sitting as still as possible, breathing in and out, Aggie tried not to allow her frustration to guide her into a failed attempt. Just when she was about to give up, she felt a lightest *touch on her shoulders and a flash of the twins' faces behind her eyelids. Nearly instantly she felt as though she was falling, her feet unable to find purchase. The only thing she could do was scream.*

Aggie fell for what seemed like forever; she felt a bit like Alice falling down the rabbit hole, and the longer she fell the less scary it seemed. It gave her time to look around where she was. The sky was a strange shade of reddish-orange, similar to Ahael, but the coloring was off just enough to know she wasn't there. She was somewhere in the demonic world, because she saw the sun and the lava moon hanging in the sky like it was high noon. Fast approaching was the first sign of anything that resembled ground. The trees were ablaze just like Ahael; Aggie wondered if she were really in a demonic place or if her brain just improvised on some of the aspects of the only demon city she had seen.

Moments before impact, her body slowed to a gradual stop and she was placed on her feet. Thankful for the improved landing, Aggie mentally patted herself on the back for getting that this time. Quickly, she stood and brushed her clothing down, even though it wasn't marred or out of place at all.

Aggie knew she was in a demonic realm, but had no idea where. After walking for what seemed like forever, she sat down on a blue rock with a few spots which made it resemble a robin's egg. In the back of her mind, she worried a giant bird was going to swoop down and attack her in an effort to protect her young. Something moved in the distance, causing Aggie to flinch. She worried that a bird was attacking. When she braced herself and raised her hands to somehow magically attack, surprise hit her when she saw a woman walking toward her.

Relief washed over her as she felt a strong sense of déjà vu. She had done it; Aggie knew her inner self was walking toward her.

Knowing her inner self would look like her, Aggie let her guard down. She anxiously awaited her visible demonic changes. Her Fae self was equipped with ears of Fae descent. Mathius didn't have any strong demonic features, and part of her wondered if her Demon self would be the same since he was the reason she had been gifted her powers.

The woman who approached her would have startled her if she hadn't been expecting to see a twin version of herself. In that case she was almost a replica, but the newest arrival was different and Aggie saw it the moment she came into focus. Her forehead sported deep V-shaped wrinkles in four sets. They didn't mar her beauty in any way, but added a new element. Her facial contours were still the same and the curves of her body still matched her own. And when she spoke Aggie realized even her voice was like an echo of her own.

"I wondered when you would figure it out. Your Fae and I have been placing bets on when you would get here." The snark in her voice reminded Aggie of when she loved calling the guys out on their shortcomings.

"I think part of it wasn't my fault. Mathius was a bit overzealous and wanted to teach me everything he had ever learned. That took some time to get through, and I think we only made it a fraction before we needed to try something new." Aggie's shoulders dropped in defeat.

"It's about time you stood your ground. This is the best way to interact with any of your new selves. We can teach you what you need to know, and while you might not know the extent of your powers upon leaving us you will know how to access and maximize your reach." Aggie glanced away for a moment then felt something heavy weighing down her wrists. Lifting her arms, she found that a pair of gold gauntlets was now clasped around each arm. They were nothing too fancy but she was captivated by the fact that, at first, they had felt weighted, but the longer they remained the lighter they felt.

Aggie glanced down at her golden cuffs and they rippled at the thought. Mathius' power was seated in the ability to manipulate matter. The cuffs, as she learned after waking from meeting her beautiful, demonic self, were her way to always have something to manipulate. Her Fae bracelet had automatically and naturally changed to a dainty anklet. This way she always had a piece of her alter egos with her at all times.

CHAPTER TWO

Eckard started, but hesitated for some reason and started shifting on his feet. "I knew your mother." Aggie knew the guilty uncomfortable look well and wondered what he was hiding.

"And?" Aggie prompted, but he wouldn't look at her. Which made her more than worried.

"I'm your father." Eckard's last words were spoken on a whisper and she barely heard him.

"What? My father? Seriously?" She stuttered and stammered, her words disjointed into broken questions. Taking a moment to inhale deeply, she found her voice. "This isn't some movie and I'm not Luke Skywalker. You can't just show up here and drop that bomb and expect me to take it blindly without some sort of explanation." Aggie started pacing and her breathing picked up. There was no way she could have predicted that, on the day she was walking down memory lane, the man she wanted to know the most about would suddenly fall into her lap—or her Gateway, as the case may be.

"Let me explain. I was exiled from this house by your grandmother years ago, regardless of your mother's wishes. You were just born, and for some reason unbeknownst to us your Gran always had it out for me." Aggie still felt like he was hiding something but his words seemed true enough, so she let him continue. "I loved your mother and you with all my heart, and it nearly killed me to be separated from you. So one time, when I found out you were out of the house, I would show up and just watch you from a distance."

"Do you realize how creepy that sounds?" Aggie asked dryly, hoping he understood that he sounded like a crazed stalker. Even if he was her father, Gran wouldn't have acted lightly in any case. Unfortunately, she couldn't sense any ill in him or will to do her harm. He seemed genuine, if not just from his words then from his mannerisms, too. His feet were shuffling like he was uncomfortable, but how many times does a man meet his long-lost daughter and have to explain it to her? Not to mention he answered her when she asked this time; it had to be a good sign that he didn't dodge her question.

"I'm sorry. I knew if I approached you your mother would run, as your grandmother had won her over in time to her way of thinking. They never explained to me what my wrongdoing was. Once, she saw me and scooped you up so fast it was as though you were never there." His words were full of remorse and sorrow. Those of a father who had truly known loss. Aggie felt for him, and against her better judgement she caved.

"Say I was to believe you; how would you prove all of this is true?" Aggie's stance relaxed a bit and she was less on guard. She always could call her powers on a moment's notice, so there was less concern.

"Aside from our similar features that I'm sure you have already noticed, and the fact that we are both left-handed, which I know from watching you all these years." He answered the last part before she could question it and the words caught in her throat. He hadn't stopped watching her after her mother had passed. "I could prove it to you because we both share something no one could replicate. Behind your right elbow is a mark that is only worn by those of my bloodline. The Gnash family is known to bear their family crest upon their skin as a badge of honor. It is passed from father to child."

Aggie knew the mark to which he referred and had assumed it was a birthmark, and so never gave it another thought. It was hidden enough that most didn't even know it was there. How did this man, this stranger, know of its existence unless he spoke the truth? Still not responding or moving to show him this mark, Aggie stood like a statue and waited. Rolling up his sleeve, Eckard displayed his left wrist. On that patch of skin was a dark patch in the shape of a crescent. The same image that she bore on her right arm, hidden away from view and forgotten about. Anyone who had seen hers in the past assumed it was a tattoo, and she never corrected them. Stunned, Aggie absently ran her fingers over her own skin that bore the mark he just showed her. Was there any way it could be a coincidence?

Silence filled the room as Aggie processed this information and Eckard just waited for her to speak. No words came to her except how impossible this all seemed. Just minutes before she had been in the attic and stumbled across a picture of this man from years before. The weatherworn picture suggested it from a time long forgotten. Now this strange man was standing in front of her, admitting what she had assumed while in the attic. Her father? Could this really be? The room practically vibrated with unsaid words. Neither even began to speak, and even though Aggie had a thousand questions she didn't know where to start.

Saving Aggie the torment of deciding, the room began to fill with magic from multiple points. The fact that her house didn't shake or do anything strange, must mean someone friendly or at least someone the Gateway trusted was coming. Now she knew what an intruder felt like, or at least someone unexpected. Though she wondered why it never did that when the guys came through the first time after Gran passed the control onto her. Also, she had a better idea of how connected she was to this space. With her house still hidden from view the room broke with three doorways, as though from nowhere. Aggie feared she would never get used to that.

A moment later Liel, Mathius, and Xavier stepped through their respective doorways, wearing matching looks of concern. To her surprise, Xavier was the first to react.

"What are you doing here?" He spoke mere inches from Eckard's face as he held him up off the floor by his collar. Blinking rapidly, Aggie was still surprised every time he used his vampire super speed. It was as though he moved in the time of a single breath. Once Aggie righted herself and was back on track, she realized his choice of words was strange.

"Do you two know each other?" Confusion filled Aggie's face as she glanced between Eckard and Xavier a few times. The scowl Xavier wore was matched by the looks on Mathius and Liel's faces. They were actually standing much closer, too. "What is going on?"

"I believe he asked you a question." Liel's tone was his usual level-headed one, but his expression wasn't any less fierce. No one was paying Aggie any attention or answering her either.

"Excuse me! Will someone please tell me what is going on here?" Aggie persisted, but no one acknowledged her. Her guardians were solely focused on Eckard, and Xavier hadn't loosened his grip.

"I...can't..." Eckard's words were short and stunted. His sentence wasn't finished. Aggie looked closer and saw he looked to be changing colors.

"Put him down; can't you see he's struggling to breathe? There is no way he can answer your questions or succumb to your interrogation if he passes out." Aggie was frantically tugging back on Xavier, but found it was like pulling on a statue firmly rooted in place. "I said Let. Him. Go!" She mentally reached for her demonic golden wristlets. Combining them to make a golden choker, she wrapped them around Xavier's throat and cinched down tighter and tighter until she had his attention. Her tone was so demanding that, by some miracle, it was enough to get his attention. The other two oafs were just standing there, stoic and observing. Neither one of them bothering to assist her in any way.

"Do you know who this is?" Xavier's words were spoken as though he wasn't struggling to breathe or choking at all, and couldn't understand why she would be defending this stranger. Aggie really didn't know why either, other than it went against her human nature to harm an innocent. At this point, she didn't know one way or another. "He is a traitor and has been banished from being able to travel through the Gateway unattended." His attention quickly turned back to Eckard. "How did you get in here?" He released the pressure on Eckard's neck but didn't release his hold on him. This made Aggie release her pressure on Xavier's new neckwear. She didn't pull the magic back completely, just to stay on guard if need be to call him off again.

"I was summoned by the Gateway. How else would I be here?" Xavier's expression was one of disbelief. Eckard spoke his words in a haughty way and his explanation was the same one he gave Aggie. This caused her to believe he was telling her the truth. Though, for some reason, the Gateway seemed to shudder. Almost reacting again to the words. Xavier, Mathius, and Liel's expressions gave her pause.

"What do you mean he's a traitor?" Aggie didn't know what they were talking about. "He told me he was my father and, while I don't know what to believe, it seems like, as the Gatekeeper, I should have some protection against unknown threats." Now, thinking about it out loud, Aggie didn't know if he was telling the truth. Why would the Gateway endanger her by bringing a traitor to her door? The room felt like it pulsed again and Aggie wondered if, for some reason, perhaps the Gateway was telling her something. Maybe it didn't bring Eckard here after all. It felt like the room was being opinionated, and that might have been why the door to her home was blocked. This possible reaction gave her pause. Eyeing Eckard warily, Aggie stood her ground. "Given the fact that I'm not completely sure of why you're here, I'm leaning toward believing the part about you being my father. While I don't have any of the stuff with me that I was carrying down when you chose to make your appearance and my house started quaking, I do see similarities between you and a picture I found."

Eckard preened at her words but, unfortunately for him, he didn't wait before he spoke. "I have a feeling I know what picture you're speaking of. I knew it would be the only one your mother hid away from your grandmother."

"I'm not playing games with you. I have no idea what you did or how you upset my Gran, but I'm a different person now than I was when you left. I still want to give you a chance to plead your case. I know my Gran can be a hard nut to crack, but I want a chance to get to know you, too. I'm an adult and can make that choice myself." Aggie squared her shoulders, proud that she had stood her ground and made this decision. Though when she turned around she was met by three angry glares.

As if the Gateway heard her silent plea, but before anyone had begun to explain the traitor aspect of Eckard's situation, the room began to explode in magic again. This time only from one point of entry, and Aggie let her eyes travel to the phantom glow of the mystical doorway created. As two bodies stepped through, a smile spread across her face. The door sealed behind the two broad- shouldered bodies and their faces came into view. Mitchell and Ren.

"Why didn't we get an invite to the party?" Ren's lopsided smile was so endearing, and at that moment was just what Aggie needed.

"Had I known you were free I would have been happy to extended a personal one for you to this gathering, but unfortunately it was unexpected to all of us." Aggie walked over and placed a kiss on his cheek and threw her arms around his neck.

Given the fact that he didn't come in with powers blazing, he deserved a reward.

Mitchell just scowled at her and directed his attention toward the other people in the room. "What is going on in here?"

"It seems Aggie has received an unwanted visitor." Mathius spat out the words, showing how displeased he was with the turn of events.

"Now don't speak for me, Mathius. You might be my mate, but that doesn't give you the right to speak for me. I will say who I allow into my life, and at this point I haven't seen a reason to cut Eckard out without cause. No one has given me a viable reason, and until I have one nothing will change without my say-so." Aggie didn't want to ever let anyone control her again. She was the one in charge and that's how it was going to stay.

"As much fun as this is, and I'm happy to sit here and watch you put everyone in their rightful place, we have bigger problems at hand." Mitchell's words got Aggie's attention and she turned to give it to him fully. As did everyone else in the room, including Eckard.

"The shifter realm is under attack," Ren announced. Mitchell gave him a dirty look and his jaw flexed in frustration, but Ren wasn't deterred. "We aren't sure what started it but it seems we have a rebellion underway, and if we don't put a stop to it we could lose many shifters unnecessarily."

"Are you finished, or do you want to be the one to share all the news?" Mitchell spat the words at him and it looked like Ren was fighting an eyeroll. Even though Ren was Beta to Mitchell's Alpha, they were both equally Alpha in most situations. Aggie fought back a laugh at the ridiculous situation. She couldn't imagine having a twin or even a sibling to argue with over trivial things like who got to tell a story.

Interrupting the twin shifters' usual bickering, the room filled with magic. Aggie glanced around and saw three new points of entry. Smiling, she knew exactly who was coming in to join them. Only a moment later she felt the magic dissipate, and in its place stood Gryson, the Mage Guardian. Kyrel somehow stood beside him, as though they had come through the same door, with a look of confusion painted on his face. Aggie assumed this was because she didn't return with the food she promised, only to find her here surrounded by everyone and then some.

Then, on the other side of the room, all that was right in the world settled as she saw her Fae mate, Eldon. As their eyes met Eldon's small smile greeted her, ever shy even after all they'd shared. His eyes softened. "My sweet, I've been anxious to get back to you all day." His words made Aggie's heart soar. He had begun calling her his 'sweet' soon after the Demon attack. He had helped heal all the children, and with Gryson's help they magically righted their situation so it was as though the previous few weeks were nothing but a bad memory. Eldon closed the distance between them and wrapped his arms around her. The butterflies that ran through her at his touch were a comfort now and less of an invasion. Stretching up on her toes, Aggie pressed her lips to Eldon's and melted against him, knowing he wouldn't let her fall.

"Are you two finished with your reunion? You saw each other this morning." Mitchell stood with his arms crossed, and his words popped the bubble that was their moment. Raising one eyebrow in Aggie's direction when she started to speak, Aggie chose to hold her tongue for a bit. She knew there was something bigger going on than her ongoing battle with Mitchell. She filed away her comment and would have it out with him later.

"What is going on? One minute I'm stacking boxes and the next Aggie is gone for too long and didn't return with our lunch." Kyrel's natural charm oozed from him and covered the room in a warm blanket, instantly settling the tension that had hung thick in the air from the men's altercations.

"You mean you didn't notice the minor relocation of my

house while you were busy helping me in the attic?" Aggie looked as though he had grown a second head. There was no way a person couldn't have felt that, especially from the top of the house. Kyrel simply shook his head.

"Is there such a thing as trolls?" Aggie hesitated after the question escaped. Words couldn't express how crazy she would sound now if she explained how it felt as though a giant troll was stalking her through her house and then she became locked in the Gateway. Before she could even try, Mitchell cleared his throat.

"As I was going to say before I was so rudely interrupted by all of you," Mitchell's gaze connected with each person in the room, showing his frustration, "there is a rebellion that has been building for a while now in the shifter realm among the clans. To my surprise, something has acted as a catalyst and everything came to a head sooner than we thought. They gained enough followers to their cause and now I'm not sure we can ward them off. Something feels off about all of this, but I can't put my finger on it. My wolf is unsettled about it all and I feel it, too."

"There have been raids every few days and we can't figure out what they are looking for in each clan. When they leave no one can figure out what they have taken. It seems they are just there for mass destruction. I said they were trying to weaken the individual clans, but Mitchell thinks otherwise." Ren's usual lightheartedness was missing and he was all serious. If he didn't look a bit different from Mitchell it would have been hard to tell them apart in that instance.

"Do you know who is spearheading this fight?" Mathius, ever the warrior, was first in the ring as always.

"It's not clear, but I have my suspicions," Mitchell sneered, and Aggie knew he had to have had a rival of some kind.

"Childhood friend come back to play?" Aggie teased, throwing it in his face, knowing it would set him off but not caring. This rebellion, while serious, wasn't going away overnight, and a few well-placed jabs wouldn't hurt anything.

"You could say that," Mitchell snarked. "He was never much of a friend; more like a bully. Didn't go after me but everyone else even a little smaller than him. I got in more fights with him than anyone. Thankfully, the fighting is part of shifter life, Princess. So, unlike your human school, it was encouraged to establish a pecking order. Though it is frowned upon when you are purposely attacking those weaker than you." Mitchell's words acted as a reprimand he was so good at, disguised as an insult all the same.

Aggie curled her lip in disgust but didn't grace him with a verbal response. At least not until she had something better than sticking her tongue out at him like a petulant child.

"What can we do to help?" Liel asked, always one to bring everyone back to the issue at hand and back to business.

"Initially I think a stronger presence is going to be enough, but I know that won't last forever. They are getting stronger and braver in everything they do. I can't figure out if it is actual bravery, or insanity masking itself as courage." Mitchell started making his way to the door and paused. "Who are you, again?"

"Eckard Gnash, Aggie's father." The room went completely silent at his words, since the majority of the guys hadn't been there for that part of this discussion. Outside of the original three, they were more focused on the shifter problem and not worried about the stranger in the room. Aggie realized that not all of the men were as privy to Eckard's history and for that she was grateful. While she didn't know if she could trust him as far as she could throw him, there was always the chance if she let him leave she would never see him again. No one stuck around in her life forever and most weren't for very long.

CHAPTER THREE

*B*eing more prepared for a trip through the Gateway this time, Aggie knew she didn't need to pack. Her new powers gave her a break from the need for luggage. "So which knob is the lucky one tonight?" Aggie started toward the side of the room where the twin wolves appeared. Scanning the wall, she was always enamored by the vast array before her. Having already spent some time analyzing different ones Aggie knew there were a few icy ones in this area, but to her surprise Mitchell was reaching for a smaller one almost hidden from view. One she would have overlooked if he hadn't drawn attention to it.

The size wasn't as much the issue as the coloring. It was very plain upon first inspection, though when you looked closely the details became known. It almost shimmered and looked to change from icy blues to the deepest greens imaginable. This made sense since it was a shifter realm, but there was more. In the depths of the colors were shapes. The blueish coloring showed icy shards that gave off a frosted look. Then when it shifted slowly to the greens she could see the individual blades of grass, and in the distance a forest of trees ran along the perimeter of the knob. The effect was breathtaking and made Aggie want to know more.

She had learned that each destination was reflected in a way through the doorknob. This gave her a surge of excitement and she wanted to know what lay beyond this door. Reaching out she pressed her hand to the knob before Mitchell could connect, and heard a rumble that came from beside her. Glancing up, she noted that Mitchell didn't seem too keen on her stepping into his territory without permission or explicit invitation. Shaking her head, Aggie smirked at him. "You are so territorial." This didn't stop her from wrapping her fingers around the metal and feeling the magic soar through her entire body. It was acceptance through and through. Everything about this moment felt right, like the Gateway was sending its approval over this choice. Aggie faintly heard a laugh and knew in an instant it was Ren.

Instead of barreling through the door, Aggie waited at the last second. There was always a chance that anyone on the other side would be unfriendly. Without a word she slid to the side. Mitchell just sighed gruffly, showing his annoyance with her antics.

The men slowly made their way through, following Mitchell. Ren was hot on his heels but not before throwing a sly little wink in Aggie's direction. He might be a big jokester and his brother might be a pompous ass who was never wrong, but she did enjoy watching them move. The best time to see that was when they were walking away and she wouldn't be called out for her lingering eyes. Oh, and boy did they linger on every muscle exposed by their clothes fitting them all too well. Every ripple and swell were mouthwatering, and Aggie knew what they both looked like without much clothing on. She wished for a chance to get them both still and mute long enough to take it all in as slowly as possible. The last time they had such an encounter was a not so friendly ending. She hadn't been able to get it out of her head when she had been alone with either of them. Ren, of course, would make comments about her emotions getting electrifying. While Mitchell just would remark dryly about her not being able to control her impulses. Neither were what she wanted to hear when she was drooling over their sinfully sexy bodies.

"If you took a picture of them you could drool anytime you wish." Gryson's voice sounded right beside Aggie and she startled, not hearing his approach. She was so lost in her thoughts and her daydreaming that she had forgotten she wasn't the only one in the room.

"Where's the fun in that? Then it doesn't move. I prefer the real thing." Luckily the two men in question were already through the door and couldn't hear their conversation. Aggie hoped not, at least. Gryson just shook his head and made his way through the door, quickly disappearing while laughing slightly at her thought process.

Kyrel was next in line and gave her a quick peck on the cheek, mirth in his eyes. Clearly he had heard the conversation she had just shared with Gryson. Mathius and Liel, ever battle-ready were next, but Mathius hesitated. "I'm not sure I like leaving you alone with him. I'm not happy that we haven't had a chance to talk about why, either."

"Well, if you guys hadn't come in with guns blazing we could have discussed it like civilized people. Now I guess that will just have to wait. I'll handle this from here on out. I want to be the last one out, so shoo." She flapped her hand like she was scaring a fly and Mathius scowled at Eckard before pressing a sweet kiss to her lips. It wasn't goodbye, but everyone was acting like they were just leaving for work. Aggie wondered if they forgot she was tagging along this time.

"Care to remove your handiwork from my neck? I'd hate for you to be without power if needed." Xavier stepped forward, almost acting bored now. It was as though he had resigned to her decision and wasn't going to say another word about it, and anger was beneath him. Aggie mentally reached for her gauntlets and they pulled from Xavier's neck.

"It's a pity; they looked quite stunning on you and you would make a pretty pet." She winked at him to show her humor, and a smile stretched across his face. If she hadn't known him before that moment it would have been almost scary how he could be happy and look evil all in the same breath. Well, her breath at least; it didn't seem like her vampire needed to breathe in order to survive. Aggie filed that away for a question and answer session with Xavier later. With her matter back in place on her arms, Xavier practically floated into the open doorway. Aggie secretly wished she could move with that much grace.

"I'm willing to walk through with you if you wish, my sweet." Eldon was the only one of her guys left. She hadn't spoken to Eckard since the guys started arriving, and hadn't asked if he wanted to accompany her. She didn't want to with any of the guys so they couldn't share their displeasure with her decision. She was sure they assumed she was sending him on his way upon their departure.

"I'll be fine, El. I have to check on one final thing before I step through and I can't do that completely with anyone here." She pressed her lips to his once more and it quickly turned heated. She had to force the fog away so she could think again. Breaking the kiss Aggie gave him one last peck, and he disappeared along with the rest of her guardians.

Aggie turned after a moment. The doorway had remained open, somehow knowing there were more travelers that day. Looking back over her shoulder she saw Eckard was waiting off in the shadows, most likely hoping to be ignored. He wasn't given the best reception, and once the guys got distracted Eckard was given a bit of a reprieve.

"What are your plans now?" Aggie shot the question at him without warning. She simultaneously was dreading and curious to find out the answer.

"I came here to help you. What do you want me to do?" Like a true negotiator, instead of answering her question he shot out one of his own. Unexpectedly leaving the ball in her court. Aggie knew what she wanted but didn't know if she could handle the rejection. After the response her guys had just given Eckard, her next plan might be too much to ask of anyone. Resolved that he was going to say no, she just went for it anyway.

"You could come with us—if you aren't busy, that is." Aggie spoke so fast. Anticipating the rejection she was a bit light-headed, regretting her choice already. Immediately, she started covering and saving face. "If you are busy, which you probably are, I understand. You could leave me your number and I could call when we get back. Or your address and I could write you a letter. Maybe not, since no one writes letters anymore. Does the postal system work where you're from, or staying, or whatever?" Rambling as usual, the crazy just came out without any effort. Aggie didn't know how to stop, but she couldn't have anticipated what Eckard did next.

Placing his hands on her shoulders to stop her word vomit, he said, "I'd be happy to go with you. I'm sure I could be of some help even if it is just to answer your questions when you aren't busy saving the realms." His look was one of pride, and something else Aggie didn't recognize. She was too taken aback by the response. She was so used to people leaving and letting her down that she didn't know what it was like to have someone to count on. She was speechless. Well, almost.

"Oh... okay. That sounds like a great idea. I'm not sure how much downtime I'll have, because the guys are still training me to fight and hone my new powers. I'm still very green, but being part Fae and part Demon is hard work."

"I'd be happy just to watch you, and be a part of your life for as long as you'll let me." Eckard's eyes softened.

"I really do have something I want to do, and as much as it seems like I'm throwing you to the wolves, sort of literally, I need you to head on before me." Aggie wanted to test her theory that the Gateway had been protecting her when she first entered.

Eckard didn't flinch. He just stepped through as though he knew he would be perfectly safe and had been doing it for years. The door remained open; Aggie was about to step through, but she felt a magic warm the room causing her to glance back. Just as she has suspected the door her house was wide open, as always. It had been waiting for the area to be safe, protecting her personal space from anyone unwanted. With that, she stepped through the Gateway.

*B*right. That was the first thing Aggie noticed as she stepped from the enchanted Gateway. She always took longer to come out of it, as she was certain that she heard it speaking to her and drawing her this way and that. However, this time, when she exited it was hard to adjust. They were outside, she thought, and a bright light was blinding her. There was no telling who was near and exactly where she was.

"Uh, is anyone here?" She hesitated when she didn't hear any voices or movement. She couldn't see past the end of her nose. *This is an interesting way to become acquainted with a new world.* Aggie was getting a bit nervous, knowing she was the last one through. In the back of her mind she wondered if the Gateway took her someplace else.

A shoe scuffed across the dirt and Aggie gasped. Still no one spoke. Aggie blinked rapidly, trying to adjust her eyes. Raising her hand, she attempted to block the glowing object. She felt a hand connect with her arm, nearly jumping out of her skin, and screamed. It took her a moment to settle and realize that the warm vibration was Ren. It could have been Mitchell, but he wasn't likely to comfort her in any situation, after their last panicked encounter.

"Gryson, do you think you could tone down your interrogation lamp for a moment so we can get settled into the clan?" Ren was more than calm, and it was as though he found the moment comical. Aggie wouldn't expect anything less. He found the humor in most situations. Though Aggie worried what kind of lamp he was using that was literally blinding her. What was it doing to everyone else? Suddenly, the light dimmed and Aggie blinked to rid her vision of the blinding spots that were left floating across her eyes, marring everything in her line of sight.

"What the hell?" Aggie still couldn't make out everything but she wasn't just going to stand there silent, waiting for them to sort everything. "I could have hurt myself. What are you guys doing?" Then it hit her like a ton of bricks and she went on alert. Interrogation? There was only one situation that would require a lamp to intimidate someone. Her father, Eckard, came through moments before her. She didn't warn anyone of her choice to invite him along on this unknown adventure/battle thing. As the floating lights cleared, she saw her restrained father and all the guys surrounding him. It must have escalated while she was gone.

"We thought he had done something to you." Eldon's lyrical voice met her ears and she relaxed a fraction of an inch. "You had us worried and, while he swore you were fine, you weren't here."

"Forgive me for trying to figure out a way to know my father." Sarcasm was a go-to for Aggie, but this was too much. How could they assume someone harmed her in the Gateway? Wasn't that supposed to be her safe space, controlled by her as the Gatekeeper? "I needed to know more before I just wrote him off. This was the first thing that popped into my head. Then I sent him through first as a safety precaution. In case you all didn't notice, when he arrived the Gateway locked down. My own escape was cut off to protect the Gateway, or so I assumed.

I had to know for sure. So I hung back to verify my assumption." Aggie looked between her guys. She was thankful to see at least half of them had the decency to look chastised as their gazes fell to the floor. Unfortunately Mathius, Liel, and Xavier still looked unimpressed and glared at her father.

Mitchell just looked bothered, as though the last few minutes have been wasted and he wouldn't ever get them back. Leaning against a tree with his arms crossed, Mitchell waited for everyone to pick a side. His muscles stretched and rolled across his arms and Aggie was lost in that image for a few seconds or minutes. She wasn't sure. Following the lines, she made her way to his shoulders; his shirt was sleeveless, and for that she was grateful. At least until her eyes met his and his mouth stretched in a cocky grin, as though he had just read her mind. Darting her eyes away, she was pissed that he had caught her in the act of practically drooling over him. Absently she wiped her hand across her mouth and her fingers came back wet. She tried to wipe them on her pants unnoticed, but she heard Mitchell snicker. It was an unexpected sound and, as much as she wanted to hear him do it again because it was sexy, she was fuming.

"I was right by the way. Not that any of you care." Swiftly turning her back on her men, Aggie saw Eckard still tied up but there was no rope. His restraints were invisible. "What is that? Someone let him go, because he's not your or anyone else's prisoner." To her surprise it was Gryson who waved his hand in the air and mumbled something inaudible to Aggie's ears. Eckard's hands flew forward under his own control and he rubbed the blood flow back into them.

"If you are all finished playing around, I'd like to get settled before nightfall." Mitchell turned on his heel and Aggie got the pleasure of watching him walk away all over again. "Aggie, come stand beside me because I can't have you drooling again." She almost couldn't believe her ears. Did he really just say that? "I mean it." Stomping forward she came to stand near him, but out of arm's reach. Ignoring his triumphant look that took over his face, Aggie instead took in the scenery.

If she didn't know better she would have thought she was taken out into the country on Earth. Nothing looked foreign or alien in any way, at least not until they turned the corner and she heard a stream close by. A violet stream that seemed to run in the wrong direction. Amazing and somewhat magical, it ran uphill. Her eyes lit up at the sight but she refused to ask any questions.

"Wyntra is the life flow of our realm. It runs that way because it forces the power throughout the land. It keeps the plants green and living all year 'round. The seasons don't have any bearing on this world because it is seasonally broken." It was Ren who had seen her wonder and decided to fill her in. Mitchell just walked faster. As expected he never wanted to assist in anyway, just making things more difficult. She still had no idea how she would ever be able to bond and be mated to the meathead.

Flowers of every shape and size bloomed on every hill. Some Aggie recognized and others were completely new and foreign to her. Grass was greener than Aggie could ever have imagined and the blades were soft like fur or more like feathers. That couldn't be a coincidence on a shifter world. The sky was blue but clear, and almost shimmered in the light. Aggie could imagine that when it rained the glitter fell to the ground making it shine like diamonds.

The trees lining the edge of the countryside they walked through were the start of a deep, thick forest. Aggie wondered what creatures would be living in there, and if all of them were shifters throughout this realm. Every bear, wolf, bird, or maybe bug, were really able to take an alternate shape. She hesitated calling them human because, while the twins were in human form, did that make them human?

"Your home is beautiful." Aggie's words were only a whisper but the twins were both so close they both easily heard her. Ren threw his brawny arm around her and squeezed, placing a kiss to her temple. Mitchell just nodded and marched on toward their destination.

After what seemed like hours of walking, a village appeared in the distance. Aggie didn't once complain about the trek because she knew Mitchell would just make it harder on her. She just distracted herself with the scenery and the sounds of the river tinkling in the distance.

"Is that it?" Her attention was solely focused on Ren, as he would be the only one to answer her.

"Yes, that is Galata." Mitchell's voice behind her threw her off and the awe in his voice was captivating. He actually answered her, but his tone was that of someone who was taking in this place for the first time. He was very proud of his home and it showed, even in the way he said the name.

"It's about time; I should have sifted us all there instead of this hike you have brought us on." Kyrel's words were in jest, but Mitchell's look spoke of dark and horrible things that would befall him if he spoke again. Raising his arms in surrender, Kyrel pressed on behind them.

"There is a law in Galata," Ren began to clarify, but Mitchell took over.

"There has always been a law for the demons who travel here. Wyntra prohibits any magical transportation outside of shifting ways. It is our safety protocol so they can't get the jump on us if there is ill intent." Aggie was impressed by that; it was something that she wouldn't have thought of, and for them to have had it from the start was genius. "Wyntra, might remove it after a demon has been here for some time."

The town, Galata, was quickly approaching as though they were moving faster, but it didn't feel like it. Aggie was just so happy to be close to their destination that she didn't question it.

As they breeched the edge where the first few dwellings stood she was surprised at how primitive they seemed. It was a cabin, but nothing too fancy. As though it didn't take long to erect. Simple and basic, and all mostly uniform.

The town, even though it was close to nightfall, was still bustling with life. Animals which Aggie assumed were shifted creatures lived amicably among each other. Bears and birds, wolves and livestock, nothing seemed to be unacceptable. They were walking with humans—well, beings in human form. No ill intent or fighting. They helped carry large, heavy things in their shifted form and provided food for each other from what seemed to be hunting trips. Aggie mentally filed that away; some of the creatures must be just that and not shifters. They had to eat, right?

"Come, let's get everyone to their beds, so we can get started in the morning. It will be dark soon." Mitchell's gruff words were matched by his increase in speed. As though they weren't already moving fast enough and weren't tired from the long walk.

Aggie was confused by the rush until they made it to the center of town and something dawned on her. "Is there any power here?" In place of what one would assume was a street lamp, Aggie saw torches lighting the paths of the small town. Actually, Aggie didn't know how big it was and assumed its size by the rustic nature of it. The number of people and animals versus the houses or cabins she saw was definitely unmatched.

Ren started to answer her but was quickly silenced by a growl from Mitchell. He must be wanting to spill the beans on that little tidbit.

Dropping each Guardian off in their own small hut, in the low light Aggie couldn't see the door colors but absently wondered if there was a similar coloration as in Ahael. Finally it was Eckard's turn. "These will be your accommodations. Please don't wander around unaccompanied, as most don't take kindly to strangers around here." Mitchell practically shoved him through the doorway and slammed it behind him.

"Alone at last." Ren's words were strange because they weren't alone. Mitchell was standing directly behind him.

"Come on, I'm tired enough as it is." Mitchell's words were almost whiney as they made their way to the last cabin in that section. It was slightly larger than the rest and that caught Aggie's notice.

"Where am I staying?" She had assumed there was a separate cabin for her, like in the Demon realm.

"Well, seeing as you invited an uninvited guest along, that means you gave away your own accommodations. Leaving you with little options and inconveniencing me." Mitchell sneered at her and proceeded into the last cabin ahead of her. She would have been appalled if she hadn't realized that being an Alpha was practically royalty here. Quickly silencing her reaction, she followed him ahead of Ren, who was being a gentleman.

The room was bigger on the inside than it seemed from the outside. Aggie didn't know if it was the dim lighting or an optical illusion. It was a two-story cabin, unlike the rest. Also, it seemed more craftmanship went into building it. Open wood and logs were used to create everything. Even the furniture was based from wood with fabric cushions placed on top. Aggie absently wondered what the mattress was made of.

Moving from room to room, Aggie felt like she was on a rustic vacation in the woods. There was an open kitchen and bar, with stools pressed under it. The living room faced a large fireplace; Aggie wondered if it was safe to use around all this wood. Making their way upstairs, she walked down a short hallway that boasted two doors. Both were closed, and Aggie didn't know for sure, but she assumed they were the twins bedrooms. Not knowing where to go, she just followed both men until they stepped through into one bedroom.

"This is my room but, given the fact that there are three of us tonight, I am not about to let my brother make this decision.

You can stay here with us both or take Ren's room across the hall." Mitchell was in his element and nothing short of a king, and was all but asking people to bow to him. Aggie was shocked yet again.

"I'm not going to kick Ren from his room so I can sleep. Why can't I just sleep on the couch? Even better, why didn't you offer me your room?"

"If I recall correctly, that is what I did," Mitchell drawled lazily, making Aggie think for a moment. She was tired but certain he didn't offer to sleep in his brother's room or displace himself.

"No, you didn't. You offered to kick your brother from his own space for me to sleep or we all sleep together. Given your attitude today and most days, I'm not sure I want to be anywhere near you. Ren, why don't you join me in your room?" Aggie could be the bigger person and share if need be, but she wasn't going to order someone to give up their space for her.

"No!" Mitchell roared, causing Aggie to startle. He had never lost his temper to this extent and she wondered what side of him she was seeing. "I offered you my room, and we all would share because my wolf won't share you with Ren alone tonight. He has a ridiculous need to protect you at all costs. I will shift and let him have you tonight if that is what you choose. Unless you want to be alone, and then he will likely just sleep by Ren's door." His volume tapered with his words and Aggie wasn't as upset with him.

She had a soft spot for Alpha, the name she had given Mitchell's wolf. He cared for her and wasn't afraid to steamroll Mitchell to do it. As confusing as the two might be, the wolf was a different entity all together and why Aggie had named him separately, and should have been in better control of his wolf. Unfortunately, when Aggie's safety was concerned Alpha, the wolf, wouldn't take no for an answer. That make the outburst a moment ago a bit clearer.

"I understand now. Why didn't you just say so? You're

always so overbearing and you never say what you mean. I wouldn't have questioned you if you had said Alpha needed some Aggie time." With that she pushed past him and sashayed into the room. She could have sworn she heard a moan and a chuckle as she did so.

The twins entered the rest of the way behind her and closed the door. Aggie glanced around the space and instantly knew it was Mitchell's room. If he hadn't told her so she would have guessed. It was full of all things Alpha. Rugged décor and minimal luxuries, Aggie was even impressed by the cleanliness and absently wondered if someone came in and cleaned up for them daily. It also smelled like Mitchell's Alpha musk, and Aggie found herself filling her nostrils with the scent before she could think better of it.

Happily, her gaze landed on a wooden wardrobe. Making her way over to it, she placed her hands on the front and smiled mischievously. He wanted to play games about sleeping arrangements and was embarrassed to say it was his wolf that needed her. Aggie would test that on her own. The power flowed through her and the wood warmed beneath her fingers. Quickly she opened the doors and snatched the garment from the already full rack.

"Is there a bathroom in here or do I need to use the woods?" Thankfully her joke didn't fall flat.

Ren snorted his amusement. "There is a bathroom off each of our rooms and one downstairs. Pick whichever you like." He pointed toward the door behind the wardrobe and Aggie darted in with her pilfered clothes and locked the door behind her.

"You do realize if I wanted to get into *my* bathroom I could with minimal effort?" Mitchell's deep timbre penetrated the door with ease, making Aggie smile.

"By all means, if you need to see me pee come on in." Knowing most men don't want to take away the magic that girls don't poop or fart, he would remain on the outside of that door. Snickering to herself, Aggie looked at herself in the mirror. It was strange how so much of these places had so many similarities to what she knew from Earth. Mirrors, toilets, showers, and everything right where it should be and as expected. This room was no different, and for that she was grateful. Some things were better when they were the same or typical. No one wanted to question how a bathroom worked. Where do you pee? Is this a sink?

Slipping out of her clothes, Aggie slipped into the nightgown she'd designed. Intentionally picking colors that would torture the boys. She wasn't a prisoner, but she was also tired of their games. They didn't frighten her, and for that she was thankful. This was going to be more fun playing things her way.

Unlocking the door, Aggie stepped from the powder room and leaned against the doorframe. Both shifters were lying on an oversized bed. She had never seen one like it. It was as though it was a custom size made for the Alpha's own harem. An unexpected pang of jealousy ran through her and she didn't know where it came from. She wasn't one for such tendencies in her normal life. Trying for a sultry look, Aggie popped a hip out and rested her forearm against the frame. She raised one eyebrow at the twins.

She felt their joined gaze rake over her. From her long hemline up to the raised slit that split open to her hip, exposing so much of her milky white skin. Black was her color of choice, but slashed through the silky fabric were golden mesh cutouts that shimmered like the real thing. As though she had designed this garment from the stone itself. Their eyes flowed over every curve and valley, to the deep V-line wrapped in delicate lace, highlighting her ample bustline.

Enjoying the attention of the stone-still twins Aggie just stayed in her spot, soaking it in for as long as possible. Ever so slowly, Ren leaned forward from the headboard. He was shirtless from what she could tell and, given that the blanket only covered his crotch since his bare legs had slipped from the covers as he leaned forward, breathing deeply, inhaling her scent. It was the biggest turn- on ever.

Mitchell tore his gaze from her. Like his brother, his shirt was thrown haphazardly on the back of the high-backed chair sitting in the corner beside the bed. That was all she could see because, as he rolled over to avoid looking at her, he remained covered by the blanket. Her imagination was working overtime to piece together the image that might be lying in wait beneath the sheets.

A low growl rolled through the room. Aggie blinked because it wasn't Ren who was growling. A quick glance at Mitchell told her that he was struggling to control Alpha. Smiling at him, she sauntered over to the foot of the bed. Wrapping her hands around the baseboard Aggie leaned in, and when she stopped her lips were a hair's breadth from Ren's.

"What's the matter, boys? See something you like?" Aggie snaked out her tongue and trailed it over his lips and pulled back.

Ren's hand quickly wrapped around the back of her neck and pulled her back toward him, but she didn't give in that easily. Leaning back, she pulled herself from his grasp. "Aww, come on, Sparky."

"Sparky?" Aggie recoiled farther back, hands on her hips. Part of her was questioning him while the other part was confused.

Ren snickered, "Yeah, last time we got to mess around it was similar to this." He waved his hand around the room, indicating the bed along with his brother who was actively trying not to look at her. "You changed the game plan and went all electric on us. I though the name suited you." Winking at her he leaned back and supported his head on his hands, arms bent at the elbow behind him. Cocky as ever, Ren wasn't fazed by her reaction and just waited for her to come back to them.

"Well, be that as it may, I'm planning on sleeping tonight. If you boys can't handle that then perhaps I should head down the hall." Making her way to the door, Aggie shifted her weight a bit more in her hips than normal and sashayed away.

"Wait, I think my brother is capable of keeping it in his pants. That, and I'm sure my wolf will be happier if you are here." Mitchell didn't bother to look at her, just spoke while facing the wall. His words were spoken so low it was almost a growl. She half wondered if Alpha was voicing his opinion as well. So she stopped dead at his words.

"Why doesn't Alpha just come hang out with me then? He can crawl in bed after I get settled if he needs to." With that she flipped her hair over her shoulder and made her way on out the door. It took a lot of effort to leave that tanned sexy man flesh just waiting for her to join them. Fighting against instinct, she stepped past the door and made her way down to Ren's room. It was dark but she quickly found the bed and crawled in, happy to be down for the night. The remaining days of sorting out what was happening in the shifters' realm would be more than interesting enough.

Sunlight glinting through the window, Aggie groaned at the thought of waking up. Throwing her arm over her eyes, she rolled over and tried to avoid the offending light. Burrowing down into the blankets, she was startled to feel warm fur in their place. Smiling, she lifted her arm and split her eyes open only a sliver. She was met with dark fur, and Aggie ran her fingers into the softness. "Couldn't take it, could you, boy? How long did you let him fight?" A soft bark answered her and a low rumble, like Alpha was laughing. Instead of getting out of bed, she snuggled deeper into the wolf's fur.

A knock sounded at the door. "Are you two gonna get up sometime today?" Same as before, it was Ren on the other side of the door while Alpha was beside her in bed. On some level she felt bad, but in reality the thought made her happy.

"Leave me alone, Ren. I'm happy in dreamland." Alpha growled his agreement at the door, but neither of them moved.

"Not gonna happen, Sparky. We have work to do, and as much as I know he wants to stay in there with you there's too much to do out here." When he rattled the door, Aggie was pleasantly surprised to find it was locked. She wondered if Mitchell did that before he shifted into Alpha.

She scratched him behind the ears with both hands, as though he were a house dog. "Did you guys do that when you came in last night?" Alpha's responding rumble was like a laugh yet again. Aggie couldn't contain her bubbling laughter.

"Laugh it up, you two. I'll start breakfast and meet you down there." She heard Ren's footsteps trail off, his boots knocking on the wood floor of the hallway.

Groaning, Aggie rolled over and stretched out her sleepy limbs. Alpha hopped up and shook out his fur, stretching and yawning wide, letting out a tiny squeaky whine as his muscles and bones cracked.

"Damn, I think you slept all tied up in a knot there, Alpha." Aggie crawled out of bed and headed for the attached bathroom. Alpha let out a strong bark, startling her into stopping. When she turned to look over her shoulder, Alpha ran up to meet her. His teeth clamped lightly on the fabric of her nightgown. "Easy, boy—I like this one a lot." He released the fabric and she was at eye level with him. Her eyes locked on those of the wolf and he held her gaze. Slowly he leaned forward and his nose lined up perfectly with Aggie's. Pressing lightly, he held her gaze until her vison swam and the eyes became one, causing Aggie to close her eyes to avoid becoming dizzy and falling. Alpha's grumble was on the edge of a purr. Then he licked her from chin to forehead and sat on his haunches.

Aggie burst into laughter. "Really? There we were, having a perfectly sweet moment, and you had to go and ruin it." Wiping her face, she stood and disappeared into the bathroom. Before she closed the door completely, Aggie peeked back out the crack in the door and caught a glimpse of Mitchell's bare ass. Licking her own lips now at the sight, Aggie felt a little guilty for spying on him. Then as she trailed her eyes up his naked body, she realized he was staring at her from over his shoulder. The smolder on his face was enough to make a girl stop breathing. Aggie slammed the bathroom door to avoid any further embarrassment.

After a long, hot shower Aggie emerged from the steamy bathroom, wrapped in a towel. Thankfully there was an equally as large wardrobe in Ren's bedroom, so Aggie was able to create herself something to wear.

Unsure of what the day was going to bring, Aggie didn't know what was the right thing to wear. Opting for comfortable casual, she placed her hand on the wood and imagined her next ensemble.

<hr>

*A*s Aggie's boot hit the floor as she walked into the kitchen, a pan clattered across the floor. Aggie looked up to see Ren's face and his mouth hung agape. "What is it?" She walked over and picked up the forgotten pan that at one point held what looked like pancake batter but was splattered across the floor. A wet cloth flew through the room and hit Ren square in the face with an audible smack.

"Clean up your mess, asshole. It's not like this is the first time you've seen Aggie wearing tight clothes." Mitchell's words were dripping with his usual disdain. Aggie never could understand why he was so angry with her all the time but, given the opportunity, he would taste her body from head to toe. The thought gave Aggie goosebumps.

She was wearing a tight shirt with thin straps, with a scoop-neck that accentuated her cleavage a bit more than normal. She was a woman, not dead, and the way the Guardians looked at her made her feel wanted. So she might have upped the ante a bit and her girls might have been spilling out a bit more than usual. She paired that with a pair of cutoff shorts. The weather was humid and more like summer. She figured it would keep her cool. The shorts might have been a bit short and the pockets may or may not have been sticking out the bottom.

"I'd say tight clothes, but that's a lot of bare skin that gives me many ideas of what I want to do to every inch of it." Ren licked his lips but he was already on the floor, busy cleaning up his mess.

"Given the fact that you both are here, does that mean there's food? I feel like I haven't eaten in a week." Aggie slid between them both and made herself comfortable at the breakfast nook on a stool and propped her boots up on the rungs.

"I've made pancakes and sausage, but if you want anything else I'm happy to whip it out." Ren waggled his eyebrows at her suggestively, wearing a mischievous grin.

"I think I can make this work." She reached for the plate of pancakes. Mitchell placed an empty plate in front of her and grabbed a stack of pancakes for himself, sitting down at the small farmer's table off the kitchen. "Thanks, Grumpy." She placed her own pancakes on the plate and a piece of sausage, too. Ren handed her the syrup and she smiled and gratefully took it, smothering the breaded goodness and her sausage in the sticky sweetness.

Moaning around her first bite, Aggie closed her eyes. "I could watch you eat forever, but we have things to do." Ren leaned over her and got his own bite of her pancakes. Aggie reacted out of instinct and her fork came down fast. Within a centimeter of Ren's fingers, her fork clattered against the handle of his fork.

"That's my food regardless of where we have to be, and I'm going to enjoy every last drop of this. Keep your dirty paws off my food." Aggie glared at the offending wolf and slid his fork from her plate, after she slid his bite onto her own fork and away from his clutches.

A low chuckle from the table caught Aggie's attention. Glancing over her shoulder, she saw Mitchell stifling the sound with his fist.

"Aw, come on, Sparky. I just wanted a taste. You made it look so delicious and tempting." Ren leaned over her ear, standing so close his breath danced across her skin. "I really like these by the way." He tugged lightly on her loose pigtail braids.

"What is that about any way? Channeling your inner schoolgirl?" Mitchell held up his juice glass in her direction, indicating her hair.

"No, I just figured after our long walk in the prairie yesterday and the cabin life around here, I should be working on my farm girl look. Hence these shit-kickers." Aggie slung her booted foot up on the empty stool. She opted for a pair of work boots rather than cowboy boots. Figured if anything went down she would be ready and prepared. Shoes played a huge part in a fight. It would be a little hard to kick ass in flip flops. Not that she couldn't do that, but it would make things harder.

"Prairie walk? Is that what you got out of our trip here?" Mitchell's words were growled. She apparently had stepped on his toes.

"No, it was beautiful and serene. I would be happy to be here for any time I'm allowed. I just wanted to fit in and I didn't think my demon-fighting leathers would do the trick." Aggie raised her hands in a defensive motion. It was never her intention to get Mitchell riled up.

"I have to admit the leathers you wore in the demon realm with Mathius' people were hella sexy." Ren's words broke the moment between Mitchell and Aggie as he stormed from the room.

"I'll meet you guys in town." With that, Mitchell slammed the door and left them alone.

"Well, that wasn't how my morning was supposed to go. I'll finish this up quickly and we can go meet up with the others." Aggie started shoveling food into her mouth, regretting her argument with Mitchell. She didn't mean to disrespect their home and people. She just knew it was vastly different from that of Mathius or herself. Those were the only places she had seen so far. While the shifter realm was very Earth-like, it wasn't her home and she had yet to figure out how they differed.

Upon finishing her breakfast, Aggie slid the stool back and jumped down to the floor. "Okay, let's start over and see if I can un-piss off your brother before the day is over." Walking past the sweeter of the wolf twins, she walked into the living room. She had laid her overshirt on the back of the easy chair. Flipping the plaid shirt around her shoulders and tying the bottom half together covered the majority of her exposed skin.

"You really went all out on that outfit, didn't you?" Ren tugged at her collar, laying it flat and smoothing it out.

"I don't do anything small. Now that I can conjure up an outfit on a whim," Aggie leaned in close again, her voice dropping to a husky tone, "I might as well go all out. What else can I control one hundred percent?" Ren leaned in to close the distance between them but Aggie held fast. Sealing her lips to his in a kiss, but not lingering. "Now let's make quick work of this and show me around this little town." Spinning around, her pigtail flipping over her shoulder, she headed straight for the door of the oversized cabin.

Waiting outside were all the guys except Mitchell. Her father was also standing out there, a bit father out in the distance. A small smile broke on his face she started toward them. Something out of the corner of her eye caught her attention—a small movement. Pausing in her tracks she looked in the direction of the distraction, and saw a small group of children was playing in a circle. It looked like a version of duck, duck goose, but it wasn't quite the same. Then, out of nowhere, one of them turned into a small dog and chased the children around. Aggie started and ran toward the group. "Stop it!" she screamed at them. All the little faces froze and turned toward her.

A hand snaked over her shoulder, pulling her back and stopping her progression across the yard. "Wait, *parum praesetes*; they're just playing." Gryson's words stopped her cold. She always loved the way he used her nickname in Latin, but that wasn't what stopped her.

"Playing? But he shifted and went after them. I thought…"

She stopped and just stared at the children, who had run off to continue with their game elsewhere.

"Shifters play in both forms here. It is a part of our culture. We interact with each other on both levels from an early age. When children find they are able to shift, they tend to not have much control. So, in excited times, they shift without warning." Ren made his way to her side to explain.

"You're saying this is every day for you guys?" Aggie was stunned and didn't know how to react. "I'm sorry. I guess I'll just try and adapt quickly and not scare anyone else."

"Well, I'm digging your adapting so far, Love." Kyrel's fingers drifted across her exposed cleavage.

"Easy, lover boy. I'll be just fine without any sexy mojo you want to spew. I think now is far from bedroom time and we have work to do here. I'd hate to think what they would think of us if as soon as we got here we slunk away and stayed cooped up for sexy time." Aggie stepped on in toward the center of town. She was sure there was something she needed to do or could do to help. Worst case, they could train or something to pass the time. Surely there was plenty of prep for them if a war was coming their way.

She let her eyes travel. People were walking up and down around the cabins, each doing mundane things. One lady, who looked to be in her mid-forties with her hair tied up in a severe bun, was hanging laundry on a clothesline. Another woman, who looked close to Aggie's age but with long blond hair braided back out of her face, was working in a garden at the edge of a cluster of houses. A man who might have been a young grandfather in his late fifties, with dark hair just starting to gray at his sideburns, was splitting wood with what seemed to be a young teenage boy following behind him, stacking the logs. Everything seemed perfectly normal and very Earthly. Aggie was having a difficult time differentiating between the two.

Each person who was working relatively alone was met by other members of this tiny society. The woman hanging laundry was met by neighbor. While the work wasn't hard the basket was full and her neighbor had a baby on her hip. On Earth, she would have been considered a young housewife. The girl working in the garden leaned back on her heels and wiped the back of her hand across her forehead, some of her braid coming loose around her face. Walking past her was a small group of teenagers, who stopped and exchanged a few words. The next thing Aggie knew was each of the teenagers joined her in the garden and got to work pulling weeds.

A woman came out of the house closest to the garden, carrying a tray. It was laden with a metal pitcher and filled with glasses of ice. She walked over to the garden and filled them with a yellow liquid Aggie assumed was lemonade. Smiling, she kept walking and made her way to the man chopping wood. He spiked the ax into a larger log and lifted his leg onto the same log to steady himself. The man's shoulders were broad, and if he'd been on Earth Aggie would have said he looked like a bodybuilder. Leaning and setting his elbow across his knee, a smile broke out across his face and he gestured to the boy, who stopped stacking. The woman carried over the tray and filled the remaining glasses with the same drink as before.

These people all lived in a different world, but they coexisted better than humans. Aggie didn't know what to think about how people just helped and counted on each other here. It was beyond her understanding. In her experience, people always left or bailed or just plain disappeared. She had never counted on anyone, not completely.

"Where are we, Mayberry? This place is unreal. I'm not sure I know how to act here." Aggie was backing away from the scene in front of her until she backed right into something firm. Over her shoulder she looked and saw Liel, stoic as ever.

"This place is as real as you and I. Flesh and blood, shifters who take care of each other. It is a bond of trust amongst the shifters," Ren supplied from his place, never having moved.

"What are we supposed to do? I feel so out of place." Aggie

was being transparent, but leaving out the part about her trust issues.

"Why don't we start by taking the tour?" Ren spread his arms to indicate his home and smiled charismatically. Aggie couldn't help but share his smile. He always had that effect on her. They all had things that she enjoyed; Ren's was his good humor, regardless of the situation.

"I'd love a tour. What about everyone else? Are you going to join us or do you have other plans?" Aggie turned to face her little motley crew. They were all staring at her with differing expressions.

"I'm not sure about everyone else but I plan to spend my entire day with you by my side." Eldon's words were soft but his eyes were piercing and passionate. His love for her was without limits and it made her feel the butterflies all take flight at once. Though his touch was usually necessary as their relationship grew, it was just the knowledge of how he felt making itself known.

"I'm with him, and that sounds like a near perfect day." Kyrel was always going to jump on that bandwagon. He never liked to do actual work, and preferred to spend his days lounging if he couldn't be having sex of some variety.

"I think I should find Mitchell and gather any information that he has on this rebellion. Mathius, you're welcome to join me." Liel had backed away from Aggie and was a bit colder than normal. Not knowing what to make of it, Aggie decided to step toward Ren since he was her tour guide anyway.

"Yes, I suppose that is the best course of action. Some of us need to stay focused." Though he didn't look angry, his words were forced and he sounded vaguely jealous. He was her newest mate and, unfortunately, she had spent the least amount of time with him. Sidling up next to her lover, Aggie slowly wrapped her arms around his neck.

"Mathius, the choice is yours. It's always yours. Remember, I've been sitting at home for a while since our... encounter.

You've been off fighting battles and keeping things safe in your demon realm. That was your choice and what was most important, but remember you chose that. So don't punish me or pretend that you have any reason to be mad at me." Her hands slid down his chest slowly, and as she leaned in toward him his lips crashed against hers. She let him deepen the kiss because his body had a way of communicating with hers. The vibrations he caused before were deeply seated and everything was right in the world just feeling him around her. Soon the kiss slowed and Aggie was back to her senses. She shoved him, hard, away from her.

"What was that for?" Mathius was startled and confused.

"I mean it, don't blame me for your choices. We might be mated, but you aren't allowed to treat me like our separation and what little time we spend together is my fault. Make your choices, but don't drag me down with you." Aggie turned on her heel and stalked away from him.

"On that note, anyone not want to go hang out with Aggie?" Xavier's words caught her off guard, his words usually few and far between.

CHAPTER SIX

Walking among the shifters, Aggie saw more of the helping nature that Ren spoke of. Xavier sidled up next to her, and she looked back to see her father trailing behind everyone.

"Did you guys say something to him?" Aggie demanded to know, and turned her attention to the vampire next to her. "Wait, how are you out here in the sun?" There hadn't been much sun to be concerned of in the Ahael; there was mostly cloud-cover and storms, so Aggie never questioned it.

Xavier smiled a tight-lipped smile. "Sun isn't a concern for my bloodline. Only turned vampires have that little aversion; those of us who are pure have little that will harm us. Younger purebloods are sensitive to light, but it won't kill them. I've been around a while." That was all he said about the subject.

"So the folklore about vampires is inaccurate?" Aggie pressed. They didn't have a close relationship but he was obviously interested, so she was planning to put forth more effort in respect to them all.

"Folklore is just that. Lore." It was like pulling teeth to get information out of Xavier, but that didn't deter her.

"Are you going to tell me anything? If you don't burn to ash in sunlight, and clearly you don't sparkle, is anything I've heard true? Should I avoid silver or crosses? Perhaps garlic on my pizza is frowned upon?"

"Only time will tell if anything you know is accurate. Seeing as I can't read your mind yet, it is hard to say what you know." Xavier was speaking in riddles but Aggie picked up on one word.

"Yet? Are you saying a time will come that you could read my mind?" Aggie was getting worked up. She had already experienced the voices in her head, and that was almost too much. Not sure if she could handle just one person reading her thoughts, there were always one or two things a girl should be able to keep private.

"It is always possible upon mating or sharing blood." Cryptic. If Xavier was one thing, that was it.

"Sharing blood? Won't that make me a vampire and weaken me as you said, making me a turned blood-sucker?"

"You have so many questions, Wee One. Let's leave some things to the imagination or to surprise us along the way." Xavier, ever the proper one, was still wearing a suit in this environment. Aggie wondered if he ever wore casual clothes. Gryson, who usually dressed nicer, was wearing a pair of jeans and Aggie licked her lips at the sight. They hugged his ass in a way that made her interested to see if the muscular lines were true to form. She wasn't complaining about Xavier's suit, but it didn't seem location- appropriate.

"Do you own anything else to wear?" she blurted, true to her character, not letting herself wonder too long without asking out loud.

"Are my clothes displeasing to you?" Answering a question with a question was true to Xavier's character. Aggie fought an eyeroll.

"Seriously? No, you look amazing as usual, but isn't this place a bit rugged for a business suit? Are you planning a hostile takeover of the rebels' cooperate headquarters or are you going to battle?"

"That would be ridiculous, but I don't usually get dirty when I fight. I prefer to keep things clean and put together. If it would make you happy I could go change into something you deem more appropriate." His voice never wavered, and it was as though he was actually waiting for a response to his seemingly ridiculous question.

"Uh, maybe later. Now about my dad..." Aggie left her question unsaid, because he'd heard it already and chose to not answer.

"Your father is merely feeling out his surroundings. Mathius, Liel, and I scared him enough the first go-around. He doesn't know how he fits here, which he doesn't. I won't tell you what to do but I will say this one time only: you shouldn't have brought him with you."

"What do you know?" Aggie hadn't had a chance to find out what caused Xavier's outburst the previous day when he saw her father. She wasted no time in getting answers.

"It is not my place to say, as it was before my time. I know the story of the Gateway history and how the Gatekeepers were chosen. Your family has done it for many years and it used to be a shared job. No longer is that the case, and I know your father's family used to be joined to it as well. I know the Gateway severed that connection years ago. I'm unsure of the exact reason, but I knew as soon as I smelled his blood it was that line. My family is very old, but I wasn't always the Guardian from the Porphyrian Realm. That is my home, named after the Vampire Disease that created the pure-bloods of my kind. While I was trained for this role, part of my training to take on my job was to know the tainted bloodlines that would harm our people or the Gateway. The story is incomplete, so perhaps that is some-thing you should ask the man himself." Xavier bowed his head to her, excusing himself from Aggie's side.

"This is the school." Aggie startled at Ren's words and took in the slightly larger cabin, but it was still smaller than Mitchell and Ren's. The yard was filled with small children playing. It must have been recess time.

"How old are the children who go here? Because I saw what seemed to be teenagers working and walking around earlier." Aggie glanced behind her to confirm that she had indeed seen kids helping with the load around the town. Seeing them still working at their individual jobs, she returned her attention to the kids playing at the school.

"It is really just an elementary level. We teach them the basics and they use instincts for the rest. We know they have to go to Earth when they get old enough to pass Earth's standards, so they need to be able to do basic math and language skills to get jobs there. We also throw in a bit of Earth's history for good measure. By the time they reach what you would consider teenage, they are working more on survival skills and learning to handle their shifter side. As children, if they can shift it is unpredictable and very influenced by their emotions, like you saw before with the younger ones playing. They were still too young for education and their shifts are more unpredictable. By the time they get to school they have a bit more control over their emotions and less of a toddler mood swing or imbalance over something as small as a lost toy. They can be expected to stay in a learning environment and not turn on a whim." That was different from Aggie's previous assumption. They weren't as primitive as it seemed. They had some sort of plumbing in their cabins, and they educated the kids to be able to survive outside of the shifter realm.

"What's the name of this place?" Aggie wondered out loud. Xavier had told her the name of his realm, and she didn't know if they all had names or if the individual towns were different.

"Cratlian. It's an ancient language spoken by our ancestors." Ren stopped their tour as he spoke. "It means 'the changeling'. Our people are so diverse there was a time when people assumed we were changelings. The name sort of stuck for a while and since we have a menagerie of creatures living here, it was the perfect name. We are open to any shifter breed that swears allegiance to the Alpha."

"That name does sound perfect. So, these rebels, are they just shifters who wouldn't swear allegiance?"

"Something like that, but they are more like those who don't play well with others. Though I can't figure out how they get along with each other to have joined this rebellion and not be busting at the seams. I'm sure they are breaking up fights left and right."

"Has anyone figured out what they're doing in the smaller communities when they raid them?" Eckard piped up from behind, startling Aggie because she'd forgotten that she wasn't alone walking with her men.

Surprisingly, Ren actually answered him, but Xavier's face was now painted in a terrifying scowl. If Aggie didn't know him, she would have been worried. "Nothing seems to be missing, but they make quite the mess and stir up some fights. They don't do much damage, but it seems like they are testing the strength of the clans."

"So, they're looking for weak spots in the perimeter?" Eckard confirmed, catching up to the group which had now stopped walking during their talk.

"That is what the consensus is at this point. At least until we have more information." Mitchell surprised everyone as he walked up behind Aggie. He was off doing Alpha things all morning, and to Aggie's understanding was too busy to walk this tour with her.

"Do you have any close by that haven't been hit?" Gryson's face told Aggie he was plotting something. She didn't know what he was doing prior to speaking up, but his look was very calculated.

"There are three nearby villages that are loyal to me left that haven't been hit. There is no rhyme or reason as to why they are working or hitting the ones they have already attacked."

Mitchell was followed by Liel and Mathius and Aggie felt complete again, having all of her men so close. While she hadn't completed the bond with them, it was still an unspoken closeness that eased her.

"I think we need to split up and take up stations in each one of those. If we can be present for an attack then perhaps we can figure out what they are actually after. Worst case, so we don't have to spread our resources so thin and leave Cratlian unattended in case that is what their ultimate plan is, we could magically spell the towns to get as much information as possible." Aggie considered Gryson's suggestion and, after their last mission, his idea had merit. While they didn't have enough information to barge in there half-cocked, having the magical back-up would be the responsible thing to do.

"How long would it take to set up a magical booby-trap like that?"

"I'm not sure magic will fool them unless we can figure out a way to conceal it. They can smell the magical signature in some cases." The guys had drawn up in a circle right in the middle of town, and at Ren's suggestion they all fell into a communal silence. All of them considering their options and power limitations.

"What if we use Fae magic in some way? If nothing else, it could cover or conceal Gryson's spells. It might throw them off the scent long enough to confuse them." Eldon's suggestion was valid and timely. Aggie was still new enough to the magical essences she possessed that she didn't know all that it was capable of yet.

"That could work, but if they come in shifted already it might not matter regardless. My wolf and Ren's would smell it as soon as I broke the village lines. There is just something that will stand out that is clearly not shifter. I pick up on things that are unnatural quickly when not in my human form." Mitchell was now pacing and when he caught sight of Eckard standing away from the group, he realized they were speaking in mixed company. "Perhaps we should pick this up later in private. I think Aggie would like to see more than the center of town. Let's head out to the ring." Without clarifying, Mitchell made his way through the town of overly helpful shifters.

"The ring?" Aggie didn't want to be kept in the dark. Unfortunately, Mitchell shot Ren a look that could kill, forcing Ren to shake his head at Aggie. With no one to explain, Aggie was forced to tag along in silence. She had never witnessed Ren rendered to silence with a look from his brother. This caused Aggie's brain to go into overtime, but since Ren was essentially gagged he couldn't answer any questions.

They walked for a few more minutes and, given that the town wasn't that large, it didn't take long to arrive at an area that looked like it could have been a horse corral. Aggie tried to figure out what they would need a corral for because she couldn't fathom them cooping up any animals, given their alternate nature. With a rustic wooden fence around the circular pen, the area inside wasn't covered in grass any longer. Instead it was dusty, dry dirt that looked to have been stomped down by hundreds of feet. There was no gate to close it off, so it wouldn't function like a typical enclosure, but it was large enough to house upwards of forty or fifty people. "What is this place?" Aggie finally asked, since no one offered any explanation in the passing moments.

"You don't know?" Mitchell was still the only one to speak, and she wished Ren was allowed. "I would have thought you would have figured it out by now, given your exceptional deducing skills, Princess." Typical Mitchell was back and she hadn't helped this morning at breakfast to improve his mood. What had she ever done to him that he treated her with such disdain? He was an asshole above everything else in every situation.

"Why would I know what this is? Aside from a horse corral, I have no idea. It's obviously not that. Unless you use it for some crazy witchy rituals, I have no clue." Aggie looked to Ren for help. He was still not speaking. "What did you do to Ren?"

"He is just falling in line." Mitchell smirked, folding his arms over his broad muscular chest. His shirt was stretched tightly across his large muscles and Aggie had to tear her eyes away from the temptation. Until he was in a better mood and treating her better, she couldn't justify rewarding him in anyway.

"What the hell does that mean? He's a living being and has the right to speak whenever he wants." Aggie was fuming and hoped that he wasn't impaired permanently because of his brother's ass-like tendencies and need for power. She never saw Mitchell as power-hungry but today she was seeing him in a new light.

"I just think you have the tendency to rely on him to supply you with information too often. While I know you may not have the resources to come up with an answer on your own, sometimes others are capable of helping, too. Ren takes too much pride in being your favorite source of support. Regardless, I want you to learn to trust everyone the way you say you do." Aggie felt like Mitchell had slapped her in the face. He was always rude, but this was a new level.

"I trust all of you and you each have different skills that work better in certain situations. I trust you each to do your part but is it really my fault that he typically pipes up before any of the rest of you? Liel has given me his fair share of information. I don't play favorites, and even though Ren is very helpful I'll take information from anyone." Aggie's hands had found their way to her hips in a defiant stance.

Mitchell leaned down, and got a mere inch away from Aggie's face. "Prove it, Princess."

"Only if you promise to release the gag order you have on your brother. I'll let someone else explain once Ren has the freedom to make his own choices." Aggie didn't budge. She let him stay in her face and their poses never relaxed. It was a standoff that Aggie wasn't going to lose.

"Ren, can you restrain yourself from helping for a few minutes? I don't think you know how." Mitchell glared at his brother, who was strangely silent. It more than worried Aggie that Mitchell had the power to do this to one of his people. The power being Alpha had over them was beyond what Aggie had imagined. Ren nodded and the two were locked in a strange silent conversation for a couple minutes.

"Dickhead." Ren's abrupt words startled Aggie from her scowling, though Ren didn't move. He just insulted his brother in proof his ability to speak had been released. Aggie had no idea before now that Mitchell, as Alpha, had that kind of power. Now she understood a little more about swearing allegiance to the Alpha.

"Did you seriously use your Alpha power to silence your brother? You can't just carry on a conversation with me like a normal person?" Aggie was fuming and, on some level, it was frustration for Ren. Mostly she couldn't believe he would stoop so low just to seem like he was helping her learn something. There were other ways to go about it.

"It's a bit hard to get a word in edgewise with him always chiming in with his helpful tidbits. Even if he isn't the best person for the job." Mitchell leaned against the rail of the ring. Aggie still couldn't figure out what it was used for and the entire situation made her feel stupid.

"Well, unless one of you wants to let me in on this little secret, this has been a lesson in ignorance and hasn't been helpful in any way, shape, or form." She again placed her hands on her hips in a stance of defiance. If Ren wasn't allowed to help her someone needed to step up to the plate or she was going to lose it. She could feel her magic building beneath her skin and it was electric, causing the hairs on her body to stand on end. The feeling was almost akin to what they say happens before a lightning strike. He eyes widened in the newfound knowledge, but then she came to terms with it and quickly checked her features into something more normal.

"I thought you would surely be able to figure this one out, Princess. I'm sorely disappointed this time." Before Mitchell could get his remaining thoughts out, Aggie was pleased to see a streak of lightning falling from the sky. Given the fact that there was no thunder, Mitchell was caught off guard. The bolt came down and zapped him right in the ass.

He picked himself up over six feet from his original location, where he had been leaning in all of his smug glory against the rail of the mystery ring. Mitchell scowled at her and she held back a bubble of laughter as she realized that his ass was literally smoking. That was when she heard Ren burst into a fit of guffaws. Served Mitchell right. In normal society she would have felt bad for someone who had just endured a lightning strike, but in this case it was more sweet justice. Yes, she had delivered a judicial punishment to the man who thought he was untouchable. He had doled out whatever he deemed right to his brother and every other shifter. Now Aggie had retaliated, but knowing he would heal with ease there was no real threat to him. One could say it was a magical practical joke.

CHAPTER SEVEN

Finally Mitchell had healed and simmered a bit in his anger, which had resulted in a lot of yelling. He was surely not going to show any sign of weakness or that Aggie had hurt him with her magical bolt. She might have been reprimanded by the Alpha shifter, but she still felt justified and was mentally patting herself on the back. The rest of the guys didn't seem to mind either.

"Now that you've had your fun, the ring is where we train for battle. It is the largest contained space. It has been used for generations." His words showed his ever-present anger, and that just made Aggie feel even prouder of herself. She didn't bother to hide her look from him. He was welcome to stew in his anger.

"Was that so hard?" Ren reprimanded his brother. "Why did you wait so long to spit that out? Everyone else was worried you might lash out at them, so they remained quiet. I would have kicked your ass myself if you hadn't put that gag order on me. Don't ever do that again, and I mean EVER!" He raised his voice but didn't seem bothered or afraid in anyway. Mitchell looked to be fighting an eyeroll in true brotherly fashion. The banter made Aggie long for her family again.

"She needs to learn to count on more than you, brother. If you aren't around she needs to know who to look to for her questions. We all have our skill sets and sometimes you aren't the best in a given situation." Mitchell stalked into the ring and Aggie felt a magical movement as they crossed the threshold of the gate. There was definitely something that they crossed.

"What was that?" Aggie pointed at the doorway and motioned all around because she had no idea where it came from specifically. She was new to the magical elements that could be at play. There was no telling for sure what the culprit could have been.

"Those were the wards. No one with true ill intent can be allowed in this place. We want them to fight but not kill or maim here. If someone gets hurt they will heal, but the goal is to train and they aren't going to get very far if they are severely injured. They would spend more energy healing than they would in training, and that defeats the purpose." Mitchell was being forthcoming with information now that she had zapped him. Aggie wondered if they should consider keeping him in his place with minor violence more often. With that thought the arena hummed, and Aggie's skin actually got very warm. Letting go of the thought, Aggie was surprised to notice that the space cooled drastically. It was amazing how it picked up on her passing thought even after she had crossed.

"If their intent changes upon becoming engaged in the battle drills, what does the space do to counter that? Can they be ejected magically?" Her question was only partly educational. The other part of her secretly wondered if she could have been catapulted from the ring as punishment for her wayward thoughts.

"The arena will make it uncomfortable for the abuser, and unless they calm down and change their thoughts it would transition into pain. If that doesn't stop them, the pain becomes so intense they will become incapacitated so they can be removed without any harm coming to the innocent." Aggie breathed a sigh of relief, but Mitchell shot her a knowing smirk. She knew he couldn't read her mind, but he did know his realm, and Aggie hadn't learned yet what connection he had to this place.

"On that note, what are we going to do today?" Aggie shifted uncomfortably on her feet, silently thanking the gods that she had let that thought go. Not that she regretted it, but she wasn't going to think about that as long as she was inside this fencing.

"You need to learn to better hone your powers in an actual fight. I know you have worked them separately and have a basic understanding of control, or so Mathius and Eldon tell us. You need to work them with basic maneuvers and blend them seamlessly together to work like a second skin." Mitchell was making his way to the center of the ring, but the rest of the guys must have been privy to this stop since they were spreading out around the large space. Aggie had no idea why such a small community needed such a colosseum at their disposal.

"So, you're saying we're back to square one? I thought we would at least be doing something new. I feel like this is all we do in our regular sessions." Yes, Aggie was whining but, given the changes in her life, she felt she was entitled.

"I wouldn't say square one." Mitchell's look was unreadable and that worried Aggie. Then she glanced around, looking for the rest of her entourage and coming up empty.

"Where are they?" Aggie's head whipped around in a panic and then freaked out further because Mitchell was gone as well. "What the hell, guys?" Aggie screamed and her words echoed back at her. The space was so large, and now so vastly empty that she was a bit worried.

Walking side to side and backwards, Aggie twirled systematically for fear of one of the guys was sneaking up on her to catch unaware. She was thankful she'd opted for boots that morning, as the dirt slid underneath the tread loosely. She scanned the open area for any signs of movement but, unfortunately, nothing moved even the slightest. "Where have they gone?" Aggie murmured to herself. This wasn't like the last time they sped off. There was always one trying to attack her in some way and she could plan her attack. Now she had no idea where they were or what to prepare for in the least. Then, from far above, Aggie heard the loudest squawk she'd ever heard. Glancing up and staggering back to keep her footing, she saw a bird that was far larger than anything she had ever seen before. It looked vaguely like an eagle, but was at least the size of a small car. "What in the world? How is that possible?" She naturally assumed it was a shifter, but it was still an unfathomable sight. Another loud "CAW!" and the bird dove right for her head.

Scrambling for purchase, Aggie flung herself to the ground, barely keeping her face from imprinting the dust that was swirling at her feet. In the distance, Aggie heard multiple familiar laughs but she still couldn't figure out where they were hiding. "Seriously? Is this some sort of game to you all? I'm standing here, preparing to fight you, and you send a dinosaur to attack me?" She screamed into the empty desolate space and quickly realized that the bird wasn't going to give up after one shot, as he was realigning his approach on her.

"Not a game, only a chance for you to use your new skills on someone who isn't vested in keeping your skin whole." Xavier's words wafted over her like a dream. He was using his super speed and brushed past her, his words drifting on the air as he passed. She never even saw or felt him. With not enough time to think about it, Aggie had to dodge another attack from her new adversary.

"Training. That is all this is, and while they think I'm some delicate flower that will wilt I'll prove them wrong." Mumbling under her breath, she readied herself. It would be difficult to attack a flying creature, bird or whatever it was; every time it got close Aggie was forced to duck, dodge, or flee. So, she hadn't gotten a good look at it but that didn't matter to her magic. As the creature got closer Aggie summoned her demonic magic and sifted herself six feet from her previous location, causing the flying beast to skid into the ground and roll violently. Aggie then realized that it wasn't a bird at all but looked a lot like a gargoyle.

His skin looked rough and solid, almost like rock. He wasn't colored like a normal creature or human, but had almost a grey tinge to his overall tone. It would prove challenging to best a beast that was the size of a Ford Pinto and probably made of actual stone. Aggie would have to break into some creative play to pull this one off. She refused to lose, and since the guys weren't man enough to face her themselves she would do whatever it took to prove them wrong.

Calling on her Fae self, Aggie conjured up a nest for herself to keep hidden. It resembled a small briar-filled fort, with her at the center. She wasn't hiding, but the gargoyle didn't need to know that. He leapt from his place on the ground and pounced on top of her little hut. Aggie blasted from the inside and threw an elongated thorn at the creature. Bouncing off the winged beast, Aggie's suspicions were confirmed that she would need a bigger punch to seal this deal. *Perhaps I could bind his wings somehow and incapacitate him.* Aggie thought though her next step or maybe two to stay ahead of the game. This wasn't like fighting the guys at all. They attacked and she countered, but this thing was just using his sheer brute force to get his way. That gave Aggie an idea. Since the ground was at her feet, she could combine her powers in some way to create something big enough to nip this situation in the bud. She would need something to keep the beast busy.

Quickly, before the beast was able to mount his next attack, Aggie called the vines that she had immobilized the twins with in their first altercation. The winged creature swooped down and extended his claws toward Aggie's face. She had no idea if this was a calculating beast or just an instinct-driven one, so she didn't leave room for error or a new arrangement to her features. Casting the magic far and wide, Aggie grew the biggest bramble of vines she could manage and felt her magic flicker.

She used a lot in a short time, but knew that she could make up for it. The creature was wrapped tight, but he wasn't immobilized. Instead he thrashed savagely, trying to free himself.

Aggie had little time to prepare, so she used her Fae magic to call every stone she could feel to herself. Then she manipulated the demonic magic to reshape the matter of the stone into something bigger than the creature. If she could manage it before he freed himself she could possibly knock it unconscious. She didn't want to kill it since it was obviously just a pawn the guys were using to train her. Aggie then had a new idea.

Using the more creative side of her brain, Aggie shaped and molded the stones. "What are you doing, Wee One?" Xavier called out, trying to distract her.

"Just trying to use what I have at my disposal since none of you are planning to play knight-in-shining-armor," she teased back, but didn't let her concentration lapse. The beast was still trapped but was slowly making progress on his restraints. The vines weren't stronger than stone, but that was why she weaved them so thick and kept them tight.

Waving her hands around and shaping with magic, if anyone on Earth saw her they would think she was conducting an orchestra to play their greatest symphony. "HA!" She had finished her masterpiece and, with a careful eye, launched it at the gargoyle. Landing square on his head and crumbling slightly with the force of the impact was an oversized stone tulip. The giant was left, as Aggie had hoped, sleeping like a giant baby in a pile of vines and the flower fell to land between his massive claws. "Ah, how poetic." Aggie sighed as she jumped for joy, mentally congratulating herself.

"Did you just best him with a stone flower?" Ren's arms wrapped around her waist, lifting her into his embrace.

"Yes, of course I did. I used the tools at my disposal to train with what I had. It's not my fault you guys think I'm a delicate flower that will crumble at the slightest hint of adversity." Scrambling out of Ren's embrace, Aggie crossed her arms and looked pointedly at Mitchell who was walking around the aftermath and her attacker. "And as for you, it's not nice to spring an attack on an unsuspecting person. What would you have done if I had gotten hurt?"

"I suppose I would have scheduled more trainings, because your fighting skills would have needed even more work. Do you think in the case of an actual attack, that someone is actually going to give you fair warning? If you don't train and plan for someone to catch you off guard then there is no point in training. You can't practically fight against us because this lot," Mitchell's hand flourished to encompass the rest of the guys but didn't include himself, which Aggie found interesting, "can't seem to see past your allure to train you properly." He spoke with a noticeable sneer in his voice and continued about rousing her attacker. He lolled from right to left and slowly began to come to. Leaning on his right side, the gargoyle-like creature pushed his weight up on his left fist with a deep rumble that sounded more like a growl. Aggie took in the pained look on his face and assumed it was some sort of moan.

"Is that true?" The question on her lips was directed at the guardians creating a semi-circle around her and she raised her left eyebrow to emphasize that she wanted an answer. Each of guys looked instantly uncomfortable. Ren instantly dropped his gaze and scuffed his foot against the dusty ground. Mathius and Xavier took that exact moment to strike up a very heated conversation about the weather. Liel and Eldon just turned their backs on her and started pointing at the area outside the arena. Gryson and Kyrel were on opposite sides of the group and just glanced back and forth between the group of guys and realized they had nowhere to go, but just kept their gaze from landing on Aggie.

With an audible "Argh!" she flipped her pigtails over her shoulder and stormed away. In the distance by the gate that they came through, Aggie caught sight of her father. Though she wasn't ready to call him 'Dad', she still had come to terms with the fact that he was, in fact, her dad.

"Eckard, how about we leave these guys to clean up this mess and take a walk?" Aggie was done dealing with them, and since they weren't going to talk to her like adults she was going to leave and let them figure out how to grow up and come to her.

"I think that's a great idea. I'd be happy to answer any questions you might have, and we could use the time to catch up." Eckard's words were met with a rumble of a growl but, when Aggie turned to figure out who was the grumpy one making his presence known, she was surprised to find all eight of them stalking toward the gate where she was standing.

"Nope, you're all in time out. I've had my fill of all of you. Regardless of how you think I might need your protection, I don't care. I need a break and you can all take time to think about how well you want me to succeed and how you can go about doing it without alienating me and my feelings. Not everything that happens is completely about you guys." Throwing a glance at Eckard, Aggie stormed off in the direction of town. She wasn't stupid enough to be alone and isolated with this stranger, also known as her dad.

CHAPTER EIGHT

When they were a few yards away, Aggie decided to start her inquisition. "What happened that you had to leave? My mother never spoke of you, and if I ever asked about you Gran got so upset that she could have spit fire."

Eckard chuckled at her description. "That sounds like Blythe. She was never one to mince words, and when she didn't like someone she made it very clear that you were either actually dead or at the very least dead to her. Nothing could redeem that person in her eyes in any way. I was one of those people, and it was purely because of my bloodline and not me as an actual person. I could have been poor and a thief and she would have been fine with me loving her daughter. I wasn't either of those things, but the Gnash family has a tainted line and that was unforgivable in Blythe's eyes. No matter how Adalade felt about me, nothing was going to be able to change my blood."

"That sounds very unfair of her to not give you a chance to prove yourself." Aggie knew that she only was hearing one side of the story, and she had to remind herself that she needed to take what he was saying with a grain of salt until she knew for sure.

"Well, her distrust ran deeper than most things and she didn't know how to see past that. See, there was a time when the Gateway was controlled by the Wasley women and the Gnash men. While we didn't typically end up in romantic relationships, it was the balance that kept the Gateway working as it was intended. Then, after a betrayal that happened so many years ago I don't even remember the details, the Gateway severed the Gnash connection and the Wasleys were left to find a new sense of balance. I think." Eckard hesitated, and twisted his face in deep consternation as he considered his words.

"What?" Aggie pressed, worried he would try to keep this from her, which made her feel betrayed. While they had nothing that even resembled a familial relationship, she still felt that if he kept anything from her she would have lost what little trust she had started to build with him. Trust was the hardest thing for her to build because it's earned. Everyone always broke her trust, and she was waiting for that shoe to drop now.

"Blythe was always one to put her entire belief into the old ways. She was a rule-follower but she never thought that, under the right circumstances, things could actually be improved if she wavered a little." He slowed their pace but kept walking, scuffing his feet as they walked across the dirt path.

"So you're saying rules are meant to be broken?" Aggie scoffed, and tried to no laugh outright. It was a common saying, but to have a parental figure tell her that was a kid's dream come true. Unfortunately, Aggie didn't want a parent who says what they think you want to hear as a teenager. She wasn't a teenager, and the reason there were rules wasn't lost on her.

"Not exactly; I think rules should take into account all the factors before they're set in stone, just like in your case." Eckard was hedging and Aggie wasn't stupid enough to be reeled in.

"In my case? I'm not sure I know what you mean. I think the rules were followed to the letter with me, and as much as Gran and I didn't always see eye to eye I believe she did right by me in most instances." She knew that wasn't the best speech but hearing Eckard badmouth her Gran, the woman who raised her after her mother passed, wasn't going to fly.

"All I'm saying is there were likely other factors that impacted her actions, and why you had so little knowledge of the Gateway and this side of your life. Did you ever wonder how Adalade knew about it, if the position hadn't been passed on yet?" Eckard's words bounced around inside Aggie's head. She had always assumed her mother was appointed Gatekeeper at some point and that was why she was aware or that the guys knew her. Nothing else had crossed her mind at any point. Then again, it had been a rather eventful time since she took on the role.

"You're saying my mother wasn't ever a Gatekeeper? That Gran let her know about this side of our lives anyway? The Gateway had been sealed, locked, and completely off my radar until Gran died. Then it just opened. Why would a door that Gran kept locked just pick that moment to open to me?" Questions addled Aggie's brain, and she was so overloaded it wasn't an option to keep them to herself. They spilled out of her like a river without a dam.

"No, Aggie, your mother was never appointed as the Gatekeeper. She was introduced to this life as a child, though. She knew about everything growing up and that's how she and I met. I was drawn to the fact that I didn't have to hide my knowledge of these alternate realms from her. Our families were similar and it was nice to have someone I could be with and not have to lie to them." His words were pensive and his gaze lost in the distance. Aggie's heart broke a little because she hadn't known this man before now. Then the rest of her heart hardened, because she knew it couldn't last and she needed to be ready. Any man who had left his daughter for so many years without a word couldn't be counted on, no matter how much she wanted to wish otherwise. "The Gateway chose you, Aggie. It wasn't your mother's time, and even though she would have taken the role long before your Gran passed fate had other plans for your mother. Without Blythe there to open the door for you, the Gateway made the decision for her. Rules be damned." Eckard wasn't a soft-spoken man, but he wasn't a very passionate speaker either. While Aggie couldn't picture him standing up to the likes of Gran, he had caught her mother's attention. She worried that something happened in his life to break him since then.

"If Gran felt it was okay to talk to my mother about all this," Aggie swirled her hand around indicating the Shifter Realm, but was talking about everything she had been introduced to since the Gateway chose her "why didn't she tell me?" The last question was barely a breath of a whisper. This entire conversation was giving Aggie a complex. Her father left her as a baby, her mother died young, and Aggie didn't even know what caused that, as her Gran never told her. Now she was feeling like something was wrong with her.

"Honestly, Aggie, I'm not completely sure; Blythe and I were never close, but I have a theory." He paused and Aggie glanced up at him, wondering why he didn't continue. The look on his face as their eyes met told Aggie Eckard wasn't sure she wanted to know.

"Tell me. We might as well get it all out in the open while we're on the subject," Aggie prodded, but a small part of her still didn't want to know. His look scared her a little, and there was always a part of her that was great at second-guessing.

"You have tainted blood. Like I said before, if I were anyone other than a Gnash Blythe would have been dragging your mom and me down the aisle. Sadly, she was too prejudiced to see past my name and therefore she was preventing you from taking your rightful place in the family business. All because of a few rules that were clearly antiquated." His voice was raised slightly and his words were passionate. It was clear this was a sore spot with him. This gave Aggie pause.

"You're saying Gran raised me but hated me all the same?"

A tear slipped down her cheek, luckily on the side opposite Eckard so he didn't notice.

"I'm sure she loved you." Aggie could tell he was trying to backpedal but she didn't care. Her mind was running her life on a loop to look for signs of any of this being true. "I think she just had mixed views about this side of your life because you share my blood. She had to make a decision; I just happen to think she chose wrong. You were done a disservice by not being allowed to understand this side of your life before now. You have to play catch-up instead of falling seamlessly into your place."

This was making Aggie more and more uncomfortable. She didn't want to think ill of Gran, but some of the things Eckard was saying made sense. Her dad was just giving her facts as he saw them from the other side of the fence. She already had a basic idea of her side of the fence, because she had lived it.

"So if my blood is the reason Gran chose to keep this all from me growing up, why did the door open when she passed?" This was all so confusing for Aggie but she felt like she needed answers now.

"I would imagine it's the reason I was able to travel to see you. I've been blocked from the Gateway for my entire life. I met your mother by happenstance at a street fair when we were young. My family hasn't been allowed to use the Gateway for anything since we were removed from our position. I grew up with an understanding of this world and the Gateway. Our family hasn't stopped training the descendants because they never thought it was a permanent disposition." Eckard's eyes shone with something Aggie didn't recognize, but looked an awful lot like a child who had lost their favorite toy. A mix of sadness and longing.

"So, on your first trip into the Gateway, where were you planning to go?" Aggie knew that the Gateway was a place all its own. While a person might go into the Gateway, and she came to it from her home, that door was still just another access point. Her mind drifted back to when the door disappeared from view to protect her personal space. It had never done that before when she stepped into it. That thought gave her pause and was mildly distracting.

"Switzerland." Eckard's words startled her from her reverie.

"What?" Aggie's thoughts had made her forget what they were talking about that would have garnered that response. Now the only thing she could think of was a neutral party.

"I was on my way to Switzerland. I've always wanted to go but hadn't ever made the time. Figured if I was going through I might as well take a trip I actually wanted and might enjoy. You never know when the privilege would be taken away." The smile on his face made Aggie giggle slightly. Eckard really wasn't a bad guy, and from the sound of things the only reason she hadn't been able to have a relationship with him was a direct due to her grandmother.

"That sounds like quite the vacation." Then she realized that Eckard hadn't brought anything but a small bag the size of a reusable shopping bag. "You didn't pack much for your trip and, given that Switzerland is typically colder," Aggie dug back to her high school geography class, "wouldn't you need some bulkier clothes to stave off a chill?"

Eckard's warm laughter floated around her, a deep rumble that came from his chest. If she were touching him, Aggie would have felt it. "It's not cold year-round in Switzerland any more than it is anywhere else in the world. They have seasons, too." He gave her a placating look and Aggie rolled her eyes. "It happens to be spring there, so I could get by with a light jacket if need be. Though it seems the Gateway alerted you to my presence for a reason. It should only do that if you're needed, but in most cases it will let the traveler pass to their intended destination without assistance."

"What reasons would a traveler need assistance, or are there other reasons I would be needed as Gatekeeper?" Aggie hadn't fully thought about it but she knew that his trip hadn't been like the rest of the guys that had passed thought. Now that she thought about it, it did seem strange that she hadn't seen anyone else pass through. If this was such a common way to travel, then why hadn't she met anyone else besides the guardians and Eckard?

"Oh, I can't say I know the entire list or plan that the Gateway has, but I know novice travelers usually alert the Gate-keeper because they usually aren't as informed as I am and get confused."

"Well, how am I supposed to help them? I've never made a solo trip through the Gateway. I wouldn't even know how to select the right doorknob to go home." The thought sent Aggie into a panic. There was no way she thought that she could play travel agent or navigator to someone who didn't already know the ins and outs of the Gateway. Her heart started to race and she felt a slight sheen of sweat start to bead on her forehead.

Eckard placed his hand on her shoulder to stop their pace. "I can see this has you worried, needlessly I might add. You have a connection to the Gateway that's in your blood; now doubly so, in my opinion. It speaks to you in a way it does no other. Though, for any traveler, the Gateway can read their intent. If they want to go somewhere, that doorway is drawn to them above all others. Each one is different, and in some cases it might seem to glow. In others, it might just be a feeling. The Gateway speaks to each individual differently, and in a way that works best for them without feeling obtrusive or invasive."

"What if there are multiple travelers?" Aggie had never felt or seen any of these things when she traveled with the guys, and wondered if there was a connection breakdown or she didn't know what she was looking for. If that was the case, then how could she be expected to be in charge of this *All-Knowing Thing* or whatever it was. Maybe a *Being?*

"Whoever is passing through or has the greater intent. If there are multiple travelers going different directions then they will each feel a pull to their intended destination. In the case of them all going to the same place, the Gateway doesn't need to work that hard. Only whoever seems to be leading the group will need to be connected to the Gateway in that trip." Eckard was so matter-of-fact and it was as though he was giving a lecture about the subject. He was in his element for sure.

"So much to process, and I'm sure you're giving me the abridged version." Aggie rubbed her temples and tried to ease the headache that was creeping up on her. "I'm not sure how to process all of this. I had no idea there was so much involved in my new job or if I'm cut out for this. I wish Gran had prepared me for all this, even with any prejudices she might harbor." Aggie sighed audibly in frustration.

A throat clearing caught their attention, causing Aggie to turn abruptly. "I'm sorry to interrupt, Agatha, but we thought you might want to join us for some lunch. It is the least we can do, then you can ask us any questions you might have thought up about your fight." Liel wasn't beating around the bush. He also didn't show any signs of remorse for their underhanded tactics earlier. Aggie knew she should be upset with him still, but it was a part of his personality to not see or understand the little things, like why she might be still upset with them.

"While I'm not ready to let it go yet, I could eat. And since you guys are the experts on the area, I'll concede for now." Aggie glanced over at Eckard. "Are you coming?"

"I need to make a stop at my cabin to change my shoes. I didn't plan ahead for this trip." Aggie looked him over and realized he was still wearing his dress shoes, but had taken off his tie and sport coat from the previous day. He must have redressed that morning because his slacks and shirt weren't wrinkled but, then again, Aggie only assumed he was human like her. No one had clarified that information, and she filed away that question for their next private conversation.

"Well, Liel, where are we headed? So Eckard knows where to meet us when he's finished changing. Wait, where are you getting clothes?" Her questions aimed in different directions, Aggie felt a little like she was watching a heated tennis match.

"I have a few tricks up my sleeve; you just get yourself to lunch and I'll join you soon." Aggie knew he didn't have a suitcase or anything that he'd brought with him. She had gained powers to create her own clothes, but if Eckard was completely human he didn't have the same luxury to gain powers that she had. That gave Aggie pause; if the Gnash family and the Wasley families were intended to run the Gateway together were the Guardians originally supposed to share the wealth of powers, or to never have crossed that line to begin with?

"We will be at the lodge, as it is the only place to get a meal all together around here." Liel extended his hand to Aggie and she placed her in his. This was the first familiar contact the two of them had had. Aggie knew he was just being polite but this gesture felt odd, given what she already knew about the Guardians and the Gatekeeper intentions.

"I hope it's good because I haven't had any snacks and didn't pack any. Do you think I could get some Brownie or magical assistance to conjure up some chocolate or sugary goodness for later?" The question was mostly rhetorical but somewhere deep down Aggie wished it was easier to get some of her favorite junk in the other realms. She would kill for some licorice, the soft Australian kind, or a Milky Way at that very moment. There had been too much piled on all at once and Aggie needed some sugary distraction.

"I'm sure the cook will have something that will satisfy your cravings. He might even be persuaded to satiate your desire even when the lodge is closed for the night." Aggie's mind drifted on his words and she was thinking of some others who could satiate other desires when they weren't officially on her shit list. She honestly couldn't stay mad at them forever, but she didn't want them to know that just yet.

"I'm not sure what you two were discussing, but I did catch the tail end of it. I want you to know that you are right where you need to be, Agatha. The Gateway wouldn't have chosen you if you weren't destined to be the Gatekeeper. While you are forming bonds with us, you have formed a bond with the Gateway. It chose you, and in your own way some part of you accepted it long before you knew anything about all of this." He waved his arm around, indicating the shifter village. Aggie knew he was trying to gesture to the magical elements of all the newness in her life.

"It was very nosey of you to eavesdrop, Liel." Aggie wasn't chastising, because she didn't have the energy to argue with his logic. Up until Eckard stepped through and into her world, she had felt satisfied and settled in her decision to accept the role. "I'm just not sure I'm cut out for the level of responsibility that's involved. When I decided to do this there was a list of unwritten things I didn't know about, and I'm now second-guessing myself."

"That is to be expected, but you also know that you have us to lean on whenever you need us. We are always here for you." Liel's words were spoken with every ounce of sincerity that she had come to expect from him, but it didn't leave her feeling all warm and fuzzy. Her father had left, her mother had left, and her Gran had alienated her and then passed away before Aggie knew what was happening. She never had any close friends who had wormed their way into her life. She had acquaintances and a few dates here and there. No one stuck around for her, and it was still hard for her to picture the guys in that way.

CHAPTER NINE

The Lodge—Aggie wondered if that was the official name or the convenient one, based on location and design—was similar in design to the cabins. It seemed the shifters preferred to work with the means at their disposal and didn't feel the need to reinvent the wheel. What worked for the small worked for the mighty in this case. It wasn't a large structure, and the entire clan wouldn't be able to be in there all at once, but instead would have to eat in shifts. It made Aggie think of a rustic B&B that would be a perfect place to relax and reboot. In this case the bed part wasn't connected, but the Lodge was the perfect name for it.

The rest of the guys were gathered around a couple tables that seemed to have been shoved closer together. The remaining tables were spread out and no table accommodated more than six people at a time. There were probably two dozen tables spread throughout. Aggie was never good at math, but it looked like the place would seat a maximum of about a hundred people. There were few other tables occupied, but it was by no means packed. She had no idea what time it was; since her cell phone didn't work in the realms, she had gotten out of the habit of carrying it with her. Making a mental note, she realized a watch might be something worth investing in sometime in the near future.

"Have you all decided to come back to me with your tails between your legs?" Aggie sashayed up to the table, her hand still joined with Liel's. While it felt odd to begin with the connection was apparently something her body was craving, because after a few moments it felt wrong to release him.

"I'm not cowering in the least. That fight has been necessary for ages now. Landon was the next best choice, so you wouldn't hurt anyone else." Mitchell's words dripped with frustration and arrogance.

"Oh, so you're saying I hurt you guys, and I needed to be placed in the rocky version of bubble wrap?" Aggie smirked at him, knowing that wasn't what he meant. It was too fun not to poke the bear or, in this case, wolf.

"Not in the least, since you couldn't hurt any of us. Between our healing, speed, strength and overall power, most of them were more concerned about hurting you than getting the job done." He crossed his arms over his muscular chest, causing it to swell and press against his taut t-shirt. Aggie fought to keep her eyes on his face but failed. The way the corner of his mouth tipped up told Aggie she had been caught. He just tightened his grip, flexing all the more.

"Enough, both of you." Xavier's words from the opposite end of the table drew Aggie's attention. "We're here to eat and let Aggie ask questions. If you two stand there posturing all day we're never going to get anywhere. Aggie, I'm sorry we allowed you to be drawn into that fight. As awful as that was for us to do it, had you been aware the result would have been vastly different. I never want to deceive you, but I also don't ever want to see harm come to you. You held your own in the fight against Alentra in the Demon Realm, but not everyone fights with the same delusional passion as she did. Some are methodical and others are chaotic, seeming to have no end game. What I'm trying to say is it will do you good to see different fighting styles and fight those who aren't directly connected to you. While you might be mad at us, and within reason, it was for your own good that we did this today. Now, while we eat, you can ask us anything that you can think of that we can help you understand or improve in future fights."

His words made Aggie think, and even though she wanted to be mad at them he had a point. That made her even madder, because it wasn't supposed to make sense. Now her anger seemed displaced, and she didn't quite know where to go from there. Glancing over the table Aggie noticed that, as Liel took his seat, she had one of four places to sit. It was as though they'd thought this out beforehand; there was no way their seating arrangement was coincidence. She could choose to sit by any two of them. There was a space open beside each of them. The tables were too narrow to put anyone at the ends but with two, six-seat tables slid together, the second seat from each end on both sides was left open. Now she had a hard decision to make: who did she want sit beside?

She knew she didn't want to sit next to Mitchell's brooding ass, but then that meant she automatically crossed Mathius out of the running. He had the empty seat beside him and Kyrel to his immediate left. So, Aggie decided to do what any self-respecting woman would do.

"Eeny, Meeny, Miny, Moe. Catch a tiger by his toe. If he hollers let him go. Eeny, Meeny, Miny, Moe." That eliminated Ren and Gryson. Then she began again, pointing to each man as she went.

"What are you doing?" Mitchell demanded to know. Ren and Kyrel were stifling laughter, but with little effort, so it was clear that they knew what was happening.

Aggie finished her rhyme the second time, eliminating Mitchell and Mathius, and while she was a little sad for Mathius she was thankful Mitchell was out of the running. "I have eight guardians and one little ol' me. What would you have me do? If

I sit down willy-nilly, what's to keep you from thinking I'm playing favorites?" Picking up her pointing and chanting again, Aggie began to make her final decision. And took her seat between Liel and Eldon. That was probably for the best, as they were the calmer of the bunch and left her to face and talk with the rest of the table at her leisure. Though she didn't miss Mitchell's obvious eyeroll now that she had finally seated herself.

"Now that that's settled, what's for lunch? I don't know about you guys, but I'm starving. Between fighting, wait was that a gargoyle? I'm not sure, but that's what I started calling him in my head while we were fighting." Aggie's thoughts spewed out of her as usual and took her on a tangent. Shaking her head, she didn't wait for an answer but continued back on her original thought. "Either way, between fighting him and the fact that breakfast didn't stick to me as much as I'd like, I need to eat, like now, or I might waste away before all of you. I might not be super-model skinny but I'm content with my muffin top." Glancing between all of the guys she wondered who, if anyone, would answer her.

A menu was dropped in front of her as though conjured from thin air. It was generic, like in any diner she had ever visited before. Which surprised her on some level, but on another she remembered that shifters frequented the Earth Realm and spent time living there. They were bound to bring a few things back to their own people to share.

"You are perfect." Eldon whispered from his seat at her left. His words were spoken softly, but she was sure she wasn't the only one who heard him. This was confirmed by the chorus of affirmations that followed.

Before she had a chance to say anything, a man approached their table. He was rather tall, and Aggie had to incline her head to look at his face. He was just as wide as he was tall. Aggie could tell by the stretch of his shirt that he wasn't overweight, but solid with muscle. His face was familiar, but Aggie couldn't put her finger on where she might know him from.

"Felix, glad you could join us. I was hoping you didn't have anything more pressing to do this afternoon. Your help would be appreciated. Please take a seat." Mitchell flipped to his diplomatic side in a way that made Aggie think he might suffer from some sort of bipolar disorder. Not knowing who Felix was bothered her more in this case, so she let her eyes follow him and chose not to linger on Mitchell's behavior.

Felix took a seat between Ren and Gryson, across from Mitchell and Mathius. This placed him in a seat that made it hard for Aggie to see him without turning in her own. Not wanting to draw too much attention to herself she remained facing Kyrel and Xavier, but the fact that she couldn't place Felix was bothering her. She tried not to let it show on her face.

"Happy to be here and, hey, a guy's gotta eat. Not like I didn't work up an appetite this morning." Aggie had turned and was politely looking at him now since he was speaking. His voice was deep and gravely. Almost as though he had swallowed handfuls of dirt and was suffering from a severe need to drink a lake's worth of water. When he said the last part he glanced her way, shooting her wink. She stifled a laugh when a chorus of growls erupted from around the table. It didn't slip her notice that Felix was jostled slightly, and she realized that Ren or someone had kicked him under the table. Felix didn't apologize or take anything back. He just smirked knowingly.

"Wait, what did you do this morning that worked up such an appetite?" Aggie had seen people working here and there through the encampment that, while it would be considered work, none of it was particularly excessive in any way save for maybe the wood-chopping. Though Aggie remembered who was doing that, and he was far older than Felix and not anywhere as close to his size.

Forgoing his vow of silence, Ren chimed in. "Felix was your, we'll call him combatant." That took a moment for Aggie to digest.

"You're the creature that attacked me?" She knew she probably wore a look of complete surprise and should probably pick her jaw up off the table, but she wasn't there yet. Everything was still settling into her subconscious, and far too soon for her to have recovered yet.

"He didn't attack you, it was training. If you think all those who train you are attacking you, you will never learn from them. You will see them as out to get you. There is a time and a place for anger, and training isn't it. Learning from your mistakes is key. If you can't learn from them then you will never rise to your potential." Xavier was a breath of fresh air. It wasn't Liel preaching at her or Mitchell barking or Mathius dictating. Xavier was matter-of-fact and direct, but what he said made sense. She couldn't argue with sense. The others just brought out her inner child, who wanted to argue and kick and scream to get her way.

"Okay, that's a valid point. I won't disagree with you, but you have to admit it was a backwards way to throw me into that. I had no idea we were going to be training. I thought I was on a tour and then was thrust into it unawares." Xavier opened his mouth to speak, but Aggie cut him off. "No, before you scold me, I get it. The old methods weren't working, but you could have warned me we would be training at some point today. I would have worn something a bit more flexible."

"You can't always dress for battle, Love." Kyrel's hypnotic voice didn't have the same effect on her as when they first met, but he could push a bit of his magic into it and she would relax. The glassy-eyed doe that she used to become was thankfully a thing of the past. "It is inevitable that we will be attacked sometime when we least expect it. You need to learn to work with what you have in any situation."

"That makes sense, and I think I did a pretty good job of that today." She smiled, and her confidence showed as she allowed herself a moment of pride.

"You were sloppy and took too long to take him down. If he were part of an army, you would have used too much power and weakened yourself physically. The more of your powers you draw on the more likely you are to be targeted. They will push you to your limits in order to take you down quickly." Mitchell always knew how to knock her off her high horse. Not that he wasn't right, but she hadn't ever expended too much. She had always been able to draw on her power to refresh her human energies in the past. It never occurred to her that she could run out.

"That didn't happen last time, so why would you assume that it would now?" She stuck her jaw out at him a defiant gesture that she internally recognized as the petulant child she always fell back on with Mitchell's perpetual need to be right in every situation.

"The more power you have, the harder the toll on your natural body. If you use too much too fast, it will slow you down," Liel answered in his usual dry tone. It was so hard for her to see the emotional side of him in order to make a lifelong connection. He would always be the hardest to get close to. Even if his words were the most factual and honest of all of them. "Don't recover the way you should, and you may not recover at all."

A silence fell over the table, as no one seemed to want to follow that statement, but Aggie realized there was so much she didn't know. Truthfully, not considering the consequences of taking so much unnatural magic into herself by bonding with each Guardian was terrifying. What had she done, and was it all really potentially worth her life in the long run?

"I'm a gargoyle." Felix's words, though softly spoken, were loud in the silence that had descended on the table, and the unexpectedness of it took away from what would normally have been a triumphant response on Aggie's part. She truly did love being right in most, well, all situations.

Taking a moment to come to her senses, Aggie let his words sink in. Only then did she allow herself a moment to gloat. "HA! I knew it. Maybe I have a knack for these things. Is there a game show for this kind of thing here? If not there should be, and I'd call it 'Guessing Obscure Mythical Creatures'. It could be like *Jeopardy*. 'What is a gargoyle?' I'd be amazing at that game." She was letting her thoughts run amok and didn't notice the blank stares directed at her, not at first. It wasn't until Ren burst out laughing followed, surprisingly, by Felix, that she saw the mirrored looks on the guys' faces. Mitchell looked to have tuned her out and, while he might know what she was referring to, wasn't going to dignify it with a response of any kind.

"You are quite the little thing, aren't you?" Felix was still chuckling lightly, but it brought her back down to Earth… well, Cratlian in this case.

"You have no idea." Ren shook his head, but was still enjoying the moment of Aggie's random rambling. He was always in good humor and, while sometimes it bothered Aggie, this time she was thankful he wasn't abiding by Mitchell's order. Life was much better when Ren could be his usually happy self.

"My brain works in unique ways, but don't let these guys fool you. They all love it in their own ways. Even Mitchell, but he won't tell you that, or me for that matter. I just believe deep down he isn't the asshole he likes to portray." Felix's eyes nearly bulged out of his head. He might be a massive, rough and tough rock man, but clearly he still respected and had a healthy fear for his Alpha. The rest of the guys didn't share that sentiment, and Ky and Ren, but also Mathius, Gryson, and even Xavier burst out laughing. To Aggie's surprise, Liel even cracked a smile.

"I thought you were hungry, Princess. I think you should stop sharing your thoughts on things you don't understand and fill it with food, or I'm sure any of the Guardians would be happy to fill it with something else if food isn't what you desire." A look of promise flashed across his face, and as Aggie glanced at the remaining men at the table their eyes darkened ever so slightly. Her body betrayed her at Mitchell's words and she felt a flush creep up her neck. It wasn't embarrassment. She wasn't sure if she hoped they misread it or was worried they hadn't. Ky flashed her a smile and she remembered he could read her sexual desires, as they fed his magical side. That also brought back a memory of their first kiss and also the knowledge that Mitchell, Ren, and now likely Felix could smell her desire. That immediately changed her flush from desire to embarrassment in a flash of a moment.

"Food, yes. That would be a wise choice since, as we said, our morning activities worked up quite an appetite. Sorry Ren, breakfast was delicious but, if you guys are going to make me burn thousands of calories a day training, small meals aren't going cut it. Unless someone wants to run me home to stock my room with snacks. I doubt the cook here wants to stay up at all hours to sate my cravings." Her double meaning wasn't intended, but she still smirked at the thought. She hadn't even met the cook, but so far she hadn't seen an ugly shifter. It was like the magic in their genes had a beautifying effect on them. Not that she had eyes for anyone other than the Guardians and, in her mind, she wasn't sure she was enough for them even now.

CHAPTER TEN

Full beyond the point of comfort, Aggie leaned back in her chair. They were right, the shifter cook was skilled in his chosen profession and Aggie knew she would put on a few pounds staying in this realm.

"So, what's the plan for the rest of the day? It seems we knocked out training for now. I already had the tour. What else is there to do here?" Glancing around the table, Aggie realized something. "Where's Eckard? You told him where we would be, didn't you?" Aggie's attention was focused on Liel. She couldn't figure out how they had made it through the entire meal without noticing before now.

"He should have made it here. Unless he couldn't find a change of clothes. That was what he was supposed to be doing, right?" Liel wasn't second-guessing himself, but clarifying with Aggie. That was unlike him. Aggie's brow furrowed but she nodded, acknowledging what he should have already known.

"Clothes? Where was he planning on getting those? He is staying in your cabin, Aggie. If there were any clothes in there it would have been the wrong gender for him and likely the wrong size, even if he were happy to swing that way." Ren offered his two cents and showed his clear confusion as well. The mumbles that started sweeping the table told Aggie they were unsure of where he was.

As though thinking of him was a spell that conjured him, Eckard swept in through the door, slightly out of breath. "Where have you been?" Aggie asked as she took in the fact that he hadn't changed clothes.

"Can we chat for a moment?" Eckard hesitated as Aggie noticed the scowls on all eight men at the table. Felix had begged his leave after they finished eating and talking a bit more about fighting methods and strategy. "Outside?"

She decided not to look at the guys, sure she would see their displeasure. They had made no effort to hide their dislike of Eckard. "I'll be right back." She followed Eckard to the front porch of the café.

Eckard was pacing by the time Aggie made it through the doors. She knew something was wrong but didn't know enough about the man to put her finger on it. "What's up?" she blurted, making her way to him.

He startled at her words, which threw Aggie because he was the one who asked her to come out and talk. He was acting beyond strange, and not just for him, because clearly her knowledge of him was limited, but for basic human interaction.

"Oh, good. You came. I need to talk to you." His words were gruff and less compassionate than she had heard from him before. "I've been called away for some unexpected business. I was hoping you would join me and we could begin your training as the Gatekeeper." Eckard looked at her expectantly, as though he thought there was only one way she could react.

"I can't go now." She was blown away by his timing, yet his words were even and he was acting like it made complete sense. "I have a responsibility here; there's a rebellion waiting on the horizon. No one knows when they'll strike and we have to be prepared. The Guardians need to show a united front in this specific situation. I'm needed here to train and fight."

"You think they need you, but they have been doing fine for centuries without you. They just want you to be distracted from your destined role and help them because they can finally break their vow of celibacy. Men can't not think with their dicks. You need to be the brains here and realize there's something bigger. You need to take control of the Gateway in a way no one has before. You're the one with the power. The Gatekeeper is the one who will rule them all. They say women have power over a man and that isn't untrue. In this case, you have all the power. Between your legs, as well as their way between realms. No one can make a trip without your approval and they should see that for the power that it is." He was practically shaking with his passion. "You need to come home with me and train for your one true destiny."

This change in Eckard was giving Aggie whiplash. He had been so forthcoming with information in all their previous conversations and now he was preaching about some kind of takeover. It was like he was a modern-day Hitler, and that didn't sit well with Aggie. There was always a chance he was just tired and in a hurry, so it was coming across wrong. Aggie didn't know what to believe.

"I can't go with you, not right now at least. You have to understand that I've made a commitment here and I intend to see it through. I have too much invested now to back out." Her words were softer and less passionate than Eckard's, but that didn't mean she meant them any less. She didn't know where she was meant to be, or if she wanted to explore the prophesy that she learned about while in Ahael, the demon city. She couldn't fathom anything about being the Dragon intended to save everyone. That was insane as far as Aggie was concerned.

"I can't wait for you. I have a life and people who count on me as well. You aren't my only priority in the worlds. I will try and return later to offer my help, but that isn't a guarantee." With that Eckard, turned on his heel without another word and made his way out of Galata and didn't look back.

Aggie's heart was breaking as she watched her father walk out of her life again without a glance back in reassurance. She had no idea when or if she would see him again. Fighting tears she didn't want to shed for a man who'd reentered her life just one day prior, Aggie walked back inside to the guys.

Felix had already taken his leave from the table, but all of the Guardians remained. Aggie blinked a couple times to clear her thoughts and any lingering emotions. "Eckard has been forced to leave earlier than planned."

"Where did he go?" Gryson sounded concerned, but Aggie couldn't figure out if it was for her or Eckard's abrupt departure.

"He didn't say, but he was disappointed that I refused to join him. He just left and didn't look back." She didn't feel the need to explain the details of their private conversation. She knew most of the guys already had ill thoughts of Eckard, to say the least, and they didn't need any more fuel for the fire.

"I'm sorry, Love. I know you wanted him to stay, if for nothing else than to give you some closure. I know one day wasn't enough to count. I just hope you got something out of his visit." Ky was being sweet to her as usual; it was as though he didn't have a mean bone in his body. Aggie considered this and wondered if negative thoughts reacted badly to his 'spread love' mentality. She would save it for a later conversation, as this wasn't the time or place.

"Well, now that he is gone we can get back on track. Something about Eckard didn't sit well with me. His sudden appearance rubbed me the wrong way. His timing was perfect." Mitchell was being his usual brutish self, and just as inconsiderate. Gryson noticed, and stared him down but didn't say a word. Mathius, who was the closest to Mitchell, punched him in the arm hard enough to make the Alpha shifter grunt softly.

"While I don't agree with the way Mitchell is acting, I agree with part of what he is saying. I know you wanted a relationship with him, Aggie, but something is off." Xavier was speaking softly, and Aggie remembered before she had to silence his aggression over this topic with her golden cuffs now always on her wrists. Absently she rubbed circles with her left middle finger over her right one. Xavier's eyes were drawn to the motion and he smiled at her. "That won't be necessary, Wee One." "I'm just saying his behavior today was a bit suspect, and we should remember that we don't really know much about his character." He left it at that and nodded at Mitchell, who was looking all too smug.

"Okay, let's change the subject because I need a distraction." Aggie glanced at Gryson. "Since Mitchell said the magic might not fool the shifters, it sounds like we'll need to split our resources and go to the three remaining towns. Is there a magical alert or alarm that you can tie to us in case something happens in Cratlian while we're gone? I'm not sure how long we'll need to be away." Since her father left, her trust issues were rearing their ugly head again. She didn't like the idea of splitting everyone up for fear one of them would turn on her, or leave her like everyone else had. Nothing was harder than watching people walk away from her. Now she would have to watch six of the guys go in a different direction. "Also, while this is against my better judgement, can we set up a communication system like we did in Ahael? Would that spell even reach that far?"

"You're volunteering for that?" Gryson looked shocked and Aggie shrugged. There was a part of her screaming "NO!" but another part of her needed to feel that connection regardless of distance. It was something she almost welcomed, just to have that connection with the guys.

"Don't get me wrong—the idea completely creeps me out. But how else are we going to know if something's happening between the villages if we're all split up? Also, I would prefer it if one of you would teach me how you were blocking your every thought from me." Aggie shuddered at the thought of that little worm-like creature going back inside of her.

"That will take more than a crash course, Princess." Mitchell was such an ass, but he was probably right. Aggie was getting tired of his mouth.

"Lose the attitude unless you have helpful things to say, Mitch." Her words were laced with exhaustion. The fight was catching up to her, lumped in with her emotional stress over Eckard. There was still so much to do, but the need for a nap was starting to overtake her.

"That wasn't attitude, it was fact. You want me to sugar coat everything for you, you're dreaming. This isn't the place for daydreams. We need you on your game and not fantasizing about what you think should be happening." Mitchell leaned back in his chair and crossed his arms. Aggie found herself wishing he would tip over. The thought gave her an idea.

With a mere thought, Aggie created a vine and snaked it between his legs without drawing attention to what she was doing. The vine looped around one of the rear legs all in a few seconds. When she knew she had a tight enough grip, Aggie mentally pulled the vine. The Alpha shifter was caught off guard and the chair started to fall. He reached for the lip of the table but a second too late. The prank was already in motion and the result was priceless.

Aggie burst out laughing, though the tables obscured her view of the audible impact. It was the perfect move, and while Aggie enjoyed the moment she knew she would never get away with that again. Mitchell would retaliate eventually.

With a growl, Mitchell got to his feet and reset the chair on all fours. "You'll pay for that, Princess."

"I don't know what you're talking about. How did I do anything to you from all the way over here?" She had destroyed the evidence as soon as she tugged and the chair began to fall, the vine disappearing without a trace. "Is it really my fault you never learned in school what happens when gravity takes over?"

A hush fell over the group, though Aggie knew most saw the humor. It was time to get to work and Aggie had only delayed the inevitable. "I think if I use a stronger device it will work." Gryson broke the silence, bringing them all back on track to their plans.

"Device? You mean worm, right?" Aggie's lip curled in disgust as she thought about the creature piece that had been in everyone's heads.

"Yes, it is easier to think about them in a less creature-like way to handle working with them. They are the tools of my trade as I work my magic. Do you think it is pleasant using frog eyes and human brain matter in spells?"

"Ewww, brain matter? Seriously? Don't ever use that in anything you make for me." Aggie was struggling to keep her lunch inside her stomach.

"We use worse than that, but if I think of them as ingredients and devices then I can compartmentalize the thoughts they induce." Gryson didn't put her at ease but the idea made sense to her, and she knew that would be her new goal in thinking of his spells.

"Well, do you have to do anything special to get the stronger device?" Eldon had been quiet up until now, just observing and taking in information.

"I will have to make a trip back to my lab. I keep all my supplies there and only carry a few things with me when I travel, for emergencies." Gryson patted the pocket of his coat before remembering he had dressed down for the day. He chuckled at his mishap. "Well, they are in my cabin."

The thought of traveling to Gryson's home was intriguing. "Will that take very long?" She wondered if they would have to postpone their plans for any length of time.

"No, just a short while to gather supplies. The Gateway does all the work in this case." A look flashed across Gryson's face like a lightbulb had just flashed inside his head. "Would you like to accompany me?"

Aggie's eyes grew wide and a grin spread across her face. "Really?" She looked around at all the guys before realizing she didn't need anyone's permission. She was a grown woman and the Gatekeeper. "That would be amazing. I'll need to change clothes. What's the weather like there?" Aggie was so excited, her thoughts were running away with her. "What's it like? You said it was amazing but, really, that isn't a great descriptor. Will we run into anyone else while we're there? Do we have time to look around?"

Laughing at her excitement, Gryson answered, "Calm down, Parum Praesetes. I will show you all I can, but we don't have a lot of time. It won't be the last time you visit my home. You will want to dress for fall weather on Earth. It isn't cold but it isn't exactly warm either."

Bouncing up and down in her chair, Aggie excitedly declared, "I need to go change. Now. I have so many ideas and I want to put my best foot forward, as they say. I'd hate to look out of place." Jumping up from the table, she was chased from the café by a chorus of laughter.

CHAPTER ELEVEN

*A*fter a dilemma about which cabin to go to, Aggie ended up in what was originally hers. She didn't know what it looked like, but it seemed Eckard hadn't left a trace of himself behind. If a forensics crew had come through, Aggie wondered if they'd even find a stray hair or fingerprint. It was like he was never there.

Not letting this deter her from her mission, Aggie walked over to the wardrobe. Similar to the one in Mitchell and Ren's cabin, it looked hand-carved and ornate. More so than one would think anyone would put the effort into in this shifter camp. While they had cabins, it still felt like if they needed to uproot and move to another location it would be within their expectations. Not yet ready to conjure her clothes, Aggie thought about it for a moment.

Gryson had told her to think Earthly-fall style. She threw some ideas around in her head and after a few moments had an idea. She wanted to be comfortable as she was going to have to walk back to the Gateway location, and she still didn't know what to expect when she crossed through into Gryson's world. She hadn't even though to ask him the name, something she intended to rectify as soon as she reconnected with Gryson.

Placing her hands on the handles of the wardrobe, she saw they were twisted and carved into the shape of wolf heads. Aggie thought that was ironic, given the fact that not all the shifters here were wolves. The natural hum of her magic flowed through her as her design was created on the other side of the doors.

As she opened the doors Aggie felt like a magician presenting her great reveal, only without all the smoke and mirrors. The garments hanging on the rod were everything she had envisioned. A hunter-green cable-knit sweater, slightly over-sized so it would fall nicely over the jeggings she had created. Over the top of the hanger hung a mustard-yellow cowl that Aggie was dying to see on. Resting in the bottom of the wardrobe were a pair of leather boots the color of milk choco-late. Just dark enough; she hoped the lighter colored dust didn't collect on them too much or she would look like she rode in from the Wild West. Chuckling to herself, Aggie turned and made her way to the shower. After that fight, she was a hot mess and needed to freshen up before donning her new, fashionable, appropriate outfit.

Leaving the door open just a crack Aggie had no concerns, as she wasn't sharing a room any longer. Twisting the handle in the shower and letting the water warm the space, she sighed with anticipation. Aggie unfastened her hair and shook out the braids she had put it in that morning. Just as she was about to remove her clothes, Aggie heard a faint knock at the door. With a roll of her eyes, Aggie strolled back into the bedroom and pulled the latch open.

Xavier stood on the stoop, looking pensive. "What can I do for you?" Aggie held the door open to invite him in.

He proceeded into the room and his ears perked up. "Am I interrupting?"

"Only trying to get cleaned up a bit before I take off with

Gryson." She motioned to the small chair that was sitting beneath a lamp. The space resembled a reading nook, but without a bookshelf seemed wasted. She sat down on the bed. The room was laid out much like a hotel room in its simplistic nature.

His eyes flashed with something akin to desire but he quickly tamped it back down. "I can understand that, so I will try to make this visit brief. I wanted to apologize for my previous behavior. I know we aren't that close yet, but I am still very protective of you. You are my intended mate, and I will do anything to keep you safe. Eckard has a reputation in our world. The best way to describe him in a way you would understand is probably a pirate in your world. He is a bit of a scavenger and has minimal morals to keep him in check." Aggie knew her eyes were wide in shock. She had no clue what to say to that. "I saw him standing there with you alone and I reacted on instinct."

The thought of him being so primal and defending her on instinct, Aggie had to admit that alone was a turn-on, but it wasn't right to attack someone unprovoked. "I can appreciate that, and thank you for being honest with me. I want you to know I still don't condone your behavior, though. Eckard seems to have been genuinely trying to help me, or at least get to know me as his daughter. While I don't have blood proof, there are enough physical characteristics that I'm inclined to believe him. That said, I don't trust easily, having been burned so many times in the past. It's something I'm actively working on. I'm intrigued by your natural instincts; it piqued my interest."

"I could do a little more than pique them if you would let me." In the blink of an eye, Xavier was kneeling in front of her with his hands resting on her knees. The abruptness startled her, but he balanced her quickly with one hand. Leaning so close in the motion, she could feel his breath on her lips. Without another thought, Aggie leaned forward and pressed her lips to his. Soft and supple were the only words that broached Aggie's locked-down mind. The distraction of kissing Xavier was more than enough to keep her in the moment. His lips were the perfect opposition to his hard muscles and firmness of his body that she had felt on previous occasions.

Xavier didn't wait for permission; he pressed further and leaned into her and his fingers tangled into her loose tresses, holding tight at the roots. The action put him in complete control of the kiss. Angling her head to give him better access, he ran his tongue along the seam of her lips, begging entrance. She didn't falter as she opened to him. His tongue dove deep and plundered her mouth. Their tongues battled, wrestling as they got acquainted. A moan bubbled up from Aggie's throat and Xavier leaned her back slightly, further causing her to find her balance with her hands on his shoulders.

Xavier's other hand traveled up the outside of Aggie's shirt, but quickly found her covered breast and kneaded it softly. It was as though he was holding back and wanted to do more, but was waiting for her to lean into it. Aggie's mind caught up at this point and she moved her hands over his expansive chest. Normally clad in a buttoned shirt, Aggie found herself disappointed that she couldn't access him so easily. Xavier broke their kiss for only a second as he tore the shirt from his body.

Leaning back, he changed his trajectory and lined up with her neck. A small gasp escaped her as his lips connected with her skin right where it met her shoulder. He chuckled softly while placing a series of kisses there.

"Did you think I was going to do something else, Wee One?" His tongue lapped once over the area and he hummed his pleasure. "I won't bite you yet, but soon, very soon I will and you will love it. Right before you climax, my teeth will pierce your skin and you will soar to new heights." The thought made Aggie long for it even now, as his lips hadn't left her neck.

His hands hadn't moved from their chosen places. His right hand regripped her hair at the nape of her neck, placing her neck right where he wanted it and he latched on to her skin, but still no teeth. Aggie hadn't known she ever wanted such a thing until that moment. He body craved it and wanted nothing else. His other hand found her nipple beneath the fabric and plucked and squeezed until she cried out in pleasure.

Without warning, Xavier scooped her up from the bed and carried her bridal-style to the bathroom.

"What are you doing?" Aggie was in a state of confusion. Xavier's kisses were enough to render her completely stupid.

"I'd hate for you to run out of hot water while we're getting better acquainted in the other room." He placed her on the counter and began to unbutton her shirt.

"Just shut the water off. I can be a little late; Gryson didn't say when we were leaving," she reasoned, but it seemed Xavier had other plans.

Not saying a word he continued to remove her shirt, his movements painfully slow. One button at a time, and with each expanse of skin his lips found a way to connect. Her head lolled back in pleasure and simply decided to go with the flow.

Once Xavier had divested her of her shirt, he made quick work of her bra and slowed his progress there. His eyes ravaged her bare skin and didn't waste any time suckling her exposed nipples. In a moment of wanton pleasure Aggie pressed her breasts up closer to him, indulging in the luxury of his focus.

Her hands placed behind her to help keep her balance on the countertop, she felt left out of the exploring. Locking her legs around his waist, she pulled with all her might and locked his core with hers. He groaned. She clearly felt his hardened length right where she wanted it most. Leaning forward, she felt blindly for his jeans button. She wasn't willing to give up the pleasure of him feasting on her breasts. Before she could get them unfastened, he pulled his hips away with his vampiric strength and broke her legs from his waist.

"You are an impatient little vixen. I have plans for you yet. First we need to remove the rest of this offensive clothing so it doesn't get any wetter." He popped the button of her denim shorts and slid them from her waist, pulling her from the counter in the same smooth motion. Her panties were soaked and completely ruined. It was another reason she was thankful for the ability to create clothing from a thought. Perhaps she would think up something ultra-sexy to go beneath the clothes she had waiting for her, post- shower.

"I think this little game we are playing is weighing in your favor. I feel I should get some visual pleasure as well." Aggie pretended to pout, but in reality all the guys so far had been very gracious lovers and she didn't want for anything. Though, in this case, she wanted to see more of Xavier before she reached a point of no return and couldn't appreciate the view.

"Who is to say you aren't going to win in the end?" Xavier halted his process and leaned back, allowing her to admire the vast expanse of his chest and pectoral muscles. They weren't overly bulky but she knew he held massive amounts of strength beneath them. He was lean and entirely edible. Aggie had so many ideas as to what she wanted to do to him. Xavier had other plans, however. Her gaze was distracted by the movement of his hands as they latched onto his own waistband. Biting her lower lip, Aggie knew she was holding back drool. All she wanted to do was see what was beneath those pesky jeans. If she were lucky, he'd let her roam a little before continuing with his plan.

With a flick of the button he had them open and off before she could finish her inhale. His erection was standing at attention, begging for her to taste him. As she began to lower to her knees, a flash and a gust of air caused her to freeze. In that same moment the air hit her lower lips in a way she hadn't known possible. Only then did she look down and see that her soaked panties had been torn from her, leaving her bare to Xavier's hungry stare. As her eyes met his she realized that her panties were now caught in his teeth, and he smiled like a cat who had caught its prey.

With a long inhale his smile grew. "Oh, Wee One, I want

nothing more than to have that smell invade my nose forever. You smell exquisite and I could survive on you alone."

"Oh, I think that you'd die of starvation if you tried to feed off of my juices forever." She teased, falling the remaining inches to her knees. His cock was at eye level, and oh so tempting. Giving in to her primal urges, her tongue snaked out and caught the glistening liquid building on the tip.

"Oh, that's all I've dreamed and more." The words were more of a murmur, but Xavier heard them with ease. His ears could pick up a whisper carried on the wind.

"You have dreamed of me, Wee One?" He grabbed her hands and pulled her to her feet and straight to the shower. She started to stop him from pushing her into the water, but didn't when she saw him following her under the spray. "I will clean you off and dirty you again. It will be an honor and a privilege if you'll let me." It was the first time he had asked permission, and for that Aggie was grateful. While she knew that taking any of them meant an addition of power and bonds, she couldn't say no to this perfection standing in front of her. He was all she wanted, and everything she needed in that moment.

He produced a washcloth from nowhere, or that's what it seemed because Aggie saw nothing but the cloth appear. He began to lather it with the soap and Aggie watched his motions with rapt attention. She couldn't pull her gaze from his hands and waited in anticipation of where it would go next.

Lowering the foaming cloth to her skin he started someplace tame: her shoulder. Her face must have registered her disappointment because she heard him rumble with a soft laugh. He worked in slow and agonizing circles, cleaning her thoroughly, but avoided all the areas she wanted him to touch. Her breasts ached to be touched and he simply grazed the edges of them or ran down the middle to get to her stomach.

As he worked circles around her belly button, she leaned back to encourage him lower. Instead he turned her and proceeded to clean her back, but that didn't stop her from pressing her ass into him, hoping he'd take the hint. He did clean her there, to her surprise, and kneaded her tight muscles, eliciting a moan from her. Bending over a little more, exposing herself to him, she hoped he would skip all else and focus on her center, but again she was disappointed.

Xavier knelt, his face eye level with her aching core. She hoped and silently begged that he would touch her. Instead he started at her feet and began to work up to each knee in turn. Slowly, and it felt like an eternity later, he finally came up her thighs and with a feather touch brushed the cloth over her pussy. The feeling nearly made her collapse with pleasure. Never in her life had she felt a sensation so intense. It was like he was playing her body like an instrument made only for him. He knew which buttons to press and when they needed to be pressed.

He soaped her up and had her on the edge in a short time. Aggie had never been this close so fast in her life. These men were going to be the death of her if they were all this amazing. Though, death by orgasm wasn't a bad way to go.

When she thought she couldn't take anymore he removed the cloth and plunged two fingers deep inside of her, eliciting a gasp of pleasure from her. His lips instantly sealed to her clit and he hooked his long fingers as he pumped in and out of her, easily hitting her sweet spot. Once again, before she could climax her pulled away from her and rose to his feet. Grabbing the shampoo from the shelf he proceeded to wash her hair, once again avoiding what she needed most.

"As much as I'm enjoying your methods at cleaning me, are you planning on keeping me in suspense much longer? I'm not sure I can take anymore almost-there moments." Aggie knew she was begging but she couldn't wait any longer. She needed more.

"I think this sweet form of torture will be your most memorable yet. I want you to remember me while you're away. I won't leave you writhing, though, because I'm not sure I can trust you to wait until you return to satiate the growing need." Rinsing the suds from her long dark locks, he wasted no time. Grabbing her by the hip to angle her just the way he wanted, he plunged his rock-hard pole right into her more-than-ready slit. He didn't stop until he hit the farthest end and held her locked for her to adjust to his size. The full feeling was what she had needed and she cried out, her voice echoing off the shower walls. She threw her arms around his neck and raised her leg around his hip to lock them together. The last thing she wanted was for him to pull away again.

Much to her pleasure he slowly pulled from her, and she gave him a little room in hopes he wouldn't disappoint her. She felt every ripple and vein along her channel as he emerged from her. It was a perfect fit and she missed the fullness instantly. He moaned as his dick twitched inside her, indicating how much he loved the feel of her tight around him. Unable to wait any longer she rocked her hips and took him back inside her, and his delight vibrated from him. Not letting another second pass he increased his rhythm, bringing her back up to the edge of climax. He inclined his head and she was too lost in feeling to realize what was happening. Then, as promised, his open lips molded over her neck and she felt his teeth graze her skin. She felt a prick and realized that in the heat of the moment the pain she thought she'd feel wasn't anything close to pain. She felt the pull as he sucked on her neck and it tipped her over into the strongest orgasm she had ever felt in her life. It ripped a scream from her, but anyone who might have heard her wouldn't ever consider it a scream of terror. It was obviously a scream of pleasure.

It felt like only a moment later that Xavier came right behind her with a cry of his own.

Still trying to catch her breath, she teased, "Wow, this water heater has to be powered by magic. There is no way we would still have hot water at my house." Xavier just smiled, and kissed her senseless once again.

alking the path back to the Gateway entrance, Aggie kept looking at her skin. Xavier had left long before Gryson came to pick her up. Aggie wondered if Gryson knew, but she hadn't said anything. The walk was quiet and she was looking for any signs of differences to her body. She didn't feel any different, but that didn't mean anything because with Mathius it was the following morning.

"You are very quiet. I thought you were looking forward to this trip." Gryson sounded unsure and perhaps a bit hesitant. Aggie instantly felt bad. She had been neglecting him without meaning to.

"I'm sorry, no, I am looking forward to this. It's a bit like an adventure." She pushed a lot of emotion into her words so there was no doubt in Gryson's mind that she was ready and excited to see his home. "What's the name of it?" She didn't know what to call it, and hated constantly referring to different places as realms. While as a whole that was accurate, there seemed to be different towns and villages for each separate place she went. No doubt his would be no different.

"Tarlvey." Gryson still looked at her with uncertainty. "That is the name of my coven. It has been around for centuries and my grandmother is still at the head."

"Being part of a coven, does that mean you being a Mage is uncommon?" Aggie wasn't sure if it was rude to ask, but given it was just the two of them walking it was better to learn now. She could always apologize later.

"While Mages aren't unheard of, it is more expected to have a Witch in the royal family." His eyes were downcast and his expression forlorn.

"Is that why you took the role as Guardian over the Mage realm?" She had no idea why his face had constricted in such a way, but she hoped her direction of thought was wrong.

"It was the expectation of the throne. Only the females in

my family are allowed to rule or take the throne, as the case may be. If by some chance, like in my case, a male child is born, it is their destiny to be a part of the Guardian brotherhood. We have a choice, but it is strongly encouraged." They were still walking slowly, but Gryson had started dragging his feet as though the stirring of these memories was the most difficult thing he'd had to experience for a long time.

"If you're strongly encouraged, but not forced, what's the alternative?" Aggie was scared to know the answer.

"I was offered a position on staff, but to take that means no education and erratic powers. Being a Mage isn't a natural disposition. Even while we have natural powers, the ability to control them is something that must be engrained into them as a form of intense training and education." Folding his arms behind his back, Gryson straightened up and began to increase their pace.

"You're saying they would leave you in a state that could harm others just because you decided to go against their way or their plan for you?" Gryson nodded. "That is the craziest thing I've ever heard. So, you were born a disappointment in their eyes and the only way to regain favor was to do what they wanted and sign up as a Guardian?" Again, Gryson just silently bobbed his head in assent.

She turned to face him and stopped, cutting off his path and causing him to stop abruptly as well. Without thinking it through, she cupped his face in her hands and leaned up on her toes, planting a kiss of reassurance on his lips. It didn't take him long to respond in turn as his lips began to move over hers. The kiss didn't last long, but Aggie felt she got her point across.

"You are special to me. I'm sure the guys could have been fine with someone else, but it wouldn't have been the same. You are needed and they care about you in their own ways. You're right where you should be. I hope you never regret that choice, even if it wasn't much of a choice to begin with." She ran her fingers lightly down his brow.

"You are amazing." Gryson kissed her lightly on the tip of her nose. "My family isn't as bad as they sound. I wanted to do this and not just because the alternative was less than desirable." A slip of a smile quirked up the side of his mouth. "I wanted to be a Guardian because I grew up knowing about the honor of the men before me. I wanted to be just like them or at least aspire to be like them. It was the only thing I ever wanted as a child. The opportunity to be there to protect the people and take care of those who can't do it themselves." The faraway look in Gryson's eyes told Aggie he was reliving the childhood dream in his mind.

"I think that's wonderful. Now can we get a move on and get to this Gate. If I don't get to see your home soon, I might not be able to change my perception of it after that story." Aggie winked at him and captured his hand, and took off running like a child across a playground.

CHAPTER TWELVE

Stepping through the door into Gryson's world was like stepping through into the future. Aggie didn't know where to look. The buildings towered over her, and she felt like she was deep in the heart of an Earthly city. It bustled with people headed to their lives. Children being tugged by parents in a hurry to get on with their day. What seemed like businessmen and women with their heads down and rushing. The difference was everything seemed so much more advanced. They had streets with vehicles that seemed to hover over an invisible track. Those who were supposed to be driving did so without the use of a steering wheel or hands. Something that resembled a train flew low overhead, Aggie couldn't help but duck in response, even though it was plenty high enough miss her entirely.

Eyes wide with wonder, Aggie struggled to take it all in while allowing her brain to make the connection as to what she was actually seeing. A group of people approached a nearby building that stretched into the sky far past the clouds, making it so Aggie couldn't see the top of it. There didn't appear to be a door anywhere in sight. "What are they doing? They can't get inside there."

"Just watch." She could hear the amusement in his voice, but didn't let her eyes wander to his face to confirm her assumption. When all the people had fully stopped they all just began to rise into the air. It was as though they were riding in an invisible elevator, but that wasn't the end of the wonder. As they reached specific floors of the building, many people started branching off individually to their own personal stops. It was like a strange version of Tetris that ran not only up and down but left and right as well, using people of different shapes and sizes instead of blocks. Then Aggie allowed herself to focus on individual passengers on this strange Tetris elevator. When one would approach their stop the window would become less reflective, as though it had disappeared entirely. Each person would just walk through without hesitation and enter the door-less building.

Everything in this place moved seamlessly and was the most amazing place Aggie had ever seen. She was a country girl at heart, but she could appreciate architecture for what it was, art. This was the most modern artistic concept and everything, not only the people, emitted some form of life.

"This place is more than I could have ever imagined." Aggie's words were a mere whisper but she knew Gryson heard her because he hummed his agreement.

"It is certainly something spectacular. I never tire of coming home and seeing it all, but watching you take it in gives me the chance to see it with fresh eyes." He snaked his arm around her waist and pulled her in close to his side. "I've been so anxious, hoping you would love it as much as I do." Gryson placed a soft kiss to her temple and she leaned into the connection.

"Thank you for bringing me here. I wouldn't have wanted to miss this for anything." Aggie waved her hand out, indicating all the seemingly impossible things as far as the eye could see.

"Yes, in its own way. The cars as you know them are called Halos here. They are controlled by thought. The transit is controlled the same way." Gryson pointed to the sky where the train had literally flown by before. "There is no need for a track because they fly it according to who is on it. The driver doesn't have designated stops, but just feeds off the thoughts of those who have boarded." Aggie considered this and couldn't contain herself and her mouth fell open of its own accord.

"Are you saying they can read minds, or there another worm situation here?" Her nose curled at the last thought. Even though she had decided to allow that creature inside her head again, even the thought of it still grossed her out.

"Things you grow up with are seen as less taboo and have less stigmata when you aren't raised with prejudice to them. Here it isn't unheard of to place them in as a child to make rearing easier; keeping tabs on people is a bit easier as well." His face had gone distant on the last part and Aggie placed her hand on his cheek to bring him back to her. She didn't know where his mind drifted to but after hearing about his childhood, even the shortened version, it couldn't have been a happy place.

"Do you have one from childhood?" Aggie wondered, but a part of her knew that he didn't.

"I did, but when I became a Guardian I had it removed. I told them it was because I didn't want anyone having a link and gaining knowledge of the other Realms and gaining too much control. That was only a fraction of the truth." Gryson stopped and Aggie didn't want to press him. If he wanted to open up to her, she knew he would when he was ready.

"Where's your home? Is it close by?" Aggie assumed that he had picked the Gateway door that would lead them as close as possible. A part of her wondered why there weren't locked doors that led them straight to each Guardian's home. That would save time. That made her brain wander for a moment, wondering if she, as the Gatekeeper, had the ability to create new doorways. None of the guys would likely know the answer to that, but perhaps Eckard did. She once again regretted him leaving before she had a chance to formulate any valid questions for him to test his knowledge of the Gateway.

Pointing at another tall building off to their left, Gryson replied, "That is where I live. This was the closest doorway." Aggie followed the invisible line of his finger. It resembled a condo or apartment building in like New York and she wondered if there was a doorman. Looking more closely, she realized it was another door-less building.

"Why do the buildings not have visible doors? Wouldn't that make it tricky to visit friends or receive mail? I can't imagine addresses are very fun to sort out: *3rd floor, 17th window to the left of the really tall building in the middle of town.*" Aggie pursed her lips and scrunched her nose a bit and spoke with a fake high-pitched voice not unlike a schoolmarm. She pressed invisible glasses up on her nose and placed her free hand on her hip impatiently. It didn't last, as she couldn't hold back her laugh. It exploded from between her tight lips and Gryson joined her with a laugh of his own.

"That isn't exactly how it works. The lack of doors is an added level of security. The windows only open for the owner or someone who is granted access, like if they work in an office."

"So, similar to the bedroom doors in Ahael?" Aggie registered the similarities and wondered who had created that idea first.

"Yes, in a way, but it is a faster system and magical, almost like DNA coding. And the postal system doesn't work the same way as it does on Earth. Addresses aren't required. The magic finds the person a message is intended for and travels of its own accord. My people are also not the type to just pop over to someone's home for a visit. If there is a gathering it is usually royal or public and carried out in a venue. So, a person's home is essentially a haven of peace, quiet, and sanctuary."

These ideas were foreign to Aggie's human mind. The idea that people weren't social in the same ways made her wonder how friendly the people would be if she ever met any of them.

This wasn't a social visit but more like a grocery store run essentially.

"Well, let's get this show on the road and get up to gather what we need." Aggie was anxious to see inside Gryson's personal space after he basically said no one goes inside people's homes. "Have you ever had visitors in your home?"

"Not often, but the guys have all been here a time or two. They have their own space inside mine. It is deceptive in size." Aggie didn't know what Gryson meant but the fact that the other guys had been here eased her mind a bit.

They approached the building; Aggie didn't know what to do, but followed Gryson's lead. As though he noticed her trepidation, he reached down and took her hand in his own. The warmth that spread between them was almost tangible. Since Aggie had started taking on magic of her own the feelings that used to assault her when the men touched her skin to skin had dissipated, and everything just felt right as though she was where she was meant to be. Gryson brought them to a stop inside a square of concrete which, looking at the mold from the spacers, seemed to be the perimeter of the invisible elevator, but nothing else gave away any clues of what was about to happen. If Aggie hadn't already witnessed it she would have assumed she was just standing on average, run of the mill concrete. No doors or glass or magic passed over her skin. It was all normal to her eyes.

Without warning, outside of a slight squeeze from Gryson's hand, the ground was pulled away from her feet and she felt like she was floating on air. A small squeak escaped her lips, as she wasn't a fan of heights. Elevators were okay because they had walls. Roller coasters had secure seatbelts and lap bars. That didn't always mean anything to her illogical brain because Ferris wheels freaked her out, too. Their flimsy rope seatbelts and swinging carts were unsafe in her opinion. She always wondered if the closed-in Ferris wheels wouldn't result in the same panic. So in this case it was unprotected heights at its best. No seatbelt, no walls, no protection outside of Gryson's hand wrapped around her own. She closed her eyes in a panic, as she did when she rode a roller coaster. After a few seconds the speed slowed its ascent, and just before it stopped completely they were jerked to the left. The motion made Aggie wrap her free hand around Gryson's arm and pull herself in close for any protection he could offer her. It felt like the ride lasted for an eternity, and she never once was brave enough to open her eyes. She felt the bouncing of Gryson's chest and she chuckled at her reaction.

"We're nearly there." He spoke softly above her head and his free hand came up to caress her hair and embrace her slightly in comfort. A moment later the ride slowed to a stop and Aggie opened her eyes one at a time, cautiously. They were still suspended in the air and the distance from the building would require them to step wide into the window when it opened. Waiting patiently, Aggie still refused to release Gryson from her terrified grasp.

"What's taking so long? Why isn't it opening?" Her eyes remained open but the tension was still wound tightly in her body.

A second later the window disappeared. Aggie was thankful it was wide enough for both of them to step inside at the same time. Only when her feet were firmly planted on something solid did she release Gryson's arm from her death grip. "I'm sorry, I was weaving the magic and letting it include you as a person accepted to enter."

"Oh, that was sweet of you, but I'm not sure I'll ever be able to ride up on my own. That was unnerving." Aggie admitted her fear freely.

"I am happy to ride with you whenever and as often as necessary, but if anything were to happen at least you know you could pass through if need be. You always have a place to be here, just like in the other guys' realms." Aggie hadn't considered that before. She had never traveled through the Gateway on her own, and hadn't thought about an escape route in case of emergency. Now that she had, the thought had merit.

Taking a moment, now that her nerves had settled, Aggie let her eyes travel the expanse of Gryson's home. They were standing in a sort of entryway. The thought was foreign to her because, given the fact that they were standing by the window, it would normally be deep inside an apartment like this. In this case, the place had almost a reversed look as she stood in the entryway. To her left was a sitting space, she would call it a living room, but aside from the chair and sofa filling the space there were no other familiar pieces. She had no idea the purpose of the room outside of sitting. A small open kitchen was placed behind this sitting space, with a breakfast nook positioned to break the two. Directly in front of her was a long hallway with many doors. She couldn't see the far side of the other two rooms, as they were combined, but this hallway seemed to go on for days and looked to have enough doors for many people.

"This is the place I was telling you about. The guys each have a room here, as do you. It is expected for each realm to have a place for us to stay. It is easier to keep them in a place where the resident Guardian to keep an eye on them." He quieted to allow her to take it all in on her own. Aggie glanced back at him, his expression unreadable. She wondered if he was worried she wouldn't like it or wouldn't accept him for who he was in his own space.

She turned and leaned up on her toes, pressing a kiss to his lips. "Thank you." Her words were a whisper against his mouth.

"For what?" Gryson's brow was furrowed in confusion but he had placed his arms around her waist to hold her against him, not yet ready to release her.

"Bringing me here. It's nice to see the other sides of you guys, and not just because you're under attack from one thing or another. This is a chance to see you for you and not you under duress." Aggie wished over the previous few weeks one of them had thought to take her on a weekend getaway or just a break from reality that was her life at home. Sometimes reality got old, and what better reason to escape than to spend quality time with her men.

"You are welcome in my home, in my life, in my space anytime you wish. I'm happy to have you here." Leaning down, he closed the gap between them. They hadn't made it past the entrance to his home but Aggie didn't care. She was lost in this kiss that Gryson was pressing deeply into her, and the passion she felt behind it was clear. Her hand came to rest on his shoulders to balance herself, but she also knew Gryson wouldn't ever let her fall. He pressed the flat of his hand to her back, holding her tightly to the length of his body, and she felt every delicious inch of him. He usually wore dress shirts like Xander, but his softer cotton shirt left little to the imagination. All the highs and lows of his muscles were so tempting, and while he kissed her into oblivion she let her hands roam. Circling over his pectorals and across his puckered nipples, Aggie let her nails drag slowly over the peaks and felt his abs flutter and realized how sensitive his nipples were. She decided to exploit that a little. Quickly, Aggie found the hem of his t-shirt and her hand disappeared beneath. His hands gripped her hips and held her tightly, not letting her back up too far. She didn't want to escape his embrace or ever end this maddening kiss. When her fingers made it back to his nipples she didn't waste a moment. She took both, one for each hand, between her thumbs and forefingers and rolled them slowly. She heard a rumble come from Gryson's throat as he growled his approval. She was intrigued and lightly increased her pressure slowly until she had him pinched tightly between her fingers. He flinched only slightly, but he moaned his pleasure and his mouth broke from hers as he nipped her bottom lip roughly.

"You are such a tempting morsel, Parum Praesetes. I don't know if I can resist you any longer when you play my body like it is your own instrument. I'm yours and I want you more than anything else at the moment." His mouth descended to her neck, biting gently and laving the area with his tongue. He suckled her skin and she remembered her encounter with Xander from that morning. The familiar ache between her legs called to her. She should feel bad for wanting to be with them both so close, but they had all discussed how this was to be expected, and her only rule was to not have sex because she was told she had to. This felt right, just like it had been with Xander and Eldon and Mathius, all in their own time.

"I don't see why you should have to resist anything. Do you have a bedroom, or are we going to put on a show for any of your neighbors as they pass by to get to their own windows?" Aggie grinned up at him and noticed his ears brightened a bit. She tweaked his nipples one last time to draw his attention back. He growled at her and lifted her from the floor, hurrying through to what she assumed would be his bedroom.

Gryson didn't slow his pace as he crossed the threshold of his bedroom. Aggie didn't even spare a glance as he carried her there. She was more interested in teasing her lips across his neck and behind his ear. Hearing him growl in frustration as she thoroughly worked him up while he was desperately trying to navigate the distance to his room safely. Suddenly, Aggie was flying through the air and Gryson was hot on her tail as she bounced on the plush mattress.

"You are quite the little vixen, Parum Praesetes." Aggie loved the way Gryson's nickname rolled off his tongue, and she preened at the sound.

"I don't know what you're talking about. I merely was occupying my time while your hands were otherwise engaged. I could have just sat there but where would the fun be in that?" She looked up at him and fluttered her lashes innocently. Shrugging her shoulders slightly, she stared at him with a slight challenge.

"You just know that I'm entitled to return the favor." Gryson leaned down and licked the length of her neck, his tongue running the length of the overly sensitive vein in her throat. A moan escaped her lips as it reminded of her of her earlier tryst with Xavier. Feeling slightly guilty for thinking of another guy while she was there with Gryson, Aggie placed a hand on his chest to stop him.

"I have to tell you something." Her words were soft and hesitant. While the guys had originally stated that they were expecting to share a mate it still seemed wrong to throw it in their faces, especially on any of their first times together.

Concern flashed across his face. "What is it?" Gryson cupped her cheek and rubbed his thumb back and forth in comfort. That didn't assuage Aggie's guilt.

"Earlier, before we left the shifter realm, Xavier and I—" Aggie stopped, unable to finish that sentence for fear of what might happen.

Gryson leaned down and pressed the sweetest kiss to her lips, surprising her by his reaction. She hadn't finished, but one could easily deduce with little effort the end of that sentence. "Oh, you have nothing to worry about. I'm always happy to share with my brothers and fellow Guardians. We told you it was destined and our fate when we took on these roles. Never ever doubt that, or our feelings toward you."

"Feelings for me?" Aggie repeated. "If it is destiny or fate or whatever, how am I to know how you truly feel about me? It could easily be faked or magically induced. I don't want any of you feeling as though you're forced to do anything. I might not be your typical old-fashioned girl, but on some level I want love to be the foundation of my relationship, or relationships in this case." Her voice rose slightly as she passionately expressed her position. Aggie couldn't believe this was the first time she had considered, or at least voiced, this concern. She had already slept with and bonded with three of the guys. *What kind of whore am I, that I would sleep with and attach myself to three guys before considering that it could all be some kind of cloak and dagger magic controlling them.*

Her thoughts were now pounding in her head, filling her with uncontrollable doubt. She was connected to a third of the guys and hadn't even let the dust settle on the one before she was jumping into bed with another one. She didn't even know what new powers were brewing inside of her. Perhaps wielding two new powers at once would prove not only difficult, but harmful. Control was hard enough to maintain for two, so adding more could only prove more challenging. Regret washed over her and settled in the pit of her stomach. Curling her legs up, she made herself as small as possible. Embarrassment washed over her like a sickness. No longer in the mood, but feeling ashamed for taking advantage of her position between the guys, Aggie imagined herself as small as possible and she shrunk inside herself.

"Never. Ever." Gryson's words were punctuated and crisp, and his intensity caught Aggie off guard and she startled. "Doubt my or any of the guys' attachment to you. It isn't magically induced or fate, or anything but true to you. You, Aggie, are the center of each of our worlds. I know I can speak for the others as well because we have discussed it. When you were stuck at home while we were away, they all expressed at different times how not being near you affected them. We all would talk about you and how you have made us feel."

Looking up over her bent knees, Aggie set her chin on her flattened hands. "Just a thought, but why didn't any of you think to express those thoughts to me directly? It might help alleviate my concerns about your intensions or attachment. That being said, I can't imagine Mitchell ever saying anything to anyone about me that wasn't something snarky or dickish." Aggie smiled, but that didn't make her words any less true. She wanted to convey that to him, but she also didn't want this to turn into a fight. Her ovaries had been working overtime and now, after letting her reality check soak in, it seemed crazy to continue their escapades.

"It is not my place to speak for the others, but I'm ashamed that I let you feel like I didn't care for you in any way. You are the light I have sought for years. When I had let doubt wash over me and settle, you appeared and my heart chanced at hope that you would accept me and everyone else. Because of you I felt complete for the first time in my life. Even though we haven't consummated our bond, I know that when that time comes, even if it isn't now, as I'm aware we have lost the moment, it will be the most powerful mating in the history of Mages. I'm happy to have you as my queen, and I will endeavor to serve you and make you feel as royal as you most certainly are. I'm all the better for having you in my life, and I hope to find thousands of ways to show you." Gryson ended his beautiful speech with a flick of his wrist, reminding Aggie of an Earthly magician, but it was punctuated by some muttered words under his breath that she didn't catch. He waved his hand over his skin and an image appeared there on his arm just above his wrist for all to see.

She leaned forward to get a better look and gasped. "Is that a tattoo of some kind? How did you do that?" It was an exact replica of her face. Her hair was slightly over her left eye, but didn't block its appearance. Her lips were frozen in what seemed to be a little gasp caught in a moment of time.

"This is the first moment I saw you and it has been imprinted in my brain. This is a magical imprint and, unlike a tattoo, can't be removed by any means, human or magical. This is how I will show the world and you my feelings for you when I can't show them first hand with you by my side. I love you now and always will. It might have been destiny but you are my choice then, when I made my oath, and now that I have met you and gotten to know you." A tear escaped Aggie's eye and she quickly swiped it away with a flick of her wrist.

"I love you, too." Her words were a mere whisper, but Gryson heard her and leaned down and pulled her towards him. His kiss was full of much emotion and Aggie poured her heart and soul into him as well.

All too soon Gryson broke the kiss. "Oh, and about Mitchell —don't sell him short or write him off just yet. There is more to that wolf than meets the eye. He just has a harder shell than that rest of us. You will get through to him, I know it."

Aggie let that sink in. She remembered their limited interactions and recalled a heat that was just under the surface, but each time Mitchell ended the kiss or connection abruptly and killed the moment by opening his mouth. She considered the fact that he might be deflecting his true emotions. "Are you saying that Mitchell has stronger feelings for me, or that not only his wolf has formed an attachment to me?" Raising her left eyebrow at Gryson, she pressed him for more information.

"Again, I can't speak for him, but I just want you to know that there is more there than meets the eye. He has an entire clan to lead and needs someone strong at his side. You are definitely that woman; I know that, and on some level so does Mitchell. He just has the weight of everything on his shoulders and won't release that until he is ready." Kissing her head one last time, Gryson scooted to the edge of the bed. "What do you say we pick this back up again later? I think now we should get the supplies I need and head back before they wonder if we have been attacked and in some sort of danger."

"Danger? I'll show you danger." Aggie leaned forward and pinched his nipple again, hard. He growled but it wasn't entirely in pain or frustration. There was an undercurrent of arousal. "You do like that, don't you?"

"I have a certain affinity for pain." Gryson's lips tipped up in a lopsided smile that spoke to a bit of embarrassment.

"I like that, as I can get a bit violent on occasion. It's nice to know I have someone to play with. Mathius leans that way but he likes to inflict it more than take." Aggie worried again about mentioning one of the other guys, but quickly let it go when an intrigued look flashed behind Gryson's eyes. "Oh," Aggie leaned up and whispered in his ear huskily, "do you like that Mathius likes to play rough? I think I'm going to tell him and let your little secret out." She knew she was playing with fire and their time for games was over, but she was happy to tease him just a bit more.

"Come on, you little vixen, we have work to do. I will have you before the day is out if I have my way." Gryson didn't tell her no about Mathius and she decided that her time with Gryson wasn't over, and she was going to try to include Mathius in their next encounter. She could just see Gryson tied up and Mathius doing all kinds of unspeakable things to his body. Heat ran through her, and if her panties hadn't been soaked before they were now.

CHAPTER THIRTEEN

Gathering supplies took surprisingly less time than Aggie expected, and before she knew it they were back on the path to get to the Gateway from the Mage city. Aggie was still impressed with what seemed to be mass amounts of technology but, in reality, was just magic that radiated from everywhere.

"How does this much magic not adversely affect the people living here?" Aggie wondered out loud.

"What do you mean?" Gryson's puzzled face was adorable, and Aggie realized once again that not everyone thought like she did.

"It's just that in an area that, say, is overloaded with technology of any time period, on Earth there are adverse reactions. With cars came pollution, building cities reduced oxygen due to lack of trees, electronics and modern simplistic tech brought about obesity. There's always a negative reaction to the positive easier movement. It's not all fun and games. So, is there a negative recourse because of all this magic, or have you somehow risen above human nature?" She wasn't sure she wanted to know the answer to this, as it could change her perspective of Gryson in some ways. He never seemed to have a better attitude than others, but this could prove her wrong.

"I guess you could say the Mage culture is lazy due to prolonged use of magic, but they just invent new ways to combat it. So if waving a hand to turn on a light becomes the new norm, then they have to come up with a socially acceptable way to force people to get up and move around and basically exercise. As you have seen we like our creature comforts, and if we have magic why shouldn't we use it?" While his answer wasn't what she expected it was just what she needed to hear.

"That's basically what we do on Earth, but it's hard to get society on a global scale to participate after prolonged laziness."

"That is where a dictatorship comes in handy. The queen orders it and they listen, or else they may not survive the punishment. Not that the queen would order anything like stopping the use of magic, because then she would have to adhere to that law just the same." Gryson smirked, thinking of his family.

"So, your mother is a regular everyday Queen of Hearts? Does she have an affinity for the color red, too?" Aggie always loved that story and, in some ways, it was as though she had stumbled into her very own version of Wonderland with all the strange things she had come to know. Her eyes trailed over Gryson's face and saw the confusion wash over his features.

"What do you mean? I suppose she does love a little bloodshed when warranted, but never needlessly. I don't think she takes their hearts, though. That wouldn't be very ladylike, and my mother is a lady first and foremost." It was cute how he justified that and still defended his mother. Aggie almost wanted to bask in Gryson's adorable side a little longer but his face was still scrunched up. She needed to enlighten him before he hurt himself overthinking it.

"No, it's a reference from a children's book on Earth, *Alice in Wonderland* by Louis Carroll. The Queen of Hearts is the antagonist and she's always ordering the decapitation of those who angered her or disappointed her. She would scream, 'Off with his head!' and everyone was terrified of her, except Alice." Reminding herself that it was just a story and nowhere close to a parallel to her current situation, Aggie sighed.

"I see, this sounds like a story I should read as you seem to have an attachment to it. I would love to dive deeper into your likes and dislikes. I want to be a part of your world as you have jumped in headfirst into ours without another glance. You are the strongest woman I know and I want to know more about you and what made you who you are." A pang shot through Aggie's chest at his words. He really was the sweetest man in the entire world—well, realms in this case. She once again regretted not spending more one on one time with the guys before now. She obviously had misjudged them all in some way or another.

"I will make sure you have a copy as soon as I get back home and can grab you one. It will be my first priority." Stretching up on her toes, Aggie pressed a kiss to his lips. Gryson's hand wrapped around the handle and they stepped through into the Gateway.

As if it sensed Aggie and no threat along with her, the Gateway opened up to the normal room filled with every doorknob imaginable as well as the door to her home. "I have an idea," Aggie started. "Care to extend our trip just a little longer?"

"What did you have in mind?" Aggie saw a flash in Gryson's eyes and she knew he was thinking with his other head again. That didn't bother her but, unfortunately, that wasn't her plan.

"Well, you've shown me around in your world, but none of you have done much exploring in mine with me. If we hurry and I pull you into my sift, we can go on a quick shopping trip." Aggie waited, her eyes hopeful that he wouldn't turn her down. The fear of rejection was strong, and something she worried she would never be able to shake.

"I think that is a great idea. I will take every spare second you are willing to spare me. If I could spend every waking moment and even the sleeping ones with you, I would accept in a heartbeat." Gryson took her by the hand and pulled her into her own house. He set down his sack of supplies and turned to face her. A breath burst from her. Aggie hadn't even realized she was holding it.

Taking hold of his hand, Aggie grabbed her purse from its spot on the wall and sifted. They arrived in the back of the bookstore. Aggie was silently hoping none of the employees were on break. It wasn't time efficient for them to drive or she would have happily prolonged this little excursion. Breathing a silent sigh of relief, Aggie straightened her clothes and dusted off invisible dirt.

"What are we doing?" Gryson's voice behind her startled her because she was wound tighter than a top. She'd never taken the guys anywhere, let alone one of her favorite places to sit and think. This might just be a store to some people, but to Aggie it was an escape. This is where she came when she felt alone in the world. Her mother was gone, her Gran was distant, and her list of friends was nonexistent. She was liked by people, but for some reason most steered clear of her. Now she knew it was because of Gran and how she was protecting something inside their house. She didn't want to risk it being discovered, even by Aggie. A bitter taste filled her mouth and Aggie quickly brushed the thought away.

"We're going to get your book." She pulled him around the building, a strange feeling of elation working its way through her body. She was practically giddy, and it was a strange feeling for her. As they approached the building Aggie noticed it wasn't a busy night, and for that she was grateful. They would get in and out quicker this way. Then she wouldn't feel as guilty for taking this tiny detour. This was as much for her as it was for Gryson.

"I haven't spent much time in the human realm. I have minimal knowledge of things such as this. Normally if I need something at home, I just conjure it or have someone else retrieve it. I know such things exist, but even when in the other realms I am not the one sent to fetch things like this." Aggie smiled up at him; she was giving him a new experience beyond just a new book or a date with her.

"How very princely of you." Grinning at him, they entered the building. She quickly glanced back and took in his initial reaction.

"This is a store for only books? Why are they sold like this? In the other realms there are places to read, but if you need a book you just take it. Then return it when finished." Aggie smiled at his innocence.

"We have those as well. They're called libraries. We can borrow books and return them when finished. This is for people who like to retain their copies of the books they love or use frequently. What do you do if you want to keep a book indefinitely?" The thought of not being able to own books was gut-wrenching for Aggie.

"You can keep books you take, but if someone else requires it then it re-shelves itself in the warehouse." Gryson didn't seem to understand why that would bother Aggie.

"You say that as though he books have a consciousness and know when they need to move and where to go."

"In a way they do; they're written in magical ink, at least in Tarlvey and others in my realm. So, the books know when they are needed. So, if I were there and a book I required wasn't on my shelf, it would appear within seconds of me looking for it. The only time one needs to go to the actual warehouse is when you don't know the exact book you need." Aggie was impressed and realized they didn't need to own books if they magically relocated to the most needed person or home.

"That is an efficient use of space and time. Though this

book, as magical as it might be to me and many others here on Earth, wasn't written with magic ink. You'll have to find a home for it on one of your shelves. The only way someone will be able to get their hands on it is if you allow them entrance to your own library or you hand it to them." Taking a deep breath, Aggie inhaled the scent of paper. The distinct smell of new books. Not the musty old smell of forgotten books but something fresh and clean and clearly loved.

"I know just where this book will go." Gryson patted his lapel pocket without another word. The gesture was sweet but Aggie wasn't sure if the copy the bookstore would have on hand would fit.

Walking through the store Aggie quickly found the right section and scanned the books listed alphabetically, silently thanking the book gods that that was the uniform system. Quickly her eyes landed on the collector's edition mixed in with countless reprints. Aggie always loved the decorative covers, and let her hands mindlessly travel to capture the beautiful representation of art. The images depicted Alice falling down the rabbit hole with the Cheshire Cat looking on, along with the White Rabbit and a symbolic chess piece Queen of Hearts. It was captivating.

"This is it," Aggie whispered with awe of the magic that would be found within the pages. It was more than Aggie remembered.

"May I?" Gryson, always so thoughtful, asked, and she passed the book over to him without a word. He carefully, so as not to break the spine, making Aggie smile, flipped through the pages, taking in the illustrations. "I will cherish this for as long as I live." With a wave of his hand the book shrunk down to the size of a pocket watch. The thought made Aggie shiver at the irony.

"Wait, we have to pay for this. You're going to have to right it to its actual size and then you can shrink it again." Gryson's eyebrows rose and Aggie saved him from speaking and embarrassing himself. "Here we have to exchange currency for that which we're going to keep. You're royalty and I'm sure don't have to purchase anything; it's just brought to you. Let me do this for you, please." Gryson waved his hand again and the book righted itself. Aggie quickly took it and scurried to the counter to pay. The process took little to no time, as there wasn't a line.

"Do you want a sack?" the cashier asked as she pulled the receipt from the register.

"No, thank you." Aggie smiled sweetly and thought of the magic that was about to happen so Gryson could fit the timeless piece of literature and art into his pocket. Then Aggie realized he was still wearing his casual shirt and hadn't put on his suit jacket that day. Turning to face him, after scooping up his gift, she queried, "Where are you going to put this?" They were already making their way to the door, so his answer didn't worry her.

As the door closed behind them Gryson's clothes changed. He now was wearing his signature suit, sans tie. Placing his hands over the book in Aggie's hand, it shrunk quickly before she let go. The sensation startled her and she shrieked slightly and the book fell through her fingers. Gryson's magic wrapped around her and the book froze in midair. Aggie was again thankful that the parking lot was empty. She simply stared at the moment frozen in time and couldn't bring herself to move. A part of her wondered if he had frozen her as well.

"I intend to keep it close to my heart. That way when you and are separated for any length of time, it will give me a reminder of you no matter where I am." With that he plucked the tiny watch-sized book from the air and slipped it right into his inner jacket pocket. Clasping his hand, Aggie didn't bother to walk around the building and decided to sift them back to her house from where they stood.

"I'm glad you like your gift. Now I think we have to cut this short and get back before they send out a search party."

Setting foot into the Gateway, Aggie saw a form walking through exactly as they crossed the threshold, but the house didn't seal.

"Too late." Gryson's words were punctuated in humor and Aggie saw who had crossed through to meet them.

"Where have you two been?" Mathius was alone, but he didn't sound happy.

Holding up his supplies Gryson explained, "We got the supplies, but it was Aggie's first time in Tarlvey so she had to take a little in before we left." He didn't mention their near coupling and Aggie wondered why. "Then when we got back Aggie needed to pick something up, so we took advantage of our location and ran one last errand before coming back."

"You have been gone for hours. We need to be ready to depart by tomorrow morning. It is a long journey and we need to be prepared," Mathius groused.

"We will be ready and still have plenty of time to sleep and prepare." Gryson winked at Aggie and she remembered his promise. Warmth flushed through her and Aggie felt her cheeks heat.

"What happened between you two? She is acting strange." Mathius nearly growled the words and Aggie decided to test the theory.

"We made out a little and then I told him I had sex with Xavier." Aggie didn't cower or flinch, but held her ground and stood proud.

"Of course you did; I would've had trouble keeping my hands off you if we were alone, too." The change in tone was unexpected and Aggie thanked the gods for letting that work out. Mathius leaned in and nuzzled her neck, nipping lightly at the sensitive spot behind her ear.

"I also learned something new," she whispered, but knew all the guys had excellent hearing and it wouldn't stop Gryson from eavesdropping.

"Did you now?" Mathius didn't release her but leaned back

and looked her in the eyes. His own were lined in sliver, like he had activated his magic.

"Yep! I learned that Gryson takes quite a liking to pain play. I thought perhaps…" She trailed off and Mathius' eyes flared full silver, and she could feel the magic rising off of him. She wasn't sure if this was a good development or not.

"Did you hurt her?" Mathius' attention quickly shifted to Gryson, an accusatory tone in his question.

"Hey, don't get mad at him. You can't tie me up and like it rough yourself and get mad at someone else for leaning the same way. And for your information, he leans toward the receiving end and not the giving. So stop jumping to conclusions and acting like a jealous bastard." This wasn't going as planned. Aggie was regretting even bringing it up.

"You like it?" Mathius asked in wonder, and his volume dropped to just above a whisper. "Then if my Aggie has deemed you worthy and you share my predilections, I think we can work with this. Is that what you were hoping to accomplish?" Mathius had turned his attention back to Aggie with the last question and she got a little shy. "Don't be coy now. I saw your face when you mentioned it and I could smell the arousal on you. You want to add him to our playtime, don't you?" Aggie nodded, and blushed fiercely. Talking about sex was one thing, but this was far beyond that. They were talking about some of the more taboo bedroom activities. She had gone out on a limb even bringing it up.

"If Gryson is willing, that is," Aggie added as an afterthought. It wasn't fair to assume any of the guys wanted to be included with each other's sexcapades. That wasn't fair for her to act like that. It was bad enough they were forced to share with seven other alpha male personalities.

"I don't see why not. I'm game." Aggie's eye flashed and her panties were toast. This was going to be a fun night if they could get back in time.

"Then let's get back before they send anyone else. I'd like to not have to share Aggie any further tonight. That means you have to get to work or we won't have time to do anything. Is that clear?" The command in Mathius' voice was directed at Gryson and he bowed slightly before responding. It was the perfect submissive move, and how quickly he fell into it made Aggie's sex clench. She wasn't sure how this would work out, but if she had her way it would end in a lot of orgasms between them all.

CHAPTER FOURTEEN

It was late afternoon when they arrived back in Galata. Not much had changed but the lighting of the sun. The clan was still working on this and that. It still amazed Aggie how helpful everyone was to each other. It seemed like a seamless system that didn't require much thought.

Ren walked up beside her as though he sensed her coming back to town. "Did you two have fun?" He winked at her knowingly. "I tried to keep Mitchell and Mathius from freaking out too badly in your absence. I knew you were perfectly all right in the hands of Gryson." It was as though they were all connected already, and Ren was the inclusive of them all when it came to encouraging each other. He hadn't even had his opportunity to mate with her, not for lack of trying. She was developing an affinity toward the shifter, but it was the connection with his brother that worried her. More than once their attractions had been shared by Mitchell. Then, like a switch, turned off just as quickly. A girl could get whiplash with how fast he flip-flopped on his emotions.

"How long is it going to take you to prepare your concoction?" Aggie turned her attention to Gryson and ignored Ren's implication.

"It will take a few hours. I will come and find you when I'm finished. We will wait to ingest it until right before we set off on our way. That way we can have our own thoughts with minimal effort for as long as possible." The look he gave her was pure heat, and Aggie was sure that she wasn't the only one who noticed when a couple of sounds that were strangely similar to muffled moans came from around her.

"If that's the case, I'm going to take some time and try to connect with my inner self again." She didn't elaborate, but none of the guys surrounding her seemed concerned about it either. She leaned forward and pressed a quick kiss to Mathius' lips. He pressed his advantage and captured her in his arms. Deepening the kiss, Mathius groaned into her mouth.

"You are a temptress of epic proportions. I'll be anxiously waiting until later." His words were a mere whisper, meant only for her. As he released her Aggie knew it was with reluctance, as his fingers lingered—pulling her slightly back—but didn't hold her back. Gryson waited patiently for his turn, but still opened his arms to her. As her fingers disconnected from Mathius, she practically fell into Gryson's embrace.

Squeezing her like he was afraid if he let go she would be lost to him, Aggie found herself snuggled into the crook of his neck. She inhaled his scent; it was almost herbal, mixed with a musk that was all him. She assumed it had something to do with him working with his potions and different natural ingredients all the time. She committed it to memory. The closer she got to each of them the vibrations she used to feel when one of them touched her was more an extension of herself, and now felt like a completion of herself upon contact. The more time she spent with them the more she felt at home, and that she was right where she was supposed to be.

Gryson's lips came down on the top of her head and she leaned her head back to see his face. His chocolate brown eyes held such warmth, but since she hadn't spent enough time with all the guys one on one there was still some mystery hidden there. She knew more about them, but their relationships were so new that she still felt like there was so much she was missing from him and all the guys. Remembering his words, that all the guys had discussed their level of feelings for and that even Mitchell had more layers it seemed than an onion, Aggie's heart warmed. Rising up on her tiptoes, she sealed her lips to his soft and perfect ones.

With each passing moment she wondered how she held out so long, and had still held out on some of the guys yet. She had a small connection to each of them and there was still a level of her figuring out the best timing to make new advances.

Their kiss ended far too soon for Aggie's liking, but Ren was right there in all his cocky pride, scooping her from Gryson and wrapping his arms around her and embracing her so tight.

"Hey," she rasped, "I need air." Her words were simplified and stunted because her airway was being squeezed into the size of a pin, or at least that's what it felt like. She had no clue how big it was in reality, all she knew was it was being squeezed by a very strong shifter and he wasn't relenting. She decided to take matters into her own hands. Given the fact that she had taken on a gargoyle that morning, this pup on his own wasn't much of a threat. This time she opted to avoid her magic since he was just playing. With her arms trapped beneath his, she bent her arms at the elbows and started poking him in each of his sides at alternating intervals. Going out on a limb, she hoped he was ticklish.

Ren didn't move an inch. "You could work on your massage techniques in my bedroom. We can detour there now if you'd like. Your inner self will be happy to wait for you to hone a different skill." He taunted her with his usual ease but never relented even an inch. With one last effort, Aggie extended her elbows to fully straight and gripped his hip bone right where his leg and hip connected. Squeezing ever so slightly, as her pressure increased Ren buckled and released his grip.

"Ha! I win. You should up your game if that's all you've got. I didn't even have to tap my magic for that one." With that she finger- waved at the three hulking men as she sashayed her way to her cabin.

The door clicked behind her, and Aggie just looked over the sparse room. There wasn't much to their cabins, with the exception of Mitchell and Ren's. She didn't need much, and since the guys used these rooms on the run it was more of an escape or a small vacation spot if Aggie used her imagination a little.

Then she remembered why they were there. People were dying. They were being threatened. Mathius' people were being attacked relentlessly and the enemy went as far as involving children. Now Mitchell's clans were being raided and attacked, left in shambles because a bunch of rebels decided it was within their rights to take instead of help. This small village, Galata, was a well-oiled machine. Aggie wondered if there was some kind of schedule that kept everything running smoothly. People just helped each other and things got done. If they all just took what they wanted, how would this way of life be different?

Taking up residence in the center of the bed, Aggie made herself comfortable by crossing her legs Indian-style. Inhaling deeply, she tried to center herself. It had been a busy day and so much had changed. This was the first opportunity she'd had to come to terms with the fact that she had actually mated with Xavier. She had no regrets, but it was still a process each time she made that commitment. Closing her eyes, she focused her energy inward and did all she could to relax and find her center.

What felt like hours later, Aggie felt herself fall into her inner depths. What should be getting easier was proving to be more and more difficult because she had to fight through the emotions that were building with each new layer. Drawing from each of the new mates wasn't the hard part, but more wondering if taking on a new mate automatically imbedded unplanned emotions or to even go as far as love them. She wanted to make choices and there was an underlying fear that it was a forced, fated, emotionally- charged reaction. That gave her pause and trepidation and caused her to overthink things. If she was being forced, then were the guys being forced as well? Was she roping them into something they didn't want? All her emotional triggers were flying off the handle.

Opening her eyes Aggie found herself in her head space but, as usual, it was different. Taking a deep breath, she began to look around. This time it was dusk, not unlike reality. She wondered if that played a factor for her and made a mental note to remember the time of day in her real life and her inner worlds. Shadows draped every inch of this place. Surprisingly, it wasn't creepy and had an ethereal magical feel to it. Like one would take a walk well after sunset but it wasn't quite dark.

I should walk more in real life. I feel like I'm missing out on subtle beauty. This place is amazing. Aggie walked and took in the area. It could have been the edge of any forest, but without the definition of daylight one couldn't make out the descriptive features that made it unique.

A quiet rustle of the grass was the only alert that Aggie had to the fact that she wasn't alone. She spun around and came face to face with an ashen version of herself dressed in a sexy wrap dress. Aggie almost laughed when she saw it was a blood-red. Surprisingly, she rocked the color. That was normally a color she avoided because it was too flashy and drew too much attention to herself. She liked to hide in the shadows, and aside from the occasional date here and there peopling was too much for her.

As her inner self came to stand directly in front of her, she caught the slightest glint of a fang. "I'm gonna need to figure out a name for you. I've been considering calling you Izzy."

"Why would you call me that?" Her words sounded slightly muffled and Aggie realized that the process of talking with one's mouth full of fang would be challenging at best.

"I.S. doesn't sound like a real name and I can't call you IS, but Izzy is close and sounds like a real name." Aggie felt a bit ridiculous having this conversation with someone who changed so frequently. "That is unless each of *you* are a different person individually and then this entire process doesn't work." She felt like she was rambling and talking nonsense.

"I am you and you are me. I am merely the representation of who you need to get in touch with at this given moment. In this case, I chose this form because it is easier." With a wave of a hand she changed the entire environment and she was now standing in the Fae version of Izzy's dream fabrication. Her clothes changed into the mossy dress; she really did have a thing for wrap dresses. Another flick of her wrist and they were in the Demon version, and the robin-egg rock was right next to her. It was tempting to sit, but Izzy seemed to be enough like Aggie that she would likely change the scene again and knock her on her ass. It was definitely something Aggie would have done, given the power.

"So, it works then. You are now Izzy, at least to me." Aggie wondered if her sanity was anything to be worried about after this conversation. Most people don't typically talk to themselves quite like this, and if they did there were special hospitals and restraints that weren't for sexual fun.

"If you must; now, can we get back on track? You came here to discuss your newest addition to your growing list of powers. I would imagine you have some questions." Izzy in this form was growing more and more impatient, but her physical presence didn't move or waver. She was still as a statue and her mannerisms reminded Aggie of Xavier's.

"I haven't actually encountered any of my new powers yet, nor have I tried to access them. I'm honestly not sure what to expect. Should I plan on needing blood now?" The thought made Aggie gag. No sane person would voluntarily drink blood, and Aggie's body hadn't actually gone though a metaphysical change. So, she really hoped that Izzy wasn't going to ruin that idea in her head.

With a snap of her fingers Izzy made an ornate goblet, not unlike what Xavier favored to drink his brew out of. Taking a long sip, Aggie worried for the response that would follow. As Izzy lowered the cup a droplet fell from her lips and dribbled slightly. Her tongue flicked out quickly and grabbed the drop. Izzy wiped the bare spot with her finger and seductively licked it off. Aggie thought about it for a moment and realized how alluring the move was, and thought about how she could apply that in the future.

"You are safe from any new diet changes. Your body doesn't require blood to partake in the increase of power." Aggie released the breath that she was holding in anticipation.

"That's the best news you could have given me. I don't even want to know what that tastes like. No matter what Xavier says, I would prefer to steer clear of such things." Aggie observed Izzy and envied her ability to stand so still. While she herself swayed back and forth, shifting her weight from foot to foot, already tired of standing in one place for too long.

"That can't be the only concern you have about the vampire powers coursing through your veins. You're not that skilled at this game yet." Izzy's tone was the only sign, once again, that she was growing impatient.

"I'm sorry if I'm occupying your time and keeping you from anything pressing," Aggie snapped at her and didn't feel in the least bit upset about it, because this was a meeting inside her head. What else was Izzy going to be doing with her time? This was probably the most enlightening conversation she'd had, well, since the last time Aggie needed her help. "I don't have a clue what I should be expecting or looking for. I haven't watched Xavier that closely or seen everything he's capable of. So in answer to your question, no, I don't have any other questions. I would prefer you just tell me what I should be looking for and see if I have gained them or not."

Izzy smirked at her. "I like it when you get sassy. It gives me faith that you can handle all these things that life is throwing at you. It affects us both." Izzy was starting to sound more and more like she was less of a figment and more of an actual entity. This concerned her slightly.

"Us? What are you saying?" Aggie wasn't sure she wanted to hear the answer to that question.

"You are human. I'm your magic. We don't exist separately anymore. If you die, then I die. I can't protect us with out your help. We have to work together." The smile never left her face and, in light of the conversation, that made Aggie a bit uncomfortable.

"Okay, then." Aggie hesitated, but she knew their time was actually limited and the idea of holding this inner state for too long scared her. *What if I get stuck here? What if someone attacks me while I'm here?* Not that she expected anyone to be in her cabin, but if there were another instance where she had to come in and perhaps wasn't in the safest of environments, could she be harmed? Would the magic warn her and protect her by sending her back to reality? "Let's get this sorted before my body decides to take a nap." She really didn't know what her body did while she was in with Izzy. The first time she did it Mitchell, Ren and Eldon were there and they didn't say anything strange happened.

"There are a few things you should be on the lookout for, not limited to any one or two. You could just as easily have gotten all of them. There is no telling with these powers in an add-on situation. This is like getting a stack of pancakes and it depends on how hungry your body actually is versus how big your eyes are. You body will only be able to take in so much magic at any given time. The overflow will just do that, flow over your body and not be consumed. I can't tell you how starved you were at the time of consumption." Izzy painted a pretty picture and Aggie wished she had eaten before taking this plunge. Her stomach growled and Izzy actually snickered.

"You should be looking for enhanced speed. Limited disturbance, which is what you seem to think of as Xavier's ability to disappear in the shadows. Also, watch for an increase in strength. That will come on quick and unexpected if you do get it. You could easily throw a grown man through a window if you don't learn to rein it in quickly." This thought gave Aggie pause. All of these powers were things she would be happy to have. The ability to be super-fast, or have even more strength would be ideal for someone as small and petite as her. She was so used to just accepting that she wasn't quite up to par or suitable in any given situation.

Now she could add the ability to spy around and simply disappear into the darkness. These were all things she secretly hoped for, that with each addition of new powers she was slowly becoming a more useful part of the team. The Guardians weren't noticeably lacking before she came along. On some level she feared she had slowed them down in some ways. So many insecurities and so little time to rectify them all.

"So, these are all manageable, but the only one I need to be on the lookout for is the strength. Although, I think throwing Felix or even Mitchell through a window would almost be worth the damage." Smug wasn't ever a good look, but Aggie was going to let it soak in for a moment and use it to practice her 'take that' face for when or if it actually occurred.

"I might have to agree with you on that one. I would like to see a few of those pompous asses put in their places. They always think women are inferior. I would just like to throw our own abilities back in their faces." Izzy's comradery was actually what Aggie needed, though this still felt odd and gave her some serious delusional thoughts. It took a lot to retrain a lifetime of beliefs of what the definition of crazy really was. This was one of those moments.

Aggie scratched her head as she tried to come to terms with all this new information. "Are there any concerns besides windows in this aspect?"

"Not with this one; you should be pretty on top of your game for this one. The previous training will help you adapt pretty quickly." Izzy folded her arms over her middle and popped her hip out. This was the first time she had moved anything besides her lips or arm to take a drink.

"Is there anything I should be aware of? Any problems with mating too close together? I almost mated two of the guys in one day before I made the move to come and converse with you. I got to thinking perhaps not allowing myself to come into each power individually might pose a challenge." Aggie remembered she had plans with Mathius and Gryson later, and it was still early and her powers were untested.

"That is up to you, and only you can make that decision. I can't help you with that or give you any guidance on the matter. You are my first human encounter and I don't have anything to reference any of this to. You and I are unique in and of ourselves. While there are others before in years past that have shared our situation, it isn't like I have a way to communicate with them from beyond. Unless one of your suitors has the power of necromancy, I'm not sure we will ever know." Izzy was a wealth of information and for that Aggie was grateful, but this time she wished it was less of an unknown and more of a just ask Google opportunity.

CHAPTER FIFTEEN

Blinking her eyes open Aggie found herself back inside the cabin, still perched on her bed. The sun was fully set and the room was bathed in darkness. She had no clue how late it was or how long she had been under the spell of her meditation. Glancing around the room, something felt off. The space seemed to have shrunk. Not physically, but like there was less space. Given the right setting of silence and darkness, you could tell when someone was in the room with you. The air moved differently and even if they weren't moving and making noise you knew they were there.

Unsure of where the light was or a way to spark it without setting fire to something important, Aggie made a mental note to practice that skill. "Who's there?" Her words came out sounding strong and bolstered, and for that she was grateful, not moving from the bed for fear of walking straight into the culprit. She didn't feel like she was in danger, but it was still unsettling.

Silence met her and she grew worried. Then, after a few seconds of contemplating what she should do, a light flickered and ignited a lamp. Xavier stood there, cast in shadows. Aggie mentally kicked herself because, out of all the guys, of course it was the one who could bend the shadows around him, literally obscuring his entire body into nothingness.

"How long have you been here?" Aggie didn't admit that his little magic show had startled her, not wanting to give him any satisfaction at having the upper hand.

"I passed Gryson and Mathius on their way back to prepare for tomorrow. They mentioned you were in here connecting to your magic and I thought it might be wise to have me on hand when you came back. That way, if you developed any questions, I'd be available to answer them." He was sitting in a wooden chair across the room, pressed right about against the wall. It looked to be the uncomfortable kind, but Xavier didn't bat an eye. He just sat ramrod straight and completely still. Aggie thought it must be nice to not feel the need to scurry and shift as one's body grew numb after sitting in a position for too long.

"I'm not exactly sure what questions I have, since Izzy answered a lot of them." Thinking about what she might need to ask, Aggie didn't realize her slip.

"Izzy?" Xavier didn't move, but Aggie could see his left eyebrow bend upwards in question.

"Oh, ha! I'm sorry, that's what I have decided to call my Inner Self. It was a logical derivative of I.S., but it probably sounds crazy to anyone else outside of my head." She waved a hand at him, as though wiping the slate clean and encouraging him to move on as though she hadn't said anything. Xavier sat still, as though what she said hadn't penetrated his silent exterior, but then a rumble of laughter bubbled from him. Aggie could almost feel the vibration of it in the darkened room. Sound carried to her like he was sitting beside her.

"That is a clever choice. Now, then, if she answered all of your questions, what are your plans?" Aggie didn't have plans, well, not so to speak. She needed to know what time it was before she made any new arrangements. It had been the far edge of dusk when she went to visit Izzy and now it was dark. It could have been only thirty minutes or it could be the middle of the night.

"Had Gryson finished his concoction yet?" Time was relative, and the only thing that truly mattered was if anyone was waiting for her. The fact that only Xavier was here led her to believe that Gryson and Mathius were still working. Not sure what Mathius was doing except keeping Gryson company. That gave Aggie pause and she mulled over the idea that perhaps they were using their downtime for other activities. The worm juice couldn't be a constant preparation the entire time. Aggie imagined it to be like cooking or baking; there was time in between where it just had to sit with the occasional stirring or just checking for doneness.

"They are still hard at work. It will be a few hours yet. I've only been here for one hour." Aggie winced and instantly felt bad that he had been sitting and watching her in the darkness for so long.

Immediately, Aggie got up and placed her hand on the wardrobe. "Then let's go for a run. You could probably use some mobility after having to wait on me for so long." Pulling her hand away from the wood, Aggie lifted the latch and opened both doors. A pair of tennis shoes that practically glowed in the reflection of the firelight blocking out any color that might have been on them, save the reflectors, lay in the bottom of the cabinet. Hanging up was a pair of tight, black Lycra pants with mesh cutaways zig-zagging across them. Aggie had a pair similar at home so it made imagining a style easy. Beside that was a navy-blue tank that read "Bite Me", but she kept that hidden from Xavier while stifling a giggle at her own humor.

"You want to run? You think you can keep up?" Xavier stayed seated and didn't make any sudden moves. He simply crossed his arms across his chest, the motion causing his arms to bulge, and Aggie's eyes were drawn to his chest. Licking her lips quietly, she started to change. There was no longer a need for modesty and the only concern was if he would let her get the new clothing on without pouncing.

"That is the question, isn't it? I need to know what I'm capable of, and Izzy is never one hundred percent sure. She allows me a way to access my new magical abilities, but can't promise the extent of my skill. In this case I don't need any grounding. I just need to test it out. She thinks speed and your ability to fold into the shadows like a ninja are some to look out for. She also said strength increase might be as well, but I'm secretly hoping to accidently try that out on Mitchell. Don't tell anyone." She winked at him as she slipped the tank over her head. His eyes traveled down to the words printed and she waited to see his reaction.

In an instant, he was standing beside her. "I'd be happy to, Wee One. Though, if we are planning to explore your new talents then I suppose the responsible thing to do would be to tackle that first." He kissed her neck in a place Aggie thought he was imagining piercing her skin with his teeth. She ran her tongue over her own teeth and sighed. On some level she wished she took on visual characteristics of her new power and could show her new forms as well. Sadly, Izzy was the only one who gained that side of the powers upon transition.

"Then let's get this show on the road. This isn't my only engagement this evening, and after this run I'd like to soak in the tub for a bit before I have to do anything else." Not once saying what her plans were, Xavier never asked. Instead he reached down and grabbed her shoes and threw them at her one at a time. She quickly slipped them on and tied the laces. "I'm not a runner, so let's hope this comes easily or I'm going to be in pain and exhaust myself before we get very far."

Slipping out of the cabin, Aggie realized that even though darkness had befallen the village people were still milling around. They had started a fire and kids were roasting what looked to be marshmallows and meat of some kind. Another night, she would be happy to join them and curl up by the fire.

A cool breeze nipped at her exposed skin. "This wasn't well thought out." She turned, ran back inside, and used the wood to create a hoodie for herself. Nothing too heavy but something to keep the chill from her skin.

"Now you have disturbed my view of your perfectly-shaped breasts. I wanted to watch them dance as you ran through the woods." Aggie barked out a laugh that echoed across the inky sky.

"You did not just say that. Ren I would believe, but that isn't where I expect you to take a conversation." She followed Xavier as they made their way to the edge of the tree line. A part of her wondered if it was a wise decision to learn super speed with obstacles, but she quickly pushed the thought away. There was always the chance she didn't gain that power and they would then be able to work and perhaps cultivate her new ninja techniques.

"Is Ren the only one allowed to appreciate the view? I thought that, as your mate, I outranked him. At least for a little while." A devilish smirk crossed her vampire lover's face and Aggie knew he was kidding, but it did stir old concerns back up. They were all supposed to be okay with sharing and so Aggie tried to focus on that.

"No, you are most certainly allowed to enjoy them, and I encourage you to do so and not to be a stranger. I just didn't expect you to be so blunt about it. Everyone here has shifter hearing or some kind of magical ability. So I can pretty much guarantee everyone within this area is privy to our conversation." She began to stretch as they breeched the edge of the woods. It wasn't like she knew what to expect or even what she was doing. Now she had to look the part or perhaps she was going to get hurt. That was the last thing Aggie wanted. She also didn't want to look like a fool. The latter was harder to accomplish. This was the same reason she didn't ever want to work out in a gym environment. She was afraid people would look down on her or think she wasn't adequate and shouldn't be there. So any exercise she took up was done in the privacy of her own room.

This time it wasn't avoidable and she needed Xavier's expertise. "So, what do I do?" Aggie turned her attention back to Xavier who was leaning against a tree, looking suave. That was when she noticed he was wearing one of his suits again. "Hey, how do you run in those clothes? I would think they would grow uncomfortable or run wrong with extended or increased speeds."

"It's not the same as running as a human. You don't rub in the same ways and the friction isn't enough to set your clothes on fire. I'm not The Flash, but I do have the ability to move rather quickly. I actually have to think about everyday things so I don't move faster than a human or even demon eye can see. It is a skill and advantage, but it requires patience to hone the skill." He pushed himself off the tree, not even once concerned with a possible snag or that the dirt might have marred his pristine look. "You start by moving." Gesturing toward the clearing, Xavier nodded his head in encouragement.

Aggie was suddenly very nervous. The way the trees cleared here it was like she was a horse on display. Originally, she was glad that she didn't have to go to the arena and practice this, but somehow the intimacy of being alone with Xavier watching her every move was even more nerve-wracking. Shaking out her hands, Aggie started at a walking pace and began to work her way around the clearing. Not a perfect circle, but enough space to work up to a faster speed.

Quickly, Aggie worked up to a light jog. She wasn't exactly out of breath, but her breathing increased and she was panting a little. She wasn't sweating and she was just getting a little warm. The hoodie was a perfect afterthought.

Growing impatient with her pace, Aggie pushed herself a little harder. Her vision blurred and the wind increased. Her stomach lurched similar to a roller coaster ride. Unable to focus, Aggie did the only thing she could think of. She rolled. Dirt and leaves wrapped around her just as fast as the wind did before. Slower than she hoped, her speed reduced and she twirled to a stop—oddly, right at the feet of Xavier.

"That was an interesting development, Wee One. Perhaps we should work on your coordination. I had no idea you were so clumsy. Perhaps we should get you a seeing eye dog to prevent any further mishaps. I bet Ren would be happy to tackle that task." He grinned from ear to ear, thinking he'd made the funniest joke. Unfortunately, Ren wasn't here to get the jab directly.

"Hey, I'm not sure Ren would appreciate your tone, but he would take the job on regardless. That said, I'm not a klutz. The powers kicked in and knocked me for a loop. The only logical thing I could do was stop, drop, and roll." Aggie had gotten to her feet, albeit with a bit of difficulty, as she was scratched all to hell from her tumble in the woods. There were other ways she would have preferred to take said tumble, and less painful at that.

"I didn't see any sign of fire. Am I wrong, or is that not the standard method of extinguishing a bodily fire?" Raising a perfectly groomed eyebrow at her, Aggie didn't know if he was being condescending or literal, but chose not to go there.

"I'm not on fire, but I could have been. I was moving so fast the world went wonky and I didn't know what else to do. I couldn't focus and make anything out. I'm lucky I didn't take you down with me." Aggie brushed the loose leaves and grass off her clothes and wondered how the guys never seemed to look dirty even after a fight. It was as though they repelled dirt or just were too intimidating for it to attack them.

"It had nothing to do with luck, my dear. I ran over when I saw you falling. I didn't realize you did it on purpose, though. That thought never occurred to me, as I wouldn't have done that myself. It was certainly an unexpected turn of events. We are going to have to work on that skill before you are ready to use it in combat or even to escape a game of tag played by four-year-olds." Aggie didn't like what Xavier was insinuating but she wasn't going to argue with the basic idea of his statement. She needed to train, but that would take time.

"Right now, let's focus on discovery and less on training. So, would you like to take me on a spy mission?" Hands placed on her hips, she cocked one to the side and put on her best badass face. She knew this would be fun if she had developed this skill.

"Did you have a particular one in mind or did you want me to lead the way? Most of the guys are in their own cabins for the night and working on individual things." Xavier left the ball in her court; she could have let him pick the destination, but a deliciously evil idea came to mind.

"I want to spy on Mitchell. Supposedly he acts different when I'm not around and, as much as I'm perpetually attracted to assholes, I would like to know that he isn't always one." Aggie turned and started to walk back to the village. "Any reason why we can't make that happen?"

"Only problem I could see is if you haven't developed that particular set of skills and he catches you outright. Wouldn't it be better to try for someone who would be happier to find you sneaking outside their rooms?" Xavier didn't sound like he was favoring one choice over the other, just giving her options.

"I'm willing to risk it. I want to challenge my abilities since I'll only have a little time to hone them before we get thrown to the wolves, so to speak."

"In that case, you will need to feel the shadows crawl over your skin. They will become a part of you, not unlike your own skin. It will wash over you and bathe you in darkness." Aggie didn't know exactly how to accomplish this. She tried to feel it but the moving shadows of the forest made it difficult to pull them over her entirely. They continued to walk toward Mitchell's cabin and she practiced the entire way. It wasn't that she couldn't do it, but it was hard to hold in place.

"What am I doing wrong?" she growled softly. She didn't want to draw attention to them both. It was growing late and darkness had fully covered the sky, but the moon was high and bright in the sky. Aggie silently wished she could black out the moon.

"You're doing nothing wrong. It is working, but until you improve your speed it will be hard to dart between the lightened patches." He was being sweet and encouraging, but Aggie wasn't feeling it.

"So you're saying I should be able to tip-toe behind the trees like in the old cartoons?" Xavier looked confused and Aggie just shook her head, choosing not to explain.

They arrived at Mitchell and Ren's cabin sooner than she had hoped, and she felt underprepared. Aggie wasn't a quitter and she was going to try this regardless. Walking around the house, she quickly realized Mitchell was in his room. And from what she could tell from the window, he was alone.

Silently she unlatched the door, letting herself into the house. She opted to leave it open slightly to avoid the click of the latch later. Tip-toeing deeper into the house, she was pleased to find that her footsteps were nearly silent. It was more like she was gliding in socks across the floor without a single creak. Smiling to herself, she worked her way up the hall and soon found herself outside Mitchell's room. She felt the darkness of the hall wash over her and she loved the taste of success without the moon to interrupt her. It was easy to wrap herself in darkness like a blanket.

Placing her hand on the doorknob, she wished she could turn completely invisible and walk through the wall. A flush sounded and she knew she had a small window of time to get into the room without being seen. Twisting the knob, she slipped in and tucked herself in beside the wardrobe's shadows. Again they embraced her like an old friend, and it got easier the more times she did it. Taking a moment to level out her breathing, she looked over to the window and saw a quick flash of Xavier's face letting her know he was watching. That made her feel better since it was now or never, as Mitchell was coming out of the bathroom.

He was wearing only a towel, and Aggie realized he had just gotten out of the shower. She tried to keep her thoughts in her head, as her body wanted to react. She knew the moment she failed. Mitchell's nose twitched and she cringed. After a moment, she realized he wasn't putting much effort into finding her because the towel was pleasantly tented, though his erection was still hidden from view. Aggie silently wished she had Gryson's powers, as she would be able to make the towel drop with a flick of her wrist.

Glancing down at his new situation, Mitchell sighed. Much to Aggie's surprise, her wish came true as he flicked the fold in the towel and it fell to the floor. He stood there in all his glory and just looked at his offending member.

"Now is so not the time for this. I have too much to do tonight." He grumbled his discontent to himself, and without another word gripped his erection with a tight squeeze. His eyes fluttered shut, and he dropped his head back to look at the ceiling. A moan escaped and he mumbled something. Aggie had to strain to hear the word, "Aggie." It may have been a mere murmur, but it was still unmistakable. However, it sounded more like a prayer than the curse he usually made it.

With a twist of his wrist he growled and released himself. Trying with a massive amount of effort to ignore his reaction, Mitchell sat down at the desk. Unfortunately, no amount of distraction could deter his dick. Aggie watched with rapt attention. She watched as his hand dropped to his lap again and brushed his erection. It was almost a mindless gesture but that meant that when his fingers, almost like magic, started pumping slowly he was lost to the sensations. His thumb grazed over his sensitive tip and he practically purred his delight. Aggie knew if she watched this for too long she would be a puddle of sexual desire on the floor. She had to stay in control.

"Aggie, you are going to be the death of me." Mitchell's

words rang through silent room and Aggie's breath caught. Did he know she was there? Was he just toying with her? "Yeah, just like that. I love it when you squeeze me. You are so tight." With wide eyes, Aggie released her breath slowly. He was jacking off and imagining her. This wasn't even close to something that Aggie would ever have imagined. His moan rolled through the space and he reached up and flicked the light, leaving the lamp on the desk as the only light in the room. The shadows were extended throughout. Against her better judgement she stepped from her hiding place and kept the darkness pulled around her.

"I love you on your knees. I want you under me more than anything." Aggie crept closer to this scene and kept to the shadows as Xavier had said. A quick look to the window told her that he was gone. He was either giving Mitchell his privacy or he didn't want to watch him in this state. A groan and his hips thrust of their own accord. Mitchell was lost in the moment. Aggie was being drawn in by the scene. Her control was wavering but she couldn't look away. This was the single most attractive thing she had ever witnessed. She had seen the guys lose themselves to Kyrel's leaking before, but this was different. It was completely and solely a natural effect, and all because of Mitchell's attraction to her.

She never expected him to feel this way about her. He always acted like it was a bad decision and she wasn't worthy of him. His eyes were closed and his head back, soaking in the pleasure. Before she knew what was happening, she found herself kneeling on the floor between his legs. Not yet touching him, she gathered her thoughts and what she was planning to do. His hand was firmly gripped and pumping a solid rhythm on his cock. She leaned forward, her tongue snaking out, and licked the tip quickly.

Mitchell's eyes flew open and met her gaze. Neither said a word. Aggie didn't know what he was thinking but he didn't stop stroking his cock. She was there and he was there. It was like he was just coming to terms with it. Still not speaking, Aggie grabbed the collar of her hoodie and pulled it over her head. The weight of her breasts felt enormous and the angle mixed with the scoop of her tank left them on display for Mitchell's feasting eyes. With his free hand, he reached up and gripped the center of her neckline and yanked it down, dropping her round, full teasing globes into full view.

She didn't wait. Pushing forward she leaned into his throbbing, and much larger up close, distraction, wrapping her lips around it above his hand. She slowly lowered her head; his hand released in time with her mouth, capturing each new inch. Hard as a rock, she couldn't imagine how he had held on so long with his ministrations. Not letting a moment pass, and not needing to work up to it, she bobbed her head at the same pace he had before. He was thrusting into her welcome mouth, fucking her face. She felt herself flood her own panties and he roared his approval of the scent of her arousal. Her clit throbbed itself and she reached into her own pants to rub herself. This was about him, since she'd interrupted him and snuck into his space. That wasn't going to stop her from pleasuring herself, too, though.

Any girl who couldn't give head and get herself off wasn't skilled enough. This was a huge turn-on, and would be a waste of perfectly good material.

"You like that?" Mitchell whispered. He leaned over her body and his hand slipped beneath the material and over her ass. His finger grazed her seam and she moaned, the sound vibrating Mitchell's cock. "You like that, too, I see." He didn't penetrate her but teased her puckered hole all the same, working her up. She used that tension to work her fingers faster and her mouth sucked tighter. His reaction was instant and without warning, because that was Mitchell to a "T", he flooded her mouth. She swallowed as quickly as he shot off and took every last drop, never one to be wasteful. She found her release a moment later. It was so intense she was left quaking.

They had this moment where minimal words were shared, but her mouth was full so she couldn't answer him anyway. She leaned back, releasing his still-half-hard member with a pop. Sitting back on her heels, she waited to see what he would say. Realizing it was her turn, she opted for snark. "Don't try to feign ignorance. You like me and I will no longer be treated like a second-rate citizen." She squared her shoulders and stood to her feet. She wasn't beneath him.

"I never said you were second-rate. I was simply letting you choose. It wasn't my decision to force you into anything. I never said I didn't like you either. I do find it fun to tease you, regardless, and that won't stop, Princess. I will push you harder than anyone, and you are better for it." Aggie was shocked. This wasn't what she expected him to say at all. While it wasn't a confession of undying love, he was a bit more transparent now. But just as unapologetic as ever.

"Now, care to enlighten me as to why you are in my room? Not to mention, how did you get in here?" Mitchell crossed his arms with a knowing expression on his face.

CHAPTER SIXTEEN

Aggie walked away from Mitchell and Ren's cabin in a bit of a daze. He never once harped at her or snapped for her sneaking in. While he hadn't known she was there, he'd seemed to come to terms with her sudden appearance rather quickly. It wasn't common knowledge that she had sealed the deal with Xavier, and the guys didn't bat an eye when she gained new powers. It was as though there was a silent understanding between them all. This entire way of thinking was foreign to Aggie, and it was hard to grasp without question.

Before she could make it to Gryson's cabin a commotion stirred, and people a mass of people burst out of the forest and made their way toward Mitchell's cabin, blowing past her violently. She caught only a few murmurs.

"We have to hurry they are hurt!" one man of large stature bellowed.

"Of course, we are going as fast as we can." A female who was very trim and lithe gave her a feline look.

That was when Aggie noticed they carried a few people on portable stretchers.

"If we could have only seen them coming," another mumbled as he scurried to keep up with the crowd.

Aggie wanted to see what was going on but thought the injured might need help, so she rushed to Eldon's cabin. Xavier had said they were all in for the night. Gryson would have wrapped up his mental worm potion by now, and from the looks of it their night was ruined for pleasure and they would be needing it sooner rather than later.

She knocked on Eldon's door, but he took a moment to answer. Aggie could hear a shuffle and the scuff of feet on the floorboards. The door finally opened and he was standing there in soft leather pants and without a shirt.

Surprisingly not winded from her jaunt, she urged, "Come quick! There's a group of shifters and they have injuries." Her sentence was stunted and not very informative, but Eldon just smiled and never questioned. Turning back, he grabbed his shirt from the chair located in the same place as the extra one in Aggie's cabin. It seemed they were all mirrored after one another for simplicity.

"Take me to them." He grabbed her hand and she pulled him toward Mitchell's cabin. By the time they arrived the group was already inside, so she just dragged Eldon inside without knocking or announcing their presence.

"What are you doing here?" Mitchell was back to his gruff tone and sounded accusatory. It was as though he had forgotten she had left his bedroom and him in a very exposed state not long before.

"I passed them outside and I thought Eldon's services might be required. So, I took it upon myself to help," she stated matter-of-factly, hands on her hips.

Ren was sitting with some of the injured and motioned for Eldon to come over. Aggie couldn't tell the extent of their injuries, but they didn't look old or aged in anyway so they must have been pretty badly hurt to not be able to make the journey. She also wasn't sure how far they had come either.

Mitchell's eye lit with something Aggie hoped was appreciation, but it faded as quickly as she caught it. He turned his attention back to the man who seemed to be the leader of the group. He was as broad as he was tall and had a trim beard with some salt and pepper tone. His hair was cropped short in a buzz cut that conflicted with his mountain man appearance a bit. He stood ramrod straight, as though he had a military background, as he awaited a command from his Alpha.

"Before we were so rudely interrupted, you were saying the rogues attacked your village. Are there others in Nolar that we should be concerned with?" He was in full Alpha mode and Aggie wasn't going to call him out. She saw the flash and knew he was putting on a front. The stab stung a little, but he was in the moment and she wouldn't fault him. For now.

"No, we brought the worst of the injured with us. We feared if we were attacked again, they wouldn't be able to defend themselves. Those who stayed are fortifying our perimeter. We were attacked without warning or provocation. We tried to defend ourselves, but it seemed more like they were looking for something in our ranks and not out to actively harm us. Unfortunately for us, we are a prideful lot and didn't want to just roll over. We wanted them gone and to leave us in peace. We have heard about the destruction they have wrought on other villages. We didn't want to have to perform extensive repairs and potential loss because of their carelessness." Aggie thought, after watching this man, he resembled a badger. Though he was quite large for a man, and most shifters had some similarities to their alter. His sheer size didn't scream small woodland creature. He had more girth than that of something so small.

"What's your name?" Aggie was so good at blurting she didn't think it was necessary to implement a filter. Given the severity of this situation it might not be relevant, but the look Mitchell was shooting at her said shut up, and that just made her all the more inclined to stay the course. That and calling him 'that guy' in her head was getting old.

"Tartan, my lady." He bowed slightly and the action confused her. Was this guy from back in time? She wasn't mated to either of the shifter guardians, and so she didn't think that her scent or whatever was a giveaway as to who she was, if anyone. Not that she knew that was even a thing, but deductive reasoning said it might be. Horror crossed her face as a thought went through her. She hadn't slept with them but she had done stuff with them, and some of said stuff was done not even an hour before in this very cabin. She knew everyone had a strong sense of smell and they hadn't exactly left a lot of time for things to settle before barging in on Mitchell. The Alpha caught her attention and had the audacity to smirk at her, confirming her suspicions.

"Tartan, you said they were looking for something in Nolar. Any thoughts as to what it might be?" Aggie was choosing to overlook the new development in her love life and getting back to the matter at hand.

"There was discussion but it is purely speculation," he hedged, but Aggie wasn't going to allow that. If he was going to assume she was in authority as the Alpha female in the room, then she would manipulate that.

"Enlighten me to popular belief, and let's discuss that speculation. I promise I won't take it as a strong resource, as speculation can cause us to run off course." Aggie settled herself on the arm of Mitchell's chair and he stiffened at the gesture. Aggie smiled sweetly, enjoying the tension in the air. He didn't say a word to move her. She was enjoying playing this game since he so quickly jumped back into his asshole nature.

"It is rumored that a set of scrolls is kept in each of the realms to pass on the ways of our people. Inside those scrolls is said to be the secrets of the Gateway. No one has ever seen these scrolls, and they are so ancient that they have become more of a children's bedtime story along with lore of old." Tartan seemed to say the last bit quickly to cover up any possibility that he might believe the stories.

Aggie thought about this for a moment. What use would it be for the rogues to have this information if the scrolls did exist? Also, Mitchell was the Alpha and hadn't mentioned them before. Again, this was all theoretical information.

"It isn't anything that ever occurred to me, but that could very well be what they are looking for. Though I can't figure out why they would risk all this on a fairytale. The only purpose for those scrolls was if for some reason the race was wiped out and someone might not know how to access the Gateway system. We have kept it active in our history and still use it to this day. If you know where the portal points are, it is just second-nature." Ren was the one to reply, but Aggie was surprised to see he was standing at the front door. "I'm headed to gather the rest of the guys. Some of this is important for them to hear, too. It sounds like our plans have just been moved up to now instead of in the morning." With that he breezed through the door, and seconds later he was gone and attention was back to the problem at hand.

"If they're operating off a fairytale then why attack these smaller villages?" Aggie wondered out loud.

"Those are our older villages and they are still inhabited, but tend to run on the small side. They don't have the same security measures in place because they are mostly families and not as many fighters. That and if something that old were to have been sequestered away somewhere for safety or otherwise, it would be in one of our oldest villages." Mitchell was putting some thought into it and that told Aggie it was worth considering as well.

"So, if you were to put it somewhere, where would you stash them?" Aggie wasn't necessarily asking anyone in particular but more the room. Eldon was still healing the last of the injured shifters and they were starting to move around and find seats that weren't laid up. He was beginning to look tired. She wondered if there was a way to share energy levels since she could draw on Izzy to help her. Though the more powers she used at once it seemed harder to recoup. This would be a question to try later.

"I would say out of all of them, Pantal or Farnack would be the most logical choices. Though they are a farther distance than the ones we thought they would hit. Nolar was on that list, but these are closer to the mountains and have more cave structures. If I were going to store ancient scrolls, I'd want them more temperature-controlled than just buried under a hut." As Mitchell spoke, Tartan nodded his agreement.

"It would seem most prudent in my opinion, sir. Nolar, while we are an older community, doesn't have the necessary holdings for something so valued. I also think our elders would be privy to it. I can't imagine that, in whatever village it is located, someone wouldn't be aware of something like that. Even if they don't know exactly what it is, they would know where it might be stored." The remaining guests muttered amongst themselves, all with differing opinions but all basically the same conclusion. The scrolls, if they existed, would need the utmost protection regardless of anyone's individual knowledge.

"So how close together are Pantal and Farnack?" Aggie concluded they would need to travel there next. There was no choice but to try and get these scrolls, if they existed, before the rogues could get their hands on them. "If we can get our hands on them then perhaps we can make it known we have them and draw the fight to us, and save the remaining villages the heartache of attack." Aggie knew this alteration of their plans would take time, but if she could protect any other villages from destruction and or injury then it would be worth it. No one should have to be subjected to this.

"They are within a half a day of each other; we can reach Pantal by the Gateway, but it won't bring us directly to it. The Gateway was never intended to be used as direct travel. The ancestors requested that the gates be placed outside of villages for protection. Should the Gateway ever be compromised, a single village of Cratlian would be safe from mass invasion.

Allowing them a chance to protect themselves." Mitchell was being forthcoming and not condescending at all. She hadn't moved and was still sitting practically on top of him. Ren came back at that moment, trailed by Mathius, Gryson, Liel, and Xavier. Last through the door was Kyrel. He was thankfully off his cycle and not currently leaking, but Aggie didn't know how often he did that. She hoped it wasn't like a monthly PMS. They each acknowledged the new arrivals with a head nod or a smile. There weren't enough seats for everyone so the Guardians stood abreast of each other in front of the now-closed front door.

That many men of notable size and mass were a bit intimidating to say the least, but the shifter visitors took it in stride so Aggie didn't mention it out loud.

"Okay, then, it sounds like we need to go ahead and plan to head out as soon as possible. If we don't announce our intentions beyond this room, then I don't see that we need to take an army with us. Am I wrong?" Aggie suddenly realized that they guys weren't caught up and nodded at Mitchell, who quickly filled them in on the latest events.

"It seems Aggie is correct. We should make arrangements quickly and get this treasure hunt underway." Xavier's analogy wasn't incorrect and Aggie suddenly found herself picturing him in a tri-corn hat and goatee. It wasn't a bad image for him. The dark vampire pirate. Aggie wondered if there were any books on the subject that she could use purely for research and not for added material.

"I imagine the nine of us should have this under control. If you aren't needed here, Mitchell, I think Ren's and your expertise of the terrain will be necessary." Kyrel was thinking out loud, but at this point it was a free for all brainstorming session as they all sorted out plans and needs.

"I can't see why they can't hold down the fort without me. They do any other time I take off on a Guardian mission." Mitchell's tone was dry, tinged with annoyance at the insinuation that his people were somehow incapable of defense when needed.

"I don't think anyone thought they couldn't, it was just a question out of courtesy of their needs." Liel was playing Switzerland and it made Aggie smile. He was always spewing facts, so it was nice to see him with an understanding of emotions tensing around him.

"I agree; no need for anyone to get their panties in a twist." Aggie focused on Mitchell and noticed his nostrils flare and a hint of remembrance in his eye. She noticed her slip and then got lost in the memory of their games from before. It wasn't the time or the place and she shook the thoughts loose. "I mean, let's get ourselves sorted. Eldon, did you get everyone here taken care of for now?"

"Yes; aside from them needing a bit of rest, they will be fine. No one had life threatening-wounds. Just severe." He looked exhausted and she decided that figuring out how to share energy was now at the top of her list. She needed to consult with Izzy before she did anything, though.

"All right, Mitchell or Ren, can one of you get them sorted for places to stay while we gather supplies?" Aggie was back in her element. She was bossy by nature and secretly loved it that no one ever stopped her from taking charge.

"I'll get them where they need to be. Rian has some rooms in the lodge that should be sufficient." He motioned for everyone to follow him and soon everyone was cleared out. The remaining Guardians took their seats and began planning in detail.

"Do you think we should still use the potion?" Gryson asked the group. "I'm leaning toward yes, but I'm open to thoughts."

"I'd hate for your hard work to go unused," Aggie said, but the part that she was thankful to not have a worm in her head was left unspoken.

"Even though we aren't going to be separated it would be nice to have that as a backup plan, or at least in case of emergency. What if one of us gets separated or we need to split up for any reason?" Liel's query rang through the room.

"I agree with Liel. I'd rather not lose someone when we could have a way to stay connected, and find them sooner rather than later." Mathius glared at Aggie, but she didn't feel any anger off him. More like concern.

"It couldn't hurt in the least." Kyrel smiled at her and it warmed her, though everyone was looking at her while talking about getting separated.

"Are you guys saying you don't think I can hold my own in this situation or in light of danger?" Aggie was offended and hurt that it seemed they all agreed on this one point.

"Not that we don't think you are capable, but the thought of losing you is too much to bear. I for one would feel better knowing you could still communicate with us." Gryson, sweet as ever, tried to soothe her hurt feelings.

"It could just as easily be one of you who is lost or hurt or in danger of being held captive." The look they all gave her was one of a resounding 'really?' and Aggie was just as frustrated. After thinking about it for a moment she admitted to herself that they were right, but she was staying mad at them for good measure. Crossing her arms across her chest in a defiant manner knocked her off balance. She slipped off the arm of the chair and right into Mitchell's lap.

"Now isn't the time, Princess." He growled the words and picked her up, setting her back on the arm, as though she had fallen on purpose. She harrumphed her discontent but didn't say another word, choosing instead to sulk.

"It sounds like we all agree that we will stay in each other's heads throughout this journey and there won't be anyone at a disadvantage." Mitchell sounded every bit the Alpha that he was and left no room for argument. That didn't stop Aggie.

"Except me, who can't block her thoughts," Aggie grumbled like a pouting child. Everyone ignored her and dispersed to go collect supplies.

"They will all be back here within thirty minutes. Anything you might need to do to be ready, I suggest you get on with it." Mitchell's tone was still as rough as ever, but Aggie was too upset to argue. She tore from the room and back to her own cabin.

Quickly, she sat down on her bed and crossed her legs. After a mental pep talk, she fell into herself quickly. Time was a luxury she didn't have this time, and there was no way she could delay.

Opening her eyes, she found that Izzy was right there. It was like she knew they had to hurry.

"Okay, what is it now? I was hoping to get in a nap before we left." Aggie wished she could read her thoughts as well as she gathered information from general awareness.

"Why can't you read my thoughts since you're a part of me?" This wasn't the reason she was here, but the question seemed valid.

"I'm a part of you but I'm not you. I'm aware of what happens around you but I don't live in your subconscious the way you think. I don't read your thoughts or desires. You are you. I am me. That's the difference. I'm aware of what happens around you so I know you're preparing for a journey and, soon after, a battle. What do you need from me now?" Izzy seemed impatient and Aggie knew she needed to hurry, so she let it drop.

"Is there a way to transfer my energy to the guys to help bolster them after they've used their powers? Eldon could use a top off, as he overdid it healing the shifters earlier." Izzy considered this and it took her a moment to answer.

"While I help you regain your energy, you know you don't have an endless supply. Some of your powers are easier to recoup because they have grounding, like the Fae side is earth-based and you can draw from what's around you. Though your vampire powers aren't grounded, Xavier could use your blood to access your essence. Similarly, you could use your Fae energy and connection to the earth to boost Eldon. I would suggest touching him skin to skin while in contact with a grounding agent." Aggie thought about this and it seemed valid enough. Of course, everything they did was a bit of trial and error as Izzy had mentioned before.

"Any idea how that would work for the others?" Aggie knew time was dwindling, but she was going to use every second she could for this one because the guys were her number one priority always.

"Mathius will be tricky, as your skill is metal-based. I would say some testing would need to be done in order to figure that out. I'll keep considering it and we'll discuss it with each new addition." With that she snapped her fingers and Aggie jolted out of her Izzy mind-meld. Such a transition shook her a bit and she took a moment to regain her senses. Her eyes were swimming and the room was out of focus. She felt like she was drunk with the worst possible hangover.

Aggie decided that hangover treatment might be the best in this situation. She placed one foot on the wall and one on the floor and attempted to refocus her vison back to normal.

"Whoa, note to self, never fall in and out so quickly. I feel like I'm Dorothy in the *Wizard of Oz*, people come and go so quickly here." She chuckled to herself but the action caused her stomach to roll. Breathing deeply, she attempted to pass the feeling without getting sick. Her time was running and she knew the guys would be waiting on her soon. She changed her clothes quickly, into all black leathers with longer sleeves this time to ward off the nighttime chill that had begun to creep into the air. Without the sun to chase it away, this was going to be long night.

"Too bad I can't just snuggle in for the night with one of the guys," she mused. She also thought she should apologize and reschedule with Gryson and Mathius. "Is that the proper thing to do when one is juggling eight guys? Or would it be better just to say, 'damn the luck, maybe later' and see how that goes over?"

CHAPTER SEVENTEEN

In a rush she blasted out the door and headed back to Mitchell's cabin. They hadn't said there was an official meeting place, but it was best to assume they weren't going to leave without their guides. Aggie stumbled across the threshold clumsily, nearly colliding with her favorite grumpy Alpha shifter. Oddly enough he didn't catch her; however, he did shoot his arm out abruptly to stop her, but it was more like a firm shove in the opposite directly.

"Watch your step, Princess. If this is how you are going to be all night on such little sleep, we aren't going to get very far or get much done." There was no compassion in his words, and Aggie fought the urge to snap back at him or stick out her tongue. She needed to work on her adulting skills and stop acting like a child when she got mad. She was in fact quite tired from her day and there was going to be no relief for her.

"I could use a super-charged coffee if anyone has one. Wish there was a magic spell that could whisk away my exhaustion." She gave a pointed look at Gryson but he shook his head in the negative, though he did have an apologetic look on his face. Then he pointed at the side table.

Aggie glanced over and nearly knocked Mitchell over once again, because a steamy to-go mug of what she could only believe was coffee waited for her.

"Thanks for the warning, Gry," Mitchell grunted, and stepped out of the line of fire. "Now that the Princess is happy, are we ready to head out?"

Everyone muttered or nodded their agreement and they all walked out of the cabin. Aggie clutched her coffee in a death grip, worried someone would take the life-giving brew from her.

They headed toward the Gateway, and Aggie noticed Eldon was bringing up the rear. Setting pace with him, she nudged him with her elbow and did something no one would have ever expected. She handed him her coffee.

"What are you doing? I'm not going to drink your coffee; you need it more than anyone." Eldon pushed the cup back toward her.

"No, just take a sip, I insist." Aggie pushed it back and reluctantly Eldon wrapped his hand around it, connecting with hers. That was exactly what she had hoped would happen, and at that exact second she pulled on her connection to nature all around her and flooded it into Eldon as best she could. It wasn't particularly graceful or skilled, but the way his eyes widened she knew something was working.

"What are you doing?" Eldon asked, but she didn't answer him. She didn't know how long she had before he broke the connection, and she didn't want to draw attention to them at the back of the pack. She just pushed harder and overloaded herself and therefore Eldon in turn. His color brightened and his shoulders lifted. She could tell it was working. After a couple minutes of the connection she released the power and let it seep back into the earth.

"Feel better?" Aggie asked wryly, and pulled her coffee back because Eldon dropped it the moment the magic settled. She immediately took a sip and sighed her contentment.

"What did you do?" Eldon asked in disbelief, looking at the

part of his exposed arms and skin that he could see without a mirror.

"I just gave you a shot of *five-hour energy*." She knew he wouldn't get the Earthly reference, but it didn't change her use of it.

"I don't want you taking from yourself. You are already tired enough." Eldon was always so concerned for her safety, and that touched Aggie deeply. She slowed and Eldon followed suit.

"I love that you're thinking of me, but don't worry. I talked to Izzy about this and figured out that my weakness of being human seems to be your gain as my mate. I can give back to you using my powers, in the same way that the grounding of the elements replenishes me." She quickly stood up on her tiptoes and kissed his lips sweetly. They didn't have time for much else and for that Aggie was sad, but they made short work of catching up to the group.

They walked and talked for a minute which, judging by the glance Mitchell had just given her, was wise. "I never thought I would say this, but he is almost too Alpha at times." Aggie grumbled her discontent to Eldon, who locked his hand in her free one. She still wasn't willing to completely give up on her coffee. She wasn't sure what she would do with the cup once empty, and so she was nursing it rather than carry around an empty cup.

"Thank you." Eldon disregarded her mumble even though she was sure the entire group of magical beings heard her effortlessly. She resented them for that power, too, since she hadn't gained even an inkling of that with her newfound powers. She was also thankful they hadn't taken their mind-meld yet, because she was in a particularly grumbly mood.

"You're welcome, El. I would do the same for any of you given the chance, and I didn't want you going into this unprepared. Who knows what we'll encounter and, if my coffee will reboot my exhaustion, you deserve a pick-me-up as well." They strolled after everyone and it surprised Aggie that they didn't move any faster. That gave Aggie an idea and she gave Eldon's hand one last squeeze and high-tailed it up to Xavier's side.

"Hey, Ninja," Xavier looked at her and gave her a puzzled expression. "Oh, I'm trying on nicknames for you, as I don't have one yet. I haven't written that one off yet, just so you know. I wondered, since this area to the Gateway is relatively straight, why are we walking?" She raised an knowing eyebrow at him and shot off into the darkness. She was thankful for the moon this time, as she wasn't trying to avoid it by sticking to the shadows. Focusing on the path directly in front of her, the open layout was helpful. While she wasn't perfect by any means, she was better than the small clearing they used at first. She wasn't up to full speed but the trees blurred past her into a mass of color. Making out individual images was challenging, so she stopped trying.

"This seems to be easier, Wee One." Xavier's voice startled her but she realized he was keeping pace with her and his face was the only thing clear amidst the darkness.

"Straight open layout, even that can't trip up my natural clumsiness. Human curse I suppose, we can't be flawless in anything. I'm sure a tree will surprise me, or a rabbit, and I'll go tumbling to my doom before too long." Aggie noticed that carrying on a conversation while running wasn't difficult. She wasn't winded at all, and on some level it just felt like she was taking a stroll and using very little energy. In her human form running wasn't something she volunteered to do, and would likely only be doing so given a zombie apocalypse or attacker chasing her. Even the latter was less likely, as she would have given up any hope of surviving an attack and succumbed to whatever fate had lined up for her.

Soon Xavier started to slow and Aggie took that as a sign. She followed suit and realized that the Gateway was just ahead. They didn't slow quite to human speed, but her vision cleared and she was able to make out her surroundings. As they drew closer, she saw three figures standing beside the Gateway. However, she couldn't make them out.

"Do you see that?" she asked Xavier, and he confirmed subtly that he did. Had he not been beside her she wouldn't have heard his soft "Uh-huh." Surely, he was trying to avoid being overheard.

She opted to stay silent and take her cues from her not so friendly vampire mate. As they approached, she began to recognize the figures but didn't understand why they were there. She saw Felix, Tartan, and one more unknown companion she had the yet to meet.

"To what do we owe the pleasure, boys?" Aggie spoke now that she recognized them, startling them. That was when she realized she was still moving faster than their eyes could see and she probably sounded like a ghost. Quickly she reduced her speed and their relaxed faces told her she came into view. Xavier did the same and they both stopped a few feet from the group.

"We heard you were going looking for the scrolls and wanted to lend a hand. We may not be able to help you find them exactly, but if there is an attack of any kind you won't be pulled in too many directions. We can help protect the villages while you are distracted in the caves." Tartan seemed to have taken on the role of leader, or maybe it was a natural disposition for him. He wore the title well.

"Who's your friend?" Aggie nodded at the mystery guest, who stood just as broad as Felix except a little shorter. He looked like he could hold his own in a bar fight or work as a bouncer. She certainly didn't want to pick a fight with him or meet him in a dark alley alone.

"This is Ulnack. He is one of Galata's strongest warriors. He has won the stadium games the past five years. He heard us talking about coming along and insisted we let him tag along," Felix answered, and Aggie thought she heard a bit of attitude in his response. She decided she needed to ask later if they weren't necessarily the best of friends and, if not, perhaps a type of rival.

"Well, it isn't my place to say, for that we'll wait on Mitchell, but I'm happy for the extra man power. There was a niggle in the back of my mind," she wondered if that might be Izzy, "that told me this might not be the trip we're planning it to be."

"We are at your disposal, my lady." Tartan bowed so deeply she worried he might fall on his face. What surprised her was the other two followed suit, like she was some sort of royalty. Then she remembered, Mitchell always insisted on calling her Princess. Perhaps there was more to the nickname than his usually snark.

Soon the world flickered and Mathius, with Mitchell in tow, and Kyrel with Ren, appeared from the darkness. Without a word, Mathius and Kyrel disappeared just as quickly as they arrived.

"We thought this was where we would find you," Mitchell grumbled, and Ren grinned in his signature way that made Mitchell's words less abrasive.

"You are getting pretty good at that. I want to race you the next time we have a free moment." Ren's challenge made Aggie beam.

"I'm not sure even you could outrun me," Aggie taunted with ease and her muscles relaxed, not realizing she had tensed upon their arrival.

"Not me. Wolfie." Ren used her name for his wolf and it warmed her heart. It was as though he never had a name for him before and her blessing him with one was second-nature for him.

Mathius chose that moment to wink back into view, carting Gryson this time, and the pair made Aggie remember their plans had been rearranged by this trip. She wondered if the choice of passengers was on purpose or not. Kyrel appeared a second later with Eldon. Now that everyone was present, Mitchell decided to address the additional guests.

"Decided you couldn't let us leave without the cavalry?" He let a smile slip and she knew he was joking almost with old friends. "Also," he redirected his focus to her alone, "next time you decide to take off, give us a warning. It took us a moment to figure out you were gone because you weren't in front." His jovial tone was gone, replaced by scolding. Aggie wasn't going to let that fly aside from Mathius in the bedroom.

"Don't talk to me as if I'm a child. We all ended up here and all the faster for it. I don't know why no one considered sifting before. It's not like I couldn't have done that myself, only easier as I've had more practice. I just decided before going off into the great unknown I should probably train a little harder on my newfound powers." She threw in a bit of poking there and rubbed in the fact that she and Xavier had done the deed that afternoon. Reminding him that he still hadn't had that full honor, and the few bedroom activities they'd had would be all he got for a while due to use his renewed assholeish nature. She had hoped their little tryst earlier would have softened him a bit, but it seemed only his dick was softened. She fought an eyeroll and turned her attention back to the guests.

They quickly picked up on the shift and Tartan replied, "We figured a little extra man power, or animal if needed, couldn't hurt."

"Glad to have you. I assume your affairs are in order?" Mitchell said that like it was a passing statement.

"What is that supposed to mean?" she blurted, and Mitchell groaned.

"We always sort our affairs before going on a mission of this caliber. It is the logical course of action." Mitchell's condescending tone was starting to get on Aggie's nerves.

"None of us have any family left, so we are happy to lend our skills to you." Felix must have sensed the change in the atmosphere and his words were rushed, as though he was trying to get it out before an argument started. Aggie decided that Felix wasn't so bad and she could tolerate him. He was a bit of a peacemaker, and for that he got a pass.

"All right, then, let's get this show on the road. I have had one too many plans interrupted this evening, and would like to get something accomplished tonight." Aggie wasn't leaving any room for argument, and they had too much to accomplish to get caught up in lengthy discussions. If these guys wanted to tag along and risk themselves at the hand of who knows what or who, then it wasn't on Aggie to stop them.

Taking the initiative, Aggie placed her hand on the knob and it warmed beneath her touch. The Gateway responded to her and for the first time she understood exactly what the guys meant by it just knowing. She had clear intent and, while it wouldn't let them travel to Pantal directly, it would take them into the Gateway first. This wasn't the first time she had traveled through alone, but it was the first time she had led the pack and it was she who dictated the travel. The feeling was strong and she could feel the pull. The give and take and tug of the Gateway gave Aggie a new sense of the connection they shared.

Seconds after taking that step, she felt the solid floor of the now-familiar Gateway underfoot. She opened her eyes and took a deep breath. The doorknobs on the walls were just as she left them; but, then again, she didn't think they could move or be changed in any way. Her thoughts fluttered to Eckard for a fleeting moment. Did he have any trouble passing through the Gateway? She recalled the room closing down and barring entrance to her personal space. Was the room telling her something then? Should she be concerned about the man who claimed to be her father? Was he not who he said he was?

So many thoughts, and yet so little time. Aggie's time was limited and her considerations cut short when the guys all started flooding the space. It was always amazing how the room never really felt small with them all inside. Even now, with an additional three large men filling the space, it still felt roomy. Almost as though the walls were just a suggestion. Normally, one felt the air shift in a room or it would become claustrophobic when filled with so many bodies. The Gateway didn't do this at all and it gave Aggie pause.

"Now, then, we should probably take this before we go any further." Gryson drew a bag from his pocket, and Aggie instantly knew what it was even though it wasn't visible. Her stomach revolted at the thought, but her mind knew it was necessary.

"Is there any way to extend or make that go farther?" Aggie's head bobbed in the direction of their three comrades. If they had allies in their pockets, it would be good to know they could communicate at a distance and utilize them as the resource they are. If there were to be an attack on one of the villages, they would have the upper hand.

"It could be thinned, I suppose, but it would be better to give them full strength ones and thin our own. Then the distance wouldn't be a problem. Since we will be close at hand, our own clarity won't be a problem." Gryson scratched his chin thoughtfully as he theorized.

"Aggie gets a full one," Mathius barked, as though he needed to say the words before anyone else, probably Aggie, recommended another course of action.

"I agree, but with others in the link it would be wise to give her a crash course and help her build a mental wall." Kyrel smirked at her and Aggie shot him a glare, even though she was grateful for the suggestion. She always hated being easily read, but the fact that with this they had a direct route into her mind was unsettling. Nothing was just for her when they did this. Girls aren't that hard to figure out but they do like to keep some things to themselves, for sanity if nothing else.

"Then who gets the watered-down versions?" Aggie didn't know if there was a good way to go about it. "Do I need to go get some straws?" She flicked her eyes to the open doorway in the room and realized the room didn't shut down like it did with Eckard. No threat assessment must have been done in this case.

"No need, Mitchell and Ren have their own shifter connection. Does that include those under your command?" Xavier posed his question to Mitchell and Aggie was intrigued. This was the first she had heard about the connection, but it made sense. She had seen enough movies and read enough books to know there had to be some basis of truth to their mental conversations with the Alpha.

"Only with me. Ren can't communicate with them. It is the Alpha's right to have complete control and command over his legion. Once someone swears fealty to the Alpha, the connection is made." Mitchell folded his arms over his chest and he seemed to grow in mass. It was as though talking about his Alpha side brought it to the forefront. He now appeared every bit the Alpha in this room. Even though each of her guys had their own Alpha instinct Mitchell was a living, breathing representation of that entity twenty-four-seven.

"Well, that solves the dilemma then. Shall we get this over with so I can throw up in my mouth?" Aggie didn't sound excited but she got tired of talking about things quicker than the guys. She was becoming quite the woman of action and less chatter.

"If you throw up, you are just going to ruin all my hard work." Gryson handed her a vial and proceeded to pass the remaining ones between the guys.

Pinching her nose, Aggie didn't justify Gryson's words with a response. Knocking the vial back like a professional shot taker, Aggie was confused. The liquid didn't taste bad at all. Her tongue snaked out to lick her lips and tasted the roof of her mouth a couple times in confusion. "What was that?" she finally asked after everyone had finished ingesting their own.

"Since I had time to gather the ingredients, I grabbed something to help make it more palatable. It wasn't a particular flavor but just something that coats your tongue. Each individual reacts differently to it, but it tends to come across like a forgotten flavor that was tasty at one time or another." Gryson wore a look of pride that he had surprised her.

"So, similar to a timararoo." Aggie remembered the cake-like dessert that she had in Ahael at the festival. It was the tastiest delicacy but it also brought forth a memory long forgotten.

"Similar, but the memory of this flavor is fabrication and less of something you have actually tasted. It tricks your brain into registering it as something you like. That saves me from having to change it for everyone. It works for everyone the same way." Gryson swallowed his down and Aggie felt the link click into place. The feeling of everyone in her mind was instant and just as overwhelming as last time. Though they were quickly locked away, the instant flooding into her senses was almost enough to drive Aggie to her knees. Everyone else took the connection in stride and Aggie secretly wished she could look even that suave while enduring something so blatantly painful to her senses.

"Aww, she thinks we look suave." Ren's goofy grin overtook his face and Aggie cringed, instantly regretting drinking her vial. Her thoughts were once again sent through the hotwire that was connected to each of them. The rest of the guys were trying at varying degrees to stifle their laughter and smiles. Those not connected, Felix, Tartan, and even Ulnak, were not succeeding either, but at least they didn't hear it firsthand from her thoughts.

"Shut it, you!" Aggie pointed a finger at Ren and he stopped his laughing, but his smile remained. "And you," she pointed next at Kyrel, "you said there is a way to make a wall. That is your first task when we get into Pantal; teach me." Her words left no room for argument but Mitchell wasn't going to let it go.

"Yes, because anyone hearing your sexual fantasies is the least of our worries on the list of priorities we have on going on today." He had a way of speaking such that his eyeroll could actually be heard. Aggie didn't care what he thought; there was only so much she could put on display and still keep her head held high.

"I'm sure he can find time in between our travels if we can't use the Gateway to get us straight into Pantal. I imagine we will have time." Her hands flew to her hips in a defiant motion and she felt an instant boost in her confidence when she could put him in his place. But Mitchell wouldn't let her have the win. It wasn't in his Alpha nature.

"Oh, as you were so kind to have pointed out, we could just sift from place to place." His defiant look was holding firm and she knew if she were to win it wouldn't be easy.

"Actually, since the shifters are the only ones who know where we are going, the sifting will prove to be difficult as we don't have a location planted in our minds to get us to the right location without much effort." Kyrel came to her rescue, and she breathed a silent sigh of relief. "After we have seen it, we will be able to move around quicker."

"Ha! See? Now, let's get through and get this party moving. I'm so over this part already." Aggie knew she was acting childish, but when it came to Mitchell she had a tendency to fall back on her youthful ways. She didn't have any siblings, but if she did she imagined their arguments would have gone a lot like this.

CHAPTER EIGHTEEN

The Gateway dropped them out in what felt like the middle of nowhere, but Aggie was somewhat used to that after the hike to get to Galata. This time, though, it was more of a rugged desert terrain, and Aggie wished that they had stronger technology here. A car or even a horse would be more preferable.

"Shifters can't ride horses." Ren acknowledging the thoughts in her head was getting old, but reinforced her position. She didn't need them hearing everything, and only what she projected. A niggle in the back of her mind, what she was starting to learn was Izzy, told her she had everything she needed within her to block this. The only thing was to figure out how.

"Why can't you ride horses?" Aggie knew they were bigger in stature overall, but that didn't mean a horse couldn't support them.

"They scent us before we approach and our animals make them nervous. Some are predators and, while we wouldn't necessarily attack them, we do hunt and feed in our alternate forms. They have a natural aversion to us." Ren's words made sense. Aggie couldn't imagine being a horse and how confusing it would be to smell a deadly animal in the air and not be able to see them.

"I can see that, but wouldn't it be just as easy to train the horses that shifters aren't the enemy?" She thought it was a valid point. Horses were trained all the time in her world, so why wouldn't the shifter realm be able to do the same?

"That would be a lot of natural instinct to train away. It is easier to avoid the situation entirely. While it isn't necessarily impossible, it isn't looked highly upon. How would it look to have an Alpha thrown from a horse because he didn't want to walk? Not to mention we could all shift into our alters for added speed if the situation called for it." Hating to admit it, Aggie agreed that Mitchell had a point. The smug look that was now plastered on his face angered Aggie further.

"Ky, we need to get to work. Everyone else can lead the way and we can fall back and work on this block. If I can't get it in place before we reach Pantal, I'm going to lose my mind." She grabbed him by the arm, tugging him back to the end of the group. That allowed everyone else to pass them, and for that Aggie was grateful. She didn't need an audience watching her try to learn this seemingly impossible task. It was bad enough that they would hear her missteps and probably ridicule her for them. Ren wouldn't likely pass up the opportunity.

"Are you ready?" Ky pressed as he and Aggie found a pace that was much slower than the others. Aggie was purposely creating a gap between them.

"Yes, where do we start?" Aggie didn't stop. She glanced at Ky, who smiled at her. His smile was breathtaking and Aggie found herself lost for a few moments. Then the niggling in her brain came back and she realized she was swooning within earshot of all eight of her guys. No one said a word, but Aggie flushed in embarrassment. "We start now. No more delays."

"Of course, my love. Look within yourself and find your center, much like when you fall into your inner self, but don't let yourself fall." Aggie couldn't close her eyes to focus like she normally would, so she took a few cleansing breaths and focused on the path ahead. Not taking her eyes off a set point a little in the distance, this allowed her to stay on the path and not lose her balance. In and out she breathed as she looked deeper on the spot in her vision and began to look through it. Now without taking her eyes from the trail, she was actually looking inside herself and creating an external link to herself. Her center hummed its approval and Aggie realized it was Izzy responding.

"Okay, I've locked in on it. Now what do I do?" She held tightly to Izzy's warmth for fear that any distraction would cause her to falter and lose the connection.

"Now I want you to imagine one brick being placed around that center." Aggie scrunched up her face and she considered how she would do this. Imagination seemed to be more literal when she spoke about her center. She didn't want to lose her direct line to Izzy either. Then, slowly and cautiously, she placed an invisible brick on the perimeter of her inner self. Then she waited to see what would happen. When Izzy didn't throw out any cause for alarm, Aggie placed another one.

"That's it, keep going all the way around. Completely close it in and all around it. Don't let anyone in and you will be blocked from us." Ky's words were just what she needed, and one by one she placed brick after brick.

When she had a small dome created but hadn't sealed it yet, Izzy sent a spike of pain through her. Aggie cried out in pain. "What was that?"

"What do you mean?" Ky didn't feel the sharp pain that pierced Aggie, so he was confused. Aggie wasn't in pain any longer but the feeling was vibrating through her at a dull level. It felt like a warning. Then Aggie realized she had done something wrong. She was about to wall off Izzy completely. She wouldn't have access to the outside world.

"Okay, my inner self didn't like that plan, but I have an idea." Aggie pulled back some of her bricks and restarted, this time building them in a way that she had a mental door with a latch. Then, on the opposite side, she left a hole for a window and imagined a thin sheet of glass being placed inside. This made Izzy happy again and she warmed inside Aggie's chest. Placing the final brick to close in the roof of her space, she settled back and threw a few thoughts into the atmosphere.

Mitchell is an asshole. Mathius is a sexy beast who can tie me up and fuck me stupid. Wonder what it would be like for Xavier to taste me, blood and all?

No one blinked or made any movement to question her stray thoughts. So, something must have worked.

"Okay, now that I've got that done, what do I do when I need you to hear me?" Ky's face brightened at this and she wasn't sure why.

"You are a quicker study than Mitchell gave you credit for, my love." Mitchell heard Ky and turned to glare. He didn't dignify this with a verbal response. "Now, if you need us to hear something, you can do one of two things. Focus on the lot of us prior to thinking or focus on one of us and we will get it first, or possibly only one of us if you do it right." Aggie didn't know this was an option and wondered why no one mentioned it before.

Focusing her thoughts on everyone, she asked that question, *Why didn't anyone care to mention the isolation option before?* Waiting patiently, she glanced between the guys and, at first, wondered if it she'd done something wrong. Then, one by one, their faces changed and they looked back to her.

"You couldn't isolate the entire group to block us, so there was no need to tell you what else you couldn't do. It seemed a bit cruel." Eldon's sweet voice trilled over her and washed her in his warm caress. She loved the feeling of his words, how they not only hit her ears but her heart and soul as well. Thankful to Kyrel's training, that last part only made it to Eldon because he filled her entire mind at that exact moment. He blushed, and she wanted nothing more than to kiss him, but he was still a bit of a distance away.

Now that she knew about the isolation factor, she thought up a perfect idea. *Too bad you're too much of an asshole to get over yourself. We could have had some fun before.* She knew she was playing with fire, but Mitchell's eyes flew to hers and they were full of fire. Though, in true Mitchell form, there was no response. He couldn't say anything out loud, and to say one in her head would be admittance. She knew he had feelings for her, but there was still something holding him back. She worried it was something she wouldn't be able to overcome. He needed to get past this himself.

"That is enough playing around. She is clearly on the right track for now. I'm sure she will falter here and there or lose it in the heat of the moment," Mitchell alluded to their moment, and that surprised her more than anything, though he didn't continue or give anything away. "I would either like to discuss our plans or walk in silence, because this chatter is really starting to get on my nerves." Once again, Aggie thought the last part was more for her because she had directed that thought to him and him alone, and she had stirred something. Neither of them needed to be thinking of such things in this particular moment, so she nodded her agreement.

"Once we get to Pantal, where are we going from there? I'm sure the scrolls aren't hidden in the town." Aggie was flying blind here and had no idea what to expect.

"More than you might think. This region is very dry and has very little plant life. As you can see the trees are limited, and they actually have their supplies brought in or they barter outside of their area for fresh food. We have stronger crops in Galata and other villages around. So, the people here live more in cave-like dwellings. So, while we think that it isn't in the village directly, they are still interconnected." Ren was chatty as usual, and for once Mitchell didn't berate him for it. Mitchell was likely just as happy to stay quiet in this instance. Aggie had given him much to think about.

"So, the village is in a cave system of some kind?" Aggie's eyes widened. She didn't have claustrophobia per se, but she also hadn't been in a situation where she had to be underground for so long either. She had heard about places built into cave structures on Earth, but the idea always freaked her out. What if there was a collapse or flooding? Would there be a way out or would those people be trapped and ultimately killed? The thought sent chills over her skin and she rubbed at the covered flesh.

"Are you cold?" Ky misread her reaction because she was now walled off, so Aggie smiled and shook her head. There were positives to keeping her thoughts to herself. She never wanted to show them any weakness, and this unsubstantiated fear was one of those she wanted to keep hidden.

"They have built a few of them in the cliffside and it works for them. It's not for everyone, but it is stable and carefully maintained. They are safe from predators and it is also likely why the rebels didn't attack them first. The scrolls are likely hidden in there somewhere, but they went for the easy targets first. I just hope we can use our magic to find them before anyone else gets any bright ideas." Mitchell seemed to have sensed her concern, and in his own gruff way set her a little more at ease. Just like with that kiss in Ahael it was unexpected, but usually followed with his natural snark. "Now, let's move a little faster or it will be dark when we get there. Cave entrances are hard to find in the dark."

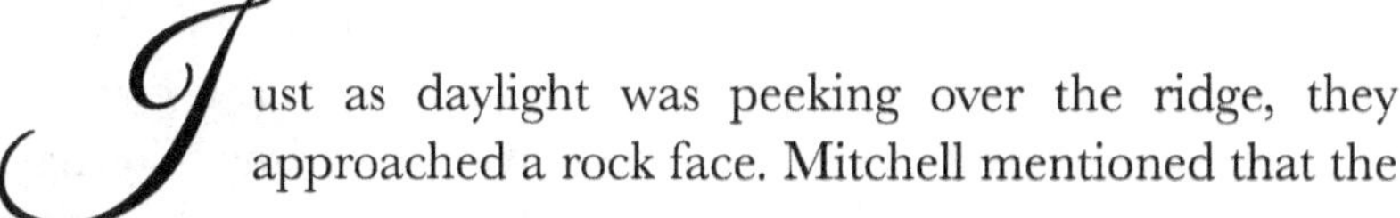

ust as daylight was peeking over the ridge, they approached a rock face. Mitchell mentioned that the cities were underground and built right into the cliffs, but Aggie had no idea what to imagine until she came face to face with the phenomenon.

The rock was nothing to write home about, not too tall and not exceptionally wide. The only strange thing was the multiple cave openings running the length of it. Some of them were gated, but not all, and that struck Aggie as odd.

"Why are they not all protected? Wouldn't it be logical to gate all or none?" She kept pace with the guys but slowed her pace as she took in the area. The terrain would prove to be rough and uneven with the growing hills as it rose into the cave entrances. Not something one would take on lightly or unprepared. The guys tackled this like professional hikers and Aggie did her best, but found herself stumbling every few steps.

"Agatha, allow me to help you." Liel always insisted on using her full name, and Aggie was adapting to it. He lifted her arm by the elbow in an effort to help her balance.

"The gates are just to keep unwanted traffic isolated to a few guarded openings. The colonies here only have so many people available on protection detail. This is just a safety precaution. They can guard the open areas and leave the gates to protect the other spaces. That doesn't mean they can't use them themselves, though." Tartan spoke very clearly, though softly, and Aggie almost missed what he said before she could tune her ears to his words.

"That makes sense, I suppose. I just would think it would have been easier to not have so many openings." Aggie clung to Liel's arm like a cat trying to avoid water.

"The openings serve a dual purpose," Liel said from her side, and his voice was steady and strong. He always had a way of knowing things. Aggie couldn't fathom the wealth of knowledge locked away inside that head of his. "They are also a natural light source. It doesn't work throughout, but it covers a little way and they don't have to have too many alternate sources."

"Alternate sources? Like torches?" Aggie was confused, but Liel's choice of phrasing seemed purposeful. He always strived to make things as clear as possible, even if that meant too much detail that it was confusing.

"I'll let you see for yourself when we get inside. It is harder to explain than it is to see firsthand." Aggie scrunched her face up in confusion. Liel loved to explain things in painful detail. This was highly unlike him and she wasn't sure if he was working an angle or not. They hadn't had the strongest relationship, as she found him more annoying than anything most days.

They continued toward the mouth of the open cave. The group slowed as the guards came out to greet them. "Who goes —" the guards started, but stopped short as they saw Mitchell and, of course, Ren. "Oh, Alpha, we didn't know you were coming today." They practically stumbled over their words, trying to be respectful and show allegiance to their Alpha. The one on the right was shorter but stocky, and Aggie would bet money he shifted into some kind of pig. His short hair was buzzed close to his head and stuck up all wiry. The one on the left was tall and thin, making the pair look a little like Mutt and Jeff. He was lanky and not very intimidating, with red hair and freckles. Aggie could picture him as an older version of Opie. Then she reprimanded herself for reducing him to a cliché.

"This trip wasn't planned; more of an expected vacation. Unfortunately, there is less pleasure and more preparation. We need to speak to the elders. It is rather urgent." Mitchell had squared his shoulders and risen to full height. Aggie was always impressed with how he seemed to have a professional Alpha stance versus his everyday look. Then she also thought it was funny that he was referring to this as a vacation. Of course, how much free time does an Alpha of an entire shifter community have to himself?

"Right away, sir." The guards spun on their heels and started back toward the cave. The stockier of the two moved to the side and took up his post at the gate, but the redhead continued on and everyone fell into step behind him. Liel stayed with her, and she hung tight to his arm as though her life depended on it.

Farther into the cave the natural light faded, and the cave seemed to emit a warm glow. It was beautiful but still low light, and not ideal for anything that required strong focus. Aggie thought about this and realized reading a book down here would be impossible. No matter how hard she looked she couldn't find the source of the new ethereal light.

They kept walking. She took in everything and had to admit that in this new light everything sort of had a romantic feel to it. She never thought she would think of a dark, dank claustrophobic cave as anything close to romantic. The space was supported by giant stone pillars cut from the rock itself. They were wide and probably the thickness of four to six grown men and stuck to the ceiling and floor. They were placed every few hundred feet and between them sat the houses. Just like city blocks, each opening between the pillars held two houses. They were uniform little blocks of space and everything looked as it would have above ground. They had just used their resources and created this little town beneath hundreds of feet of rock.

Then she realized that there were small street lamps at the end of each city block. She wasn't close enough yet to see what was powering them. Aggie had her money on magic.

"How far do we have to go to get to the elders?" Aggie whispered to Liel.

"I'm not sure, but I would guess that they will need to summon them regardless. It will take a few minutes once we get there for everyone to arrive. We didn't exactly warn any of them we were coming." Liel tapped the side of his nose in a knowing gesture. Aggie thought all of this was strange for Liel, so she decided if they had a few minutes she was going to find out.

"What are you doing?" Aggie tugged on Liel's arm and forced him to look back at her.

"What do you mean? I answered your questions and I'm

being helpful as always." His eyes were wide and he looked uncomfortable. Just then Aggie heard a snicker and she glanced up to see Ren and Ky huddled close to each other, watching them.

"What did you two do?" She wasn't yelling but her words echoed through the cave and she made a mental note to keep her voice down. In this case, the echo worked to her advantage. The two quickly turned around and dropped their heads. "Liel, what did they do?" She decided she would go to the one person who wouldn't try to shift the blame or topic.

"They told me you might be more comfortable around me if I tried to be more like a human. So, I did some research and am trying to fit in more with your model of what I should be or what is expected of me." He spoke softly and Aggie could see his embarrassment wash over him even in the low light.

"Liel, you are who you are and I'm adjusting to it. I don't have a preconceived notion about any of you. I don't want anyone to change themselves into what they think I want. I want you all to be who you are, regardless of your quirks." Aggie had stopped walking and pulled Liel to stop next to her. "Besides, if you change on me, I will be back to square one on figuring you out, and you are a constant that I need. So, do me a favor." She paused and waited for him to acknowledge her words. When he nodded, she continued. "Don't ever stop being you." With that she surprised them both by kissing him on the cheek. They didn't have a strong romantic relationship but she hoped that would change soon, because Liel was the odd bolt in her toolbox of men.

Quickly, they caught up to the group as they were approaching a larger building. "This is our council building. I'll leave you here to get settled after your journey and then I'll summon the elders." The guard opened the door and guided them all inside. There was a waiting room of sorts just inside the door and Aggie was grateful for a place to sit down. "I'll have some refreshments brought in for you all." With a slight bow, he left them alone inside.

Sitting down in the nearest chair, Aggie didn't wait on any formalities. Arching her back, she pressed her fingers into the center of her back to stretch it. "Ahhh, I'm so stiff from all that walking. Not enough sleep and a long hike are not a good recipe for my muscles." Aggie moaned loudly and the room grew silent. When she opened her eyes, but hadn't yet moved, she realized she was pushing her breasts out into the direct line of sight of every man in the room. Three of them weren't even part of her little harem, but that didn't stop them from taking in the sight. Quickly she righted herself and smoothed out invisible wrinkles on her clothes. "Uh, sorry. I'll just sit here and keep to myself."

"Fat chance of that," Mitchell mumbled under his breath, but Aggie caught sight of a small tent in his pants alluding to his half- erect cock from her tiny display a moment before. She left it alone since she was trying to be quiet.

"What should we plan on here?" Mathius brought them all back to business, as that was his nature. All business, and play-time was still just as controlled. That made Aggie remember their broken plans and she resolved to get back to them as soon as possible. She wanted to live that moment more than anything and was more pissed than ever that the rebels' plans had gotten in the way of her sex life again.

"Well, these three," Mitchell indicated their new additions, "are going to stick around here and help make preparations. When or if we end up in Farnack, they will come along and do the same for the townspeople. The women and children need to be made safe and the men of fighting age can be set up to protect and patrol. Then we are going to hope that the Elders of each community have a good idea of where the ancestors would have stashed the scrolls of importance." Mitchell loved being in charge and Aggie could see that plain as day in his eyes.

Just then, a group of six men and women walked into the building. They all nodded and said their hellos. Given that they were shifters it was hard for Aggie to tell their ages, but it seemed like these must be the Elders, if nothing else because they were the first to arrive. A couple of them broke off and let themselves into a closed door. Soon they came back out with trays laden with drinks and bowls of fruit and light breads.

The remaining four people gathered around the room and took empty seats. One of the men gestured for the rest of them to take seats as well. Mitchell remained standing, as did Ren just a half step behind him. Both stood with their arms crossed and looking very intimidating.

"Elders, we're sorry to spring this visit on you. We have much to discuss and need your help." He proceeded to give them the shortened version of the current events and why they had found themselves at the Pantal caves.

---

*T*wo hours later, the sun was bright in the sky. Unfortunately for Aggie, she wasn't basking in its glow. Instead, she was squandering away her day underground, inside strange cave systems. While waiting on the Elders to gather them any supplies they might need and information on where to start, Aggie wandered around a little. The cave-town of Pantal was much like any other place, if you looked at it and couldn't see the pillars.

If she focused on one house at a time they seemed like small houses, but with a desert landscape for their yards. No grass could be seen but sand was built up as one would a basic front lawn area. Some of the houses even had items in the yard that made her wonder if children lived there. She saw a kind of makeshift swing set built out of some larger tree limbs. The thought warmed her heart. Nothing stopped these people from surviving, and she couldn't see where their lives had suffered for their living situation. While she couldn't imagine living in a place like this, these shifters had definitely made the best of their situation.

Walking up the street, she had an idea. Her next goal in mind was to check out the light source. She slowly approached the lamp post and hesitantly placed her hand on the outside. She remembered this was her approach when she worried the doorknobs in the Gateway would harm her upon touching them. When her hands connected to the metal-like material that made up the lamp, it was cold beneath her fingertips. So cold that she recoiled in surprise.

"What in the world?" she said aloud, and once again jumped in surprise when a deep, scratchy, unused voice answered her.

"Fireflies." She twirled around at the sound of the voice and gasped slightly when she saw Ulnak. He stood there in silence after speaking only that one word. He had never once spoken since she met him and, if she thought about it, mixed with his looks, it gave him a very serial killer persona. That gave her pause as she realized she was standing on the edge of the street alone with a man she knew nothing about.

"Uh, Ulnak, you startled me. Where did you come from?" Aggie was getting down to the important things, and less about the fact that she thought he might have addressed her question when he first approached.

"I followed you out when you left the council building. The guys were all preoccupied, but they watched you leave. I knew they couldn't be here, so I thought I would be of most use watching you." Ulnak glanced at the ground nervously and Aggie felt for him. He was definitely the strong, silent type.

"Can I ask you a personal question?" Aggie hesitated, but she didn't want to stand there alone with someone she didn't know much about.

"I..." He paused slightly, as though he were thinking. "...guess you can."

"I don't mean to pry, and I know there are social protocols for this question, but I'm really not good with all that. They guys usually buffer for me so I don't come off as rude or stupid." She thought again how to word it but she figured she had warned him and the direct approach was the best way. "Since they aren't here to do that, I'll just ask. "What is your alter ego?" Knowing he was a shifter it was easier just to blurt and not speak in too much code.

He chuckled but, standing this close the mysterious lantern, she could see his eyes darken. That concerned her more than anything and she took a half step backwards. Her natural instinct was telling her a small gap between them would give her room to run if need be. Once nothing stood in her way of a speedy escape, given her vampiric powers, she looked back at him expectantly.

"I'm a pit bull." She looked at him funny, unsure of how such a domesticated dog was also a shifter.

"Seriously?" She didn't know what else to say. This was probably the last thing she expected him to say. Most all of the shifters she had encountered were more of a wild species and he was clearly the polar opposite.

"Afraid so; my past is a sordid tale that I'll tell you if it will make you more comfortable. I mean you no harm, and neither does my animal. He smells the Alpha on you and therefore knows you as his mate."

"We aren't mated." Aggie was quick to correct him, and she didn't exactly know why. He was obviously trying to calm her and make her at ease with him, but this was a point she needed him to know.

Raising an eyebrow at her in question, he replied, "Is that so?" Aggie panicked instantly. The last things she wanted was for any of Mitchell's people to think poorly of him or that he was weakened in anyway. It was bad enough that there was a rebellion brewing, and the one who was leading seemed to be a rival to the standing Alpha.

"Well, it's bound to happen eventually, but we just haven't gotten here yet." She filled in the last part right at the end of his question and he laughed.

"Don't worry, heiress; you are under no threats from me. I'll not advance upon you in that way and neither will anyone else who is loyal to the Alpha. His scent is enough to ward them away." Ulnak was warming up to her and she felt less frightened by him, but his alter was a different story. Her body visibly relaxed at his words, but she still remained at a distance and ready to run if need be. "Not to pry further or make you uncomfortable in anyway, but if we are to spend any time together it would be wise for me to know who I'm dealing with. In my world, pit bulls aren't the friendliest of species."

"That is understandable. I'm happy to share my story, but know that my life hasn't been one of sunshine and roses. Would you care to sit down?" He motioned toward a bench that Aggie hadn't seen before. It sat in the shadows a little way away from the lamp. Stepping ahead of him, she checked her surroundings to be sure she had an escape if need be. When she was satisfied, Aggie accepted his invitation and sat down on the rustic bench that was very basic, without a back or arms, but big enough for two average sized people or three small children. He joined her a moment later but stayed far enough away from her so they didn't touch at all.

"I am an orphan, but in shifter culture that doesn't matter. Families in the clan take on any children who are left without a family to raise them. So I didn't lead a life any different from any other shifter child." Aggie's heart still broke for him as he started his story. "When I came of age I left for the human realm, Earth, to spend my time there just like all my friends at the time. We had gone together, and stayed together for a time as we adjusted to their ways and culture. It wasn't anything like we expected and none of us listened to our parents to have much of an understanding. We were just happy to be on our own and taking in this new and exciting place."

"That isn't unlike Earth. Our teenagers think life away from their families will solve all their problems and they can make their own life choices," Aggie chimed in, and reassured him that he wasn't in any sort of wrong and in that their cultures were the same.

Nodding, he continued, "After a few months, I had gone out late to stretch my animal. It wasn't unheard of for me to do it in the daylight, because as you know mine is more domestic than some. It wouldn't be a surprise for someone to see a dog running around. I just chose to exercise him mostly at night to avoid anyone seeing the shift at any time. Unfortunately, that night was different. It was a warm summer evening and more people were out than I expected at such a late hour. I ran into an alleyway to shift and walk home in my human form, and someone followed me. I heard them enter behind me and that is the only thing that stopped me from shifting back right away. I cowered behind a dumpster and tried to stay hidden. Unfortunately, my animal's coloring is predominately white, so the light caught on the patches and gleamed brightly. The human found me much quicker than I'd hoped, as he had entered the alley with the intention to follow me and not just be in there as well. I watched him warily and was surprised when a rope appeared in his hand. I was trapped and didn't know what to do. It was shifter law not to shift in front of any humans. I also didn't want to attack him for fear of being caught as well. I froze. My youth was part of it but it was mostly fear of repercussions, as the laws on Earth are different than in Cratlian." Aggie feared she had an idea of where this was going but she let him continue without commenting.

"I tried to dodge the approach, but he had me cornered. I had nowhere to go, and when I attempted to leap around him he grabbed me by the middle. Before I knew what hit me, I had a rope looped around my neck and choking me. The harder I struggled the tighter the rope cinched. I couldn't breathe, but I fought with all I had. I knew that nothing good would come of being in the custody of this human. No one in their right mind or a decent person would do this to a helpless animal. I'm stronger than a normal animal, but the lack of air was a real deficit. So, I didn't last long before I had to stop or pass out. I knew I needed to stay conscious if at all possible so I could find a moment to escape." The sadness in his voice was evident and Aggie didn't blame him in the least. This was high on her list of the worst things one could imagine happening to another person. She wanted to save him even now from his darkest memoires.

"You don't have to continue if you don't want to. I understand. We all have things that should remain buried." Aggie was holding back tears for this young boy from long ago.

"No, you need to know." With that he continued his dark tale. "He tugged the rope one last time after he realized I had given up my fight. *'Come on, mutt; let's go!'* he barked, and I knew to obey. At that point, compliance was going to be key to my survival. I followed to avoid the tightening of my restraints and we walked back to his van. When I hopped in without the need to be provoked, he released the rope and sealed me into the windowless van. Without the possibility of escape, I lay down so I wouldn't get knocked around the moving vehicle. He brought me to a warehouse, and in the back room when we entered I could smell other animals. None like me, shifters, but all of them canine for sure. I didn't know what was happening, but I have now lived to regret it." Aggie saw where this was going. It was obvious that he had been caught by dog trainers who were using the dogs for the fights. Her heart broke for him.

"They shoved me into an empty cage and I was trapped in my animal form. They left me there and didn't return for days. None of the animals were fed in this time and there was no human interaction. I wondered how long it would be before they returned, and when they finally did only three dogs got fed.

The room had easily a dozen or more. I didn't know why until the fights began that night. Every one of us ended up in the ring." His eyes fell, as the memory was vivid in his mind. Aggie hurt for him and wished he didn't feel the need to tell her this story. No one should have to relive such a horrific life event just so people will trust them. She remained silent since he had insisted before, but she was still breaking inside for him.

"It was a bloodbath, and some didn't survive the ordeal. I only survived because I was more than they were. Though winning meant I had to take another's life. I was only thankful that it wasn't a forced shifter fight. It still hurt to kill a living being and another animal. Even though it wasn't a shifter we felt like kindred spirits." He paused and sighed, like he was taking a moment to remember the lives lost. "This carried on for months. The more I won the more often I got fed, but not enough to really garner any strength. I took so many lives, and after a time I became numb to the effects. Even now, I don't recall the sheer number of kills I had. I basically blocked it all out and retreated inside my mind. I let my animal have complete control and I went feral for a long time. I was vicious and violent and allowed no one near me. They had to shackle me before opening the door to my cage after I started taking swipes at the handlers. I was their prized possession and was treated better than any other dog in the warehouse. New ones came and went and none of the ones that were there when I first arrived remained. There were always new faces and new smells for those I couldn't see from my new home of bars. I couldn't escape, so I just adapted as best I could." A tear slipped from Aggie's eye as she tried to listen to all he had endured. No one should ever have to go through that.

"Didn't any of your friends try to find you? How long did you have to stay there?" She wasn't downplaying his life, but if she could skip over details that hurt him and affected her so deeply, she would try to save them both as much pain as she could.

"They couldn't track me as soon as I ended up in that van. The metal blocked the smell. Then, since I wasn't released into any open areas, they couldn't pick up my scent. I was lost to them, so they just moved on and assumed I was either dead or had just up and left them for my own reasons. I can't blame them, because it really was a lost cause." He again sighed as he remembered his friends. Aggie wondered if they were lost to him forever or if they ever rekindled their friendship. "I was in captivity for three years. I was the best fighter they ever had, but they thought I was reaching the end of my prime because they were used to regular Earth dogs and not the prolonged aging of a shifter. So, they began entertaining offers from security firms. It didn't take long for them to accept a pleasing offer in what I believe was five- or six-digit range. I didn't understand yet what their currency was back then, and so I didn't pay close attention." He crossed and uncrossed his legs, clearly uncomfortable, and Aggie reached out and placed her hand on his arm. He settled and then continued.

"I was sold to a drug cartel that needed me to guard their stash. It was an easy job and I got fed on the regular, so I didn't fight them much. After a time they became complacent, and that was just the opening I was looking for. They stopped chaining me up and just trusted that I would stay because I was getting fed and was taken care of. I did for a time, to earn their trust and gain some weight and strength back. It didn't take long, and then one night a few weeks after my arrival I made my move. I knew I could take any of them alone and the only downfall would be if they had a weapon. So I planned to avoid as much as possible. I stalked the perimeter and looked for a weak spot. I knew I still couldn't shift until I was away from there, as they wouldn't hesitate to shoot an unknown male on their property. Not long into my search, I found a bend in the fencing and I squeezed myself through, never once encountering another person.

"Even though I was feral and had been in my dog form for

years I was tired of the constant killings, but would still do whatever necessary to survive. Once I was a few miles away, I stopped. My conscience never left me and I quickly called to my animal and he allowed me to take back over with minimal fight. He was confused and it took some cajoling, but he let me back in and we soon fell back into old habits. We are bonded, and deep down we know that sharing is better than trying to handle the burden solely as one or the other.

"While he was still violent, he kept that side to himself. I stretched my body and sat down on the cool ground, naked as the day I was born. I stayed there for a while to formulate a plan. I knew I couldn't go back to civilization without clothes, but I didn't know exactly where I was and where to find supplies. I waited until nightfall and kept my human form, stayed in the shadows and walked. Eventually I came upon an old cabin that looked empty. Inside were a few clothes, dusty and deteriorated with age. I figured the cabin hadn't seen an inhabitant in a while. I decided to stay for a while to get my bearings back. I hunted for wildlife and gathered wild fruit for food. There was a creek nearby for water that kept me sustained and not dehydrated. It was years again before I saw another human, and I've never had a comfortable relationship since. I soon returned to the shifter realm and here I've stayed ever since." At the close of his story, Aggie had a newfound appreciation for him. She didn't fear him or his alter. She knew he had been through Hell and back just to survive, and would do anything he could to remain that way and protect those he deemed worthy.

"So, fireflies?" She didn't even say a word about his story, but moved on so he knew she trusted him.

He chuckled softly at her antics. "Yeah, they capture fireflies, and in captivity they shine brighter in this lower light. They make perfect torches in this environment. They swap them out every day so they can get food, and they make happier workers that way." Aggie wondered if he allocated their entrapment to his own experience and that's why he knew so much about them. Instead they just sat together on the bench in companionable silence, and took in the nearly alien world around them. She was still captivated by the fact that someone decided to create a town in this strange place. That there was no fear of possible dangers in doing so.

CHAPTER NINETEEN

ramping through the darkened cave tunnels, Aggie felt like Indiana Jones. She wondered if around the next bend they would have to turn and run the other direction for fear of being flattened by a giant stone rolling toward them. Chuckling to herself she proceeded to follow Mathius, who had taken up residence as their guide.

"I can see in the dark," Mathius had said when they started their walk. The deeper they were, the harder it was to see.

"So can most of the guys. I'm probably the only one who can't see straight down here." Aggie wished that, along with the other seemingly random powers she had already garnered, a better nighttime eye would have been one of them. She really didn't know for sure if Eldon, Liel, or even Gryson could see in the dark, but they weren't mentioning it one way or the other. Aggie assumed they didn't want to rub it in that she might very well be the only one in that predicament.

"The first alcove is up on our right. That is where we will look first." Mathius was holding a makeshift map that one of the Elders had drawn up for them. Aggie was surprised that Mitchell let Mathius take the lead, but Mitchell did have a lot on his plate lately. Perhaps he just wanted a few moments not to think about all of it at once. They turned the corner and the space widened into another sort of room. There were shelves and boxes all organized throughout.

"How do we know where to start?" Aggie was glancing around; the space wasn't huge, but they had it well organized and many boxes were stored here. She worried this was a wild goose chase.

"There will be some obvious signs of being in the right area. Since they are in such a well-kept system, there should be a way to rule out certain sections by time period alone." Liel was getting back to normal and Aggie relaxed instantly when she heard his casual, analytical tone. She was still mad at Ky and Ren for telling him to change his ways before. She might not have seen him for the friend that he was before, but she certainly did now. The fact that he was willing to go through the effort of attempting the ludacris idea in the first place gave her hope for their eventual relationship.

They naturally broke apart and everyone took on a small section of the room. Each one checking boxes and coming up empty. They didn't know exactly what they were looking for, but there was a sense of understanding and everyone jumped in to help. It didn't take long to realize that this area housed more of the modern documents and that they would need to travel further back to get to what they needed. Aggie still thought it was odd that the shifters had a written document that explained the inner workings of the Gateway.

Once again following Mathius, they all strolled at a steady pace, lost in thought. The sudden turn of events kept everyone on a more somber note. There was a real possibility that they would be in a war for control sooner rather than later.

"So, this rebellion, how long has it been brewing?" Aggie drummed up a small conversation and posed the question to anyone willing to answer. She knew that this was deeper than just a passing chat. Unfortunately, it was also probably the only thing that any of them were thinking about. The more they knew about what they were dealing with, the better.

"There have always been a contingent of people who didn't like the hierarchy. Just like in any society that is expected to fall in line. There will always be those who think they are above the law and will fight them tooth and nail. This is no different." Mitchell just kept walking and didn't bother to stop as he answered. His words were choppy and broken as he forced them out. It was like he knew them, but they were also words he didn't want to believe.

"So, there isn't a particular time in history that the rebellion just came to be? It has always just been in one way or another? That's awful. What's to stop them from attacking before now? Did they have a stronger following in the early days?" Aggie really wanted to know, but she could see the muscle tick on Mitchell's jaw. One side of her wanted him to answer and the other side wanted him to calm down.

"Every year there is a fight for Alpha. Every year Dranton comes to fight. He believes if he can win out over me and take control, then the rebellion will finally see the light of day. They have always been there for those who don't want to fall in line, but what they don't realize is Danton will be a tyrant and the power will go to his head. That is why I regret this fight every year. It isn't a fight to the death, but it is a fight to yield. He fails every year, and leaves a little more damaged each time." Regret was something Aggie never imagined she would hear come from Mitchell's lips. She couldn't make out his eyes in the firelight that Gryson had, following near her to keep her from tripping over her own two feet or a loose rock. The sound was unmistakable, and that made her instantly want to console Mitchell. She held back though because Mitchell wouldn't take to that kind of compassion well at all.

"Was Danton picked on as a child?" Aggie wondered if there were deeper issues at play here.

"His father was an Alpha many years ago." Ren took on the

task of telling this tale. "Everyone expected Danton to follow in his footsteps, but when the time came to fight his father for the role he stepped down. No one wants to fight a family member for something like this, but it is tradition. So when he refused, the next in line was called to fight. That was Mitchell and me. I yielded to Mitchell since he is the oldest, but because we match each other in a fight against one another I became Beta without much effort on my part. Danton didn't like to see his father fall, but he didn't sign up for what he called archaic practices. So instead of swearing allegiance to Mitchell, he ran. His father has since passed on, and Danton was an only child. There is no family left for him, except the pack as a whole." Aggie wondered why there was such a sob story going on for the enemy. Mitchell and Ren were clearly close to Danton, and his betrayal of their practices was a slap in the face to them.

"Where do these rebels stay that you guys don't have a run-in with them anywhere and everywhere you go?" Aggie was desperate to find out what she could about these interlopers.

"They are on the move a lot. We don't necessarily seek them out because, contrary to popular belief, it isn't a priority for us to have control over every shifter. We are wiling to protect and fight for those who swear fealty to the Alpha as head of the clans. Those who don't just don't have the same benefits. It isn't like a civil war that we are fighting, and every time we encounter one or two a fight breaks out," Mitchell scoffed, and Aggie bristled at the thought. She didn't understand the inner workings and politics, but he didn't have to act like she was somehow subpar because she didn't know.

"Fine, I'll drop the subject seeing as you can't carry on a civil conversation and not belittle me in the process," Aggie huffed, and stormed past him and over to Eldon, who reached out for her and drew her in close under his arm. A protective wing outstretched around her.

"If you all would stop coddling her she wouldn't be so damn soft when it came to controversy. She isn't going to be battle-ready if she keeps up this naïve act of good versus evil. There isn't a cut and dried answer for that, and sometimes the enemy is a friend who has been misled. Nothing can prepare you for a fight against someone close to you. She needs to harden herself to that before she can wrap her head around what we might be facing." Mitchell roared his anger and Aggie flinched. Did he really mean that they would be fighting rebels who were friends of theirs? Her stomach rolled at the thought of facing a drawn line and finding familiar faces on the other side.

"It's true," Ren started. "We don't always know who is on the side of our enemy because, in this type of war, they could be keeping things close to the vest. That means that they could be living amongst us and we not have a clue. Then they take the information they learn on a daily basis back to the rebels. That is why we don't leave our plans out there for anyone to intercept and why we made our move to come here so quickly. That's not to say that the rebels haven't already gotten wind of it and are on their way here." When Aggie thought of it that way, she realized the danger they were in. Anyone could be the enemy, and that thought terrified her.

"How do we know we haven't been sent on a mission to find something that isn't here?" The thought had crossed her mind a few times, but she hadn't wanted to voice it until now.

"That is always a possibility, but I think the best bet is to keep looking and hope for the best. We have a few more places left to check and then we can decide if we want to proceed." Mathius had set a brisk pace and they were closing in on the next storage bay. "We also have to consider that the scrolls we are looking for don't even exist. That could still be just an old wives' tale. Mitchell and Ren, you guys did say there was no firm evidence to prove they existed to begin with." Aggie hoped that wasn't the case because, otherwise, people were getting hurt for nothing.

"Here's the next one on the left." Mathius pointed up ahead and Aggie let the conversation drop. They had a purpose for being so deep in these caves, and she was planning to pull her own weight.

Once again, they all dispersed and started going through the stacks and crates. This section seemed to be older, as the crates were filled with straw as a packing material. This gave Aggie hope. She dug deeper into the box that she was working on and pulled out page after page of what looked to be shifter history. She read a few lines: "...*as was in the time of the Great Artimus, the Lion. He was the first Alpha and has kept us from harm. Those ways will be upheld until the end of time. Those who choose not to follow the old ways will be shunned and turned away from our family. They will not be allowed to partake in our sanctuary and will be made to live in the outer lands.*"

Aggie didn't know what she had found, but it seemed this was one of the original documents that were recorded when the first Alpha was established.

"I think I might have found something, but not we're looking for." She startled when the paper was snatched from her and she twirled to see Mitchell standing beside her. "Hey, I was reading that."

"It is faster if I read it and let you know if you found something or not," Mitchell grumbled to her as he skimmed the page and read the information quickly. While he may have been right, Aggie was still disappointed that she wasn't being allowed to read it herself.

"Well, is it of value, and are we in the right area?" She tapped her foot softly on the floor, showing her impatience and frustration at his antics.

"We are getting closer. If the scrolls are anywhere they would likely be in the same place as our origins. All we can do is look further here and hope we can find something." Aggie didn't like the wishy-washy answer that Mitchell just gave her, but it was the closest thing. Just then his eyes went distant. The low light was unable to block the golden glow that they emitted, and Aggie knew that meant he was tapping into his powers.

"What is it?" she asked, glancing around and between the

twins the most. No one said anything, and the shifters grew alarmingly quiet.

Almost as quickly as he froze, tension locked up in Mitchell's shoulders. "Something is happening in the Pantal. Tartan just alerted me to a commotion, but no news on what it is. He is rushing to investigate." Aggie's gut dipped down as reality sank in. Their time was limited.

"Since we don't know anything, I think we should use our time wisely. We left the Three Musketeers in charge for this reason. They can handle most anything thrown at them. The best thing we can do is find the scroll." With that, she got back to searching. The crate she was working in still had some things in it, so she continued there. One by one the rest of the guys followed suit. Each had filed in around her and started pulling their own crates from the same section she was in. It seemed logical to her that this was the oldest records portion, given what she had already found.

After a few minutes, Gryson whooped and pulled out a sealed scroll from his crate. Aggie wrinkled her brow in confusion; she couldn't figure out what had got him all riled up over a sealed scroll he hadn't even opened yet.

"What did you find, Merlin?" Aggie was trying on new nicknames and she wondered if he would get the reference. He looked up at her and beamed, not countering the name in the least. She took that as a good sign.

Waving the parchment in the air, celebrating on his own, Gryson quickly brought it over and placed it in Aggie's waiting hand. "This has to be it," he whispered, almost in awe. Something about that moment seemed monumental.

She flipped the sealed document over a few times in her fingers; the only thing that made it different from any other wrapped page in the remaining crates was the image on the seal. It was a door wrapped in a heart, and an old skeleton key placed at an angle across them both. The heart was almost like a shield in front of the very plain and generic door.

"That is the Wasley family crest," Liel pointed out as she stared at it longer than any other piece.

"Family crest? Why haven't I ever seen it before in my life?" Aggie ran her fingers lightly over the wax blob and felt the indentations of the images pressed into it. In her entire lifetime she had never seen anything like it, and she was in awe of it. Something about it made her want to feel it and touch it and never let it go.

"You wouldn't have, as it is only known in the realms. On Earth your family crest would look much different. I'll show you the two side by side some time." Liel wasn't being fake, and that was what Aggie liked about him. He was still just being himself, and this was just something he could share with her on his level. That was the connection she needed with each of the guys, something they could have just for them.

"So, if this is my family crest then you think that this is the right scroll, because nothing else would have my crest?" She wasn't sure if this logic was correct but, on some level, she guessed it made sense. Running her hand over it one last time she glanced back up at the group, silently asking for permission. She didn't want to break the seal unnecessarily, but they needed to know for sure what was beneath that limited protection. Pressing her fingers under the paper, the warmth of power welcomed her like crawling into a cozy bed on a cold winter's day. It was familiar and she welcomed it.

"I guess I just need to break this open and we'll all know for sure." She lifted her finger slightly and the wax popped up, the scroll free to be opened. No one reached out to take it from her, and it was then that she noticed they were all perched in one way or another around the space waiting for her to open it.

Unraveling slowly, Aggie's breath caught at the image she found beneath her fingers. It was some kind of picture message and map mixed into one. The more she looked, the more details appeared to her. It was clearly a map of all the Gateway points around the shifter realm. She recognized two of the pinpoints as the places they had traveled between already. There were a handful of others scattered around in places she had yet to see. Though, on a deeper level in the map, there was a recessed image. As she tilted the paper it formed into a clearer image and Aggie gasped, dropping the parchment. Thankfully Xavier had fast hands and he snatched it out of the air as it fell.

"What is it, Wee One?" he asked as he pulled the page back into view. A few of the guys gathered around him and they all had varying responses, but none of them were as surprised as Aggie.

"Don't you see it?" Aggie pressed as she watched them all take in this mysterious scroll.

"This is a map of the key points that are grounded by the Gateway," Mitchell replied coolly. "I don't know what you saw that caused you to panic."

Aggie reached up and tilted the paper like one would a holographic sticker, and she watched as their eyes lit up in understanding.

"That is a dragon," Mathius whispered, his obvious astonishment on display for all to see. "Is this about the prophecy?" Mathius referred to the woman from Ahael who had a vision that one day Aggie would be the dragon warrior.

"What? A dragon?" Aggie was confused because that wasn't what she saw at all. She quickly snatched the paper and turned it up and down, back and forth. Once again, she was surprised to find that the image changed. She also saw the dragon that Mathius mentioned, but when she turned it back the other direction she saw the image that had scared her. It was like she was staring at her own reflection.

"There." Aggie pointed at the image that was holding fast now that she had stopped moving it around. "Do you see that?"

The guys all pressed in around her, their presence reassuring, but the image on the ancient parchment was disconcerting. How was it possible that she herself could have been depicted hundreds or even thousands of years before? She looked between each of the guys and they all shared a look.

"That is definitely an unexpected turn of events. It is probably a good idea that we found this before anyone else. It seems the secret that was hidden all those years ago for control over the Gateway was right in our grasp all along." Kyrel usually didn't weigh in on such things since he preferred to be the lover, not the fighter. Though he could be just as fierce as the rest if the need arose. Now his eyes were glowing slightly and she could see the determination lying there. "I think we need to hold this pretty close and not show it to anyone until we know what and who exactly we are dealing with."

"I think you are correct. I'd hate for anyone to think that Aggie was their golden ticket to all power." Ren's eyes were also glowing slightly and she could tell he was holding Wolfie back. Her two shifters were very protective in their own right, but their wolves were even more so.

"So you guys are just going to glance over the fact that my face has been plastered on a map for gods knows how long ago, like this isn't somehow catastrophically impossible?" Aggie couldn't believe the words even as she said them. It seemed completely insane to say it out loud. Nothing like this would ever have been considered a few months ago, let alone actually believed.

"It's not that we don't want to address it, but we you have to remember that we have grown up believing that you existed. Not only that, but that you were made to be a part of our group and our mate. We have a different level of understanding when it comes to what fate is capable of. There is no doubt in my mind that there is magic on this map, but I also don't find it hard to believe that fate knew about you before you or your family knew about you." Liel seemed perfectly sound in his thought process, and that wasn't unusual. Aggie was still having a difficult time coming to terms with it all.

"I'm tired of you guys talking in riddles. Why can't you just tell me what's going on? Is this a magic thing that just picked my face by default, or is it that it knew who I was before?" Aggie threw her hands up in frustration and her voice was increasing in volume. All she wanted was a straight answer for once.

"That, none of us can say. It's no different than the prophecy about the dragon warrior. While you are believed to be that dragon, and I'm leaning toward that even more now, no one knew for sure who it was. Then, in Ahael, when Navian's mother used her powers and saw you as the Dragon Warrior. All things are pointing to the same outcome here, and it is hard to deny." Mathius stood with his arms crossed across his broad chest, and Aggie allowed herself to be lost in the view as she took his words to heart. She had to admit things were all falling into the same line of thought, and she would be lying if she said she wasn't beginning to believe that this wasn't a coincidence.

"While, I'd love to sit here and beat this horse until it is dead," Mitchell's words rang through the cave because he was practically shouting. Not that it was necessary because no one was speaking but, clearly, he wanted to be heard above all else. "We have bigger problems at hand. Now that we have found the scroll, we need to get back as quickly as possible. It seems a small scout team has been sent to Pantal. Felix was able to send them running before they breached the cave entrance. That won't keep them at bay forever. We need to regroup; I don't know about you guys, but I don't want my back pinned in against these cave walls. I want this done on my terms." He tore from the alcove and started back in the direction of Pantal.

"Would it be better for us to sift there?" Aggie quietly offered, and she was thankful that, so far, they hadn't been separated and needed to use their link. She was secretly hoping it would stay that way.

"Only if we go in full groups." Mathius was always trying to control the situations. She wondered how so many Alpha males coexisted like this. Each of the guys was a leader in his own right. Someone would have to back off occasionally to allow for others to make final decisions. This wasn't a dictatorship, but still some had more valid points than others at times and someone had to be the deciding vote.

"Well, with Aggie, three of us can move at a time. That means we can stay in groups of three throughout the transition and stay protected." Ky wasn't a strategist, but he did have a point. Aggie agreed with him wholeheartedly and the others followed her lead.

"Who's going in first?" Aggie was just going to jump right in and hope to get this train moving faster.

"Mitchell and Ren need to have a presence, so we should be sure they are in the first wave." Gryson was systematically dissecting the situation at hand. "Even though no attacks have been made, there is no saying that they don't have reinforcements close by. So Eldon, perhaps you should jump in on the first run as well. With your sword skills and healing abilities, you would be the next logical choice. That leaves Xavier, Liel, and me to protect each other here. It's not like we will be waiting long. The question is, who should protect the scroll?"

"I'll protect it, obviously." Aggie didn't want anyone to see that scroll, and if she had it in her possession she could prevent anyone else from getting their hands on it and know it was safe. She wondered if there was a way to cast some sort of spell over it. "Gryson, do you think there's a spell you could do that will help keep it hidden from those who haven't already seen it? Then, even if something happens to me, it's still protected."

"I think I could whip something up when we get back to Galata. That won't help us now, though, so keep it close and make sure it is well hidden. I don't want that falling into the wrong hands." The rest of the guys started shuffling and the three who were headed out first were quickly taking up their places in front of Ky, Mathius, and Aggie. Ren was lucky, or perhaps they just drew straws, and was standing in front of Aggie with his radiant smile.

"Care if I board the Aggie Express?" She was sure that was

an inuendo of its own sort but she didn't care. He was still her lighthearted shifter and she would accept him for who he was and appreciate that small aspect of his character and personality.

"I suppose, but only if you pay the toll." She was being cheeky and she knew it, but their time was short so she wasn't going to let it go. Slowly she puckered her lips, and when his connected with hers she sifted them using that simple connection. Skin to skin contact was all that was required to transport another being along with you. She just decided that this was going to be a different form of contact than normal.

They reappeared quickly, and Mathius with Mitchell, and Kyrel with Eldon, were standing beside them. They had chosen the same gathering place that they had met with the Elders. This time Ulnak was guarding the door with an unrelenting look of concentration. Aggie didn't know what he was waiting for, but he was clearly on edge. Felix was perched on a chair; for a flying shifter this was ironic, and he looked slightly silly for his size. He looked like he could take flight any second, but the room was covered by a stone roof and she wondered where he was planning to jet to. Tartan was standing in the corner, discussing something with a couple of the Elders who didn't look prepared to fight. Aggie wondered if they were only there for the protection that the three shifters garnered.

"Quickly go back and get the others, and we will plan our next move while you're gone." Mitchell was barking orders and Aggie thought in that moment it was the sexiest thing she had seen. He was truly in his element.

Aggie sifted back without a word and instantly was back deep within the cave. The remaining three Guardians were patiently awaiting their transportation. Mathius and Kyrel were there a moment later; Aggie assumed they waited for more information before disappearing back into the depths of the cave.

"Everyone is on red alert back there. We had better get back before anything else happens." Mathius had seen the same as she had, and she was relieved to have interpreted everything correctly. Being new to this world was definitely challenging when it came to picking up on certain social cues. She was glad that something was working if she was picking up on them in the correct context.

"Okay, who's with me then?" Aggie prompted, and Liel appeared before her. Little did she know this was a planned move by Gryson and Xavier. When she didn't move right away, Liel spoke.

"I'm ready and I can pay the toll as well." He puckered his lips and Aggie felt her own tug up at the sides. He must have heard her conversation with Ren, and now she wondered if Gryson and Xavier had put him up to it. She started to ask as much, but then thought better of it. If he was ready, then who was she to judge him? She leaned up on her toes and pressed a kiss to his lips. The feeling that exploded in her chest was unexpected. The Fae magic was swirling around her and she was a bit dizzy. It was enough that she lost her focus on where they were going and, much to her surprise, they didn't land inside the council building.

Her feet weren't on solid rock of the cave, but a softer squish of fresh dirt. The grass was unexpected, as the area around Pantal was mostly desert and dry land. When she opened her eyes Liel was there with her, but they were standing in a forest.

"Where are we?" Aggie whispered, but the look of panic on Liel's face wasn't reassuring.

CHAPTER TWENTY

$\mathcal{L}$iel had never looked panicked the entire time Aggie had known him. So now that he wasn't his calm, cool, and collected self she didn't know what to think. The only thing she knew was they weren't where they were supposed to be. The woods were quiet, save for a few animals that skittered and squeaked up high in the branches of the trees. They had to be quite a ways away from Pantal to see this much green life. Their first priority was to figure out where they were before anything else. Then find out what caused them to be derailed.

"I haven't the slightest idea where we are." Liel somehow kept his voice steady, and Aggie didn't know if he was calming down or hiding more of his emotions under a trained guise of having it all together.

"Well, I didn't bring us here on purpose. We need to figure it out, because I don't want to sift us back and be even further derailed in the process." Aggie was doubting her abilities, and that wasn't a good place for her to be at the moment. She needed confidence in her powers to make them work, and doubting herself wasn't going to get them anywhere. Then an idea clicked in her head.

Can any of you hear me? she projected through the link, in hopes that they weren't too far away to be heard.

Liel's eyes brightened, so she knew he heard her, and in his state of panic she guessed he hadn't thought of the link and the resource it presented. A few long moments passed and a faint sound bounced in her head.

Where are you? It was Mitchell who answered, but it was quickly followed by a cacophony of replies.

Aggie?

What is going on?

What happened?

Can't you get one thing right? She couldn't identify everything that was said; the few things that came through were a jumble, but the latter question was clearly Mitchell. He was the only one who would condemn her like that over one tiny slip-up. The rest would understand or create a justifiable reason for the mistake.

Her heart melted at the sound of their voices in her head. Even Mitchell's assholeish nature made her smile. *Be quiet, all of you. I can't hear you all at once and keep track of your voices and questions. Liel and I are fine physically, but we have no idea where we are or how we got here. I didn't sift in any way different than I have in the past or when I moved Ren moments ago.*

Well, I don't care where you are at this point. I want you both here. So sift again and get here now. Mitchell had taken charge over the conversation again and clearly was back in command mode.

Aggie agreed that they needed to get back, but she was nervous it would happen again.

"He is right, we need to get back. Do you want to give it another go and see if we can make it this time?" Liel's words rang true and she knew they were both right. She was just unsettled.

"Yeah, let's give it another go. But this time let's try it the traditional way." She grasped his hand and closed her eyes. She imagined every little detail of the council room. She had painted the picture in her mind in such detail she could have crawled around inside her own replica. The world moved around them and she knew they were traveling. Nothing felt different from normal, but when she opened her eyes they hadn't moved an inch. Something was keeping them there and Aggie worried it was her own insecurities.

"That didn't go quite as planned," Liel jested, and smiled to reassure her. She smiled back, but it didn't reach her eyes.

"What are we going to do now?" Aggie whined, and just wanted to fall into a heap on the ground and pout. She knew that would get them nowhere, but sometimes a girl just needed a good wallowing session.

Liel opened his eyes and met hers. Leaning forward, he pressed a kiss to the tip of her nose. Nothing romantic about it, and yet Aggie felt her insides twirl. He was reassuring her and, even though his own fear almost got the better of him when they first arrived, he was slowly coming back to himself.

Seems we have a bigger problem. Liel was the one speaking to the group, and this time he included Aggie so she could hear the conversation. *Aggie seems to have a block, or someone has figured out how to interfere with this part of her powers. Mathius, have you ever heard of someone who had the ability to block a demonic sift?*

It's not easily done, but there are ways to block a sift or redirect one. It takes a serious power pull, though. Whoever is doing it isn't going to be a shifter. Mathius' words scared Aggie. Someone was likely doing this to her, and if that was the case then who and why were the next questions that she needed answered. Unfortunately, the guys weren't likely going to be able to answer that.

Then I suggest the two of you find cover and start doing some recon. Someone wants you right where you are and you need to find out who. Mitchell's thoughts were sent to them both since they were all joined in the conversation. Aggie's stomach dropped at the idea of seeking out whomever was trapping them there.

We will stay in contact this way since we know it works at this distance. I had hoped we wouldn't have to use this and it was a mere safety precaution. Once you know something let us know. We will work toward getting things under control here and head back to Galata to prepare for the final attack. I want this battle fought on my terms. The passion that vibrated from Mitchell's words gave Aggie chills. This way of communicating was so much more intimate; she could almost feel his compulsion and that he truly meant what he was saying. He was tired of fighting this battle and would do whatever it took to end it now, once and for all.

Coming out of their mental conversation, Liel and Aggie shared a look. Aggie knew that between them they would keep each other safe. She was worried, though; if someone had tapped into her Demonic powers and essentially blocked her or took control over them, what was to stop them from doing the same with her other powers? Did that mean she didn't have the safety net of Izzy?

"Well, I suppose we should start scouting around and see what we can see." Liel jerked his head to indicate that he wanted her to follow him. Aggie wasn't ready to discuss what they had learned from Mathius. She needed to think about who all she knew who knew her and would have access to such powers.

Silently, she followed Liel between the trees and she used her new Vampiric powers to keep her footsteps light and silent. She was thankful that she had worked on honing those powers with Xavier the night before. Everywhere she looked, everything seemed to be just like any other forest. Grass and exceptionally tall trees grew up everywhere, and some of the paths were over-grown and riddled with vines and thorns. The animals she heard were in the distance, but none really made themselves known while they were walking. It was uncomfortably quiet where they were, and as they walked the sounds moved further away. It was as though the woods even knew the danger that lurked silently around them. That gave Aggie chills, and she stepped a little closer to Liel to ease her mind of the fear that was brewing.

"How do we know we're going the right way?" Aggie finally

asked, and hoped Liel didn't get offended at her question. She wasn't distrusting his abilities, but they could just be going on a blind chase and become further lost. She couldn't just sift, as they would probably end up right where they started from yet again.

"My people have a connection to the forest, similar to Eldon's Fae. The difference is we communicate on a separate plain, almost an opposite one. Whereas Eldon connects to the plants and nature around him, I connect to the sub-particles between them. So I can sense disturbances in the path that aren't natural. This is the path that was last used in these woods." Aggie had never heard Liel describe his powers in that way. It was almost scientific. "My people live in woods similar to this, but our realm sits between the one that others see naturally. You have to know where to look to find the Elven realm. It is all around you, and yet you might never touch it."

"That might be the most amazing thing I've ever heard. You never talk to me about things like this, and I feel like this is the most I've ever learned about you." Being alone with Liel, Aggie was feeling like it was easier to open up and be real with him.

"My people don't see ourselves as anything wonderful. We protect the woods and nature from a distance. We don't do it for gratification, but to protect our own realm by default. In a way, that makes us selfish in our own rights." Liel kept walking and following the invisible line that his powers allowed him to see. Aggie thought for a moment and wondered what it would be like to share his powers in any form. To see this trail that only Elves could see because it existed in another dimension. The thought was enough to give Aggie goosebumps.

Much sooner than Aggie expected, because she still didn't hear anything around them, they came to a clearing. Staying behind the brush line, they looked out into a camp. People were milling around, some tending to small fires and others preparing weapons by sharpening or cleaning. Aggie found it odd that a group of shifters, if that was what they were, would need so many weapons. Weren't they weapons in and of themselves?

"Do you think those are the rebels?" Aggie whispered, for fear of being overheard. She didn't know what powers she was dealing with but, if they were shifters or any of the other magical races, improved hearing would be a given.

"I'm not sure; some of them seem to be shifters, but not all of them. I find it odd that they would have aligned with any other races." Liel looked like he was looking through some kind of enhanced glasses, as he squinted slightly to see deeper and farther. "I count at least three different kinds of people down there. Shifter is the majority, but not the lone species. They must have figured out a way to bring others to their cause, and only controlling the Gateway in the shifter realm isn't the end of their plan." The thought sent a shiver through Aggie. She was the Gatekeeper, and her family had always protected the Gateway. Even now, with her limited knowledge of her role, she never felt like she was in control of it. More like she just was a bridge to keep things balanced. The Gateway protected her when it sensed danger or any unknown. Eckard was an unknown and it sealed off her life from him. Now these rebels, shifter and non-shifter alike, wanted to change that balance. That didn't sound like a wise plan.

"How do you know what they are from this far? I doubt you're smelling them like Mitchell and Ren would." Aggie followed his line of sight, out into the crowd of people camping out in the clearing. Liel's nose wasn't twitching, and that was her first clue there was something else at hand here.

"I can see their auras," Liel replied simply, as though it was no big feat. Aggie just stared at him in disbelief.

"Their auras? Seriously? Are you some sort of medium or psychic or something?" She was dumbfounded. He was acting like that was no big deal, and for him it probably wasn't, but for Aggie it was mindboggling.

"It's nothing," he downplayed, and Aggie was done. She was

tired of him not owning his amazing abilities. Prior to now she really had no idea what his skills were, other than resident information guru.

Grabbing his face, she made him look at her. "That isn't nothing!" she exclaimed in an effort to get her point across. "You tell me you can track people just by looking for a disturbance in the force, and now you can sense what they are by looking for them to glow in the dark? No one can do that, and it's extremely helpful. You sound like the best tracker I've ever met. You're better than the Indians, and they can pick up trails days old, but you can sense anything out of place." Not releasing his face, she waited for him to acknowledge what she was saying. Then she had an idea. Still holding on to him, she opened her link to him and pressed her feelings into him. She wanted him to know the awe she felt as to what he could do. Valued member of the team aside, this was truly an amazing skill.

She knew the moment it hit him because his eyes grew wide and the tops of his pointed ears tinged pink. His ears were a strong point, unlike Eldon's dulled, blunted point. They must have been related on some level of their race, but she would question that later. There were more pressing issues at hand.

"There are a few demons, some mages, many shifters, and what looks human, but there is something off about them." He was owning his powers now and had squared his shoulders. Aggie worried that before now he had felt like his powers were a lesser part of him. That thought process baffled her, but she let it go for now.

"What do you mean off?" She would have thought he understood his powers in a way for them not to be confusing even to him.

"I'm not sure; they are shining like humans, but from this distance it is like they are tinged slightly differently. It's a faint underlying color. Perhaps they are crossbreeds, but I don't know how they would have ended up here." Liel was focusing hard, but Aggie just redirected her attention to the group ahead of them. They were a few hundred feet away, and any attempt to approach them would have them seen. They would have to approach at night, but she didn't really want to do that with just the two of them. Then again, perhaps they could spy for their own side and get some information and recon done, giving them the upper hand.

"Can you hear anything they're saying from here?" She hoped they wouldn't have to traipse through the enemy camp to get anything from them.

"Not from this distance, since my hearing isn't as good as a shifter's. I can hear better than a human, but even this is too far for me." Liel's face fell, as though he had let her down. She instantly felt like she had kicked her favorite puppy, and her heart broke for him.

"No worries. We'll get through this. When night falls or at least at dusk, I'll use my new vampire powers and see if we can get anything we can use. If we're stuck here, we might as well use it to our advantage." Liel nodded somberly, and Aggie knew he was still feeling down and beating himself up about all of this.

Opening up the link between all the guys, she decided they could use their time wisely and relay what they had learned.

We've found the rebel camp but we still have no clue where we are. We might use our time before nightfall to figure that out, but not sure if it will be worth it. They seem to be in the middle of nowhere and we might not be close enough to anything identifying to figure it out. Aggie waited for anyone to respond, opening the link wide so everyone including Liel could share information.

Don't get yourself killed. Mitchell was always so encouraging and confident in her abilities. She really found it endearing. Well, almost.

Your confidence in my abilities should be higher, given the fact that you didn't even see me coming. She alluded to their interlude the previous night, but didn't give anything away.

No one saw you coming, Wee One. Even though Xavier knew what she was referring to and had excused himself from witnessing anything, he decided to take it back even further to her own coming out party. Well, not party, but that first meeting in the Gateway was quite the event.

Playing along she continued. *I'm a ninja at heart.*

Let's get back on track, Liel interrupted, and Aggie hoped he wasn't frustrated with the banter. Now was clearly not the time but, given the stress of the situation, a little was warranted to calm everyone's nerves. *It seems that we have encountered the rebels, yes, but there is more to that then meets the eye. Upon closer examination, they seem to be recruiting. I'm not sure about everyone, but there are shifters, as we all knew. In addition to that there are some mages, demons, and some kind of human crossbreed.* He let that all sink in, and he and Aggie just waited for a response.

I suppose those who were loyal to Yavari and whatever master she served could have been easily swayed to join this cause. Aggie could hear the betrayal in Mathius' tone even across the link. She could practically feel it herself. This link was a blessing and a curse. The underlying emotions were unable to be blocked once the link was open.

I can't imagine who would have wanted to follow her, with her child kidnapping tendencies. Surely people would have seen right through her crazy. Aggie's heart went out to the kids who were kidnapped. She had really fallen for the little girl, Raleigha. She was the sweetest thing and, thanks to Gryson, her spirit wasn't broken after the entire ordeal. Aggie hoped she would grow into the sassy, opinionated little demon that Aggie saw deep down inside her.

At least we have seen the threat from the demon realm and the shifter realm, but I'm baffled trying to figure out where the Mages came from. We haven't seen any kind of revolt or attacks in Tarlvey or the surrounding areas. Gryson sounded livid at the thought of anyone of his kind being a part of all this chaos. *No one has heard anything in the rumor mill either. Mother would have alerted me if anything had come up. Now I'm going to need to send a message back and get people digging into it.*

Learning this couldn't be easy for him, and Aggie wished she could comfort him in person.

Should we try and sift back to you and then figure out what the threat is here later? Would it be better to be together and prepare? Knowing they needed information, she wasn't sure if this was a good suggestion. However, on some level, she needed them to tell her to stay put in order to feel right about it.

No, there's a threat and we need to assess it. While I don't like it that you guys are there alone, we'll work with what we have. You two keep an eye on each other. You can each hold your own in a fight. I'm glad you've had some extra training recently. The pride and concern in Mathius' voice were warring with each other. She knew he preferred to keep her in a bubble, but it wasn't like she hadn't proven herself. Not to mention, she'd had an addition of powers since her first fight.

I'll protect her with my life. Liel's bolstered words were endearing, but that archaic attitude was where they were all falling victim.

You most certainly will not! I'm quite capable of holding my own and we'll protect each other. I appreciate the gesture but as I had hoped I made clear on numerous occasions, I don't want you guys dying for me. Imagine life after that. I would have to live with the fact that you died for me, and that if I weren't the one in danger you would still be alive. I will not have that on my conscience. She might have been speaking into the link and in her mind, but she put her hands on her hips and gave Liel a look that told him she meant business. She glowered at him and pursed her lips. She wanted him to feel and see her wrath.

We all know you are capable, but you have to understand that none of us could live without you, contrary to popular belief. So, given the choice between you and us, at least the others wouldn't die from a broken heart if one of us dies for you. I think we can all agree that none of us wants either to happen. So give us a little credit that, if it were a life or death situation, we would know the difference. Otherwise you are required to pull your own weight and defend us all the same. It took a lot for any of these guys to admit that a woman would be defending them, as it went against all of their Alpha tendencies. She could respect that and she felt a chorus of affirmations flood the link, and she knew they were all in agreement. She could give them that small allowance.

Deal. We can just hope for small mercies, that it's never a choice between you or me. I might just freak out and blow everyone up. She didn't even know if that were possible but, given her unpredictable aspects of her powers, the sheer emotional overload might just backfire and cause a catastrophic explosion. No one needed to experience that if it were the case.

Leaving the link open, a silence fell through the group. It seemed no one wanted to continue planning and no one wanted to be the one to sever the connection. Being so far apart from her mates and potential mates was almost painful. For once she was actually thankful for the worm in her head.

The waiting game was hard, and it seemed to take forever for nightfall to settle in. Aggie waited until the shadows were far and wide so she could have more areas to hide in. She was still new to this side of her power, but she knew she could fool a shifter if the situation arose, and silently thanked Mitchell for the practice.

I didn't give you practice knowingly, so I'm not sure I'm the one you should thank. Perhaps you cohort in crime? His words drifted over their link and she knew from the blank look on Liel's face that he had projected those to her and her alone. She chuckled softly to herself, but didn't reply to him. She needed to keep her head in the game, and the last thing she needed was to be distracted and get caught in the act of spying. She was channeling her inner Xavier and silently asked Izzy for all the help she could get. Her center warmed and she knew Izzy was awake and ready to go.

"Okay, you stay here while I go and dig up what I can. I'll keep my link open so you'll know if something is wrong. You can watch the hordes and warn me if someone is lurking where they shouldn't be or where I might stumble upon them." Aggie's stomach was in knots. She had trained with Xavier and tested her powers, but never in such a high-stress and important situation. If she had been caught previously it would have just been friendly banter or a slap on the wrist. Now it was her life at stake.

"You have my undivided attention, and I will be your backup. Should you get into trouble let me know and I will be by your side." Liel was loyal to a fault. He really would get himself captured if that's what it took so she wouldn't be alone.

"Let's hope it doesn't come to that." She patted him on the shoulder and leaned up and pressed a kiss to his cheek. It settled her stomach slightly, but not enough.

Then Liel stiffened and quickly wrapped an arm around her waist, tilting her chin with his free hand.

"You will be safe, regardless. You know what to do, and I will be your eyes where you can't see. Together we will get through this." To punctuate his words, he sealed his lips over hers and she molded to him. The small action helped her to relax and trust in them both.

You will be fine, Wee One. I know you can do this, and anyone who can outwit an Alpha shifter can handle a bunch of rogue asses who don't know which way is up or down. They don't have anything on you in this case. Xavier's words of encouragement sealed her fate. She was going to do this one way or another and prove Liel and Xavier right. She felt the confidence in his words and it bolstered her confidence.

"Let's get this show on the road." Aggie called her powers to her and stepped out of the cover of the wood and into the cover of the shadows. She felt them wrap around her, encasing her in darkness. They covered her completely, and it felt like a blanket wrapping around her in comfort and protection. She walked effortlessly and believed she was encased in the shadowy darkness.

The closer she got to the encampment, the stronger the voices became. One thing she wished her powers had lent her was the improved hearing of her mates. Unfortunately that was still on human level, and so she had to get even closer to make out individual words and not just murmurs.

Feet soft as a feather and quick as lightning, given her vampiric speed, she crept closer to the rebels' tents. It wasn't very late and they looked to be preparing for dinner. Like any good camp, they seemed to have a small group fixing something for everyone. That meant that soon everybody in the camp would be passing this tent. Aggie decided to take up residence in a small alcove around the edge of the tent. A small bush was nestled between the canvas of that and a neighboring tent. She tucked herself in beside it for added cover.

"The Master says we depart in the morning, but we are waiting for something. He won't say what." A voice trailed over to her from one of the cooks.

"How will we know when it arrives, if we don't know what it is?" A female voice this time.

"It doesn't matter to us. If you believe in the Master and his ways, then you won't question him," the man scolded, and Aggie winced at the sharpness of his words.

"I don't doubt him at all. I just want to know if we should be looking for the arrival of something. Not knowing makes me uneasy," she replied with a bit of sass. Aggie could understand her perspective. She wouldn't want to be caught unaware either.

"The army marches out tomorrow regardless. So I guess whatever's coming isn't our concern. The way the Master is speaking it sounds like whatever is coming will be a strong element in helping us win this war."

"Doesn't Dranton still need to fight Mitchell for Alpha rights? How could someone else help us with this war?" This female was throwing out valid points, but Aggie didn't know what they were.

Liel, can you tell me what these two are? I think understanding what everyone is will help me keep up with their conversations.

They are shifters, but the crowd approaching is mixed. So that is fair warning.

Turning back to the conversation, Aggie was right that knowing that they were shifters was important. They were following this 'Master', but they still kept up on shifter politics.

"Dranton's fight won't happen if there's a cluster of shifters rallying against us. It isn't time for a shifter transition, and therefore no one will sanction the fight for Alpha. They also won't accept Dranton if he wins the fight until it's sanctioned." The male shifter's voice was low, and had only enough pitch to make each word audible.

"We are strong in numbers, and we will win this war with or without this mysterious thing that is coming. Doesn't the Master have faith in our numbers?" The female was gruff and her voice was only slightly feminine. If Aggie hadn't caught a glimpse of her, she would have assumed it was another male that was speaking.

Soon the group of people Liel mentioned approached and the conversation died. She would have to wait and see if any others joined or started new conversations.

The murmur of the crowd was overwhelming and made it hard to pick up individual conversations. They were all louder when together and she struggled to pick out individual voices.

"Have you seen her yet?" A familiar voice broke through the crowd as it approached the tent. Aggie was stunned and wasn't sure she'd heard correctly.

"No. I have had scouts out all day to look for her, but no sightings as of yet," a softer male voice replied.

"We need to find her before we leave or we will lose the upper hand. They will do anything if we have her, even turn over the control to you even for a little while if they think it will free her." The familiar voice trailed on and she needed to see him in order to believe her ears. Unfortunately, if she moved to see him her cover would likely be blown.

"I don't need her to win that battle. Mitchell is weaker now that he has her around, that's for sure, but she isn't the only way in. The mere distraction alone would be enough. We don't even have to have her to prove we have her. Just being missing is enough. The Mages are blocking her powers since you provided the hair to connect to her. Now she is at our mercy regardless." The unfamiliar voice was cocky, and the fact that he thought he could take on Mitchell told Aggie this must be Dranton.

The attitude alone made her hate and distrust him. He actually thought that Mitchell could be distracted to the point of losing the most important fight of his life. He must not know Mitchell that well if that's what he thought.

"Aggie is the key. They will all lose themselves for her. She is their weakness, not their strength. They were stupid to have followed the prophecy and form a mate bond with her. Now they're all weakened because of her." Aggie didn't know if this were true, but she knew they all would bend over backwards to save her. They couldn't even train her anymore for fear of hurting her. This hit home, but what made matters worse was that the voice she was hearing belonged to Eckard Gnash, her father. The betrayal stung far more than the possibilities he was spewing.

Then it clicked what Dranton was saying: she was trapped because Eckard betrayed her and used her own DNA to help the Mages create a potion or spell that has trapped her and Liel in this foreign place. She didn't even know where they were.

She relayed all of this through the link and a chorus of 'dammit' and 'fuck' played on repeat back to her. All the guys were pissed, and she felt it radiating through their connection.

You need to get out of there. You are too close if they are looking to capture you. I can't have you and Liel separated if you don't even know where you are. Mitchell was playing protector and bossy asshole. That was a lot of hats to wear at once, but in this case Aggie agreed with him.

Now that I know what they've done, I'm working on a counter spell to track where you are. I'll have you out of there before they find you, but until then stay out of sight. Gryson was Mage royalty, so she had no doubt he would follow through on his words. His powers alone were a strong rival to however many Mages Eckard had on the payroll.

I never trusted that asshat. I will rip him apart if I ever get my hands on him. Mathius had never pretended to like Eckard. He would have killed him on day one if that had been an option, but Aggie had rose-colored glasses on back then. Now she was going to have to come to terms with the fact that the man behind all these attacks and apparently the ones in Ahael was none other than her father.

She reeled at the thought, and remembered he had wanted her to join him before he left. He wanted her to hone her powers over the Gateway. Was he trying to take control even then?

Enough, all of you. We have obviously been duped, but this isn't the end. I'll fall back to Liel and we'll keep to the shadows. I'll keep him from being spotted. Gryson, work fast. I don't know how long we can stay hidden. They're determined to find us and embark for Galata in the morning.

She didn't wait for anyone to respond; it wasn't necessary. Keeping out of sight and staying safe was the priority now. They were planning to use her as leverage against Mitchell and the rest of the guys. She wasn't having any part of that. If the guys could pinpoint where she was, Mathius could sift and pick them both up. Her powers might be blocked by her own DNA, but that didn't mean she couldn't tap into anyone else's. It was like being one hundred percent human again.

This was her new goal and priority. The rebels didn't know she had overheard them and, clearly, the last resort for them was to bluff with an ace in their pocket. Well, if they could cheat at this game, watching them crumble while calling their bluff would be priceless.

CHAPTER TWENTY-TWO

Aggie snuck away from the rebel camp, enjoying being the vampire ninja that she was. She sent a quick note of appreciation through the link to Xavier.

Wee One, I will teach you so many things when we have more time. I can't wait to spend some free time with you and let you experience all that it means to have vampiric powers.

She preened under his words and was thankful she had him. Thankful for all the guys who, until now, she'd taken for granted. They were always there and vying for attention at every turn. She worried they were only there for their connection and eventual pairing, but now that she was separated from them it was clear. They were just as anxious and worried as she was, and were actively trying to get her back. She could feel their emotions through the link and knew their true feelings. They wanted her, not just because of fate and what they were waiting for but because they wanted her for her. They longed for her to be close and keep her safe. They needed this to feel complete.

It didn't take her long in her distracted state to get back to where Liel was waiting. He embraced her as soon as he saw her, catching her off guard.

"Agatha, I could sense you but now that you are back with me and I can see and touch you the weight of guilt is off my stomach. I hated sending you in alone, even though it was the best way to gather information. I didn't like doing it." He breathed his words into her ear and she didn't know what to say. He didn't usually show affection outside of the time Ren and Ky had tricked him into being more so. This felt genuine and less forced. He really was worried about her, but he showed his trust by letting her go.

"I'm glad you let me do it, Liel." She never shortened his name in any way, mostly because he never shortened hers. It didn't feel right to give him a nickname when he seemed so keen on using her full name as almost his own nickname for her. It felt right when he did. "You guys keep me in such a small bubble, I worry you don't have faith that I can do the things my powers have now allowed or you've trained me to do. The fact that you trusted me enough to do that means more to me than you'll ever know."

"I believe in you, Agatha. I just have to train myself to let you do the things we know you are capable of. The thought of you getting hurt sours in my gut like bad wine. I don't ever want that for you." Aggie squeezed him back as a reply. She knew they struggled, but the fact that Liel was trying meant the world to her.

"We need to find food and cover. I haven't eaten since our snacks at the council in Pantal and I'm starving. I love being in Cratlian, but seriously, you guys haven't fed me enough. I feel like every time we get remotely settled there's an uproar and something dragging me away. I'm going to have keep a bag on me always with snacks to balance out the times when you guys are starving me." She winked at Liel to let him know she was kidding, but she really did need to eat more. She felt herself losing weight from the lack of chocolate and salty goodness she was used to having so readily available. Her stomach chose that moment to rumble its agreement.

Liel chuckled at her train of thought. "Only you would worry about your stomach at a time like this. We need cover of darkness and to cover our scent to hide from a massive battalion of shifter rebels. If we don't, we won't be rescued before they capture us and use us for leverage against our own people."

Aggie realized that she was being selfish and close-minded, but she didn't care. "I'm not saying we shouldn't hide, but along the way can we at least find some berries or something on a nearby bush? I just need a snack, or my stomach is going to give away our location regardless of how well we hide." Her sorry-not-sorry attitude was all she had left. She wasn't going to change her own personality just because their lives were on the line. That wasn't who she was and, in reality, they were either going to hide or be found. There was no in between for them. She was just being true to herself in the process. There was no sense in lying to herself or to Liel about their situation. He knew as well as she did what they were in for.

"All right, let's go find a place to hide and maybe some mud or something to help cover our scent. If you had your Elven side, I could pull you into the veil and we could hide there." He mumbled the last part and Aggie wondered if it was an afterthought or part of a dream he wished had happened. He never spoke of feelings before he wrapped her in a hug when she returned from her information gathering mission. Now he was sharing his what-ifs with her.

"Unfortunately, we don't have time for such activities." She hinted at the possibility of sexcapades and Liel turned back to her in surprise.

"Unfortunately?" he questioned, but left the question hanging.

"Surely you don't think I haven't thought about it with you or any of the guys." Aggie held her ground but kept walking as they talked, bypassing Liel's frozen form. She couldn't understand why he thought she hadn't considered it with them all. "I might have acted on urges with three of the eight of you, but it doesn't mean I haven't considered my position with you all." She cringed at her choice of words as Liel caught up with her and raised his eyebrow in question. Clearly, he'd picked up on her word choice as well. "I mean, where I stand." She emphasized the word 'stand' and glared at him a little. She wasn't mad, but he couldn't fault her for certain words when she was operating on a nearly empty stomach. Her thought process was split.

"I just never considered being a part of those thoughts. We hardly spoke before now, and the others seemed to garner more of your attention." He spoke honestly, obviously baring his heart. She never intended for him to feel left out, but they had a different relationship since she didn't know how to relate to him. The facts guy always had a detailed, analytical answer for any question.

"When you guys told me about your oath, I thought you were crazy. Now I have to realize that there's so much more to all of you than just fate sealing it for you. You've had to put your lives on the line, waiting around for me. Now I've asked you guys to wait longer while I get comfortable with the idea, but you've had countless years to come to terms with it yourselves." Aggie stopped and realized she was opening a wound inside herself that she wasn't planning to get into. "So, yeah, I've thought about you all," she ended simply.

"You deserve the right to process this at your own pace. I can't expect you to have the same feelings for us overnight. I'm willing to wait until the end of time for you to be ready." Liel's championing and chivalrous routine was extremely sexy. He wanted her safe and was willing to give her the time she needed. Those words were music to her ears. He followed her through the woods, by her side, matching her pace. Silence fell between them as they walked. She didn't know what to say to him, and he didn't seem to feel the need to talk as they explored the area.

Aggie saw dense trees and foliage everywhere. It was dark,

and she still didn't have the luxury of night vision. She really hoped that would be one of her powers to come. Her human vision had adjusted, and she could see better than before, but it wasn't perfect.

"Here," Liel snagged something off a nearby bush with a quick flick of his hand, "these berries are safe to eat. They might not fill your belly, but they will help."

Aggie reached out to take them and their fingers brushed. The more time she spent with him, the more her body reacted to these small touches. She couldn't make heads or tails of the timing, but she decided not to question it. He was here and they were alone. That probably had a lot to do with the way she was reacting. She would see what happened when they were back in a normal environment.

"Thank you." Pulling her hand back, she smelled the berries and the sweetness hit her nose. The smell was potent and she worried they were overripe, and another part of her brain realized that didn't matter. They would be super sweet and that was her favorite thing. Popping the first one into her mouth, she slowly bit down. The juices burst into her mouth, flooding it with flavor. She had never tasted anything like it. They didn't taste like any berries or fruit from home. Still sweet as she expected, but the flavor was so bold as it filled her entire mouth. Swallowing the first bite reluctantly, the flavor lasted on her tongue even after the berry was long gone. She only had a handful and wished they had time to pick enough that she could eat until she was miserable and sick.

"These berries are wonderful. I've never tasted anything like them! Do you know what they are called?" She glanced over at Liel as she placed another berry on her tongue. She did it slowly so she could avoid possibly dropping one of her precious snacks.

"I don't; let's ask Mitchell or Ren." She felt him open his thoughts as the question bounced into the inner world only her and her men were a part of. She silently, and to herself, thanked the powers that be that they had the forethought to make this connection to each other. Who knew they would have gotten separated, but it was good now in afterthought.

Those are parnical berries and they only grow in one place in Cratlian, Ren replied in their mental link, though he didn't say where.

Care to enlighten the rest of us? Aggie pressed as she opened her own link to connect with everyone. She loved the feeling of all of their emotions flooding her, though it was too overwhelming to leave open all the time. They were all in a panic, and worried about her being gone and so close to the enemy. They were all leaking it to varying degrees. It filled Aggie's heart and gave her a sense of relief to know they were concerned for her safety.

Oritan. The word came from Mitchell, and his tone sounded furious.

Doesn't that make it easier to rescue us? Aggie didn't understand why the location would make Mitchell go from worried to angry in a matter of a few seconds. She could feel it coming off him in waves even in his silence.

We know where you are, but not your exact location. I would have to be able to know how far away you are from a particular landmark and hope it isn't guarded before we could just come and get you. Until Gryson breaks the spell grounding you and severing any location blocking magic they have in place, Mitchell clarified, but still didn't explain his anger.

I've been trying to scry for you in between breaking the spell, but you are blocked from me seeing you. Whoever they have on their side thought far enough ahead and even closed the back door option. Aggie couldn't help snickering, and she noted Ren struggled as well, but she covered it better than he did.

Back door? I really wanted to get in the back door. He snickered through his words, and Aggie couldn't help but join him.

Not the time, brother. We have bigger problems at hand. That city is the closest city to the west of Galata. Liel has already pinpointed demons, so that means they will be able to get to us quicker than we originally thought. Our time is dwindling and we still have no idea where they are. I also don't like that they have been hiding basically in my backyard. Aggie felt pain radiate through the link, coming from Mitchell.

What just happened? she asked the group. There should be no reason for Mitchell to be in pain. He hid his emotions normally but couldn't hide anything from her through the link. Something else none of them probably considered before agreeing to it. Then again, the connection was more important than their secrets.

Mitchell just punched the wall. It wasn't very forgiving, but I imagine that the local carpenter, Trenton, won't be thrilled to need to repair it. Aggie winced at Ren's words. Mitchell was always volatile, but this was still a lot.

You'd better not hurt yourself before all this starts. You'll have to fight Dranton before this will all end. I need you at your best or else he'll have the upper hand. I'm not losing this fight because you decided to lose your temper, Aggie scolded, and put enough fire into her words that he felt them rather than just heard them. She wanted to be clear that she wasn't going to have any tantrums in the heat of their turmoil.

Princess, you don't have to worry about this. It is just a scratch and will heal over in a few minutes. Mitchell's words were deep and dark. Like he was lording over her even in her thoughts. *Dranton is the lesser in this match-up, you and I both know it. I don't need to prove that to you.*

Regardless, you don't need to throw a tantrum just because he had the upper hand for a little while and was able to keep them hidden. Now, what do you need from us for you to find us? Gryson, can you bring your supplies along and finish breaking the enchantment on me? I feel like we'll all be in better moods if we're together and have more manpower, in case they find us before Gryson succeeds. Aggie also would just feel better having everyone close by rather than spread between here and there.

I can bring everything with me, but there is always a chance that the enemy is camped out where we want to meet. Gryson had to point out the obvious.

Yes, but we can't exactly just say, 'Hey, we're over here by this parnical bush' now, can we? Aggie wasn't in the mood for obvious, but what else was she to do? They needed to come up with a solution.

We can't sift anywhere unknown, Mathius reminded, and Aggie felt his own disappointment with his own abilities. They had to figure out a way to get there. They were originally just going to focus on Aggie and, with their connection and being Mathius' mate, it should have worked. Now, without knowing exactly where she was, they couldn't sift safely. They might end up in Timbuktu.

Then Gryson will just have to crack the code and you guys will be able to find us. The priority is safe travel, and Liel and I will be safe until you get here. I know that in my heart. We'll find a place to hide and stay there. Then, she added as an afterthought, *Oh, but when you do get it sorted, can one of you pack a snack bag for me? I'd hate to be stuck anywhere else without the option of food.* Aggie's stomach growled and she ate another berry. They were a find placeholder, but wouldn't sustain her for very long. They guys all shared a laugh and she was thankful she could lighten the mood for a moment. They all knew about her obsession with food and didn't even question her for a second.

They walked a little further and Aggie could hear the faint trickle of water in the distance. "Do you hear that?" She glanced at Liel hopefully.

"Yes, I imagine that is the River Wyntra. We saw it by Galata on our way into Cratlian. It is likely just a few more yards ahead of us." Aggie wanted to run to reach it.

"Is it safe to drink?" Not that she was actively thirsty, but if she was hungry then she probably should drink something, too.

"Yes, it is, but I was thinking it might provide another resource for us." Liel was being vague as they walked. Aggie was still surprised they hadn't happened upon any of the rebels who were supposed to be looking for them. In some part of her brain she wondered if they were actually looking, or they had just told her father that to appease him. Perhaps they had so much faith in their mages that they didn't consider that they could fail. She let that thought slip into Liel's mind and he looked to be considering it.

"That is possible, but we should still find cover. If they are looking, we can step into the water and wash away any scent we might be leaving behind. At least it isn't the cold season. A little dampness won't kill us, and we can travel by river. If what Mitchell and Ren say is true, we can head East up river and at least be a little closer to Galata. Even if we have to walk, we at least know which direction to travel." Aggie beamed at the thought that he gave her idea merit. While it was a little thing, she was thankful they were giving her ideas credence. In a situation like this it wasn't like her normal barking orders about what they should do. This was a hypothetical situation that he thought was valid.

"I'm glad I can swim. How deep do you think it is?" Aggie wasn't worried about drowning, but more of exhaustion. With her powers blocked she couldn't tap into them to boost herself. That and now that she thought about it, she hadn't felt Izzy since before the sift.

"It shouldn't be too deep, we should be able to walk most of the way, but wade in deeper if we need to hide." That gave Aggie a bit of relief. She wasn't used to these conditions and didn't want to wear herself out too quickly.

"Well, let's get to it so we can have a bit of cover." Aggie increased her pace in the direction of the sound. When the beautiful purple river came into view, she sighed in relief. It wasn't just the beauty, but what it represented. Freedom. Home. Getting back to her guys. All things she desperately wanted more than anything.

Dipping her toes into the water, she stepped in slowly. The current wasn't moving too fast, but it was there enough to give her pause. She reached down and cupped some water. Taking a drink, the cool liquid slipped down her throat. She realized then it was dryer than she had originally thought.

"Oh, that tastes almost sweet. I never imagined a river could taste this way." Gathering more into her hands, she gulped down another mouthful.

Liel did the same. "It is the magic that runs through it. The magic that sustains each place it touches. The villages are blessed, if only to see it from their lands. Some are too far out to truly benefit, but they transport it back and forth."

They both walked deeper into the water, and the fact that it flowed uphill was astonishing to Aggie. She couldn't fathom how it did that; it could only be described as magic. The water flowed past her as she waded in deeper, and when the water reached their knees Liel encouraged them to begin walking with the current.

"This is the way we need to go. I'm not sure exactly how far we have to go, but at least we will be headed in the right direction. When they break whatever is blocking you, we will at least be in less danger when they come and grab us." Liel grasped her hand as they walked. Aggie chalked it up to the fact that he was just helping her balance. Then, after they walked for some time, his thumb began stroking the back of her hand slowly. She chose not to acknowledge it, and instead she just enjoyed the feeling of him letting his guard down.

A twig snapped in the woods that they had come out of. They had walked for a while but hadn't escaped the woods yet. Aggie stiffened and Liel tugged her hand as they froze. The water was all she could hear—no more movement from the woods. Her heart was beating so fast she was sure Liel could hear it next to her. If it continued it would beat right out of her chest. She couldn't fight what she couldn't see, and if there was a threat it was still in the shadows. Thankfully the darkness worked to their advantage and they didn't have to hide much just yet. Though Liel pulled her to her knees as they crouched into the water.

Another crack sounded and they knew someone was out there. The distance was hard to judge because things always seemed louder in the dark. Though it did seem rather close. Aggie crouched lower into the water until only her head was above the surface. Liel was still crouched at his knees, looking like he was ready to pounce on any hidden threat.

The footsteps, now not hidden the same way, grew closer. Aggie knew that they would be seen in mere moments if they remained, and she knew they couldn't submerge themselves for long and not draw attention to themselves eventually. In a last-ditch effort, she sent out a thought to all the guys.

Someone is here. We're going to be found.

CHAPTER TWENTY-THREE

Suddenly, as though a mirage, Kyrel and Mathius were standing with them in the water. Aggie gasped at their sudden arrival.

"You're here," she whispered, the words tumbling from her. She wanted to leap from the water and embrace them both. Then her situation came back to her and she held her ground.

Kyrel placed a finger to his lips as he gripped her arm and pulled her to him. She came up from the water silently as he lifted her slowly out of the water. Mathius gripped Liel's arm closest to him. In the blink of an eye, they were gone. When Aggie's vision came clear they were standing in Mitchell and Ren's cabin, surrounded by everyone.

"Aggie!" they all cried out at once in relief. She was so happy to see them all, she felt the tears escape before she sobbed loudly. Kyrel still had her wrapped up as he indulged himself and hugged her deeply, pressing a kiss to her ear. She continued to cry out her happiness to be home with her guys. She realized in that moment that it didn't matter where they were. As long as they were together, she would be home.

"Thank you," she whispered into Kyrel's neck. Her tears were still falling but she had grown quiet. Her thoughts were so jumbled and she couldn't sort through her feelings. Then she quickly glanced around and saw Liel safe and sound, just like her.

"When you called out, I pushed everything I had left into the spell and it just snapped," Gryson said softly. He sounded exhausted and Aggie knew he had indeed used all he had in order to save them. She gathered up all the strength she had and shuffled over to him. Throwing her arms around him, her lips met his softly but passionately. She poured every bit of emotion she was feeling into that kiss. She wanted him to feel it all and know that she would be forever grateful for everything he'd done.

"I'm glad you did. I wasn't sure how much longer we had but I knew, as close as they were, we couldn't hide ourselves any better." Aggie spoke to the room but didn't completely let go of Gryson. She needed a connection to him, or at least one of the guys in that moment.

"They weren't following our scent like I imagined, and I wish I knew what they were doing. They came back on us too quickly and I didn't know how else to hide us." Liel's words were spoken in defeat. Aggie felt bad that he felt like he had no control in that situation. They were both in danger, and there wasn't anything either of them could do.

"All that matters now is that you're home, the spell is broken, and they have no control over you." Mathius' gruff words were filled with emotion. They all were on the edge of their control.

"I am just happy we're back in one place." Eldon's lyrical voice was just the music Aggie needed. She breathed out all the tension that she was holding on to and sagged into Gryson. Eldon reached out and pulled her to him, essentially stealing her from Gryson, though Gry didn't stop him. He understood what Aggie meant to each of them. Eldon wrapped her up and held her tightly. It was as though he were afraid she would escape or be stolen again if he let go. Then again, the last time was right under everyone's nose. So his fears were warranted.

Soon she felt a pull from the other side, and she looked up. Ren stood there. She went to him willingly and Eldon released her without complaint. They were all acting like a fluid being, passing her through the ranks. Each one getting their fill and relaxing at the touch. Like they each needed to feel her to let their bodies know she was real.

Then came Mitchell, the one she knew had feelings but never showed them. To her surprise, he actually pulled her to him and tucked her head under his chin. Leaning his head so his cheek rested on the top of her head he inhaled deeply, taking in her scent slowly, one second at a time. As he exhaled, the tension fled from his muscles with each passing moment. Then, as suddenly as it began, Mitchell ended it, pulling away from her and letting his brutish nature take over.

"Now we have a war to prepare for, and we all could use a good night's sleep. I'll have Ulnak keep watch over the encampment. If anyone gets close, he will alert me." Dismissing them all with his words, they all slowly started for the door.

Mathius, who had a short welcome for her, stepped up behind her and draped his arm around her neck. "I don't know about you but I'm wound pretty tight and could use some help relaxing. I bet someone else could use the break, too, as he has worked extra hard tonight." She followed his gaze to an exhausted Gryson. Aggie then remembered they'd had plans before this all happened, and wondered if Gryson even had the energy to do anything but sleep.

When Gryson met their gazes alternately, he must have gotten the idea. "I might have leaked that thought to him," Mathius clarified, and Aggie remembered they were all connected. She just hoped she could keep the link closed under such extreme circumstances.

The three met in Mathius' room. Aggie hadn't been in this cabin and was surprised that, while it looked just like hers, Mathius had put his own twist on things. She realized that he had everything they needed already prepared.

"Did you get bored while waiting for Gryson to free me?" Aggie grinned at him, knowing he was going into dominant mode and she was poking the bear.

Smiling wickedly, he replied, "No, Dearie, you must have forgotten that we had made plans before to tango together." This was the first time Mathius had called her anything other than Aggie, and the nickname dripped from his lips in a dark way that made Aggie's panties wet.

"I hadn't forgotten, but I didn't know you would go to so much trouble. Where should we start, Sir?" Aggie fell into her role seamlessly and was thankful he hadn't punished her for her cheekiness.

"I want you both on the bed. Though I think Gryson will be getting the attention first, seeing as he has had the most stress tonight. He can lie back and enjoy. Don't you think?" Aggie nodded and climbed up on the bed. "Aggie, do you think you could undress him while I prepare a little something special for him?" Aggie's eyes grew wide, but she was more than up for the task at hand. No answer was needed as she got to work on her given job.

She reached for his shirt. The buttons were already half undone, showing how stressed he had been trying to free her. As she undid the buttons further, she pressed a kiss to the exposed skin as each inch came into view. Gryson reached his hands up and cupped her face. They continued like this until she had his shirt fully open. She ran her hands up his stomach and chest, pausing to pinch his nipples because she knew how much he enjoyed it, and he moaned his pleasure.

"I don't believe I asked you to tease him but, seeing how responsive he is, I rather enjoy hearing him. I think I'll let you continue." Mathius reached over and pinched the nipple closest to him. Gryson cried out because he pinched it hard. His erection was now visible in his slacks and Aggie glanced at it and then to Mathius, silently asking for permission, and he nodded. She reached her hand down and flattened it on his tented pants, pressing down slightly and tightening her grip as she brushed it. She worked her way up and reached the clasp holding his pants shut and flicked it open. She was thankful he hadn't had on his normal belt, as that would have slowed her down.

Mathius pushed Gryson's shirt from his body and off his shoulders, leaving him bare from the waist up. Then he leaned down and pressed his lips to Gryson's and kissed him soundly. His tongue lunged powerfully into Gry's mouth and they tousled and battled each other. She could see Mathius' enlarged cock press against his jeans and knew it was uncomfortable. She also knew he wouldn't release it yet. He enjoyed being in control, and he would only bare himself when he was good and ready. They kissed for a while and Gryson's hands found Mathius' hair. Mathius followed suit. His hands gripped tightly in Gry's hair and he arched into Mathius, groaning through their sealed lips.

Aggie was so engrossed in watching that kiss she had forgotten she was supposed to be undressing Gryson. Blinking back to reality, she resumed her task and knew that their display was the hottest thing she had ever seen and that her panties were ruined.

She slipped his zipper down as Mathius broke the kiss. Gryson whimpered his disappointment.

"Enough of that; you will get everything you need and deserve tonight and Aggie will be helping me. Then you will get to watch me pleasure her before I let you have your way with her." Gryson's eyes lit up and Aggie was intrigued. "Does that plan work for you, Dearie?"

"I think that is a wonderful idea, Sir." Aggie reached in and palmed Gryson's cock beneath his underwear. She squeezed it firmly, causing him to flex his hips and pump up towards her. "I think he likes the idea, too." She leaned down and flicked her tongue, catching the bead of cum there, and purred her pleasure as Gryson groaned. He knew she was teasing and that it would be a while before Mathius allowed him a release. She ran her fingers beneath the edge of his pants and underwear before gripping and ripping them down his legs, exposing him to the room.

"Hmmm, yes, I think that will do nicely." Mathius openly gazed at Gryson's cock's standing salute to them both. He reached forward and stroked it, and a growl could be heard under his breath. Then he reached up and captured Gryson's right wrist, and in a flash had him strapped to the headboard. Quickly repeating the motion, it didn't take long for Gryson to be completely tied to the bed. Though his legs were free, Mathius didn't seem worried about that much. He rubbed the front of Gryson's chest. "You want me to pleasure you or Aggie first?" He pinched another nipple and, to Aggie's surprise, in his hand was a tiny little clamp. "You are so responsive to this, I want to push your limits." His hand brushed over the other side and in his hands appeared another clamp. He attached them both at the same time and Gryson arched hard and cried out at the sensation.

Aggie watched the two interact, and she could see as Gryson settled into the pain and moaned as Mathius flicked and rubbed his nipples. "I want to see Aggie," Gryson managed to say through his torture, even though he seemed to enjoy every minute of it.

"Oh, do you, now? Is that because you can't handle this?" He pressed one of the clamps down harder and Gryson cried out, but when Mathius soothed it with his tongue Gry's cries turned to pleasure-filled moans and he pulled at his restraints. Clearly he wanted to participate but couldn't. Aggie took that opportunity to divest him of the rest of his clothes and took off his socks and pants in one last pull. Naked. He was stark naked and Aggie was as turned on as ever, watching Mathius lick and lap at Gry's skin. They were both enjoying the moment and Aggie was enjoying the show.

"I just need to see more skin, and not only my own," Gryson squeaked out, and Aggie began to pull her top over her head. A willing sacrifice to them both. She wanted anything and everything they planned to do to her. She stood from the bed and lowered her pants slowly. Not the best striptease, but still more than just getting ready for bed.

When she had nothing on but her bra and panties, she decided to tempt them both a bit. She reached down and stroked her folds slowly. She wet her lips with her tongue and then drew in her bottom lip and nipped it lightly with her teeth. Pulling the fabric of her panties to the side, she wanted one of them to have to remove them along with her bra. She then wet her fingers with her own juices.

"She seems to be ahead of us wouldn't you say, my friend? Should we let her get away with teasing us?" Gryson shook his head, as Mathius was stroking his cock now and he was fighting against the pleasure. He didn't want to come unless he was sheathed inside of Aggie, or Mathius. At this point either would do, but he didn't want to find his release at the hands of anyone. He let that thought go to the two of them and Aggie's eyes shot up in response. A slow smile spread across Mathius' face and it was a little sign of his darker side.

"I..." Aggie started, but before she could get the words out Mathius was on her.

"I think you deserve to be punished for trying to get ahead of me." His words were a growl and she was captured by his hands. Locked in his grip she couldn't move, but he left her hands on her pussy, and with his own he flicked her nub sharply. She cried out and then moaned. The sensations were in contrast with each other. Then in a flash, she was face down on the bed, still trapped but now between the bed and Mathius from behind. His massive cock was pressed against her ass and he pumped it once for good measure. "You will feel this here tonight." His promise struck her with fear and arousal. She knew how large he was, and he had hinted at venturing there before, but she still had yet to experience it.

A sharp smack to said ass brought her back out of her thoughts. The slap was followed by his hand soothing the stings softly. "Thank you, Sir," she replied as he reached for something on the bedside table. From her vantage point she couldn't see what it was, but she heard him slide it off the table and take it in his hand.

He pulled her panties down just enough to expose her ass; she felt the leather fingers against her ass, and the sting was worse than before. Crying out she looked at Gryson whose excitement was clear between his legs, and his eyes were shining. He not only enjoyed receiving but was enjoying her being in the same boat. "I think you both look perfect. Gy, my brother, you all tied up and clamped? I considered putting something on your dick to entrap you. Would you like that?" He looked confused, as though he had never considered such a thing. "Aggie, you want me to constrict him further. It will be harder to put it on him, as he will need to be softer. Do you think you are up to the challenge?" Mathius didn't let up on the pressure trapping her to the bed, but then she realized he wanted her mouth on Gryson's cock. She remembered he was fighting his release because he wanted to be inside her but, then again, he would be inside her mouth. She nodded her agreement.

Mathius let up on her slightly but, when her hands moved to climb up on the bed, Mathius captured them. "I think you have too much freedom." With that she felt a soft rope wrap around her wrists behind her back. He was fast because it only took him seconds to tie her into submission. She was still not allowed to stand, but Mathius lifted her by her bound arms and settled her between Gryson's legs.

She lowered her mouth to his standing erection and licked him slowly from shaft to tip. Then she flicked her tongue over the hole, nipping at it lightly with her teeth. Then she surrounded him with her mouth and began to suck and pump, tangling her tongue around the shaft and focusing on the throbbing vein. His legs wrapped tightly around her and held her head in place, but that didn't stop her. She sucked harder and flattened her tongue to the vein and pressed firmly.

"No, no, you forget who is in control tonight. It isn't either of you." Aggie feared she had done something wrong and braced for punishment. When none came she was surprised, but soon Gryson's legs were pulled away and pulled toward each corner of the bed. Aggie leaned back on her legs to watch. Mathius, with one hand on each leg, snapped him into cuffs that were affixed to the footboard. "Now you won't be able to interfere with Aggie's mouth. She will bring you to your release. Don't worry, though, I'll happily get you back hard again myself, when the time is right." Aggie saw Gryson's cock twitch in excitement at Mathius' words. She realized just then that the kiss was only the beginning. Mathius and Gryson were both totally into this, and that turned her on even more. Falling back to her face she happily took his cock again and pumped and licked and teased it until, not long after, he was shooting his hot release into the back of her throat as he came with a yell.

"Very good, Dearie. Now, would you let me do the honors?" Mathius had a small metal device in his hand. "Or do you want to try?" He saw her eye it with intrigue. It was metal and she could manipulate it without touching it. This would be fun. She nodded and focused on the material.

It floated in the air toward Gryson's not exactly deflated cock; it still was full, but not standing at complete attention. That was okay because she could reshape this if need be to fit him. She purposely didn't focus on warming the metal; she wanted it to be cold when it touched him. She wasn't disappointed by his reaction. The temperature of the metal caused him to flinch immediately upon touch. Wrapping the metal around his cock, she fixed it in place; she had never seen a cockhold in person but she knew how it worked. He wouldn't be able to go fully erect until it was taken off. He would press against it from the inside as his body warred with what it knew to be true. Worse than being pressed against a pair of rough jeans, this metal wouldn't give an inch. As she clicked the lock in place, Mathius pinched both his clamps harder and pressed another sexy kiss to Gryson's lips. Aggie wished there was a way for them all to feel that attention at once.

Mathius broke the kiss that kept Aggie turned on and then some. "Now then, Aggie, you have been a good girl. I think it is your turn. Though I think you need a little encouragement as well. I plan to take your ass tonight, but I know it isn't ready. So, I will prepare you slowly." He reached into the drawer of his bedside table and pulled out something. Aggie recognized it immediately and was impressed by the size. She had never seen a butt plug that large or shaped quite like that before. "We will work this in slowly, but as we work over the rest of you, your body will have time to adjust to this." It was shaped like the tip of three dicks, each one stopped and tapered off into its own place to cause it to hold in place by her tightened hole. The girth was the size to match Mathius's own cock. "The was molded after me. So I know if you can take this you can take me." His words sent chills through Aggie and her nipples puckered beneath her bra.

"I will do my best," she swore to him, but underneath it she was still a little nervous.

"Excuse me?" Aggie realized her blunder quickly and covered for herself.

"Sir. I will do my best, Sir."

"That's better, now let's get rid of these offending clothes. I'm disappointed you left them on in the first place." Mathius flicked the clasp of her bra and lowered the straps down her arms. Though her hands were still tied, that didn't stop him. He just ripped the thin fabric of the straps. "It's a good thing we can just make you more clothes. Although seeing you run around without a bra under your shirt wouldn't make me sad. I doubt anyone else would feel upset either, would you?" His question was sent to Gryson.

"Not in the least bit. I'd be happy if she didn't have to wear clothes at all." Mathius grinned at Gryson's statement and nodded.

"I agree with you there, brother. Now do me a favor and suck on her tits, while I prep her from behind. We have much to do tonight and I would like to get started." He pushed her up over Gryson's chest and she tumbled because her hands were bound. He pushed her up by her ass until she fell onto Gryson's face. Her ass remained in the air as she used her legs to hold herself up. Gryson didn't waste any time getting to work on her breasts as he licked and circled her nipples, and she moaned as he sucked it into his mouth, flicking his tongue on the taught bead, but then bit down unexpectedly causing her to cry out. He quickly soothed the area and moved to her other one, giving them both equal amounts of attention.

Mathius squeezed some lube into his hand and rubbed it together. She mentally thanked him for warming it before touching it to her skin. He rubbed it on her tight hole and she reacted on impulse, flexing. "Calm down; I'll take it slow, but once we get it in I'm going to fuck your pussy hard." He said the words so calmly, as though they meant nothing to him. "Then you will be ready for when we both enter you and fuck you senseless." The mental picture of all the things he was proposing was almost enough to send her over the edge. Then Mathius pressed his thumb to her tight sphincter. Gryson leaned up and kissed her lips, distracting her from the pressing to her hole.

Mathius worked her softly, only pressing in a little way before pulling back out. Each time he was able to get in a little further. After a few pumps he fully sheathed his thumb and continued pumping and twisting inside her, causing her to moan.

"See, I knew you would enjoy that. Now for a little more." He pressed his index finger in slowly beside his thumb and soon he had his thumb and three fingers inside her. "Now I think you're ready for the next step." Aggie's thoughts flashed to that plug and she panicked. He hadn't pulled his fingers from her, so he felt her tense. "Relax, trust me." Then he pulled his fingers out and lifted her by her arms.

"What are you doing?" Aggie looked around as he lifted her upright and began shifting her forward further.

"Not that I like it when you question me," he popped her once on the bare skin of her ass enough to sting, and she was sure he left a hand print, "but I want Gryson to eat your pussy while we continue. I think you need a bigger distraction."

"It would be my pleasure." Gryson's eyes lit with excitement at the mere thought of it.

Mathius lifted her up and placed her firmly onto Gryson's face. "You two do look sexy in that position." Aggie heard him release his belt. She looked back over her shoulder; the man who prided himself on control was reaching into his pants and lifting his cock into view. He stroked it as he watched them. Gryson didn't waste any time as he licked her nub, causing her to flinch with the sensation. No one had touched it that night since Mathius flicked it. Neglected and fully aroused was not a place she enjoyed being. He plunged his tongue deeply into her and she wished their hands were free so she could enjoy more than his tongue. Mathius moaned as he stroked himself, enjoying the show they were putting on for him. Then he climbed back onto the bed and straddled Gryson's legs to get to her. His cock fell between Gryson's legs, since he left it out and exposed, though he didn't remove his pants all the way. Aggie glanced over her shoulder and turned slightly, just in time to see Mathius stroke his cock over Gryson's leg and then against the metal of the restraint. Gryson moaned into her pussy and she felt the vibration all the way through her. It was magical.

Not long after, she felt Mathius' hand on her ass. She was too far gone at this point to care as he pressed the tip of the plug, or actually his other cock, to her lubed-up star. Slowly and steadily he pressed it until it popped inside her. Locked in place, he released it and she heard the clink of the metal restraint around Gryson's cock. Mathius was releasing him.

"Don't you dare stop what either of you are doing," he growled as the metal of the cockhold hit the floor. Aggie's ass was full. Gryson was pleasuring her with his mouth and wonderfully talented tongue. She couldn't see what Mathius was doing, though.

Gryson moaned and a smack of Mathius' mouth echoed through the room as Mathius let Gryson's cock pop from his mouth. He was fulfilling a promise he had made and was helping Gryson get fully hard. Aggie was enjoying her own pleasure but the sounds of Gryson and Mathius were pushing her closer and heightening her experience. She had never been in the same room as two men, but this was now her most favorite experience. Mathius growled and the vibration made Gryson shoot upwards, but his restraints on his hands and legs kept him down. Then Mathius reached up and pushed her plug in one more round and it popped securely into place again.

Gryson worked her faster and faster in rhythm with Mathius' mouth on his own cock. Aggie moaned and cried out and soon found her release loudly, as Mathius reached up and sheathed the plug all the way into her ass, causing her to come again instantly.

Riding the waves down, Gryson licked her one last time. "That was delicious, Para Praesetes. I could live off that if you would let me."

"I agree, and now I have something for you as well now that I've released you. One last thing to seal our evening." Mathius pulled a much smaller butt plug from the drawer, but it was still good sized. "I want you to wear this while you fuck Aggie. Though I have work to do on her first." It was posed as a statement but not an order. Aggie didn't know if these guys had done this with each other or anyone else before, and didn't know Gryson's experience level. Though one look into his eyes told her he was excited.

"Does this mean…?" Gryson began, but didn't finish.

"Yes, if you'd like. I will fuck you as well, but only before you come into our dear Aggie. I want her to feel us both first." Mathius' eyes flared at the idea and that wicked smile broke out on his face again.

"I think that would be perfect." Gryson leaned his head back and sighed. Even though he hadn't found his release, the mere idea of having Aggie to fuck and Mathius fuck him was enough to send him somewhere else. He allowed Mathius to insert the plug without much effort, surprising her how well he took that and leading her to believe it wasn't his first time.

"Now, Aggie, you need to come here and ride my cock." He leaned back at the other end of the bed and kept his legs over Gryson's so they were all still connected. She turned awkwardly and realized that movement with her ass plugged up was challenging but not impossible. She moved slowly, and soon she was straddling Mathius and his enormous cock. Gryson was a tad smaller than him so this would definitely push her to her breaking point.

Mathius didn't touch her, and instead allowed her to move at her own pace as she lowered herself onto his throbbing cock. She was so full she could feel him pulsing inside her as she sheathed herself over him. When she was fully seated, she let out a breath she didn't know she was holding.

"Now ride me for a while to get used to it. Then you are mine and I will fuck you senseless. Then maybe I'll switch it up and give you a break to watch me and Gryson fuck." Gryson's breath caught and Aggie smiled at the thought. She would love that. One day she hoped they would all three fuck, with Gryson in the middle. It was a perfect picture as she imagined another round with the two of them, even before this one was finished.

She rode him slowly at first and allowed her body to stretch to fit. She was so full between the cock in her pussy and the plug in her ass. It was a new sensation, but she didn't hate it.

Without warning, Mathius caught her up and flipped her back. Her hair splayed across Gryson's chest. "Now, isn't that a picture," was all he said before he started to pump in and out of her so fast she didn't know what hit her. The feeling of her ass being full and the plug hitting that small layer and meeting the cock in her pussy with every movement was all too much, and she had just come from Gryson's magical mouth. There was no warning as it crept up and she exploded, seeing lights, flooding over Mathius' cock. It was amazing. He let her enjoy it for a minute before pulling out of her.

"Now what do you say, Gry. Let's put on a show for her while she prepares herself for us both. Think you can manage and hold out for her? I know you've wanted this for a while." The last part was spoken softly and seductively. If Aggie didn't know better, she would have said he was toying with Gryson. He leaned forward and she slid from Gryson's crotch to the foot of the bed. Mathius kissed Gryson passionately; a lesser woman would have been jealous, but Mathius opened his eyes at her and winked knowingly. She smiled encouragingly.

He released Gryson's arms and nodded to his feet. Aggie released them as well. Gryson rubbed his wrists to adjust the circulation but Mathius didn't give him long. He pushed him forward. "On your knees. I want you to be able to watch Aggie's face and see how much this will turn her on," Mathius said knowingly.

Slowly Gryson got to his knees and bent down slightly, offering up his ass to Mathius. Slowly, Mathius removed the plug and Gryson groaned his pleasure as it was backed out. Quickly, Mathius replaced it with the tip of his cock as he slid into Gryson.

Gryson opened his mouth slightly at the intrusion and groaned as Mathius filled him. "That feels amazing!" Gryson's words were full of approval and pleasure.

With a swift hand, Mathius slapped his ass hard. Aggie watched it and her eyes lit up. She knew that feeling, and she quickly found her own clit as she watched all this unfold.

"Excuse me, but you aren't showing me the proper respect." Mathius didn't pull out but he did stop his movements.

"I'm sorry…" Gryson apologized and hesitated before the last word escaped his sexy lips, "Sir." Mathius resumed immediately.

"That's better. I will have to train you better if this is how you act." His nipples hadn't been released from the clamps and Aggie leaned forward and pinched them slightly, though not as firmly as Mathius had, causing Gryson to cry out. "Oh, Dearie, you seem to have an affliction for giving and receiving pain. Do it again, but harder." He smiled his wicked smile and Aggie did as she was told.

"Yes, sir." She smiled and squeezed firmly, as hard as she could. She glanced down and saw Gryson's cock twitch happily. "I think he liked it."

"Oh, I know he did. He tightened down on my cock so hard I nearly came." Mathius continued fucking Gryson, harder and harder, and the moans and cries from Gry were the sexiest sounds ever. Aggie was still stroking her clit and her breathing was increasing rapidly. She was practically panting and was close to coming again.

"I think she is going to come, Sir." Gryson didn't forget that time, and Aggie could see the pride on Mathius' face.

"What do you think we should do to her?" Mathius asked, leaving the decision up to Gryson.

"I think we should let her come and watch her. Then we should fuck her from both ends and come all over and inside her, Sir." Aggie flushed at the words, but she was also turned on. The thoughts he put into her head were enough she was cresting and there wasn't anything anyone could do about it. She screamed her orgasm and the guys watched her and were practically drooling.

"That was beautiful," Mathius said as he slowed his thrusts. "I agree, it is time to have our way with her. Are you ready, brother?"

Gryson leaned back into Mathius' cock one last time before pulling away slowly. A bit of regret crossed Gryson's face and Mathius must have sensed it. "Next time I will fuck you until we both come loudly," he promised, and Gryson smiled at the thought.

"Now then, you said you wanted her ass; does that mean I get to fuck her beautiful cunt?" Gryson preened, and stroked her folds.

"That is the plan. Now, do you want to start us off?" Mathius waved at Gryson in a gentlemanly manner. Gryson didn't need to be told twice. He kissed Aggie soundly and she was already so far gone it was hard to respond accordingly. She wasn't going to be much help in this round and was thankful she would have support from both sides.

Pulling her back with him, Gryson placed her on top of him. Guiding her toward him, he placed his cock at her entrance and lowered her down. She moaned softly at the feel of him and he swore. "You are the most perfect woman I have ever met and this moment is more than I could have imagined."

Leaning her forward, he thrust into her up and down. Mathius felt left out and she felt him press his cock to her ass. "Now is where this gets interesting," he whispered in her ear, and licked it. She could hear the smile in his voice and Gryson matched it when she looked at him. Pressing in slowly, he went in easier since she was fully prepped. Soon they filled her every inch. There was room for nothing else. They matched each other and thrust into her, finding the same pattern so she was filled at all times. Never once was only one of them in her from then on. She was overwhelmed and she felt the tears prick her eyes. She was happy, and in no way were the tears a sign of her being upset. Gryson reached up and brushed them away.

Sooner than she had hoped, her climax was upon her and she screamed out both their names. "Gryson! Mathius!" Upon hearing each of their names it was like a trigger, and Gryson first flooded her with his release. He was followed quickly by Mathius and they both groaned her name in unison.

CHAPTER TWENTY-FOUR

The next morning, Aggie groaned. She was sore in so many places, but the memory that came with it made it more pleasantly sore. Then, even before she could open her eyes, her stomach grumbled loudly.

"Nobody fed me!" She jerked up in bed and both Mathius and Gryson startled awake at her shout.

"What?" they replied in unison, clearly not hearing what she said in their sleepy state.

"I'm starving, and after I asked for a snack last night no one brought me anything. Then you two distracted me and I never got any food." She was pouting and she knew it, but there were certain things that were important and food was a big one.

"Are you complaining?" Mathius replied with a cocky flare. That made Aggie want to smack him in the face. No, she wasn't complaining about the sex, which was amazing, but she was still hungry and running on nothing.

"Are you regretting last night?" Gryson said with a slight lilt of sadness in his voice. That made Aggie feel instantly guilty.

"No! Not at all. I'm thrilled that it happened, and I enjoyed the way it happened. Are you okay with everything about last night?" She quickly added the last part in fear that perhaps their first time together wasn't the way he had hoped.

A smile pulled at the corners of his mouth just slightly. "Last night was perfect and I wouldn't have asked for it any other way." He glanced up at her and then they darted over to Mathius, and the tops of his cheeks went pink.

"Of course, you did. Now, magic up some food for our girl and we can get on with our day. We don't have time to lounge around in bed." His bossy self was back, not that it ever left. Mathius seemed to always commandeer attention and have people falling in line behind him. "No matter how much I want to create a playback of last night," he added, and Aggie smiled. He was invested in this and did have fun the night before. She knew there was more to him than just fights, plans of attack, and the occasional romp in the bedroom.

"Gladly." Gryson conjured a cup of coffee and a plate of food. Aggie's mouth watered as she took in everything. Bacon, eggs, and pancakes, but that wasn't all. This plate was heaping, and it was as though he had picked everything he had ever seen her eat for breakfast. "Is that enough food to get you through this, or do I need to get you another plate?" Gryson asked with a smirk. He was feeling comfortable again now that they had cleared the air.

Aggie leaned over and kissed him but placed the plate in his hand, choosing to sip the coffee first. "It's perfect but, given that you didn't provide me with a tray, you get to serve that purpose." Not wanting to leave Mathius out, she leaned over and placed a kiss on his lips as well. "Good morning to you both. I'm sorry I woke you with a start, but there are just a few things I have to have in order to function."

"Oh, we know that all too well. We were all just so relieved to have you home that we got a little too distracted. I'm sorry we forgot about it. I know we will do better in the future. Not to mention, now you should have Gry's powers and maybe you can conjure up what you need with practice."

Mathius squeezed the back of her neck as Aggie's eyes brightened.

"Oh, I hadn't thought about that. I need to go have a chat with Izzy." Her own thoughts wandered as she thought about the possibilities.

"Why don't you get some food in you before you take a trip on the Fast Track to Magic Express." Gryson handed her the plate of food and she relinquished her coffee to him to hold. Taking her first bite slowly, the food tasted so good she began shoveling it in like a homeless person who hadn't eaten in days. After thinking about it, that was exactly what she felt like.

"Whoa, you had better slow down or you are going to choke." Mathius put a hand on her fork, forcing her to chew what was in her mouth before she took another bite. "New plan: I'm going to feed you and make you enjoy the flavor and not just fill your empty belly." He took the plate from her and began cutting off smaller bites of egg and sausage to feed to her. She looked at him incredulously.

"Seriously? What do I look like, an incapable child?" She gave him a scathing look, but opened her mouth as he held the fork to her lips.

"No, I just want to take care of you, and I feel like some of these guys have a leg up because they can just wave their hands and produce what you need." He gave Gryson a look and a small smile. Aggie didn't say another word but took every bite lifted to her lips and chewed slowly to prolong the moment.

They all met that morning at the Lodge. Aggie looked around at all the somber faces. Felix, Tartan, and Ulnak had joined them.

"Ulnak said he has seen the rebel army moving in overnight. They haven't moved into an attack formation, but just have gotten close enough to get a visual a few miles out," Mitchell said gruffly, elbows on the table and his fingers steepled in front of his lips. Aggie remembered what it was like to kiss those lips, but banished those thoughts from her head. They had bigger things to do and she didn't need those kinds of distractions.

"I think they are planning, and that gives us time to prepare as well. We have clans coming in from the outer areas close to here. They should be here within the hour. We advised them to come around the opposite direction from where we spotted the rebels." Mitchell was full of information, but Aggie knew Ulnak had gone to the trouble of retrieving it. He was the quiet type, though, and as far as she knew it was normal for the Alpha to do this.

"Are we just going to wait for them to attack us, or bring the fight to them like we originally discussed?" Aggie pressed him and earned a glare for it. She smiled sweetly back at him and just waited for his reply.

"The plan is to creep up on them. If we can fight away from town it would be best. That is the only way I can think of not to have them destroy what we have, as well as to protect the women and children." Aggie considered his words and felt another question needling her.

"Who's staying with them?" She was concerned for the children after the last fiasco she'd had to deal with. The last thing she could handle was if the children were hurt again.

"The women are here to protect them," Mitchell said shortly.

"They're pretty badass in a fight. So, you don't have to worry about that. The children are safe here as long as we can keep the fight out of town," Ren added for clarification, and Aggie let out a breath she didn't know she was holding.

"That's a relief. You can continue." She looked at Mitchell pointedly and he let out an annoyed sigh.

"Glad I have your permission." He rolled his eyes and Aggie tried not to laugh. Knowing that he had underlying feelings for her was really mixing up his everyday reactions.

"As soon as the reinforcements get here, we will move out. They are bringing their young and women, too. We have plenty of room for them, but it will take time to get them settled." The fact that Mitchell was so in tune and concerned warmed Aggie's heart. She knew he would make a good dad someday, if the opportunity presented itself. She shook her head slightly, as she tried to figure out where that thought had come from.

"So you're saying I have some time to kill and train before we get on the road?" Aggie was thinking she could head back to her room and get some time with Izzy before they took off, and perhaps have an additional power to throw in the pot. That was if she could get a handle on it. Then maybe she might have the upper hand in the fight. They didn't know what powers she had acquired. The fact that her father had betrayed her still stung. She was also still confused as to how he got her DNA for the spell.

Distracted, she let her mind wander to the possibilities. She wondered if there was a chance that he had used his own DNA and just hoped it would work.

"Earth to Aggie!" Mitchell barked at her, his voice sounding permanently bothered when he spoke to her directly. She was pulled from her thoughts and the scowl on Mitchell's face made her wince. "Now that I have your attention, yes, you have some free time before we set off. Just be ready, because I don't have a set time that we are leaving. It all depends on when the others get here and their families get settled."

"I think I can handle that; I'll be in my cabin if anyone needs me. Do you have any other words of wisdom to share before I go?" She raised an eyebrow in question toward Mitchell, garnering her the sigh she was expecting. When he waved her off she smiled and strolled out of the Lodge. The guys were murmuring behind her, but she wasn't worried. Whatever they discussed, she had bigger things to worry about.

When she stepped outside she inhaled deeply, letting the

fresh air wash over her. She didn't expect the air to be so fresh later today. So, she was soaking it up as long as she could.

"Can I come with you?" Gryson walked up beside her and she startled slightly. "I'm sorry; I shouldn't have snuck up on you."

"No, not at all. I just didn't expect anyone to follow me. I was just enjoying the morning. I imagine the air will smell more," she hesitated before she said, "coppery later, if the rebels don't relent quickly." She lowered her head at the reality of what that meant.

"I know," Gryson said simply, and slid his hand into hers and squeezed reassuringly. "Let's get to your cabin and figure out what you can do; that is, if I'm allowed to tag along." He lowered his head sheepishly since he was being very presumptuous by catching up with her.

"I'd be happy to have you along, but you might be rather bored waiting for me. Then again, you could probably pull me back out if we have to leave. I'm already ready to go." She moved her hand to indicate her leathers and knee-high leather boots she had donned for this occasion. "I just need to grab a weapon or two so I don't give away all my secrets just yet." She winked at him and they continued walking to her cabin.

Stepping inside, she motioned to the chair. "You can sit over there." She got situated in the center of the bed. Gryson sat in the chair as she had indicated but, given his longing look at the bed, she added, "You could sit anywhere you want. I can slide over if you want to join me over here, but no funny business." Smiling at him to show she was kidding, he stood and joined her on the mattress.

"I will watch over you while you do what you need to do. You'll be safe as long as I'm here." Gryson placed a kiss to her temple and she faced him and dropped into her head space.

Izzy wasn't wasting any time. She walked up right away and Aggie was pleased to see the field she normally walked up in was now the city square of Tarlvey. It was empty and no one else was around, but Aggie recognized it.

"Boy, am I glad for this change of scenery. I just wish there was someone here to talk to when you aren't around." Izzy was in a good mood, and for that Aggie was grateful. There were times she just seemed put out having to talk for any length of time.

"I'm sorry, do you want me to come and visit more often?" Aggie smiled at her, but Izzy knew better.

"No, you have bigger fish to fry these days and more men to bone." Aggie gaped at Izzy's candor.

"Seriously? That's all you think about?" Aggie couldn't believe her ears. Then again, she and Izzy were as close to the same person as one could get. Today she was wearing a medieval-looking cloak. Where the mages she had seen preferred black, Aggie liked that Izzy opted for a dark purple. Just enough color to be different and less like a cult member.

"Well, until you lock in all your mates I'm stuck here, changing at your will. I'd like to travel between the beings you have created inside me at my own leisure." Izzy had a point and, as of late, Aggie called on her powers at will and when she thought she needed them most.

"Are you saying when I take on all eight mates, you will be able to help me control and know better how to use my powers? Right now, I feel like I'm just grasping at straws to find the right one I should use at any given time." Aggie was excited by the idea of full control and not this basic understanding she was relying on now.

"That's the short of it. Now, let's discuss Gryson's mage powers." Aggie nodded and Izzy continued. "It took you long enough to tap into this sweet one. His magic tastes delicious."

"Tastes?" Aggie's eyebrows shot up in shock. What did she mean by that?

"Well, of course; how else do you think I consume your new powers?" Izzy popped out one hip and placed her hand on it, with a lot of sass. This version of magic really brought out a fun side of Izzy.

"I guess I figured you just got them like I did. If you enjoyed them, then what should I be expecting?" Aggie knew her time was limited and she wanted to learn as much as she could before Gryson pulled her out.

"Well, Gryson can teach you to weave his potions, but the mage powers are really much deeper than that. He is skilled in potions but that is truly a learned talent. What you should be focusing your energy on is the magic from inside." Aggie was intrigued by this and Izzy wasn't giving much away.

"So, could I conjure food like he does?" Her eyes were bright with excitement but Izzy just rolled her eyes.

"That's what you want to do? Just be your own personal chef on a moment's notice? That is the stupidest thing I've ever heard. You could bring forth a shield by just thinking about it or levitate an object to throw it across a room and knock someone out, but you want to quench your snack cravings on a whim." Izzy facepalmed herself and turned to walk away.

"Wait, wait; don't go. I'm sorry. It was just a thought. That isn't my priority, but you didn't give me much to go on and I knew Gryson could do that. I'm ready to learn or at least listen." Aggie waited, and hoped and wished that she would turn around. Izzy just stood with her back to Aggie and made her wait. It felt like forever before she turned around slowly.

"I'm not here for your entertainment. I'm here to help you and give you information. I'm the silent partner in this relationship most days. So, if you want to disrespect me and insult my knowledge and ability, then I'm not sure I want to help you anymore." She paused for a long minute and Aggie held her breath, hoping that she wasn't finished because she hadn't turned away. "But since you can't live without me and are the only person I have to talk to, then I guess I'll stay and help."

"Oh, thank you." Aggie breathed a sigh of relief. "I really didn't mean to insult you. I just recently went a really long time without food and Mathius mentioned it this morning that I might have the same ability. I'll focus on more useful things from now on." Izzy nodded to acknowledge her but didn't comment once about her apology.

"Now then, like I said, you have to focus on your energies and you should be able to move objects with your mind. You should also work on shields. That could come in handy with this fight you are about to start." Izzy was counting things off on her fingers.

"We aren't starting the fight; they've decided to press in on us and we're just keeping others safe. It's better to take the fight to them rather than worry about any more kids." Aggie spoke with passion, as she was more concerned with the lives of kids than anyone else.

"Tomato, tamato! I don't care either way. I just know it means you're going to be counting on me to save the day. I just hope you're ready for it. This will be much harder than last time because it isn't one enemy. It will be hundreds. They will be coming from everywhere. That's why I'm so glad you chose to get it on with the mage. It's going to make things a lot easier. If you practice a little you should be able to throw up a shield around a group, and that will come in handy if you have any injured that need to fall back or be healed. Too bad you didn't take on that from Eldon when you took his powers. Though, yours come in pretty handy in a fight for that, too." Izzy was beaming with pride and Aggie knew she loved talking about the powers that Aggie had acquired through her mating process.

As Aggie thought about it, she realized that sounded very clinical. She had real feelings for the guys and didn't want to belittle that at all. Each one she had found something special about, and they had wormed their way into her heart. They were determined, that was one thing that could be said about all of them. Well, maybe not Mitchell. He had feelings but he was trying so hard to fight them, Aggie was even more frustrated with him than when she thought he was just being an asshole for the sake of it. She had to have faith that one day he would come around.

"So I have an unlimited source of power by feeding off my energy, similar to when I top off when I get worn down?" Aggie didn't think that was much different to what she had been dealing with before, but just that the energy could be told to do more things.

"No, actually, the more powers you absorb through mating, the harder it will be to refill your reserves. The more power you use, the more tired you will get. You will have to seek out one of the guys. Skin to skin, like you did with Eldon, will replenish you and that works both ways. You can feed each other energy as needed." Izzy started pacing a little as Aggie realized she was counting on her fingers.

"Will any of the guys work or only the ones I've already mated to, because that will play a factor in the fight as to where we set up and who I keep around me." Aggie wondered again what Izzy was counting.

"That's what I was trying to figure out. You've mated now with four of your Guardians. They are your ideal sources for energy, but, due to the fact that you are destined to mate with them all, the other will give you a small boost. You just can't return the favor to those with whom you haven't mated yet." Aggie frowned at this news and a part of her wished she hadn't wanted to wait until she was emotionally ready for them. She wanted to protect them all, and if there was a way for her to give back to them she would take it in a heartbeat. Now she had four guys who were at risk, and there was a chance they could be seriously injured in this fight.

"What do I do about the other four?" Aggie needed options before she left Izzy and went off to fight in the biggest, most important, battle she had ever been a part of. The last time she fought with the guys it was just that. A fight. More of a one on one, with the guys backing her up and using their talents to counter other magical elements.

"That's what you have Eldon for. He's the healer of the group and it has worked for years, before you ever came into the picture. I don't know why you're so worried about them. You're just an added bonus for those who are close to you." Izzy smiled, seeming to brush this off, and that bothered Aggie. Sure, they had Eldon, and that was great, but now they had to strategically place the guys in a way to keep them all closest to who they need to heal them. Then Eldon would need to stay close to her to boost his system and keep him at his best.

Before Aggie could ask another question, she felt a tug at her consciousness. She knew it was Gryson. "Well, that's all the time we have for today. Now we have to go and fight for our lives and the lives of my Guardians and the shifters. This is going to be an epic battle that I just hope we survive."

ggie came to and Gryson was there, but what shocked her was that everyone else was, too. She was surrounded by her Guardians. Yes, even though she hadn't mated with them all, she claimed each and every one of them. Even Mitchell. She blinked away her fog and took each of them in. She didn't want to think about losing any of them, but she wanted to take them all in and commit this image to memory.

"It seems we have our work cut out for us," she started, and Mitchell scoffed quietly, but the look on his face was solemn, as was everyone else's. "I just found out that, I can replenish the energy of any of you four, like I replenished Eldon's energy." She indicated Eldon, Mathius, Xavier, and Gryson. "That means that the rest of you are subject to your regular strength and abilities and would need to stay near Eldon to get back into it. Eldon, you should probably stay as close to the middle or to Mathius, Ky, or, at the very least, me. Then we can sift you to whoever needs you. I'm just glad we're still linked." She smiled at them, but it didn't light her eyes and her heart felt heavy. This was bigger than the last fight and she wasn't sure she was emotionally ready for it. "I also found out that all of you guys can replenish my energy and strength when it starts to waver."

"What do you mean? You haven't had any trouble with that before. You have always just had unlimited coffers." Eldon's sweet voice floated to her and she closed her eyes, soaking it in.

"I guess being human has its faults. The more of your powers I take on, the more I have to balance them. That means that, while I used to draw on my internal energies or the resources around me, I have to use you guys instead. I can replenish your weakness and you all can mine. It's just to varying degrees. The four of you can top me off." Again she indicated her four mates then turned to the remaining four. "You guys can boost me, but not completely; it's like our connection will be subdued until we, well, you know." She didn't want to say it and rub anything in or make them feel bad. She already felt bad enough for all of them.

"So you're saying we have a bit of an upper hand then." Ren smiled a devilish smile. Leave it to him to find the silver lining in all of this. She was talking about them getting too weak to fight or getting hurt, and now here was Ren, getting excited. Then, out of no- where, he howled. Aggie startled at the sound because it was full volume and they were inside her cabin. Clearly his wolf was near the surface and Ren wasn't holding him back too hard.

"Easy, Wolfie." Aggie spoke directly to his wolf, knowing he was the reason for Ren's wild behavior. "That isn't all I learned, but we need to keep our connections fully open when we are out there. I don't want to miss something because you guys are unable to focus or unable to communicate verbally." She glared at each of them one by one to get her point across. They each nodded but her gaze lingered extra-long on Mitchell. His Alpha mentality was at the forefront and she knew he was locked down like a steel trap. He didn't want anyone in his head and she needed him to agree most of all, because if he was weak going into the fight with Dranton he could lose. They couldn't afford to lose.

"Fine," Mitchell said sharply and Aggie nodded, not commenting on it.

"Okay, I should have the ability to throw up a shield. I'm not sure how big, but Izzy thinks I should be able to protect any of our wounded. So it sounds like, as much as I want to fight, I'm going to be playing protector in a lot of this fight." Aggie was disappointed but she tried not to let it show on her face. If she had a role then that's all that mattered.

"I'd rather have you out of harm's way anyway," Kyrel said softly. He was more of a lover than a fighter, but Aggie knew he could hold his own in a fight. "I'll stay close to you and Eldon and try to throw out my power and cause some confusion. It should keep them at a distance from you. Eldon and I can pick off anyone who gets close." Aggie hadn't heard him discuss his power outside of the bedroom situations and wondered what confusion would ensue. It was a bit intriguing.

"I'll stay back with Felix and any of the fliers. I'll take my bow and try to pick off anyone I can from a distance before the get too close to you. If we can find a good hill it will give them a better vantage point to make their aerial attack, and any of the bird shifters will have a better view to be our eyes." Liel, in his dry, disinterested tone, was misleading. Aggie knew better, though; after spending the time alone with him by the rebel camp, she knew he was just taking emotion out of the equation. He had feelings buried deep, and around all the guys he felt more comfortable without them on the surface. She wondered what would happen once he opened up in the link with everyone.

"I like that, but don't stay off too long because if they have any aerial players they could pick you off. So stay out of sight and come in if it gets unsafe. I don't want you too far away from the group if you need anything." Aggie's gaze lingered on him and she sent him a warm look and he nodded.

"I'll weave my magic throughout them and try to disable their mages. If I can find them, I should be able to knock them out and take away any of their spells. Then we should be only dealing with the shifters and a few demons. You didn't sense any others, did you?" He directed the question at Liel, who shook his head.

"Aside from the human or half-breeds, no, but they shouldn't be at the full power of a true blood. Either way we shouldn't have any others that are of any major concern. Just sheer numbers versus whatever we have." He turned toward Mitchell to get a read on their counts.

"I haven't done a head count, but Tartan is trying to get one together. We have to count the women and children, too, but I have one of the midwives handling that for now. I would say we have close to two hundred at least. We have a decent number of people just here in Galata, but the surrounding villages were eager to help. I hated to ask, but we are a family and the rebels are threatening that way of life." Mitchell's pride showed in his eyes and it transformed his face. Aggie was attracted to him before, but this was a new and improved version that took her breath away. He glanced her way and flashed her a rare smile, and his eyes flashed golden for a brief second. She blushed being caught staring at him.

"Okay, is there a way to get a name list or some kind of register? I'd like to be able to check off names and know who goes with whom. I don't want to think about loss, but it would be naïve to think we aren't going to have loss." Her somber look returned at the thought of their new reality.

"It will take time, but I guess I can send a message to the group counting heads. We can get something put together." For the first time since Aggie had known him, Mitchell's words were soft. She didn't know what changed other than the potential negative aspects of their situation.

"Thank you," she replied softly, in relief. She wanted to be able to tell families for sure what happened to their loved ones.

"If we have a couple hundred, then we are closely matched. Then, if you add in the fact that we are the Guardians and the most powerful of our people, and our powers are combined as we work together, we have a slight advantage." Liel wasn't being cocky, just speaking factually about what they were. He wasn't the kind of guy to get a big head, but to take calculated risks and factor in all their strengths. "I will scan the field and let you know as I can what might be headed your way, so you can plan your attack accordingly." Aggie said a silent thank you to the powers that be; keeping Liel distanced in the fight was a better chance for him not to get hurt. That was one less person of her new little family to be worried about. Not that she wouldn't be concerned about him and keep checking in on him throughout the fight.

"I would like to confront my father, given the chance. So, if we can start this with a conversation, perhaps we can stop the fight before it starts." It was wishful thinking on her part and she knew that, but it was some closure that she needed if the fates aligned.

"I'm not sure that is a wise move," Ren chimed in, and Aggie just glanced at him. She wasn't mad, but she knew it wasn't the way she wanted it to go down.

"I know. I just feel like I need to know why. Not to mention I'd love to figure out how he got my DNA for that blocking spell." Ren gave her a tight smile and nodded.

"The rest of you I know I can't keep nailed down, but try to keep one of us who can sift in your line of sight. If you get hurt, I want to pull you out before we heal you and then you can go back in full bore. I don't want anyone playing tough guy or hero. If you're hurt, call for help. I want you all to stay as close to your best as we can. If your energy is waning, call for me and I'll boost you. If I need a boost and I'm pulling too much from the ones around me, I'll call for one of you to come to me. Then I can keep my shield up." She was serious, and channeling Mitchell's Alpha. Even though they weren't mated she was trying to act as much like him as possible, leaving no room for argument.

Aggie didn't mention any other possibilities of her powers because none of it had been tested, and it was going to be hard enough to figure out how to build a shield around herself let alone big enough to protect others. Izzy would help, but she didn't want to focus on too much at one time.

With everyone in agreement, they left her cabin and headed to the center of town. The rest of the shifters were gathered around.

"We have the women and children tucked away." Tartan bowed slightly to Mitchell. Aggie hadn't considered it before, but he was sort of royalty as the Alpha. She thought about this and realized that Ren and Mitchell were royalty, as well as Gryson. Were any of the others descendants of leader families? Then she remembered that Mitchell insisted on calling her Princess, and she wondered if that was more than just a nickname.

"What is our final fight-ready number?" Mitchell put his hand on Tartan's shoulder in a respectful manner, but also in a brotherly way. Aggie knew he considered his people more like his family and they were all close. He had a connection to each member of the clans which swore fealty to the Alpha. He knew each of them on a deeper level because of it.

"We have a lot of young fighters who are just of age." Tartan's face was grim, but he still looked strong. He was ready, but wasn't living in a bubble. It was obvious he knew what this battle meant. The group was scattered and Aggie saw some of the younger members he was talking about. They looked no more than sixteen, but she also knew that shifters aged more slowly than humans. So they were probably older, but they still looked so much younger than those surrounding them.

Their eyes shone, with excitement or adrenaline Aggie didn't know, but it was obvious that they had high hopes of our success rate and didn't fully grasp what they were headed into. Without checking with Mitchell she found a stump nearby and climbed up on it.

"Can I have your attention please?" Aggie shouted to be heard over the sea of voices. They all lowered their voices and all that was left were a few murmurs. "I know today isn't what any of us wants it to be. We wish we could be inside our homes with those we love and not leaving them to fight for everything we believe in." She paused and gathered her thoughts. She knew she needed to thank them and prepare them, but also encourage them. She didn't think her words through before she had them staring in rapt attention at her, in true Aggie fashion. Now she panicked because she worried Mitchell would be mad because she had overstepped. Then a sense of pride filled her; she glanced over at Mitchell and he nodded to her, showing it was coming from him. He had opened up his emotions to her so she would continue. Taking a deep breath, she continued.

"I don't know each of you personally the way you know each other. I'm the new one here. I just want you all to know I will be there in the thick of this with you. I don't know all the reasons these people have turned their allegiance to another or just wanting to be free from the control of an Alpha. They don't feel the same about Mitchell as you and I do." She added the last part on purpose and Mitchell's face flashed in shock for a brief moment. Then he schooled his features so fast she wondered if she really saw it. "I pray that our side suffers no loss, but even I know that's a naïve way to think. I've tried to prepare myself for it as best I can. I will do everything in my power to protect each of you." She focused her attention on the youth in the crowd. "If you're injured, please seek out a healer or even me. I'll have a shield raised to protect our weakest people. If we can heal you we will, but if not someone will sift you back to the foreground and try to keep you out of danger. Injuries can be healed but none of us has the power to bring anyone back from the dead." Her head lowered slightly at that admission, even though everyone was aware that that power wasn't an option. Even if someone could be brought back it would be reanimated and not the same as alive.

"Go out there today and fight for what you believe in. Fight for each other and those you love. Fight for your right to have a family and a clan that's willing to protect you. Those rebels don't have anyone to look out for them and they aren't a family. They are in this for themselves and for their own supposed freedom. Go out there and do your best, and fight with your heart." She stepped down off the stump. Everyone stayed silent and she feared she had done something wrong. Then, just as her back turned and she headed back to her group of guys, a wave of applause and cheering started in the back of the group and flowed to the front to reach her ears, so loud it drowned out any other sounds.

Turning slowly, she realized that the entire crowed was energized and the dread was gone and everyone was ready to take on this fight and win. Mitchell nodded at her and his eyes flashed gold again for a moment and she knew his wolf, Alpha, was there and his opinion was clear. The growl came through her link and she nearly missed it. *My mate.* His eyes returned to normal and he shut down the link in the same instant. Aggie knew that comment came straight from Alpha, and Mitchell didn't want her to know any more of his secrets.

CHAPTER TWENTY-SIX

*C*resting the hill that blocked them from the rebel army, Aggie found an unexpected sense of calm. The enemy was amassed and scattered around the clearing, but they didn't seem to have any sort of strategic plan. Her men surrounded her; she stood in the center, but hidden from view along with Liel. They didn't want to give away their upper hand just yet. They stepped forward and the loyal shifter army followed at a short distance, giving them the chance to address the rebel army and try to end this before it started. They got about half a football field away from the rebels and Mitchell yelled, his voice carrying with the power of an Alpha radiating off of him.

"You aren't welcome here unless you are willing to swear allegiance." He wasn't being cocky or dictating, he just needed to have a connection to trust their loyalty.

"Never! You aren't the true leader here. We have earned the right to choose." Aggie wasn't sure, but she thought the voice that responded was the same voice that spoke to her father. Dranton.

"I didn't say you didn't have a choice, but you need to leave. There is no need for us to fight." Aggie was proud of Mitchell for his diplomacy. She knew they wanted this to end if they could do it without a fight.

"You might not think that when you realize what we have!" Dranton shouted. Aggie could almost make out the smile he wore at the distance as she peeked out between Mitchell and Ren who stood directly in front of her. She was hidden from view easily, as they towered over her, but Liel had to duck down a bit to hide, given his greater height.

"What do you mean, have? You couldn't have anything that mattered to us. We are stronger than you by default. I have the Alpha powers and, as you can see, the rest of the Guardians are here, united. We are always stronger that way." Mitchell puffed his chest out and stood a little taller.

"Really? It looks like you're missing someone from your superior unit. I can't imagine how strong you could be if you aren't united as one. Then, if I recall correctly, your would-be mate and Gatekeeper is missing as well. I can't imagine you left her behind and allowed your unit to be broken by leaving someone with her for protection." He spoke as though he had something up his sleeve but hadn't revealed their bluff yet.

"My daughter wouldn't let you leave her behind. She's too stubborn for that!" Eckard shouted as he stepped forward to seal their backstory for the bluff Aggie knew was coming.

"What are you saying?" Mitchell called them out, and Aggie couldn't wait to see how this played out.

"Well, what you don't know is that we know they aren't under your protection. At least not anymore." Dranton was getting cocky, and Aggie couldn't wait to knock him off his high horse.

"What do you mean?" Mitchell kept his cool, but was portraying agitation. He was probably pretty good at that act, as she had seen him show that emotion on more than one occasion.

"We have them, and will keep them, unless you turn over your Alpha status and let us have control of the shifters.

Everyone should have the right to choose and not report to one high and mighty Alpha." Dranton's voice carried, strong and confident.

"You did *what?*" Mitchell feigned ignorance and Aggie fought a laugh. "How did you do that? I doubt *you* could have pulled one over on Liel. He would have stopped you." He put a strong emphasis on the 'you' and sneered at the word, obviously a cutting blow to Dranton's ego because he growled loudly. It rumbled and Aggie could almost feel it in the ground around her.

"You aren't as all-powerful as you want your people to believe. The Alpha can only do so much with what he has, and can't protect everyone." Dranton needled at Mitchell, causing a returning growl stronger than Aggie had ever heard. It most definitely shook the entire clearing, causing a few to get knocked off balance. Liel steadied Aggie so she didn't fall over.

"So, you think you have the upper hand because you broke us apart and took the Gatekeeper and one of the Guardians captive?" Mitchell had an edge to his voice that, on a normal day in a normal situation, would give Aggie pause. She was thankful this wasn't directed at her because it was damn scary.

"You aren't at full power with one missing, and I know some of you are probably distraught and distracted. It will be a factor in your fighting game." Dranton was feeling pretty secure in his stance in this entire engagement.

"I think you might find we are stronger than you might think." With that Mitchell and Ren stepped aside, revealing Liel and Aggie. The look on Dranton and Eckard's faces were priceless. Eckard's jaw dropped and quickly closed as he worked his jaw muscles in anger. Dranton blanched so white Aggie could see it from where she stood. "Is something wrong?" Mitchell asked, a bit cocky himself, but they did just pull a rabbit out of their hat.

"I would like to ask you one question!" Aggie yelled as loud as she could. "Eckard," she refused to call him anything else at that point because he'd lost the right to hold any title other than sperm donor the moment he betrayed her, "how did you get my DNA for your little spell?"

"I'm not even going to ask how you know about that because, clearly, your guys worked hard to break it." He sneered at her and she saw that the calm man who had come to her to offer his help was gone. "You have such an addiction to your coffee it was easy to pilfer from one of your used cups when you weren't looking." Aggie's anger boiled to the surface and Liel grasped her hand reassuringly. Her anger subsided, but it was still lingering.

"Enough!" Mitchell shouted, clearly finished with this tango. "If you won't back down, then this fight will prove to you once and for all that the clan is superior to your ridiculous band of fighters. You had to recruit from the other species in order to stand a chance. You won't make it far because we are connected in a way you can never be." With that, Mitchell leapt into the air. In midflight he shifted into his wolf and Alpha howled, announcing the charge.

Everything happened all at once. Arrows began flying through the air as the rebels advanced, each one hitting its mark and dropping the enemy where they stood. The links from the guys flooded Aggie's mind, startling her at first, but after a moment she sorted them out and mentally created channels for them so they weren't overwhelming her senses.

The birds took flight and she could hear a "caw" from different species as they soared. Unfortunately, that meant the same things happened on the rebels' side. They flew straight into each other and their claws and talons locked as they wrestled midflight. Aggie winced, worried some of their own would plummet from the air and plunge into the ground. Tearing her eyes away, she took in the fight. She never advanced, but before long she would be in the thick of it.

Eldon stood at her left side with his sword drawn, ready for any attack. Kyrel was on her right but slightly ahead of her, holding two elongated daggers. He was poised and ready to fight if need be. Aggie saw Gryson's eyes were the brightest purple she had ever seen while flinging magic into the air. The winds changed and electricity shot through the air. Mathius was sifting in and out of the crowd, piercing anyone he came in contact with his broad sword, but as it travelled through them he remolded it and curved it up as it came out. She could see the hook. Each hit from that sword wielded by Mathius eyes were as silver as his blade, and he was deadly. He didn't stay in one place long, popping in and out, and it was hard to follow him. He was a fierce fighter and she could see the command he carried with everyone that fell off his blade.

Xavier was harder to find. She sent out a feeler along the link to see if she could pinpoint where he was, but then she spotted him. He was a violent fighter, and she wasn't sure but it looked like he was enjoying himself. His fangs were elongated and anyone he got close enough to was pulled in and he bit down hard, ripping their throats clean out off their bodies. When he pulled back he was covered in blood and his eyes were shining a red so bright, he looked like a crazed serial killer. A shiver ran through her, but not in fear. This fierce side of Xavier was compelling, and Aggie had to remind herself that sex shouldn't be on her mind at that moment.

Continuing her perusal of the chaos that was raging around them, she saw Ren—well, Wolfie. He had shifted as some point and was gnashing his teeth, in a heated fight with a red panda. Aggie wondered if the size difference would be a factor or if Wolfie was the guaranteed victor. They rolled around and the fight carried on for what felt like an eternity, and Aggie gasped each time the panda got a nip in. Nothing life-threatening but enough to piss Ren off. She could feel it through their connection. He reared up on his hind legs and landed hard on the panda, and Ren's teen connected with the panda's throat and, not unlike Xavier, Ren bit down hard and the panda stilled. Ren quickly moved on to the next closest attacker and another fight began.

Aggie found Mitchell very quickly because he was pushing his way up the middle of what was an all-out brawl in the clearing. It was a little difficult to tell who was who on the field. He didn't waste time with his fights, but ended them quickly and pushed forward until he was standing in front of Dranton, who hadn't shifted yet.

Alpha growled low and loud, the sound vibrating the ground again. She wondered if that meant he was using his Alpha magic. She hadn't seen Dranton in his shifted form and didn't know what to expect. She had speculated like she normally did, but until now she hadn't known for sure. Dranton took a step forward and shifted into a snow-white Bengal tiger. He was a little broader than Mitchell's wolf, Alpha. That didn't stop Alpha from swelling up and standing his ground. Dranton's tiger roared, but it didn't have the same fear-inducing effect that Alpha had.

They circled each other and, as if some unseen force pushed them away, the rest of the fighters cleared a circle. But they didn't stop fighting. The war still raged on and the fight between Dranton and Mitchell was just a sideshow.

Suddenly, there was a flash and Kyrel appeared next to what looked like a burnt eagle. He grabbed the eagle and brought him back.

"He was hit by a bolt of electricity from one of the mages on the ground," Ky said as he lay the eagle in front of Aggie. Eldon came over and began to place his hands over the worst of the poor bird's injuries.

"It won't take long for me to heal him, and once he's close his own shifter powers will take over." With Eldon distracted, Aggie didn't want him to come to any harm. Ky was focusing on the crowd of people fighting, so would be unable to hold back anyone who might get too close. Aggie decided it was the right time to get her shield up, protecting the eagle shifter and Eldon as he worked.

She focused internally and found her center, where Izzy lived. She felt for the ball inside her and imagined pushing it out around her. When she opened her eyes there was a shimmering shield around herself, but not anyone else. She closed her eyes again and pushed it further out, and willed the shield to extend around Eldon and the injured shifter. Opening her eyes, she smiled because the protective bubble was fully encasing them. Eldon's eyes were fully iridescent and Aggie knew he was concentrating on his healing powers. The injury was bad, but with the shifter's rapid healing it wouldn't take much from Eldon to get him back on his feet.

Soon the shifter changed and he was stark naked. He was still unconscious from his blow, but he was healed enough for the shifter side to take back control. Aggie averted her eyes. She hadn't been in a situation where the shifters were changing around her. They had always been in their human forms or animal forms. So, aside from her wolves, Ren and Mitchell, she hadn't seen anyone in the act of shifting one way or the other.

Taking in the fighting happening all around her, she reached out to Liel.

"How does it look from up there, Liel?" The link was open, so everyone was hearing this.

"We are fairing well, but it isn't over yet. We have the numbers now for sure, but the remaining don't seem to want to relent or retreat." That concerned Aggie. She worried this would be a fight to the death and not surrender. She turned back to the fight and saw everyone on both sides fighting and giving their all. Thankfully she couldn't see that they had any who had fallen. Then again, the ground was littered with bodies so she couldn't be sure.

A rogue rebel started at them and a couple more followed, giving reinforcements. Aggie held the shied firm, and she noticed Kyrel's grey eyes illuminated to his magical teal and so she knew something was coming. The three men headed toward them hadn't shifted and Aggie had a thought.

Liel, what are the men who are headed toward us? They approached quickly, and she could see when Ky's power hit them. They blanched, confused, and then they looked at each other. What happened next, Aggie wasn't sure if she should laugh or freak out.

Demons. That was the only thing she heard from Liel, and she knew he was focused on throwing arrows again. The three men, on the other hand, were all over each other and with little to no preparation. Kissing and tongues and then pants were down and their dicks were erect and as hard as a piece of actual wood. It looked painful. Then, a finger or two here in the tangle of limbs and a rub here and there. One man, very tall and blonde, was bent over at the waist, taking an auburn-haired man into his mouth. The third man, broad with jet black hair, got behind the blonde man and inserted his very large cock into its new home inside the bent man's ass. His eyes widened at the unprepared intrusion and then he moaned around the auburn-haired man's cock which he was sucking for all it was worth. The blonde reached up and grabbed the balls of the tall man before him and fondled them. The standing man plunged his hands into the blonde's hair and gripped tightly.

Ky turned around and smiled, enjoying the scene before him a little too much, as Aggie noticed the tent in his pants. Perhaps using his powers was a bad idea, then Aggie worried that the men were being forced into something and it could be called rape. Ky must have sensed it and pointed to his eyes. They were his soft charcoal grey that she was used to.

My powers don't work if they don't have a natural desire. I can sense it. If they didn't want each other or have an attraction then the confusion would just make them seek out the first person who did fit the bill. I can't force anyone to do anything they don't already want to do or have considered previously. The timing is just terrible for them, and me since I can't find release myself. He rubbed his own cock through his pants and Aggie felt bad for him. Shrugging, he went back to watching the scene before him. Aggie needed to find a distraction, because now wasn't the time for her to be focusing on the hottest male threesome she had ever seen. Although the thought of three of her guys doing the same crossed her mind. Ky caught it and winked at her. She didn't know exactly what that meant, but she had hope.

She kept her focus on her shield. The eagle shifter was healed, had woken up, and was standing.

"When you're ready let me know and I'll drop the shield so you can get out." He nodded but didn't speak, as it looked like he was getting ready to shift. He did and then flapped his wings a couple times before a "caw" sounded. Aggie took that as a "go", so she dropped the shield and he took to the skies.

Before she let her attention drift, she used her gauntlets to wrap the ankles of each of the three preoccupied attackers so they couldn't move without taking their respective partners with them. Though they weren't interested in moving very far at the moment. She decided to give them a little privacy and started scanning the crowd again.

She saw Tartan. He hadn't shifted yet, and was fighting hand to hand with what Aggie assumed was a demon but wasn't sure. They had different power and all she could see was fire. Then, for the first time, she saw him shift. She waited, captivated because she always wondered exactly what he was. To her surprise a boar stood in his place when the shift completed, complete with tusks. He was a bit larger than she would have expected, based on the size she thought natural boars appeared in. Tartan's boar charged the demon throwing fire, and it seemed he wasn't the least bit afraid of the fire. He plunged his tusks right through the demon and chucked him to the side. Aggie was impressed.

Checking back in with Mitchell, she noticed that he had a few more scrapes and bloody spots on his fur. She gasped, "We have to get to Mitchell! He needs to be healed!"

Eldon shook his head. "Now that the fight to be Alpha has started, he's going to have to bear it. They won't stop for anything and it would be considered unfair or incomplete if he's healed halfway through."

"What? No! What if Dranton gets in a deadly strike?" Aggie believed in Mitchell's ability to win, but there was always a chance. She didn't know what she would do if he was hurt.

"We will just have to hope he is still alive when the fight is over and I can heal him." Eldon said grimly. Aggie hated this rule and she watched as Mitchell's wolf, Alpha, fought with everything he had. She wished with all her heart that she could boost him from here. They weren't mated yet but he was her true mate, at least one of them, and that had to count for something. She reached inside herself and focused on Mitchell's link. She didn't block anyone else but she pushed them to the back of her consciousness. She didn't know if it would work, but she figured if it did he would benefit. If not, she at least tried.

She pushed all the energy she could through the link and hoped it was enough. Her shield was down, so she could send all her focus into this. Pushing so hard and using up everything she had, she dropped to her knees with exhaustion but didn't stop pushing. Mitchell needed anything she could get to him. Since she wasn't supposed to be able to do this, it took more from her.

Mitchell flared inside the link and she felt him growl. She didn't know if it worked or not, but she watched him on the field. His head rose and he howled loudly, and a chorus of wolf howls and other animal sounds followed. It was a war cry and Mitchell's wolf leapt from the ground and landed square on top of Dranton's tiger, whose fur was already stained with blood in places all over his body.

They had both gotten in a few good hits and it made for a balanced fight. Except now, Mitchell was ready to finish it. He snarled and used his mass and strength to drop the rebel tiger to the ground. His mouth went to the tiger's neck. He pierced the skin but not too deeply.

"What is he doing? He should finish him and end this once and for all." Aggie didn't know if the fight would end but at least there would be no more challenges from Dranton for Alpha. Her protective instincts were flaring for Mitchell.

"He's giving him the chance to submit," Kyrel said quietly. They were all captivated by the fight. Aggie was still on the ground, weakened by her actions, but so happy that it worked. Or she thought. He could have just bolstered himself and given it everything he had left for all she knew. She chose to believe it was her doing since she was exhausted.

She watched, captivated by the moment, but it was like a moment frozen in time. The rest of the battle was still in full swing. Arrows still falling from a distance, birds still in flight, shifters and demons and mages using everything in their arsenal to take out the perceived threat. Mitchell was just a part of that fighting; his own fight just that much more. Then Aggie realized she didn't see Eckard anywhere.

She scanned the battlefield. Nothing. He had disappeared.

"Coward!" she muttered under her breath, and came back just in time to see Dranton's tiger rear back and try and throw Alpha from him in an attempt to break his hold. Alpha held fast and didn't give an inch. Clearly tired of the games, Aggie felt Mitchell sigh through the link. He was devastated to have to take this life. She realized that he was already mourning the losses, and the fight wasn't even over yet. Not waiting another minute she saw the decision flash through the link, and Alpha snapped Dranton's tiger's neck. Blood flowed from the wound and the tiger shifted slowly back to a very dead and naked Dranton.

Alpha let out a less powerful howl that sounded sadder than she was used to. Surprisingly, the fighting stopped instantly. There were still some rebels, but the fighters who were loyal to the Alpha outnumbered them. They were victorious, but there was a lot of death that day. And while they should be happy to have won, they were all saddened and grieving the loss of fellow members of their kind. Regardless of the reason, they still took lives and caused the deaths. They'd tried everything to avoid it and the rebels were stubbornly following blind. As soon as their leader was dead, the fight in them deflated.

Mitchell shifted back to his human form, causing the others to do the same. There was a sea of nakedness, but shifters didn't think the same and have the same modesty as others. So, Aggie tried to keep her eyes averted.

They all walked back and checked the dead for any signs of life. Those who were left of the rebels knelt down, waiting for the Alpha to decide their fate.

CHAPTER TWENTY-SEVEN

That night the shifters were back inside Galata, the mood was dark. The rebels had been taken captive until Mitchell could get them to submit. If they didn't then they would be cast out, unable to live among the clans. Aggie wished that wasn't necessary, but she understood why. The Alpha needed to be able to sense his people's intensions in order to better protect his people. No. His family.

"We need to talk." Mitchell came up behind her. His words were spoken low and startled her, as she was lost in thought. "First we need to break the link. The threat is gone and we need a minute to ourselves." Aggie didn't know what he needed, but she was a little worried. She was still tired from her overuse of her energy, but she was at least standing. She felt like she could sleep for a week, and knew if she stopped for any reason she would drop and probably be out for a solid week.

They made their way to Mitchell's cabin. The others were already there. He must have sent out a message to the rest of them through the link. She didn't question it because she was still worried about what he might want to talk about. He was a wild card she couldn't predict.

"Let's get this over with. I've had just about enough of all of you in my head," Mitchell griped, sounding angrier than usual. She didn't know if that was him hiding his grief or if something she'd done had set him off.

Gryson provided the antidote and they all took their own vial. Without any preamble they all knocked it back and, just as last time, Gryson was the last. He watched as the weird worm formed inside his vial in place of the liquid he had just drunk.

"Is it odd that I feel like my head has an echo now with how empty it is?" Ren shook his head back and forth, like something might be rattling around inside it.

"I can relate to that," Aggie murmured.

Mitchell took her hand without a word and pulled her down the hallway. They walked past Ren's room without slowing. Aggie stayed quiet, taking her cue from Mitchell. She was growing more and more concerned as the silence extended. Her mind was running crazy with what-ifs.

Mitchell finally stopped and opened his own bedroom door, motioning Aggie inside. When she brushed past him he snaked out his hand and lightly brushed her fingertips. Her breath caught in her throat at the blatant display of affection. It was so unlike him.

He closed the door behind them and leaned his back against it, sighing deeply. "What did you do back there?" His voice was full of awe and confusion. Aggie wasn't sure what to tell him because she wasn't sure she understood it herself.

"I knew you were weakening and couldn't bear it. You needed something to replenish you. I didn't know what to do. Izzy always said skin to skin contact was required, and that it only worked with mated pairs. I felt like I was restrained and unable to do anything. Then I remembered what Alpha said before the fight, that I was his mate. I figured it was worth a shot." She shrugged and tried to brush it off as nothing.

"What was worth a shot?" Mitchell was confused, and in that he and Aggie were matched. She still didn't understand how it worked. But here he was, standing before her, questioning some unknown flood of power.

"I don't really know. I just knew I wanted to send you my energy to boost yours and hopefully accelerate your natural healing ability. I knew you were hurting and it was slowing you down. I didn't know what else to do. So, I just focused on you and channeled it into you." She remembered it all and it flashed before her eyes. "When I fell, you leapt up and landed square on Dranton's back. I knew it worked."

Mitchell stood there as though he was putting everything she said together, and in a way that made sense. The problem was none of it made sense because it shouldn't have been possible. None of it should ever have happened, and yet it did. Against all odds, and without an official mating ritual, it had happened.

Instead of speaking, Mitchell crossed the room like a man in the desert seeing water for the first time. He looked like he would die if he didn't touch her. When his hands cupped her face, she gasped. He didn't initiate very often, but when he did he took her breath away. His lips sealed over hers and she lost herself in his kiss. His tongue licked the seam of her lips and she opened to him without thought. When the shock of his advance wore off, she wound her hands up and over his muscular shoulders and up the back of his neck. Her right hand worked into his hair and she ran her nails on his scalp and tangled her fingers in the black and grey hair that matched his wolf's fur to a 'T'.

Mitchell turned her and backed her up against the wall. His body completely flush with hers, she could feel his enormous cock pressed against his pants and into her stomach. She could just imagine the things he would do to her with it. She wrapped her leg around his hip and pulled him closer. She was practically climbing him and, in the kiss, she felt everything he was feeling without the need of a link. She released his hair and found the hem of his shirt, needing to feel him in anyway possible.

Before she could get the shirt over his head, Mitchell pulled away. "I want this more than you know, but I can't do it until I have things settled with my people." He took a step back to create some distance between them. "You were amazing today. The speech before the fight was perfect, and I never expected you to do that. It made my wolf come to the surface to listen to you. He was so proud of you, and so was I. I was ready to claim you right then and there. Unfortunately, shifter politics are complicated and I want to make sure the timing is right. You are my princess and I want you to know how much you mean to me. Sorry I don't always show it. I find all the guys go easy on you, and at least one of us needs to be hard in order to keep you safe." The admission of his words hit Aggie right in the heart. She had no words. The fact that he could express himself and still be her Mitchell was enough for her.

Closing the distance, she leaned into him once more. "I understand, you just let me know when you're ready. I'm yours." Kissing him once more on the cheek she left the room, leaving him to gather himself.

She made her way down the hallway and back into the main living area, and all the guys were still there. Sprawled out on the sofas and chairs, they looked like normal guys on their day off or exhausted after work.

"You guys look comfortable." Aggie flopped on the sofa next to Eldon and purposely leaned into him, and he put his arm around her and rested his bare hand on her bare forearm. She was only wearing her undershirt.

"So, did Ky tell you what he did today?" She winked at him and his eyes lit up as a smile broke across his face. Looking up at Eldon, she smiled and he burst out laughing. It was an unexpected reaction but it caused a chain reaction between her and Ky as well.

"Now I feel like we got left out of an inside joke. Care to share?" Xavier said lazily, still stretched out across his seat. The three were still giggling and the rest of the guys looked on with interest.

"He made three guys fuck each other right in front of us," Aggie finally blurted out between chuckles and then cackled full on.

"Oh, really?" Mathius sat forward in his seat. Aggie already knew how much that meant to him.

That could be interesting," Gryson added, and looked over at Mathius with a slight blush creeping up his neck.

"Oh no," Ren chimed in, "I only go as far as sharing with my brother. We don't cross swords, if you know what I mean." He cleared his throat, suddenly uncomfortable with the line of conversation, but Aggie was intrigued. She was learning so much about the guys.

"I wouldn't be against experimenting in that department, but I do prefer sinking my cock into a woman. Well, only one woman now. Though I haven't had the pleasure yet, I know it will be perfect when I do." Aggie couldn't almost see hearts in Kyrel's eyes as he spoke about their eventual mating.

"I can't say I'd be one way or the other, but I think I'm leaning more like Ren. I can handle someone being in the room but I don't want to interact with anyone directly besides my woman." Eldon leaned down and kissed her head.

"I'm not asking any of you to do it or anything you don't want to do. I'd much rather things, especially things like that, come naturally and not be forced just because you think I might want you to do something." She was serious and hoped the guys took it to heart. "I also want you guys to know that I appreciate all you did today and that I'm glad no one got hurt more than they did. Does anyone know the damage we took today?" She was afraid to say deaths, because if she said it then it made it real.

"We actually faired very well. No one was killed, but some were severely injured. We didn't see them soon enough to pull them out, but they kept their heads down and others teamed up and protected the wounded." Ren, full on Beta, smiled at Aggie. The news was better than she expected. "And no one made it back to the village, so the women and children stayed safe." Aggie sighed in relief.

"Oh, I'm so happy to hear that. Now I can sleep better tonight." Aggie leaned back and made herself comfortable.

"I know a way to make you sleep even better," Ky stated, and gave her a look that set her skin on fire.

"Are you planning to use your powers on me?" Aggie raised her brow at him and grinned at him mischievously.

"Only if you ask me nicely." He leaned forward and rested his hands on his knees. Glancing around the room Aggie took in all her men, minus Mitchell. They all smiled at her individually, but none of them offered a comment or an opinion. The foreplay that Kyrel was throwing out there was tempting. It had been a long day, and what better relaxation method was there then to let him work his magic over her?

"I guess I should ask, your place or mine?" Ky was up in a flash and captured her, but didn't bother to take her to the door. He sifted her out, and before she knew it they were standing at the Gateway.

"Your place," Ky said and captured the knob. They traveled into the Gateway and her own doorway was waiting for them.

Standing in her bedroom Aggie looked around and realized how messy it was, and embarrassment flooded her, "Sorry for the mess." She shuffled into the room, kicking things out of the way, and cringed when she saw a bra hanging from the chair. Apparently the Brownies still were following her Gran's orders and stayed out of her room.

"I don't see anything but you and I have wanted nothing more than to have you here, in your home and in your bed." He pulled her toward the bed, and when she was standing beside it he turned to her and smiled. "Do you want me to use my power on you? I will if it will help you relax, but only if you want."

Aggie considered it and wondered what it would feel like. Curiosity got the better of her. "I want to know what it's like. If you do maybe I'll understand how you use it as a weapon."

"That is very scientific of you." Ky's eyes changed to his teal glow.

"The way the magic changes your eyes is truly stunning. I love that color and it suits you." She felt the magic fall over her and it felt like a swelling of emotion. She had always been captivated by Kyrel and this just amplified that, making her lose her inhibitions, and she pounced on him. She was climbing him in an instant and pressing kisses all the way up on every inch of exposed skin. He caught her by the ass and supported her, making the climb a little easier. Settled in his arms, she pressed a kiss to his lips.

"You are the most beautiful creature I have ever seen. I can't wait to see you splayed before me like the goddess you are," Ky praised her, and his words had her fighting to remove her clothing. She nearly strangled herself trying to get her shirt off. Kyrel had to help her the rest of the way. He lay her on the bed and divested her of her pants with little struggle. When she saw his head between her legs, she moaned.

"I know what that magical tongue can do. I can't wait." The words left her and she realized it wasn't spoken in her head as she had thought, and Ky chuckled but quickly kissed her core without preamble. "Oh God, yes!" she screamed even though they were only getting started. In any other situation she would have been embarrassed, but all she cared about was letting him work his mouth over her core in the way only he knew how.

"I think I like you with fewer inhibitions. You are free, and speak your mind with little care. I didn't mind when we were linked and I knew your thoughts and feelings." Ky looked at her over her mound and she could see his smile.

"Less sweet talk and more sucking and licking. I need you to do that for me right now. You have me so worked up that release is the only thing I can do now." She heard his words and they hit home, but now all she wanted was to fuck him and have her way with him. This was just a start.

"As you wish, my love." He leaned back down and plunged his tongue deep inside her, and worked it like he would his cock. She felt him in every secret spot and wondered how he reached some of them, but didn't ask questions because she didn't want him getting distracted. He nipped slightly at her clit and she cried out, but he was just getting started. Before plunging his tongue in again she was surprised when he replaced his tongue with his fingers. Two fingers now deep inside her, hooking to hit her sweet spot, he sealed his mouth over her nub and sucked hard. Pumping his fingers in and out and stroking her just right. She climbed quickly and knew she wouldn't last much longer.

"Yes, keep going. I'm so close. I need you to let me come." She cried out what she wanted without a filter. She had never been a big talker during sex, but she loved this. It was perfect not to feel embarrassed to say exactly what she wanted.

Releasing her clit, Ky said, "I'll let you come as many times as you want. I enjoy watching you and hearing you." Getting back to it he bit her clit hard, and she lost her inner battle that she wasn't exactly fighting, crying out her pleasure. He continued and didn't give her any break. She tumbled over again and again until she lost count of her climaxes and couldn't catch her breath.

"Stop, please, I can't take anymore," she gasped, and reached to push him away. Thankfully, he listened. Mathius would have told her he was in charge and decided when she'd had enough.

"Are you ready for this, or are you planning to give out on me?" He looked right in her eyes and she actually considered her answer. He patiently waited for her to respond as she caught her breath.

"I want you," she stated simply, and he grinned from ear to ear.

"You are so wet. I love that I can please you and you show it

so easily. I could work you over and over and never tire of it."
He stepped off the bed and shucked his shirt, and Aggie tried
not to drool.

"God, you're an Adonis. How do you keep women at bay?
You probably have to beat them off with a stick." Ky reached
for his pants and unfastened them and let them fall to the floor.
He wore nothing underneath and Aggie nearly came from that
alone. "I need you now."

He lowered down and hovered over her, held up by his knees
and arms. She looked down between them, and his cock
twitched but pointed straight down to her like her pussy was a
magnet and his cock was drawn to it. "Mine," he stated simply
and let his cock enter her slowly. He worshiped her body one
slow stroke at a time, and Aggie pumped right along with him.
Since she was shorter than him, she took advantage and licked
up his neck on the next plunge and bit slightly, and he groaned
his approval of her antics. The more she worked him over, the
faster he entered her in and out. She moved to his ear and licked
the shell and nibbled the lobe gently. She enjoyed how responsive he was and that he lost a bit of his careful control. He was
fucking her fast and frenzied now that she was actively sucking
his neck, sure to leave a mark. "You are amazing and I can't
wait to spend the rest of my life with you." She came loudly,
shouting his name, and he followed her, lost in his own bliss.

S he awoke in a darkened room, Ky sound asleep beside
her. She didn't know what woke her because she
usually slept soundly and through the night. She had been so
tired the night before. She and Ky continued their play late into
the night until they both just passed out. She was still naked, and
there was a bit of chill in the room.

Deciding that she needed to go clean up, she crept from the
bed and grabbed a nightgown from the dresser. Ky never

moved. He must have worn himself out. The thought made her smile. She tiptoed out of the room and to the bathroom. Quickly cleaning up from their activities, she used the toilet and threw on her nightgown. Turning off the light so it didn't shine down the hall, she stepped from the room.

Before reaching the hallway, a hand wrapped around her mouth. She started to scream, but before she could get it out or see who had her she was lifted off the floor and plunged into darkness.

ABOUT THE AUTHOR

About the Author:

I'm a mom of 6. Yes, you read that correctly. Please don't question my life choices I'm already questioning them enough for everyone. I decided middle of 2016 that writing was something I could do and given I stay at home already I have time to try. Well, it took me about a year to get my first book out and I was hooked. I had stories flowing through my head and screaming for the chance to be written first. Now I have voices in my head daily and I worry I'm going to be locked in a padded room if I mention it to anyone, so SHHHH it's a secret. Fall in love with my voices as much as I have and just accept that they are friendly. No one is telling me to do bad things (except write unwanted cliffhangers and cause mischief.) I live in the middle of nowhere with my family and unlimited cats (females produce a lot of kittens because I let them whore around) and chickens. Sometimes I can't tell which ones are actual chickens or kids. I have a coffee addiction and I struggle to write instead of reading books on my TBR. I tend to produce book rather quickly. After my first release, I had to get the words out so my 2nd book released 5 months later. Followed by the 3rd book coming out 2 months after that (I did some simultaneous writing of book 2 and 3). My most recent release came out 4 months after that. There has been a lull between my 4th and 5th books but that was due to health reasons. You can expect me to get on track in the coming year.

If you want to contact me, you can find me at my private group, The Gateway Reader Group or at the links below:

Romantic Suspense

Dangerous After Dark

Dangerous Calculations

The Gateway Saga

The Final Link

Shifting Tides of Chaos

Standalones

Disaster in Love (romantic comedy)

You can find the above titles at Amazon or search for them via my Bookbub on multiple platforms.

www.ingramcontent.com/pod-product-compliance
Lightning Source LLC
Chambersburg PA
CBHW051644180726
48284CB00006B/1853